This rich collection of essays counters the enduring vision of South Asian Muslim women as mute, passive and docile by tracing their fiction from the 'new women' of the early twentieth century to today's 'future girls.' Rokeya Sakhawat Hossain's utopian *Sultana's Dream* (1905) provides a starting point from which to explore the contributions of Muslim female authors to fiction's convoluted genealogy in South Asia through their participation in multiple and often overlapping genres. New and established international scholars take a fresh approach to a fascinating array of fictional works in Urdu, Bengali, and English by celebrated and less renowned authors. This exciting literary journey takes the reader from horror, romanticism, fantasy, erotica, and dystopia to partition fiction and graphic novels.

—**Siobhan Lambert-Hurley**, *Professor of Global History,*
University of Sheffield, UK

In bringing together a set of brilliant new studies of Muslim women writers in modern South Asia, *Sultana's Sisters* makes a timely and important intervention in the literary history of the region. Linking genre, gender, and the genealogy of forms, the essays cover both established and little-known authors, multiple languages, and a plurality of genres from utopian fable to romance, horror, historical realism, and speculative fantasy. The editors are to be congratulated on this fascinating and critically nuanced venture, filling a gap in current scholarship by revealing the imaginative and creative range of Muslim women's fiction.

—**Supriya Chaudhuri**, *Professor Emerita,*
Jadavpur University, India

An incisive and pioneering collection of critical essays, which traces the development, expansion and cross-fertilization of sub-continental Muslim women's fiction, across different genres in the sub-continent from the early twentieth century to the present day. The informative introduction gives this further context with a discussion of Muslim women's writing since Mughal times and also engages with the nineteenth-century reformist literary movements in Urdu, including new women's journals which gave Muslim women a public platform and a new voice. This is a truly remarkable collection which makes a major contribution to sub-continental women's literature and illuminates it with new insights.

—**Muneeza Shamsie**, Author of *Hybrid Tapestries*:
The Development of Pakistani Literature in English

Sultana's Sisters is one of the most significant publications on Muslim women's writing in South Asia in perhaps a decade and will be critical reading for scholars from a range of fields. The book brilliantly opens out new approaches to the study of South Asian fiction while remaining alert to the multiple trajectories and complex subjectivities of the authors it studies. Moving quickly beyond the core canon of Muslim women's literature, Sultana's Sisters acquaints readers with authors from an impressive range of linguistic traditions and social backgrounds, thus introducing fresh nuance to key questions about what it meant to write and publish as a woman in Islamicate South Asia.

—**Daniel Majchrowicz**, *South Asian Literature and Culture,*
Northwestern University, USA

SULTANA'S SISTERS

This book traces the genealogy of 'women's fiction' in South Asia and looks at the interesting and fascinating world of fiction by Muslim women. It explores how Muslim women have contributed to the growth and development of genre fiction in South Asia and brings into focus diverse genres, including speculative, horror, campus fiction, romance, graphic, dystopian amongst others, from the early 20th century to the present.

The book debunks myths about stereotypical representations of South Asian Muslim women and critically explores how they have located their sensibilities, body, religious/secular identities, emotions, and history, and have created a space of their own. It discusses works by authors such as Rokeya Sakhawat Hossain, Hijab Imtiaz Ali, Mrs. Abdul Qadir, Muhammadi Begum, Abbasi Begum, Khadija Mastur, Qurratulain Hyder, Wajida Tabbasum, Attia Hosain, Mumtaz Shah Nawaz, Selina Hossain, Shaheen Akhtar, Bilquis Sheikh, Gulshan Esther, Maha Khan Phillips, Zahida Zaidi, Bina Shah, Andaleeb Wajid, and Ayesha Tariq.

A volume full of remarkable discoveries for the field of genre fiction, both in South Asia and for the wider world, this book, in the *Studies in Global Genre Fiction* series, will be useful for scholars and researchers of English literary studies, South Asian literature, cultural studies, history, Islamic feminism, religious studies, gender and sexuality, sociology, translation studies, and comparative literatures.

Haris Qadeer is Assistant Professor at the Department of English, University of Delhi, India. He was visiting faculty at the Department of English, Potsdam University, Germany (2019). His research interests include literatures and cultures of South Asian Muslims, refugee narratives, post-colonial studies, translations, and South Asian writings in English. He has coedited a special issue on postcolonial world literature, *Thesis Eleven*. He has translated writings by Joginder Paul, Rokeya Sakhawat Hossain, Manto, Zafar Ali, Anis Rafi, Krishn Chandra, and Taranum Riyaz. His forthcoming works are *The Silence that Speaks: Short Fiction by Indian Muslim Women* and *Medical Maladies: Doctors, Patients, and Hospitals in Indian Short Fiction*.

P. K. Yasser Arafath is Assistant Professor at the Department of History, University of Delhi, India. He was Dr. L. M. Singhvi Fellow at the Centre of South Asian Studies, Cambridge University, UK (2017). His research papers and articles have been published in major journals, including *Economic and Political Weekly*, *Social Scientists*, *Medieval History Journal*, *IESHR*, and *Journal of the Royal Asiatic Society*. Currently, he is completing a book manuscript, titled *Malabarnama: Intimate Texts and Lyrical Resistance in the Age of Disorder (c. 1500–1875)*. He has a PhD degree in History from Hyderabad Central University (HCU), India.

Studies in Global Genre Fiction

Series Editors: Bodhisattva Chattopadhyay, *University of Oslo,*
Norway and Taryne Jade Taylor, *Embry-Riddle Aeronautical University, USA*

Studies in Global Genre Fiction offers original insights into the history of genre literature while contesting two hierarchies that constrain global genre fiction studies: (1) Anglophone literature and other global language literatures and (2) literary fiction and genre fiction. The series explores the exchanges between different literary cultures that form aesthetic concerns and the specific literary, socio-political, geographical, economic, and historical forces that shape genre fiction globally. A key focus is understudied genre fictions from the 'global South' – where geographical location or language often confines works to the margins of the global publishing industry, international circulation, and academic scrutiny, even if they may be widely read in their own specific contexts.

Contributions to this series investigate the points of disruption, intersection and flows between literary and genre fiction. The series analyses cross–cultural influences in literary classifications, translation, transcreation, localization, production, and distribution while capturing the rich history of world and global literatures.

Editorial Advisory Board

- Helge Jordheim (University of Oslo, Norway)
- Abhijit Gupta (Jadavpur University, India)
- Suparno Banerjee (Texas State University, USA)
- Isiah Lavender III (Louisiana State University, USA)

Books in this series

Indian Genre Fiction
Pasts and Future Histories
Edited by Bodhisattva Chattopadhyay, Aakriti Mandhwani and Anwesha Maity

Sultana's Sisters
Genre, Gender, and Genealogy in South Asian Muslim Women's Fiction
Edited by Haris Qadeer and P. K. Yasser Arafath

For more information about this series, please visit: www.routledge.com/
Studies-in-Global-Genre-Fiction/book-series/SGGF

SULTANA'S SISTERS

Genre, Gender, and Genealogy
in South Asian Muslim
Women's Fiction

Edited by Haris Qadeer and P. K. Yasser Arafath

 Routledge
Taylor & Francis Group

LONDON AND NEW YORK

First published 2022
by Routledge
2 Park Square, Milton Park, Abingdon, Oxon OX14 4RN

and by Routledge
605 Third Avenue, New York, NY 10158

Routledge is an imprint of the Taylor & Francis Group, an informa business

British Library Cataloguing-in-Publication Data
A catalogue record for this book is available from the British Library

Library of Congress Cataloging-in-Publication Data
Names: Qadeer, Haris, editor. | Arafath, P. K. Yasser, editor.
Title: Sultana's sisters : genre, gender, and genealogy in South Asian Muslim women's fiction / edited by Haris Qadeer and P.K. Yasser Arafath.
Identifiers: LCCN 2021020116 (print) | LCCN 2021020117 (ebook) | ISBN 9780367430856 (hardback) | ISBN 9780367432508 (paperback) | ISBN 9781003002062 (ebook)
Subjects: LCSH: Indic fiction—Women authors—History and criticism. | Indic fiction—Muslim authors—History and criticism. | Indic fiction—19th century—History and criticism. | Indic fiction—20th century—History and criticism. | South Asian fiction—20th century—History and criticism. | Women and literature—South Asia. | Women in literature. | LCGFT: Literary criticism.
Classification: LCC PK5423.5.W65 S85 2022 (print) | LCC PK5423.5.W65 (ebook) | DDC 891/.1—dc23
LC record available at https://lccn.loc.gov/2021020116
LC ebook record available at https://lccn.loc.gov/2021020117

ISBN: 978-0-367-43085-6 (hbk)
ISBN: 978-0-367-43250-8 (pbk)
ISBN: 978-1-003-00206-2 (ebk)

DOI: 10.4324/9781003002062

Typeset in Bembo
by Apex CoVantage, LLC

Dedicated to

Waheed Jahan, Rokeya Sakhawat Hossain, Muhammadi Begum, Fatima Sheikh, and all early Muslim women educators

CONTENTS

CONTRIBUTORS

Mohammed Afzal is Assistant Professor of English at Zakir Husain Delhi College, University of Delhi, India. His PhD thesis is a sociological study of early Urdu novel, with special reference to the emergence of the Muslim service-class in late 19th-century colonial India. He has made many academic presentations on the Urdu novelist Deputy Nazir Ahmad in many international and national conferences, such as University of Wisconsin, Madison, USA; School of Oriental and African Studies, University of London, UK; University of Chicago, USA; University of Delhi and Aligarh Muslim University, India. He is the author of the book *Relocating Jane Eyre: Religion and Politics in Victorian Britain* (2019).

Umme Al-wazedi is Associate Professor of Postcolonial Literature in the Department of English and Co-Program Director of Women's and Gender Studies at Augustana College, Rock Island, Illinois, USA. Her research interest encompasses (Muslim) women writers of South Asia and South Asian Diaspora, Muslim feminism, and postcolonial disability studies. She has published in *South Asian Review* and *South Asian History and Culture*. She has coedited a special issue of *South Asian Review*, titled *Nation and Its Discontents*, and a book, *Postcolonial Urban Outcasts: City Margins in South Asian Literature*, published in 2017, with Madhurima Chakraborty, Columbia College Chicago, Chicago, IL. She is also the author of several book chapters.

Barnita Bagchi is a faculty member in Comparative Literature at the Department of Languages, Literature, and Communication at Utrecht University, the Netherlands. Educated at Jadavpur, Oxford, and Cambridge universities, she was previously a faculty at the Institute of Development Studies Kolkata in India (where she is Honorary Visiting Fellow). She has been Visiting Fellow at Clare Hall, University of Cambridge (spring 2013) and is now a Life Member of Clare Hall. Her areas of research and publication include 18th-century and Romantic-era British fiction (with particular interest in female-centred and female-authored fiction), South

Asian (especially Bengali) narrative writing, utopian writing, and South Asian and transnational history of culture and education. Her academic work on the South Asian Bengali Muslim writer Rokeya S. Hossain's female and feminist utopias is widely used in academic courses globally, for example in a course at York University, Toronto, Canada, on 'South Asian Literary Activism: Women Writers and Filmmakers in South Asia and the Diaspora.' She was recently awarded a British Academy Visiting Fellowship at Lancaster University, UK.

Madeline Clements teaches at Teesside University. She specializes in post-colonial South Asian Muslim art and literature and her current research explores how the condition of Pakistan's ethnic and religious minorities are represented. She has authored *Writing Islam from a South Asian Muslim Perspective: Rushdie, Hamid, Aslam, Shamsie* (2015).

Christel R Devadawson is Professor at the Department of English, University of Delhi. Her publications include *Out of Line: Cartoons, Caricature and Contemporary India, Reading India, Writing England: The Fiction of Rudyard Kipling and E M Forster,* and critical editions of *A Passage to India* and *Jane Eyre* for Penguin India and Macmillan, respectively. A Cambridge Nehru scholar, Prof Devadawson worked on Kipling and Forster for her PhD from the University of Cambridge.

Mehr Afshan Farooqi is Associate Professor of Urdu and South Asian Literature at the University of Virginia, USA. Her research publications address complex issues of Urdu literary culture, particularly in the context of modernity. She is interested in bilingualism and how it impacts creativity. She is also a well-known translator, anthologist, and columnist. She is the editor of the pioneering two-volume work *The Oxford India Anthology of Modern Urdu Literature* (2008). More recently she has published the acclaimed monograph *The Postcolonial Mind, Urdu Culture, Islam and Modernity in Muhammad Hasan Askari* (2013) and *Ghalib: A Critical Biography* (2020). She writes a featured column on Urdu literature past and present in *The Dawn*. She is presently working on a project that highlights the great Urdu poet Ghalib's textual history.

Wafa Hamid is Assistant Professor at the Department of English at Lady Shri Ram College for Women, University of Delhi. Her recent writing has appeared in the South Asian Review and JSL: Journal of the School of Language, Literature & Culture Studies, JNU among other popular publications. She also has chapters in two forthcoming edited volumes: on women playwrights in Indian writing in English and on the practices of translation and migration that confound nation-statist borders in poetry. Her research interests include comparative literatures at the intersections of language, translation and trauma studies; cultural studies and collective memorialization; gender and queer studies among others.

Mobeen Hussain is an early career researcher of the British Empire focusing on race, caste, gender, and consumption in South Asia. She recently completed her

PhD in History at the University of Cambridge, UK, entitled 'Race, Gender and Beauty in Late Colonial India c.1900–1950.' She completed her BA in English and History and MA in Contemporary History and International Politics at the University of York. Previous research projects have included tracing changes in courtesan culture in colonial India and a project on the identity politics of African-Caribbean women in post-war Britain through navigations of beauty.

Shweta Sachdeva Jha did her PhD in History from School of Oriental and African Studies, University of London, UK. She teaches English at Miranda House, University of Delhi, India. She has published on the history of the *tawaif* in journals such as *African and Asian Studies* (2009) and in edited books such as *Narratives of India Cinema* (2009, edited by Manju Jain) and *Speaking of the Self: Gender, Performance and Autobiography in South Asia* (2015, edited by Anshu Malhotra and Siobhan Lambert-Hurley). She is currently working on a book manuscript on the *tawaif*, and her current areas of research are children's picture books and crime fiction in English.

Mosarrap Hossain Khan has obtained his doctorate from the Department of English, New York University, USA. His areas of specialization include South Asian fiction, religion, and secularism, and theories of everyday life. He is the founding editor of *Café Dissensus* magazine.

Jaideep Pandey is a doctoral fellow at the University of Michigan, Ann Arbor, USA. His research is on early 20th-century Urdu periodicals for women. His interests lie at the intersection of Islam, gender, genre, and print culture. He has previously taught at St. Stephen's College and completed an MPhil in Women's and Gender Studies from Ambedkar University, Delhi, India.

Aysha Munira Rasheed is Professor at the Department of English, Aligarh Muslim University, India. She has delivered talks and has participated in panel discussions on topics of social, cultural, and literary relevance in India, the US, Italy, and the UK and has been published by reputed publishers, including Wiley-Blackwell and Sahitya Akademi. Her areas of interest include, but are not limited to, postcolonial studies, comparative literature, translation studies, and gender studies. She is a translator, blogger, and traveller, who, many a time, also gives in to her creative impulses.

Fatima Rizvi is Associate Professor in the Department of English and Modern European Languages at the University of Lucknow. Her area of interest is literature in translation and adaptation. She specializes in Urdu literature in translation. Her research papers have been published in journals of national and international repute and in anthologies of criticism. She translates Urdu and Hindi fiction and non-fiction into English. Her translation of Qurratulain Hyder's *Sitaron se Aage, Beyond the Stars and Other Stories* has been published by Women Unlimited (2021). *Shadows* *on the Wall: Pen Portraits*, a collection of Javed Siddiqi's translated essays is due to be published soon by Om Books International. She is currently co-editing a collection of interdisciplinary, critical essays on Disability Studies, *Conceptualizing Disability: Interdisciplinary Critical Approaches*. She was awarded the Meenakshi Mukherjee Memorial Prize by the Indian Association of Commonwealth Literature and Language Studies (IACLALS) for the best scholarly essay by a member of the association in 2018 and the Jawad Memorial Prize for Urdu-English translation in 2019.

Mohammad Asim Siddiqui is Professor of English at Aligarh Muslim University, Aligarh, India. He worked on American novelist Mark Twain for his doctoral thesis. His areas of interest and publication include literary theory, cultural studies, film studies, research methodology, and academic writing. He was a Fulbright Fellow at New York University in 2007. He writes regular columns on arts and culture in *The Hindu*, NDTV.com, and Rediff.com. His articles have also appeared in *The Guardian, Hindustan Times, The Statesman, The Indian Express*, and *The Pioneer*. He is also the managing editor of the project of the Urdu translation of Complete Works of Dr. B. R. Ambedkar (CWBA), a project of Dr. Ambedkar Foundation, Ministry of Social Justice and Empowerment, Government of India.

SERIES EDITORS' PREFACE

We are honoured to present *Sultana's Sisters* in our *Studies in Global Genre Fiction* series. We are particularly delighted that this book connects so well to the first volume in our series, *Indian Genre Fiction*. *Sultana's Sisters* makes an exciting and significant contribution to both the fields of South Asian studies and genre studies through its exploration of South Asian Genre fiction from the perspective of gender and religious identities. As the editors, Haris Qadeer and P. K. Yasser Arafath detailed the initial proposal, Rokeya Hossain Sakhawat's *Sultana's Dream* is lauded as one of the central texts of South Asian speculative fiction; however, even though *Sultana's Dream* is well known in literary studies across the globe, the larger tradition of South Asian Muslim women's genre fiction has been overlooked, especially by the Global North.

Qadeer and Arafath's collection brings into view the contributions of Muslim women to diverse genres, including speculative fiction, horror fiction, campus fiction, the romance, thriller, among others, from the early 20th century to the present. The contributors to *Sultana's Sisters* include many of the foremost scholars in *bhasha* and Anglophone literatures, as well as scholars studying the contributions of Muslim women. This volume not only adds to this growing body of scholarship about women genre fiction writers, but also sheds light on and challenge stereotypes about the production of fiction by Muslim women. All of the chapters of *Sultana's Sisters* are refreshingly original in their insights and beautifully written.

We believe this volume is likely to lead to remarkable discoveries for the field of genre fiction, both in South Asia and for the wider world. We are confident that the chapters in this volume will appeal to a wide readership and make significant contributions to the fields of genre fiction studies, South Asian studies, literary studies in South Asia, Muslim literature, as well as gender studies.

We are thrilled to have this ground-breaking collection as part of our series and hope the readers enjoy it as much as we do.

Bodhisattva Chattopadhyay and Taryne Jade Taylor,
Series editors, Studies in Global Genre Fiction

ACKNOWLEDGEMENT

The idea of the book was conceived in one of the pre-Covid online Skype video calls with Bodhisattva Chattopadhyay, one of the series editors, who immediately discussed the idea with Taryne Jade Taylor, his co-editor. We thank both the editors for their enthusiasm, faith, and interest in this project. It has taken more than two years of work to bring it to completion. We offer special thanks to all the contributors for believing in the project. And, most importantly, for their patience! The book is dedicated to Muslim women of South Asia, who, through the ages, have challenged a range of social and cultural norms for creating a space of their own. This book, the editors hope, will not only enable a sombre reflection on Muslim women's fiction but also challenge several stereotypical notions pertaining to Muslim womanhood in South Asia.

We acknowledge the support of various institutions and individuals who enabled the publication of the present book. We express our sincere gratitude to the staff at all of the libraries which we used for our research, including the seminar library of the Centre for Women's Studies, Aligarh Muslim University; Maulana Azad Library, Aligarh Muslim University; Ratan Tata Library, University of Delhi; seminar libraries of the Department of English and the Department of History, University of Delhi; the Central Reference Library, Faculty of Arts, University of Delhi; Sahitya Akademi, Delhi, and Delhi Public Library, Delhi. Our colleagues and friends at the University of Delhi have been supportive of the project right from its inception. We thank each one of them!

We thank Prof. Rimli Bhattachraya (University of Delhi), Prof. Patricia Hayes (University of the Western Cape), Prof. Amar Farooqui (University of Delhi), Dr. Nida Sajid (University of Minnesota), Dr. Fathima E. V. (Kannur University), Prof. Chitra Pannikar (Bangalore University), and the anonymous reviewers for reading and commenting on different chapters. We thank Labani Jangi (Anokh Somudduro) for allowing us to use her artwork for our cover. Routledge has been an encouraging and efficient host for this book. We are grateful to Shoma Choudhury, Anvitaa Bajaj, and the entire team at Routledge for their help and support, during the process of publication. Over the years that the work of this anthology evolved, our families have been extremely helpful. We can't thank them enough for unconditional love and emotional support. Apart from all these names, many more people have assisted us directly or indirectly; though we can't thank each of them individually, they all are an indispensable part of the book.

Thank you everyone!

Editors

FOREWORD

I am delighted to write this foreword, not only because Haris Qadeer and I belong to the 'Alig family,' but also because I believe deeply in women's agency that is highlighted in this book. I also believe in the power of a good story and women's capacity to produce astonishingly important and beautiful stories about themselves. Reading the stories of Muslim women novelists explored in this book can help scholars and casual readers alike use their minds and hearts to make connections and appreciate common humanity.

Stories are the stuff of life. In the Indian subcontinent, storytelling is a highly developed tradition. People tell real and fantastic stories about humans and non-humans, monsters and gods – about the seen and the unseen. Grandparents tell stories to grandchildren, mothers to daughters, and stories are shared among neighbours, between communities; the circles of the stories keep expanding. Storytelling is a currency for making human connections.

Haris Qadeer and Yaseer Arafath's edited book *Sultana's Sisters* is not just another book about stories that are told and retold. It is a book about Muslim women who created an edifice of original stories in the Indian subcontinent. These are no ordinary architects; they are extraordinary craftswomen who wrote transformative stories. In 14 engaging essays written by scholars who have delved into the craft and plot of the novels, we are invited to a virtual tour through the world of Muslim women's fiction writing, beginning from the 19th century to the contemporary 21st century. These include pioneer authors such as Rokeya Sakhawat Hossain, Khadija Mastur, Qurratulain Hyder, Muhammadi Begum, Abbasi Begum as well as less conventional novelists such as Mrs. Qadir and Wajida Tabassum, and contemporary authors such as Ayesha Tariq, Zahida Zaidi, Andaleeb Wajid, Bina Shah, and Maha Khan Phillips.

These multiple generations of exceptionally talented Muslim women novelists traverse 'the complicated gendered world of South Asia' and 'assert the existence of "speaking Muslim women",' as Qadeer notes. He calls them the 'new Muslim women' who created their 'own zones of discourses' and made Muslim women's lives visible and graspable. The ordinary pleasures and terrors of the domestic sphere as well as the extraordinary political realities of colonialism, partition, and post-colonialism are voiced and powerful narratives emerge in consequence. This book recentres the Muslim women novelists who made stories a vehicle for engaging in social and political discussions.

Each chapter explores at least one novel, the characters, the unique voice of the novelist, the reception of the readers, and discusses the craft of the novelist. But the authors go beyond the nuts-and-bolts analysis to show how the new Muslim women novelists became skilful interlocutors changing the domestic sphere, as well as claiming space for Muslim women in the public arena. The voices of Muslim women that the authors alert us to hear displace the hegemonic world of the British colonial masters and Western feminists, who have paid scant attention to Muslim women's writings in South Asia. Using the power of the pen, the Muslim women novelists dislodge the received story that Muslim women do not speak and live without agency. This unusual ability to create a presence in spaces where Muslim women were rendered absent and create a public conversation reaching out to readers across the spectrum of communities and classes is celebrated in this book.

As a historian of South Asia, I have been fascinated by the stories of colonial history and its deep echoes in the post-colonial. I had the privilege of exploring the intimate connection between colonial and post-colonial history in researching the 1971 War of Bangladesh. The leftover debris of the 1947 colonial partition of India acquired a new meaning for the people of the subcontinent in 1971. India and Pakistan went to war and Bangladesh was born in consequence. The memories and impact of the violent war that survivors, victims, and perpetrators – women and men – in Bangladesh, Pakistan, and India shared with me opened a whole new world of lived and felt history. Qadeer poignantly refers to 1971 as 'the second partition of the subcontinent.' I am especially grateful that Qadeer and Arafath were able to include in this book several novelists who inhabited and navigated the spaces between the first and second partitions for rethinking the colonial legacy of destroyed humanity in the subcontinent.

Although this is an edited anthology, I hear a common voice shared by the authors. Each author weaves the story of the novels with their story as readers. The combined voices of the novelists and the authors become a bridge connecting the story of Muslim South Asia, then and now. History and lore, personal, social, and political life are merged in their retelling of the stories, creating new spaces for the imagination to explore. And this gives each chapter in the book a valuable significance.

Reading this book will make the readers appreciate Muslim women novelists, perhaps unfamiliar to them, but authors they would want to read. I think every reader will gain new perspectives on literature produced in South Asia and sharpen their knowledge of the literary world of Muslim women's writings because of the efforts of the authors of this book.

Yasmin Saikia
Professor of History
Arizona State University
USA
Author, *In the Meadows of Gold: Telling Tales of the Swargadeos at the Crossroads of Assam* (1997), *Fragmented Memories: Struggling to be Tai-Ahom in India* (2004), *Women, War, and the Making of Bangladesh: Remembering 1971* (2011)

INTRODUCTION

I

Sultana's Sisters: Gender, Genre, and Genealogy in South Asian Muslim Women's Fiction, the title of the book, resonates with two crucial feminist texts: Rokeya Sakhawat Hossain's '*Sultana's Dream*' (1905) and Virginia Woolf's '*Shakespeare's Sister*' (1929). Writing in the early decades of the 20th century, the two authors, from two very different cultural and social backgrounds, located in two different continents, utilize the speculative mode for their narratives. While Woolf invents Judith, an imaginary sister of Shakespeare, to put forward her feminist arguments, the protagonist in Hossain's story dreams of Sister Sara, who dwells in Ladyland, a feminist utopia. Thus, it could be inferred that the 'speculative mode' in these texts is deployed by the authors to compensate the absence as well as to critique the rare acknowledgement of the capabilities of women in their contemporary societies. Woolf, while referring to the absence/presence of women in history and literature, claims: 'She pervades poetry from cover to cover; she is all but absent from history' (43). Woolf's statement could also be applied to the literatures and histories of women in Muslim South Asia. References to women are abundant in poetry written in Urdu, Persian, and other regional languages[1]; however, histories of different Muslim societies in South Asia, like other patriarchal societies, rarely acknowledge the contribution of Muslim women in the progress and development of the society.[2]

Inspired by Woolf's quest, Lawrence Lipking imagines Aristotle's sister to question the exclusion of women literary theorists. While analysing the literary histories of Muslim South Asia, the editors of the present book, fortunately, do not have to invent 'imaginary sisters' of Sultana, the first feminist heroine of South Asian speculative narratives, but along with the contributors, they are discovering and rediscovering some of the 'real' Muslim women authors, who, for various reasons, have received little or no critical attention in the literary studies. It may also be

DOI: 10.4324/9781003002062-1

worth mentioning that the exploration in this book departs from the 'searches' by Woolf and Lipking. Unlike them, the emphasis is not on symbolic sister/s of a male author/theorist but on real female authors and their fiction. The focus of the book, as stated in the second section of the title, is on three crucial aspects of 'gender,' 'genre,' and 'genealogy.' It examines the interrelationship of gender and genre and traces the genealogy of women's fiction in South Asia.

'A genre is always the same and yet not the same, always old and new simultaneously' (106), notes Bakhtin, while referring to the constituents of the life of genre. He, further, underlines the duality by delineating how in the development of literature 'genre is reborn and renewed at very new stage' (106). Over the last few decades, scholars have interpreted, reinterpreted, and revolutionized the notion of genre, and yet the term genre is fraught with confusion. While explaining 'genre as social action,' Miller claims, 'a genre is not just a pattern of forms . . . genre embodies an aspect of cultural rationality' (38); Culler observes that the activity of writing a poem or a novel 'is made possible by the very existence of the genre, which the writer can write against, certainly, whose conventions he may attempt to subvert, but which is none the less the context within which his activity takes place, as surely as the failure to keep a promise is made possible by the institution of promising' (116); and Bawarshi demonstrates how 'genres are discursive sites that coordinate the acquisition and production of motives by maintaining specific relations between scene, act, agent, agency, and purpose' (17). He explains how 'when writers begin to write in different genres, they participate within these different sets of relations, relations that motivate them, consciously or unconsciously, to invent both their texts and themselves' (17). Bawarshi's idea of 'genre function,' which is based on Foucault's idea of 'author-function,' is helpful for understanding that as a site of action, 'genre is both a concept and its material articulation and exchange' (22). Derrida, in *The Law of Genre*, elucidates his hypothesis: 'Every text participates in one or several genres, there is no genreless text; there is always a genre and genres, yet such participation never amounts to belonging' (230). For him, texts do not 'belong' to a genre; texts 'participate' in one or several genres at once. Using this hypothesis, one of the primary concerns of *Sultana's Sisters* is to investigate how fiction written by Muslim women 'participates' in one or several genres at once. A few chapters in the book also deal with fiction which traditionally may not read as genre fiction, but they 'participate' in genre fiction by sharing tropes of love, desires, and fantasies. Inclusion of chapters on such fiction in the book is important for understanding the main arguments of the book.

Merja Makinen argues that all the genres are potentially and inherently transformable. She puts forward 'a fluid model of popular discourses' (06) to demonstrate how context and audiences influence the production of literature. The majority of the women's fiction examined in the book enjoyed a wider women readership and circulation in their contemporary public spheres. Their fiction can be read as participating in one or several genres of fiction such as speculative, science, horror, romance, and young adult. However, the book in no way defines them or their readers as middlebrow. Though commenting on the readership and patterns of consumption of these fictions is not the primary area of the enquiry, but the book, at some places, also engages itself with the question of readership and Muslim women's fiction in South Asia. Fredric Jameson's idea of genre is crucial for understanding the relationship between genre and readers. For him, 'genres are essentially literary institutions . . . social contracts between a writer and a specific public, whose function is to specify the proper use of a particular artefact' (106). Like Jameson, there are other critics such as E. D. Hirsh and John Frow who demonstrate the important role that the readers play in determining the genre. Hirsch (1967) understood genre as interpretative framework, as a reader's 'preliminary generic conception' (74), and Frow (2006) claimed that genre is a function of reading not a property of a text; he stated, 'genre is a category we *impute* to texts, and under different circumstances this imputation may change' (102).

Furthermore, the book also draws upon the work of Chattopadhyay et al. to approach the term 'genre' as the 'two distinct yet intertwined uses' (01).

> The first of these refers to the formal choice of aesthetic presentation, or genre as description of narrative form: novel, short story, poem, drama, and so on. This use is to describe how things are presented. The second use of genre is to describe a collection of motifs (within any of these narrative forms) whose co-occurrence determines intertextual relations; or, genre as an interpretative label. This latter use is favored when referring to the term 'genre fiction,' and it applies to several constellations of such motifs: science fiction, fantasy, detective fiction, romance, horror, thriller, and so on.
>
> (01)

Making use of the 'intertwined uses' of the term genre, the study in the present book is on multiple investigative axes. First and foremost, as stated earlier, the book examines the evolution of genre fiction by Muslim women in South Asia. It also explores the possibilities of formation of new genres, such as partition fiction and graphic novels, and studies the contribution of Muslim women to the development of fiction in South Asia. Providing a broad spectrum of fiction, the book includes chapters on the fiction of some of the pioneer authors, such as Rokeya Sakhawat Hossain, Khadija Mastur, and Qurratulain Hyder, as well as unconventional authors, such as Mrs. Qadir and Wajida Tabassum, and contemporary authors, such as Ayesha Tariq and Maha Phillips. The introductory section of the book is divided into four parts: Section I, III, and IV are written by Haris Qadeer. They examine the socio-historical circumstances that led to the origin and development of 'women's novel' and trace the genealogy of fiction written by Muslim women in South Asia. Section II written by Yasser Arafath, explores the images and representations of Muslim women in South Asia.

II

Muslim women in South Asia

According to Lila Abu-Lughod, each country/region in South Asia has a different story for Muslims, 'In some countries, Muslims are minorities; in others, they are majorities. In a few countries, most are wealthy; in others, they are poor' (Abu-Lughod 13). However, such complexities around Muslim women remain mostly untapped in the domain of gender discourse in South Asia. Gender discourses are mostly silent about reading the stories of/about Muslim women in the region of South Asia. Similarly, the relations between the writers and the women they presented and their conversations – real and imaginary – are mostly invisible. Thus, it has been felt that there should be more engagements to go beyond the customary imagination of Muslim woman as 'oppressed' section and raise critical questions about their self-representations, prompted by social and normative contingencies in the region of South Asia. Because it is now understood that the discourse of oppression has been inadequate to unravel the realm of Muslim women writers who challenged the gendered quarters of social, political, cultural, and normative in the region for centuries. Thus, this book begins by asking how differently Muslim women writers in different South Asian countries were enchanted by the desirability of colonial modernity and the postcolonial imaginations of 'freedom' in the 20th century? It also seeks to examine the complex socio-political dynamics in South Asia that include the pain of colonial violence in the 19th and 20th centuries, and the post-partition uncertainties in India, Pakistan, and Bangladesh created significant diversity in the voices of Muslim women writers over a period of time.

Considering the act of writing as a political activism, the feminist thinkers and writers registered a range of alternative voices in the first world countries since the early 20th century. Limiting themselves in the geographical domain of Europe and Northern America, the first world feminist academic discourses, therefore, hardly noticed the complicated gendered world of South Asia and the confrontational everyday in the lives of women in the region. It was the remedial interventions of South Asia's feminists that brought forth the culture-specific invisibilities and silences about women writers in the world of academia and beyond in the region. The gender and sexuality discourses that the Third World feminist thoughts could succeed, albeit partially, in breaking gender walls in literary and historical scholarship in south Asia and in the process recast the direction of humanities scholarship in South Asia. Identified as subversive and alternative, the new discourses in the Third World countries created a non-occupied social audience across the world, while mainstream feminist scholars with Eurocentric gazes continued to refuse such audience outside of the oxidant, as scholars have pointed out (Harker and Farr 5–25).

From the last quarter of the 20th century, as South Asian feminist discourses challenged the obscurant lives of the silenced oriental female subjects in the contemporary scholarship, the remedies of such culpable absences/presences found their ways through new literatures and writers, specially from marginal communities, like in South Asia. Emerging from this newly realized literary energy, a range of new academic scholars began to re-present the 'un-presentable' voices of South Asian women from a range of geographical locations (Loomba and Lukose). New debates advanced from earlier focus, like land and property rights, and looked into the realms of violence and caste, making them central to new theorizing of de-colonial feminism, on the basis of new archives and political dynamics in South Asian regions like India and Pakistan (Loomba). Now, critically engaging with the oriental imaginations around South Asian women in general and Muslim women in particular, decolonial feminist discourses in the Third World countries examine new questions that involve family, marriage, desires, intimacy, public space, employment, education, and political as well as religious participation. Such discourses stemmed out from new critical readings of 'sexualized nature of Orientalism' (02) as Meyda Yegenoglu pointed out, and the conspicuous absences in the white feminist discourses.

In Orientalist discourses, the South Asian women lacked both literary agency and cognitive maturity for embodying un-detachable irrationality, which traced back to their putative ethnological inferiority. These discourses have a long history. They can be found in the racialized gender imaginations of the post-renaissance travellers like Duarto Barbosa,[3] cantankerous trader-ethnologists such as Francis Palsaeret, Thomas Coryat, and in the writings of ethnographically trained colonial administrators like Edgar Thurston. The women in South Asia got mutated as submissive, shrewd, sexually amorphous, morally egregious, politically un-educatable, and economically unproductive. Cloistered as the uninspiring demographic undesirables, South Asian women lacked life aspirations, social mobility, rational self-identification, autonomous voice, and public-secular interests. For example, after traveling extensively in South Asia – India, Bangladesh, Afghanistan, and Pakistan, Pelsaert made this fact very clear in a classic pre-British Orientalist comparison. This Dutch merchant, communicating with his compatriots in his travel journal, says that 'the ladies of our country (Netherlands) should be able to realize from this description the good fortune of their birth, and the extent of their freedom when compared with the position of ladies like them in other lands' (Pelsaert 66). Such early Orientalist imaginations continued to circulate across the expansive imperial grid in South Asia to the mid-20th century, stretching across four centuries.

When it comes to Muslim women in colonial South Asia, Christian missionary Orientalism played the most significant role in fixating their cultural, moral, and cognitive locations. The 19th-century missionary Orientalists' religious accounts and other writings presented Muslim women as a section subjected to a multitude of rapid freezings in their own spatiotemporal locations. They were mostly loathed for their 'ignorance' and gendered 'sufferings' in the absence of a gracious saviour like Jesus. According to one such account, the 'Mohammedan' (Muslims) believed that 'a woman must not learn to write, for she could then carry on all kinds of insubordination and intrigue' (Scott 18–19). As conversion to Christianity was presented as the only viable instrument of salvation for Muslims in missionary

Orientalists' emancipatory narratives, the Christ emerged as the immediate and palpable saviour of Muslim women as he possessed the power to 'redeem them and transfigure (their) lives' (Zwemer 272). As the saviour syndrome of missionary Orientalism became more intense in the 19th century, those women who believed in Islamic law and followed the life of Prophet Muhammad were presented to have lost every strand of autonomy, making them 'on a level with beasts of burden and no nation rises above the level of its women' (Sommer and Zwemer 299).

An early 20th-century missionary document aptly reflected on the larger European imaginations of Muslim women in South Asia. The inner life of Muslims in general and Muslim women in particular, according to this author, failed to understand the idea of 'sin' and the difference between truth and lie as they had a 'mind bound and imprisoned, without progress, without real fellowship, and permeated with superstition' (Clure 91–101). Missionary imaginations construed a putative Stockholm Syndrome among Muslim women who desired, mostly, or left unresisted their social and normative vulnerabilities. Their lives ended up like the canary birds 'that was born in the cage and never tasted the sweets of the free air' (Fuller 302). Although there were some sympathetic missionary activists who reflected the literary past and agential rationality of Muslim women and their autonomous social engagements in precolonial South Asia, the tonality, texture, and narrative designs of missionary Orientalism remained deeply accusational in the age of Empire (Aftab 91–99).

Thus, in a broader sense, Muslim women in South Asia looked permanently docile and passive carriers of imposed social and cultural dictates, remaining mute spectators for their lack of ability to claim an autochthonous selfhood. Missionary Orientalism in South Asia did not recognize the need to examine the agential capacities of Muslim women in the region, because its existence would challenge the insurmountable emancipatory capillaries of Christianity that they aggressively presented for ensuring eternal redemption for everyone. Thus, one might understand how imperative it was for them to be prejudicial in order to present their Muslim women subjects as eternal fatalists. For them they were nothing but a complacent demographic section with a multitude of undesired elements. Thus, the pasts of Muslim women, thenceforth, became inseparable from illiteracy, subordination, misogyny, sexual vulnerability, absence of property, pietistic myopia, and deficiency in nuanced aesthetics.

Subsequently, the narrative cacophony which stemmed out from such Orientalist hermeneutic imaginations influenced many generations of native scholars and a section of religious reformists who, therefore, believed not only in the indispensability of 'male acts' in creating the clusters of 'disciplined Muslim women' but also in the undesirability of femaleness in the intellectual process. Thus, arguing alongside Amina Wadud (2006), many reformists in South Asian Islamic societies and beyond failed to recognize the full humanness of their female counterparts and reduced their 'femaleness to deviant' in thoughts and epistemological practices. Subsequently, the Orientalist modernity created a good number of native Orientalists within Islamic communities as well, turning themselves into the carriers and propagators of a 'gaze' which demanded absolute purity and sexual discipline. However, post-colonial scholarship in South Asian Islam overlooked such long tradition of intellectual othering and gender clashes within various Muslim communities in South Asia.

Post-colonial scholars and Muslim feminists, however, tried to explain a long history of agential Muslim women who defied the maleness of theology and the gender of authenticating Islam. For Leila Ahmed, the literary and epistemological engagements of Muslim women in Asia started in the early years of Islam. The wives of the Prophet, particularly Ayesha, according to Ahmed, 'were important contributors to the verbal texts of Islam, the texts that, transcribed eventually into written form by men, became part of the official history of Islam and of the literature that established the normative practices of Islamic society' (Ahmad 47). Being the most erudite of his wives, Ayesha could become openly critical of the notion that women are inferior to men in many regards and firmly believed in the agility of women and their equal significance as the authenticating authority of Islam like any of her male counterparts in the 7th century. Similarly, Afsaneh Najmabadi (2005) brings into light another invisiblized history of Muslim women in Asia who continued to celebrate their agentive capillaries, following the long tradition which started in the 7th century itself. According to her, Women in 19th century Qajar Iran could exercise their agency as social and cultural authenticators by resisting the gendered theological and social spaces during the colonial period. Subverting the unilinear didactic tactics of the ulema – both reformist and traditional – Iranian women devised a range of invasive designs in their pursuit of questioning the male authority.

In South Asia, the gender subversion in women's writings began in the 16th century, identifiably with Gulbadan Bano Begum, the aunt of Emperor Akbar. As Caroline Bynum (2006) argued in the context of early medieval Europe, where women used the act of 'writing' as an instrument of becoming themselves, Gulbadan Begum used her literary skills and royal entitlements for creating a respectable space beyond two dominant gazes in the Mughal court –King and the ulema. In their pioneering work on women's writings in India, Susie J. Tharu and K. Lalita (1991) argue that Gulbadan made a warm presentation of the Mughal royal women by capturing the 'anxieties and pressures' that they experienced in the court in the 16th century (99).

In Gulbadan's *Humayun Nama* (*Ahval-i-Humayun Badsha*), we come across a range of independent women with assertive voices, strong will, and intense ability to defy and resist. According to Rubi Lal (2018), Gulbadan presented a range of Mughal women with multifarious concerns and negotiations and identified their 'difficulties of childbirth, unfulfilled desires, anticipation, marriages, love and death, war and peace, ritual and celebration.' Apart from her own celebration of female wholeness in this biography, Gulbadan made serious efforts to present other women who not only experienced 'violence, displacement, exile, and loss' but also remained 'important participants in the creation of the new Mughal royal court' (Balabanlilar 125).

Similarly, the 17th century witnessed a new phase in the gendered literary sphere of Mughal India. The literary scene of the period changed with the emergence of Jahanara Begum as the new patron of literature and aesthetic. Being a prolific writer herself, Jahanara's 'provoking panegyric poetry', and prose, according to Afshan Bokhari (2009), played the most decisive role in modifying the social imagination of female body and rationality during the period which is known to have considered 'women as repositories of male honor and religiosity' (89–90). Apparently, Jahanara's writings and patronage of literature surfaced from her innate desire to assertively create an autonomous female voice to self-represent, simultaneously, her identity as a princess and woman in a masculine court complex, imbued with perpetual internal chaos and sibling wars. She, according to Ira Mukhoty, 'establishes herself in the city as the most influential woman patron[s] of literature and poetry. She collects rare and beautiful book[s], and her library is peerless.' While travelling extensively in different regions of Modern South Asia, including cities like Kabul and Lahore, Jahanara seems to have carried her portable library (with her brother Dara Shukov) and 'must have picked up new books along the way and had scribes create new copies of especially rare or valuable works' (Gandhi 103).

Muslim women's literary engagements continued to flourish in regional courts during the 18th century. Tharu and Lalita furthered their enquiry into this period and identified the writings of Mahlaqa Bai Chanda (1767–1824), the Muslim courtesan (*tawaif*) at Asaf Jahi court in Hyderabad. Chanda's poems were compiled under the title *Gulzar-e-Mahlaqa* in the 19th century and was considered as the first woman to ever compose poetry in Urdu (Tharu and Lalita 122). Remaining one of the major educators and entertainers within the elite circle of the Asaf Jahi court, Chanda redefined the idea of femaleness in her writings. She cultivated a visible space for her self-identification and showed intense literary and social sensitivities for being, probably, the first hyperglossic Muslim woman writer in South Asia who also participated in battles and debates with important religious scholars of the time. However, she has still been considered a mere 'dancing girl' who was all about a *bad body*, as Bilkees Latif (2008) pointed out.

The path-breaking feminist intervention of Tharu and Lalita also discussed some of the pioneering works by Muslim women writers of the following centuries, and they include the literary works of Rokeya Sakhawat Hossain (1880–1932), Sughra Humayun Mirza (1884–1954) – a reformist activist who wrote a number of travel accounts (*safarnama*), and Nazar Sajjad Hyder (1894–1967) – a prolific writer and educationalist who strongly opposed to the practice of bigamy and *purdah*. While Rokeya, with her *Sultana's Dream*, wanted to take a 'terrible revenge on men' (Tharu and Lalita 340), Sughra disturbed the patriarchal structure, which vehemently opposed her ideas of women's right (378–79). Similarly, Nazar vociferously advocated for freedom for women and was very vocal about Muslim women's access to public spaces, including their right to 'walk at night,' in the early 20th century itself (391–94). Thus, this volume, along with many other writers, brought together a set of path breaking Muslim women writers who, subsequently, shaped the cognitive and hermeneutic trajectory of Islamic discursive behaviour in the region of south Asia for a long time to come.

However, one can still find absences of deep phenomenological evaluations in the existing scholarship on South Asian Muslim women, barring a few exceptions. Most of the works overlook how Muslim women writers, in the past and present, wanted to assert multiple identifications through their literary engagements. Like miriam cooke (2001) argued in a different geographical context, a phenomenological exercise becomes, therefore, necessary to identify how women writers of South Asia articulated multiple livings of Muslim women from different social strata. Thus, contributors in this volume engage the ways in which Muslim women in South Asia constructed their identities constantly and negotiated through their fragmented everyday lives. Therefore, the chapters look at the phenomenology of multiple identifications and locations in Muslim women writings by examining multiple catalysts – social, material, and political – that shaped such identifications.

The larger questions addressed in this volume, thus, include: What were the causalities that determined Muslim women writers' selection of characters and regions? What are the ways in which the communitarian and individual experiences and learning shaped their choosing of genre? How far could they define their subjectivities and female wholeness in their writing of fiction? How did they define and imagine their readers, critics, and detractors? Thus, as the phenomenology of multiple identifications and the scope of inter-textual reading stand palpably absent in the existing scholarship on South Asian women writings, this volume attempts to fill that gap. One of the principal necessities required for such analysis is the deployment of inter-textual readings of Muslim women writings in the 19th and 20th centuries within their specific geo-political and normative contexts. Such reading enables us move beyond the philological explanations.

Thus, this volume advances from a range of scholarly works on Muslim women writings in South Asia that are shaped/informed by recent intellectual movements. In light of new intellectual and inter-disciplinary discourses, emerging from multiple sites of discursive streams, scholars have begun to re-imagine the lives of Muslim women literati from diverse geographical, material, political, and epistemological spectrums. Recently, in a significant volume, Anshu Malhotra and Siobhan Lambert-Hurley (2015) brought out a number of significant writers that include the writings of Muslim women intellectuals, such as Jahanara and Nazr Sajjad Hyder. This volume tried to examine if there were 'common motivations, lingual and stylistic choices, preferences of genres, or issues that took center stage among women? Or their disparate cultural matrices resist such a reading? And what happens when gender identify itself is not stable'(1).

As multiple sites of feminism continue to shape the early South Asian scholarship on women's writing, Tanika Sarkar (2013) introduced the work on Rashsundari Debi, the first Bengali autobiographer who lived in East Bengal (present-day Bangladesh), making a remarkable addition to the discourse on women writings in South Asia. In Sarkar's own words, 't would be simple-minded to posit a straight connection between female subjectivity and female writing, to assume that the latter reflects the former in some direct, unmediated way. In-fact, for the writing woman of her generation of the first-educated, the act of writing itself would have reconstituted her subjectivity in radically new ways' (Sarkar 5). Sarkar's principal agenda was to delineate the author and her 'text of modernity' away from the conventional discourses on body, because body was not all that Rashsundari Debi had.

Similarly, even though there had been considerable writings by Muslim women, serious academic exercise to place such authors and their works had to wait some more time. Even celebrated modern works that include Iqbalunnisa Husian's *Purdah and Polygamy: Life in an Indian Muslim House Hold* (1944) and Attia Hosain's *Sunlight on a Broken Column* had waited considerable time to be placed in the larger social and normative structures of the concerned period. It was only in the late 1990s that the Muslim writers and the cultural making of their characters got initial placements in the larger theoretical and historical context (Parker). With the emergence of multiple feminisms, including vernacular feminist movements across South Asia, the structural and normative everyday of Muslim women in literature and the historical and cultural contingents that made Muslim women litterateurs since the 16th century got new lives in south Asian scholarship. Thus, new scholars began to assert the existence of 'speaking Muslim women' who created their own zones of discourses, fairly different and possibly contradictory to the male discourse which dominated the literary scene in the region (Jamil). These assertions brought forth the ways in which Muslim women in the past navigated through multiple sites of engagements – both confrontational and cordial – for creating self-designed autonomous normative frameworks and space with enormous energy and efforts. The revealing new scholarship could change the ways in which 'good Muslim women' were imagined within and outside the community and the nation state.

As the earlier writings on South Asian women were significantly influenced by main stream feminist thoughts, the re-imagination of gendered lives in South Asia Islam, as reflected in the writings of Muslim women writers, was significantly influenced by a range of Muslim feminist scholars who worked on different geographical regions in Asia and Africa. For example, a range of new scholars who worked on Muslim societies got influenced by the Moroccan feminist sociologist Fathima Mernissi (1993), who introduced a new methodological framework to analyse the gendered realities of Muslim women in the past. These women, in Mernissi's words, the grandmothers,' could devise multiple manoeuvring tactics for claiming their ritual place and social share, by envisaging multiple negotiating tools with male-centric power realms in the past (5). Generally known as the founder of 'Islamic Feminism' (a term she never used), Mernissi not only made a deep break in the ways in which Muslim women across the world thought about their identity but also influenced scholars working on Muslim women in the past and present.

Mernissi's *The Forgotten Queens of Islam* not only countered the Orientalist imagination of universally suppressed Muslim women but also enabled a range of scholars to re-examine/create new archives of Muslim women's lives in South Asia. A pertinent question she asked, 'How did the women of former times supposed to have fewer advantages than we do, manage such an achievement in a domain where we moderns fail so lamentably?', opened up a wide range of cascading questions. Along with Mernissi, an array of Muslim feminists, Amina Wadud, Leila Ahmad, Ziba Mir-Hosseini, Nasr Hamid Abu Zaid, Kecia Ali, Sa'diyya Shaikh, Saba Mahmood, and Asmaa Lamrabet, changed the trajectory of discourses around Muslim women over a period of time. Accepting impetus from such dialogues, a range of new scholars began to revisit the literary past of Muslim women in South Asia and located their narratives and imagination in light of debates around sexuality, gender, patrimony, intimacy, subversion, and various questions related to the idea of 'rights.'

III

Genre and genealogy in Muslim South Asia

Tracing the genealogy of fiction by Muslim women in South Asia is a difficult terrain to traverse. Like any other study of genealogy, this research field too 'requires patience and a knowledge of details, and it depends on a vast accumulation of source material' (Foucault 140). As mentioned in the previous section of the chapter, Muslim women in South Asia have been writing diaries, travel accounts, poetry, and autobiographical narratives from the 16th century onwards. The origin of 'women's fiction' in Muslim South Asia could be traced back to Rashid-un-Nisa's *Islahunnisa*, the first-known Urdu novel by a woman author.[3] Written in 1881, a few decades after the emergence of novels in the 1850s in colonial India,[4] *Islahunnisa* is a women-centric novel primarily aiming at reformation of women, as the author claims in the preface to the novel. She expresses gratitude to her son, Barrister Sulaiman, who, upon his return from England after completion of his education, persuaded her to publish the novel in 1894, 13 years after it was written. When the novel was first published, Rashid-un-Nisa's name was omitted from the novel; she was mentioned as 'the mother of Barrister Sulaiman.' The surrogation of nominal identity by familial identity was a common practice among the elite Muslim families. As a sign of modesty, instead of their names, many Muslim women authors used their relational/familial identity.

Though *Islahunnisa* was the first novel to be written by a woman author, it was not the first women-centric novel in Urdu literary history. Rashid-un-Nisa was in her teens when Nazir Ahmad (1830–1912) published *Mirat ul-Arus* (The Bride's Mirror), first published in 1869, a novel which is considered to be the first Urdu novel by various scholars.[5] The novel had a strong influence on Rashid-un-Nisa's young mind, and in *Islahunnisa*, she praises Ahmad for his efforts towards female education. Ahmad was an officer at the Education Department and was 'committed to the idea of female education' (Asaduddin 87). He wrote the novel for education and edification of his female relatives,[6] and it was, primarily, meant 'for private circulation' (87). The novel was submitted in a competition in response to a notification by the colonial government. In 'Prize Winning Adab: A Study of Five Urdu Books Written in Response to the Allahabad Government Gazette Notification,' CM Naim mentions five novels that were submitted by different authors in response to Notification no. 791A, dated 20 August 1868. The notification invited authors to submit their works that could serve some 'useful purpose.' One of the conditions was: 'Books suitable for the women of India will be especially acceptable, and well rewarded' (Naim 293). The notification with the promise of reward of a cash prize persuaded many authors to produce useful and suitable literature, specifically for women readers. Ahmad was declared one of the winners of the competition, and the colonial government included the novel in the curriculum of girls' schools and bought two thousand copies of the novel (Naim 300). Ahmad also wrote two more women-centric novels: *Banat un Nash* (The Daughter of the Bier), first published in 1872, and *Taubat un Nasuh* (The Repentance of Nasuh), first published in 1874. The series of novels was aimed at inculcating household art, piety, and useful knowledge among female young adults. Thus, it can be inferred that the emergence of the novel in Muslim South Asia began with *Mirat ul-Arus*, a novel that can be classed as a 'young adult novel' for female readers. Pritchett regards it as 'the first Urdu Bestseller' (Afterword) and notes that the initial part of the novel 'is marked only by the traditional romance-like opening title *Aghaz-e-qissah*' (209). Margrit Pernau reads the novel in the tradition of 'children's literature' ('Asghari's Piety' 57). It may be inferred that young women in the colonial India occupied a position of liminality – somewhere between childhood and adulthood. Pernau explains:

> One might ask whether this book about a young bride can be classified as children's literature at all. The assumption behind the question, however, is that a clear demarcation exists between childhood and adulthood. This, in turn, finds its reflection in children's literature as a specific genre that should be modified for the nineteenth-century Indian context. Asghari is eight years old when she takes over the responsibility for her parental household and that she marries at the age of thirteen.
>
> (57)

Ahmad's novel, to use Deborah Stevenson's idea, can be classified as one of the 'crossover books': the 'works that begin as titles for adults and then become the reading matter of children' (Stevenson 181). Taxonomically speaking, Ahmad's didactic novel presents ample possibilities to be read both as a 'young Adult novel' and as a novel meant for 'children.' Didacticism, a quintessential characteristic, runs through the works written for women and children. In the same vein, most of the fictions written for women in its early phase of the development of the novel in the Muslim South Asia could also be categorized under the rubrics of young adult literature. The publication of the women-centric novels by Nazir Ahmad and other male authors inspired women to write and publish their own stories. Though this could be one of the probable reasons for the commencement of a new genre of women's fiction, this was not the very first publication opportunity for Muslim women to connect with the larger community of women, through the medium of the print. By the end of the 19th century, women magazines were being published and circulated from different cities.[7] By the turn of the century, many Muslim women from the elite families began to participate actively and contribute to the social reform debates by participating in women conferences and publishing their writing in journals and magazines. Archives of women's journals are an important source of understanding lives and subjectivities of Muslim women in South Asia.

What role did the women's journal play in the evolution of the novel? What kind of writings were published in them? What are the ways in which women's journals and magazines can be understood? Published from different parts of British India, these journals, especially produced for consumption in the domestic sphere, provided avenues for discussions on various issues pertaining to women and domesticity. Shenila Khoja-Moolji (2018) analyses the debates and discussions in the two issues of *Ismat* (1911) to demonstrate how 'the two sides of the debate on the issue of women's education: those who are against it and those who want the same education for women as that for men. The latter entails going to English schools and studying the curriculum determined by English standards' (40). Established by the people who were associated with social reforms among Muslims communities, Urdu journals such as *Khatun, Ismat, Akhbarun-nisa, Mu'allim-e-Niswan, Tehzeeb-e-Niswan*, and Bengali journals such as *Saugat, Bangiya Mussalman Sahitya Patrika*, and *Nabanoor* invited Muslim women to publish writings pertaining to their own lives and experiences in their contemporary societies. But, unfortunately, as Gail Minault claims in *Secluded Scholars* (105–157), most of the journals are rarely mentioned in the histories of Urdu literature and journalism. They published articles and stories that dealt with issues such as female education, the age of girl's marriage, and the importance of her consent to marriage, polygamy, and purdah. Similarly, Azeem and Hasan (2013) show how in the times when 'the issue of modernity and the place of Islam' (03) were being debated in colonial Bengal, 'the editors of journals such as *Nabanoor* or *Saugat* appealed to women to come forward and write' (03). Apart from letters, character-sketches, reportage, autobiographical pieces, and travel accounts, they also carried 'creative writing: short stories, serialized novels, poetry on the themes 'suitable for female readers' (Minault *Secluded Scholars* 106). Pioneering Urdu novels such as *Fasāna-e Āzād* (1878–83) and memoirs of authors such as Ismat Chughtai (*Kaghazi hai Pairahan*), Bibi Ashraf (*Hayat-e-Ashraf*), and Qaiseri Begum (*Kitab-e-Zindagi*) were all serialized in different Urdu journals. The development of the genre of fiction in its modern literary form can be traced back to the popularity and circulation of magazines and journals in the late colonial period.

Literature for women

What were some of the socio-historical conditions which led to the emergence of women's novel in Muslim South Asia? In what ways did the reform discourses affect the literature written for/by Muslim women? Why did the issue of female-education become an agenda for both the traditional reformists and the modernists?

The genre of novel, in its nascent phase, was a product of the changing socio-political condition of the domestic spheres in Muslim families, and hence an investigation of the relationship between literature and reforms will help to understand the production and the consumption of literature by and for Muslim women.

In her meticulous analysis of female education in colonial India, Gail Minault (1998) refers to various 'networks of reform' and demonstrates how 'the production of literature suitable for the education and socialization of Muslim women, according to reformist *desiderata*' (158). She explains that in Muslim debates over female education, the focus remained on the improvement of domestic sphere, which by then was emerging as a complex space – the religious and the modernist reformers were focusing on the improvement of the domestic sphere by involving practical measures to promote female education. The impulse to reform the society started with the perceived decline of Muslim rule in the 18th century. For Muslim intelligentsia with a religious bent of mind, the social and religious changes were not centred on the imitation of the West but on an imagined return to the glorious days of the Islamic past. Muslim women, as the symbolic bearer of identity, had to be protected from evil influences. Pernau demonstrates how the focus of reforms was shifted to women in *Ashraf into Middleclass*:

> This delinking of Islamic identity from the ruling power and its localisation in the private sphere inevitably turned attention to the women. As long as the women were not sufficiently Islamicized, the 'Other' from which the men sought to dissociate themselves was there in the women's quarters, right in their houses.
>
> (144)

With the emergence of mass production and consumption of Urdu books from the late 1860s, various reformist texts (mostly in form of domestic manuals) were published and disseminated on a large scale. Francis Robinson notes:

> the speed and vigor with which print was taken up by Urdu-speaking Muslims, from the tracts and newspapers that were published in the 1820s and 1830s through to the thousands of books being published at the beginning of the twentieth century.
>
> (240)

The proliferation of printed texts on massive scale provided access to knowledge to a large section of the Muslim society. The print capitalism had democratized knowledge to an extent and opened up avenues for both men and women who were desirous. For instance, Bibi Ashraf's 'How I learned to read and write,' a personal narrative published in an Urdu journal, demonstrates her struggle of self-education through various printed texts available at her home. Books and domestic manuals such as Karim ud Din's *Taleem-un-Nisa* (Education of Women), Abd ul Qadir's *Risala-e-Adab-e-Nikah* (Manual of Etiquettes of Marriage), Nawab Qutb ud Din's *Tuhfa-uz-Zujain* (A Gift for Wife), Begum Shahjahen's *Tehzeebul Niswan-o-Tarbiyatul Insan* (The Reform of Women and the Cultivation of Humanity), Maulana's Ashraf Ali Thanvi's *Bihishti Zewar* (Ornaments of Paradise), and others were published and sold specifically for Muslim women. Written in simple Urdu, the language in which most of the women were proficient, these domestic manuals aimed at the cultivation of moral and ethical values, primarily, based on Islamic principles. However, not all the literature that was produced for women was religious in nature. *Tehzeebul Niswan-o-Tarbiyatul Insan* (1889) by Shahjehan (1868–1901), the Begum of Bhopal, has sections on home remedies for common illness; advices on stitching, dress-marking, and jewellery-making; and suggestion on home decoration. In her pioneering work, *Muslim Women, Reform and Princely Patronage: Nawab Sultan Jahan Begam of Bhopal*, Lambert-Hurley mentions the importance of the book: 'Considered the first women's encyclopaedia in India, this volume covered a wide variety of topics relating to women's work in the household and their status in Islam' (42).

Bihishti Zewar by Maulana Ashraf Ali Thanvi (1863–1943), which still remains the most popular domestic manual in South Asian Muslim societies, was published around the turn of the century. Barbara Metcalf, the translator, credits the book for illustrating 'a new concern for bringing mainstream Islamic teachings to women – a departure from the traditional view in which women typically were not expected to have more than a minimal acquaintance with these teaching' (01). She notes that there is 'an implicit conviction' (02): 'women are essentially same as men, neither endowed with a special nature for spiritual or moral virtue nor handicapped in any way by limitations of intellect or character' (02). Metcalf's interesting reading of the text positions gender equality as an important impetus behind the book. The book's importance, for Metcalf, lies in the way it 'challenges widely held misperceptions and stereotypes of Islamic teaching about women' (06) and also how it debunks the stereotyped image of Muslim women held by the European societies for ages. Metcalf's observation resonates with the critique of such representations by Islamic feminists such as Fatema Mernissi[8] and Mohja Kahf.[9] Both the scholars have critiqued the representations of Muslim women in different literatures and cultures. Metcalf, in her reading, appears to be critiquing the colonial obsession with unveiling of the alien culture – an aspiration to penetrate behind the veil – 'characterized by a desire to master, control, and reshape the body of the subjects by making them visible' (Yegenoglu 12).

Prominent personalities such as Chirag Ali (1884–1895), Ameerali Syed (1849–1928), S Khuda Bukhsh (1842–1908), Begum Sultan Jahan (1858–1930), Rokeya Sakhawat Hossain (1880–1932), Husain Badruddin Tyabji (1873–1973), Rashid ul Khairi (1868–1936), Sayyid Mumtaz Ali (1860–1935), and others published articles and books discussing and debating the rights, status, and responsibilities of women in Islam. Most of the writings attempt to do away with orthodox interpretations of Islam and Islamic customs. Sayyid Mumtaz Ali's *Huquq un-Nisvan* (The Rights of Women) persuaded the contemporary society to rethink the rights of women in Islam. Ali, an alumnus of Islamic school of Deoband, wrote the treatise drawing upon his knowledge of the Quran and the life of the prophet. He critiqued the supposed male superiority, which according to him was the result of ignorance of the true message of Islam. He states:

> keeping women in ignorance and isolation is not a requirement of Islam, and to say that it is betrays a lack of understanding of religion as well as a fundamental mistrust of women which is destructive of family life, of human love, and of all that the Prophet stood for in a dynamic, just human society.
>
> (Minault 'Sayyid Mumtaz Ali' 150)

Minault in her article on Sayyid Mumtaz Ali mentions how Sir Syed Ahmed Khan (1817–1898), the founder of Mohammedan Anglo Oriental College (which later became Aligarh Muslim University), was shocked with Ali's arguments regarding the understanding of the rights of women in Islam. Various scholars have argued Khan's ambiguous stand on the question of female education.[10] Khan univocally supported Western education for Muslim men, but his views on female education 'were consistent with his own cultural formation' (Minault, *Secluded Scholars* 19). In *The Education of Mohammedan Girls*, Khan expresses his satisfaction over the state of education among females and prioritizes male education over female education on the pretext of his contemporary socio-economic conditions. He urged the colonial government to concentrate on the 'enlightenment and education of Mohammedan boys' (De Souza 170), as according to him, when 'the present generation of Mohammedan men is well educated and enlightened the circumstances will necessarily have a powerful though indirect effort on the enlightenment of Mohammedan women, for educated fathers, brothers, and husbands will naturally be most anxious to educate their female relations' (170).

Many of the modernist Muslim reformers were associated with Sir Syed Ahmad Khan and the Aligarh Movement and utilized the medium of literature to articulate their concerns regarding the condition of women. Khwaja Altaf Hussain Hali (1837–1914), a poet, literary critic, and biographer, inaugurated cultural renaissance in Urdu literary tradition with his women-centric poems, such as *Munajat-e-Bewa* (The Prayer of the Window); *Chup ki Dad* (Homage to the Silent), published in 1905; and *Majalis un-Nisa* (Assemblies of Women), published in 1874. Hali created 'new' female characters – they were different from most of the romanticized and eroticized representations of women in the Urdu/Persian poetic tradition. In *Munajat-e-Bewa*, he makes a plea for widow remarriage, and in *Chup ki Dad*, he praises the important role that women play in society. Hali's poems gained recognition from the British Indian government and became a part of the syllabus of girls' schools. Apart from creating awareness through literature, many reformers translated their words into action by establishing girls' schools, though the zenana system of education continued among affluent families. Waheed Jahan and her husband, Miya Abdullah, started Aligarh Zenana Madrasa (Aligarh Girl's School) in Aligarh in 1906; Sayyid Karamat Husain, a judge from

Allahabad High Court, founded a school exclusively for Muslim girls in 1912 at Lucknow; Rokeya Sakhawat Hossain started Sakhawat Memorial Girls' School in 1909 in Bhagalpur (re-established in Calcutta in 1911); Iqbaluunissa Hussain, a novelist, established a girls' school in Bangalore; and Abdul Haq Abbas started Madrasat ul Banat, a girls' school in Jalandhar, Punjab. With the emergence of formal schools, the question of teaching a well-defined syllabus was discussed and debated, and various reformist women-centric texts became a part of the curriculum of schools for girls. The educated, thinking, new women of reformist texts inspired the early women novelists to model the characters of their novels on them.

Novel formulations in Muslim South Asia

How to understand 'women's fiction' in Muslim South Asia? What were some of the cultural determiners? What are some of the tensions/intersections that exist between women-centric novels written by male authors and female authors? What are the ways in which women novelists responded to the agenda of contemporary reforms? As mentioned earlier, many early women's fiction reverberates around the themes and narrative style of the early novels written by male authors. Thus, the emergence of women's novel can be explored vis-à-vis the history of novel in colonial India.

   In her study of the emergence and growth of novels in colonial India, Meenakshi Mukherjee outlines the complexity of understanding the process. While demonstrating the uniqueness of the process, she notes, the 'complex question of plural heritage, the multiplicity of determinants – both indigenous and derived from other cultures – that overlapped, interacted, and fused to make the shaping of this literary form a tangled and unique process' (Mukherjee, "The Epic" 596). The emergence of the novel is not merely 'a legacy of British rule' (01), and influence of the indigenous forms of oral narratives, such as the tradition of *Qissas* and *Dastaans*, or what Mukherjee calls 'pre-novel narratives,' popular in South Asia before the advent of the novel, are a quintessential part of its growth. Urdu author and translator Qurratulain Hyder hints towards the presence of a novel-like form in the late 18th century. In the introduction of *The Nautch Girl*, an English translation of Hasan Shah's *Afsana-e-Rangin* (1798), Hyder claims that Shah's text is the first modern novel written without any influence of the West, although her claim has been contested by Urdu critics such as M. Asaduddin (p. 117). Novels such as Nazir Ahmad's *Mirat ul-Arus* retain some elements of the old tradition of storytelling and bear 'a striking resemblance to the *dastaan*, in that chapters have abstracts summarizing their content while dialogues are written out in a style closely approximating that of dramas' (Oesterheld 'Nazeer' 29). The narrative mode of *Qissa* and *Dastaan* continues to be used in the 20th-century speculative novels by many Muslim women authors.[11] The novels in this part of the world have a 'tangled genealogy' (Mukherjee 'Epic' 596), and the influence of pre-novel narratives and oral story-telling problematizes the understanding of the genre of novel in colonial India.

Some of the novels in the late colonial period were written in the imitative form of European novels imported into colonial India. They may be categorized as 'borrowed' directly from the West and could be traced back to the English education of the authors, and 'through English an exposure to Western literature' (Mukherjee *Realism and Reality* 01). While analysing the consumption of European novels from 1850 to 1900, Priya Joshi mentions various novels that were adapted or translated into different regional languages; she notes, 'by 1850, English books worth £148,563 were being imported into India, and these amounts would increase greatly after the 1857 Mutiny, reaching a peak in 1863–64 of £328,024' (202). European authors such as Collins, Disraeli, Reynolds, Wilde, and others were available in many regional translations from the late 19th century.[12] Reynolds was at least translated into four regional languages; his novels had 'the special mixture of thriller/crime fiction and the fantastic or grotesque, but on the other hand the triumph of a sharp mind and logic reasoning which was at the heart of many Indian and Perso-Arabic stories about crimes and the detection of criminals' (Osterheld 'The Neglected Realm' 01). Perhaps, such similarities could be a reason for the popularity of Reynolds among the authors, translators, and readers in colonial India. Naim delineates the popularity of the Urdu translations of Reynolds' novels and demonstrates the emergence of urban Urdu '*Mistriz*' series.[13] The evolution of the genre of novel in the late 19th century reverberates with Moretti's *Law of literary evolution*: 'the modern novel first arises not as an autonomous development but as a compromise between a western formal influence (usually French or English) and the local material' (Moretti 58). The Urdu *Mistriz* series could be read as a product of the Western influence and local material. For Mukherjee, the history of early novels is littered with examples of texts 'which began as derivative ventures but far surpassed authors' limited attention by absorbing and reflecting the traits unique to their historical moment and cultural memory' (Mukherjee *Early Novels in India* 01). She cites Hadi Ruswa's *Umrao Jan Ada* (1899), which is allegedly modelled on GM Reynold's *Rosa Lambert* and Kandukuri Veeresalingam's *Rajasekhara Charitra* (1878), which emerged out of an abandoned attempt to translate Oliver Goldsmith's *The Vicar of Wakefield* into Telugu, among others as some of her examples (*Realism and Reality* 17–18)

Women fiction began in the late 19th century in Muslim South Asia, and from the beginning of the 20th century, numerous Muslim women authors – almost all of them from the *Ashraf* class – published their novels and short stories. The first generation of Muslim women fiction writers, as they may be termed, wrote fiction primarily focusing on women's roles and responsibilities and character formation. An important factor that had given impetus to the growth of women's novel was the expanding market for literature for consumption of women. Early novels such as Muhammadi Begum's *Sharif Beti*, Safia Begum's *Aaj-Kal*, Nazr Sajjad Hyder's *Akhtar Begum*, Abbasi Begum's *Zohra Begum*, Valida Afzal Ali's *Gudar ka Lal*, Tyaba Begum's *Anwari Begum*, and Jehanara Begum's (Begum Shanawaz's) *Husanara Begum* deal with the themes of domesticity, ethics and values, and female education. They share their thematic concerns with early novels by Muslim male authors, such as Nazir Ahmad's *Mirat ul-Arus*, Maulvi Karim-Uddin's

Tazkirah-un-Nisa, Muhammad Hussain Khan's *Tehzeeb-e-Niswan*, and Muhammad Zaheer-Uddin Khan's *Taleem-e-Niswan*. Some of these novels demonstrate the crucial role that Muslim male authors played in the production and consumption of literature by and for Muslim women. Didactic fiction by Nazir Ahmad and his contemporaries not only were one of the first groups of women-centric texts to be written but also represent an important milestone in the emergence and development of the novel. Novels by male authors influenced the writing style of early women authors, as Suhrawardy notes in her study, 'the influence of Nazir Ahmad is the strongest, and in some instance that of Sarshar can also be detected . . . Rashid ul Khairi's style was imitated very much during the years 1919 to 1928' (123). Though most of the fiction published by women shows the influence of male authors and *Islahi Adab* (reformist literature), their novels cannot be merely regarded as 'derivative venture.' Women's fiction may be understood as a product of the colonial modernity and indigenous reformist zeal of a class of educated Muslims in the 19th century, a crucial period in the history of Muslims in South Asia, when the 'nobility and above all the middle class which were emerging' (Pernau *Ashraf into Middle Class* xii) and the 'members described themselves as *Ashraf*, "men from good family"' (xii). The birth and emergence of novels in Muslim South Asia can be ascribed to the educated class of Ashraf Muslims in the late 19th and the early 20th centuries.

Apart from Urdu, Muslim women authors have written fiction in Bengali and English from the turn of the century. Scholars such as Sonia Nishat Amin, Mahua Sarkar, Shaheen Akhtar, and Moushumi Bhowmik have questioned the invisibility of Muslim women in the history of colonial Bengal. In *Women in Concert: An Anthology of Bengal Muslim Women's Writings (1904–1938)*, Akhtar and Bhowmik have put together stories, essays, and interviews of early Bengali Muslim women authors, such as Rokeya Sakhawat Hossain, Khairunnesa, M Rahman, Sufia Kamal, and others. The novels by Muslim women, in its nascent stage, not only demonstrate their negotiations with modernity but also debunk myths about their backwardness. While most of the early Urdu women novelists, such as Rashid-un-Nisa, Muhammadi Begam, and Abbasi Begam, with their limited literary output, emphasized on the importance of female education, modesty, and familial relationships, Rokeya Sakhawat Hossain, through her English and Bengali fiction, questioned the societal norms and gender roles in society.

These early novels are also noteworthy specially in terms of the depiction of the 'New Woman' as a cultural and literary figure in the sphere of fiction. The figure, however, is different from the Victorian counterpart, who is stereotyped in the public imagination as 'educated at Girton College, Cambridge, rode a bicycle, insisted on rational dress, and smoked in public: in short, she rejected the traditional role for women and demanded emancipation' (Nelson ix). In Muslim women's fiction, most of the literary constructs of the New woman hail from Ashraf class and strike a balance between tradition and modernity. The space of fiction was utilized by the early women authors to depict the binaries between the old and the new values in the public and private spheres. Many women authors portrayed refreshing new images of womanhood by making their characters educated and independent. Belonging to different walks of lives – doctors, students, teachers, and scientists – the new female characters question the rights and responsibilities of women in their contemporary societies and debunk the notion of confinement of women to the domestic sphere.

Though most of the literary output in this period adheres to the depiction of Muslim women's lives and subjectivities in the domestic sphere, it would not be incorrect to claim that, during the same period, many of them also experimented with the theme and form of the novel. In her study of the early Urdu women novelists, Suhrawardy demonstrates how women authors wrote in different genres of fiction. Pioneering author such as Muhammadi Begum, whose novels resonate didactic fiction of male novelists, modelled her *Chandan Har* on a free translation of Maupassant's *Necklace* (123). Suhrawardy also mentions 'several novels written by women besides those in which the influence of *Tehzeeb* was apparent' (146). Novels such as *Shaukat Ara Begum* and *Roshanak Begum* show influence of Sarshar's *Fasana-e-Azad*, depicting an alternative trajectory of development of women's fiction. Similarly, Rokeya Sakhawat Hossain's speculative fiction and Mrs. Qadir's horror/thrillers were novelty on the literary maps of women's fiction. Thus, it can be claimed that from the early 20th century, women's fiction in Muslim South Asia began to branch out into exploring the format of fiction, some of which may be read as genre fiction. Despite the volumes of scholarship and criticism available on the representation of women in literature in Muslim South Asia – spearheaded by scholarships on Nazir Ahmad, Rashidul Khairi, and Altaf Hali – there remains little acknowledgement of the literature written by Muslim women. Scholars such as Gail Minault, Siobhan Lambert-Hurley, Barbara Metcalf, Barnita Bagchi, M Asadduin, Rakhshanda Jalil, and Priyamvada Gopal have brought much-needed critical attention to literature by prominent Muslim women authors such as Rokeya Sakhawat Hossain, Ismat Chughtai, Qurratulain Hyder, and Rashid Jahan, but, to use Showalter's idea, there is a 'missing link'.[14] Showalter investigates the English literary history and explains the problem of ignoring the minor fiction writers while tracing the history:

> Criticism of women novelists, while focusing on these happy few, has ignored those who are not "great," and left them out of anthologies, histories, textbooks, and theories. Having lost sight of the minor novelists, who were the links in the chain that bound one generation to the next, we have not had a very clear understanding of the continuities in women's writing, nor any reliable information about the relationships between the writers' lives and the changes in the legal, economic, and social status of women.
>
> (07)

An attempt to connect a few missing links, by exploring some of the early as well as contemporary Muslim women's fiction, would reveal that from the early simple narratives to the experimental fiction, the female characters depicted in the Muslim women's fiction ranges from traditional, educated, rebellious, to bold feminist heroines. Genres such as romance, speculative, romance, and thriller have been popular among women from the beginning of the twentieth century.

IV

From 'New Women' to 'Future Girls'

Sultana's Sisters: Gender, Genre, and Genealogy in South Asian Muslim Women's Fiction covers the depiction of women from the new woman of the early 20th century to the future girls of the 21st century. Beginning with Rokeya Sakhawat Hossain's works as the defining moment not only in the tradition of genre fiction but also in Muslim South Asia, the first section of the book explores the early genre fiction. The four chapters in the first section, 'Genre and Early Fiction,' deal with early women novelists and the following four genres of fiction: speculative narratives by Rokeya Sakhawat Hossain, romance fiction by Hijab Imtiaz Ali, horror fiction of Mrs. Qadir, and domestic fiction of Muhammadi Begum and Abbasi Begum. The opening chapter, '*Fruits of freedom: Rokeya Sakhawat Hossain's writings as genre fiction*' by Barnita Bagchi, deals with narratives by Rokeya Sakhawat Hossain, a major figure in the history of women's activism and education in South Asia, who, according to Bagchi, eschewed realistic writing in favour of speculative mode in genre fiction. Bagchi reads not only utopian fiction, such as *Sultana's Dream* (1905) and *Padamrag* (1924), but also fabular narratives, such as *Srishtitattva* (1920) and *Nar-isrishti* (1919), and the *rupaka* narratives, such as *Jnanaphala* (1922) and *Muktiphala* (1921). Bagchi analyses Hossain's oeuvre in the context of genre fiction in Bengali, Indian, and global contexts. '*Sultana's Dream*' (1905) by Hossain outlines a feminist utopia and is one of the first speculative fictions written by a woman. Written almost a decade before Charlotte Perkins Gilman's much-acclaimed feminist utopia *Herland* (1915), it imagines a Ladyland, a place where gender roles have been reversed – men are confined to *zenana* whereas women are participating actively in universities, scientific inventions, and other productive tasks of social and national interests. Bagchi demonstrates Rokeya's belief in female knowledge and leadership as the keys to human development and progress. Shweta Sachdeva Jha's chapter 'Locating romance and women writers in Urdu literature: Hijab Imtiaz Ali's genre fiction' reads the novels of Hijab Imtiaz Ali, one of the pioneers of Romance fiction in Urdu, who is often considered as 'Pakistan's Barbara Cartland.' Ali's novels such as *Meri Natamaam Mohabbat* (My Unfinished Love affair) and *Zalim Mohabbat* (Cruel Love) were one of the early romance fiction written in South Asia. Ali's fiction not only commanded a huge readership but also inspired generations of Muslim women writers. Ali's fiction conforms to many of the conventions of the romance novel, but it cannot be regarded merely as mass-market romance with almost an exclusively female readership. Often romance is merely classed as feminized and a denigrated genre, but romance is 'a place in which women writers and their readers find a recognizable shape for their desires, apprehensions, fantasies, and often conflicted senses of identity and thus (at best) make better sense of them, personally, politically, and ethically' (Holmes 04). Jha argues that Ali's fiction can be read in the genre of romance as Hijab's fictional world has central themes of love and romantic relationship between men and women, and her articulation of desire, anxiety, and love is conveyed to readers through a range of modes and motifs familiar to the reader acquainted with Urdu storytelling and poetry, which comes close to the style known as 'Romaniyat,' or Urdu romanticism. Jaideep Pandey's " 'I'm nobody! Who are you?" Mrs. Abdul Qādir's horror fiction and the non-authorial' is an interesting intervention not only in the scholarship on Muslim women authors but also in the development and growth of novels in South Asia. Pandey's essay explores the intriguing world of the horror fiction written by Mrs. Qadir, a 20th-century 'non-author.' It is extremely rare to come across any horror, thriller, or detective fiction by women in colonial India. Mrs. Qadir's choice of her subjects and themes are interesting and intriguing. Pandey studies a new generic aesthetic that provides counterpoint to the push of modernity that one encounters in the dominant trends of early to mid-20th-century Urdu writing and demonstrates the ways in which Mrs. Qadir's horror fiction contradicts the normative understanding of Muslim women's writings. Mohammad Afzal's 'Gendering the Urdu domestic novel: Muhammadi Begum, Abbasi Begum, and the Women Question' deals with the evolution of women's fiction in Urdu and literary interventions in the tradition by two early women authors: Muhammadi Begum and Abbasi Begum. Afzal shows how the two authors contested the patriarchal discourse of the Indian reformers by appropriating the genre of the Urdu novel. The novels herald the advent of a new woman in Muslim women's fiction. Who are the new Muslim women? How is their agency represented in fiction? How do women writers negotiate with their representation in women-centric novels by male authors? Afzal, in his analysis of Urdu novel *Safiya Begum*, shows how the benefits of female education, as portrayed in early women-centric novels, are not merely confined to the good management of household affairs but extends to the study and practice of modern medicine, and reflects the aspirations of new avenues by Muslim girls.

The second section, 'Genres and modernity,' focuses explicitly on the fiction of authors who, to use Gail Minault's idea, were the 'daughters of reform,' 'who grew up going to school, reading women's magazine, and coping with accelerated social changes' (Minault, *Secluded Scholars* 266). The seven authors under the purview of this section of the book are Khadija Mastur (1927–1982), Qurratulain Hyder (1927–2007), Wajida Tabassum (1935–2011), Attia Hosain (1913–1998), Mumtaz Shahnawaz (1912–1948), Selina Hossain (b. 1947), and Shaheen Akhtar (b. 1961). Their fiction depicts a new phase in the growth and development of fiction in South Asia. Though most of the fiction by these authors are rarely categorized as genre fiction, attempts have been made by the contributors to explore the intersections/tensions that exist between genre fiction and literary fiction. Mehr Afshan Farooqi's 'Women who wielded pens: Khadija Mastur' deals with the fictional world of Khadija Mastur, who migrated from India to Pakistan in the wake of 1947 partition. Farooqi looks at how Muslim women used Urdu language to negotiate with modernity within the space of literature. She also shows how Mastur creates literary space for a new Muslim woman by fashioning her heroines as rebel women whose conflicts are with their mother and with the culture that instils internalized constraints of gender roles. Fatima Rizvi's chapter, '"Studies in [] dying culture[s]": Qurratulain Hyder and Urdu fantasy fiction in self-translation' examines the fantasy fiction of Qurratulain Hyder, the grandame of Urdu literature. Hyder's narratives such as *Confessions of Saint Flora of Georgia* and *Roshni ki Raftaar* (The Speed of the Light) contributed to the genre of fantasy fiction in Urdu. Hyder's fiction demonstrates an amalgamation of her inheritance of the indigenous, oral traditions of the Urdu/Persian languages romantic *dastaan*, replete with the fantastic. Rizvi's essay examines how Hyder's fantasy stories evolve by means of a suspension of disbelief, most of the time, on the part of the reader and at times on the part of the protagonists. She also studies how Hyder employs the fantastic as a vehicle projecting a larger concern – recreation of cultural ambience and/or the historical past along with a will for preservation of endangered/dying languages. Wafa Hamid's '"The Forbidden City": An exploration of Wajida Tabassum's magazine fiction' examines the depiction of women's lives and body politics in the magazine fiction of Wajida Tabassum, an Urdu author famous for her bold and feminist stories. Hamid shows how in Tabassum's fictional world, 'home' is a space for oppression and confinement, but with a potential of agency, and how her stories challenge the dominant narratives about Muslim women by bringing forth the questions of sexuality and sexual agency of women. The last two chapters of the section explore possibilities of development of new genres in South Asia and demonstrate the intersections that exist between history and production of literature. Many partition theorists look at the partition not merely as a historical event but as a socio-political process that is still affecting the dynamics of South Asia. With authors still writing literature about partition, it can be argued that partition literature can be treated as a distinctive genre. Though partition fiction would rarely be categorized as 'genre fiction' in the traditional understanding of the term. Partition fiction also makes use of modes and motifs of genre fiction: Salman Rushdie's *Midnight's Children* (1981) utilizes speculative mode of narration; and fictions such as Veera Hiranandani's *The Night Diary*, Irfan Master's *A Beautiful Lie*, and Gavin's *Surya Trilogy* are specifically written and published for young adults. It cannot be refuted that both reading and readerships of fiction have become quite complex and hybrid in the contemporary times. The two partitions (1947 and 1971) in South Asia played a major role in redefining identity of the Indian sub-continent. The informed intervention of feminist scholars such as Urvashi Buta-lia, Kamala Bhasin, Yasmin Sakia, and Ritu Menon has situated the discourse of gender and partition at the centre of the multidisciplinary partition studies, which have variously revised the official national readings of the partitions. However, as Lambert-Hurley notes, the experiences that are 'often neglected were the particular experiences of Muslim women' (117). Though the question of Muslim women and partition appears to be in 'a realm of virtual anonymity' (Ali 248), the trauma of partition has been documented by Muslim women authors in both fictional and non-fictional forms.[15] The last two chapters offer interesting insights on the growth and development of the genre of partition fiction, particularly how the authors responded to these two socio-historical events. Mosarrap Hossain Khan's essay '"1971 Novels" in Bangladesh: Women's writing between the popular and the literary' looks at how the '1971 novels written by Muslim women intervene in the established genre fiction in 1971. He studies Selina Hossain's *Hangor Nodi Grenade* (A Shark, A River, A Grenade 1976) and Shaheen Akhtar's *Talaash* (The Search 2004) to examine how women writers of '1971 Novels' appropriate and expand the possibilities of the genre, and outlines how both the popular and literary novels draw on tropes of heroism, cowardice, villainy, a well-marked enemy, the collaborators, and a utopic future. Mobeen Hussain's chapter, '*Sunlight on a Broken Column* and *The Heart Divided* as Autobiographically inspired realist texts: Navigating gendered socio-political identities in genre fiction,' studies two crucial texts to portray the plight and predicament of Muslims during the 1947 partition of India and Pakistan and its aftermath. Hussain demonstrates how both the authors borrow from indigenous storytelling traditions to inscribe rich detail about their gendered cultural worlds into English-language narratives and show how both the personal and public lives of Muslim women become important for both the authors.

The last section of the book – 'Postcolonial genres' – explores some of the emerging genre fiction. The market and demand for the production of literature have expanded in recent years, and the influence of genres such as graphic novels could also be seen on the fiction in Muslim South Asia. The chapters covered in the last section of the book deal with contemporary developments in the themes and forms of fiction. Christel R Devadawson's chapter, '"Obedient Daughters' and the deployment of graphic stereotypes,' studies how Ayesha Tariq's *Sarah: The Surprised Anger of Obedient Daughter*, through the medium of graphic novel, represents the world of contemporary young Muslim women. Since the publication of Marjane Satrapi's *Persepolis* (2000), a graphic memoir, the genre of graphic fiction has played a crucial role in influencing women to tell their stories through the graphic medium. Tariq's graphic novel is the first such representation by a Muslim Woman from South Asia. Devadawson, in her analysis of the novel, unpacks the conversations that develop around the genre, the nation-state, and the constituency – defined by age and gender. Mohammad Asim Siddiqui's chapter, 'Contemporary politics and prehistoric past through popular genres: Maha Khan Phillips' novels,' examines *Beautiful from This Angle* and *The Curse of Mohenjo Daro* and focuses on different subjects employing different genres. Siddiqui shows how Phillips engages with the idea of history and power in 'realist' as well as 'realist-fantastic-thriller' modes. He examines how the author addresses the impact of 9/11 on Muslims across the globe, and deals with the question of terrorism and the misrepresentation of issues in media, in Western media in particular. He demonstrates how the novel explores the world in binary terms, conceiving the East as backward and the West as the beacon of light, and how Phillips' fiction revolves around the experiences, or ordeal, of a Muslim woman who is living in a Muslim land where women are a suppressed lot. Aysha Munira Rasheed's 'Occupying educational and intellectual space: Woman as radical flâneuse in Zahida Zaidi's campus novel *Inqilab Ka Ek Din*' looks into the expansion of women's physical mobility as a by-product of the movement and concludes that Zaidi's bike-riding independent female protagonists, despite being rare, and avant-garde, are a possibility and a potential reality. It might be speculated that Zaidi's heroines were modelled on the female characters of Victorian university fiction.[16] Madeline Clements' 'Making sense of conversion to Christianity in 20th-century Pakistan: Two women's co-authored autobiographies as crafted accounts' is an interesting reading of literature of religious conversion in post-colonial Pakistan. She examines two 'crafted account' of turning to Christianity, 'written' by Muslim women with the help of western co-authors or ghost-writers, demonstrate a desire on their protagonists' part to make narrative sense of personal experiences of spiritual inspiration and affiliation, social exclusion, fellowship, and homecoming. The last chapter of the section, 'Feminist futures in the speculative fictions of Andaleeb Wajid and Bina Shah,' by Umme Al-wazedi, examines three 21st-century novels by two contemporary authors. She studies the portrayal of 'alternative futures' in Andaleeb Wajid's *No Time for Goodbyes* (2014) and *Time Will Tell* (2014) and in Bina Shah's *Before She Sleeps* (2018). Al-wazedi explores the ideas of time travel and dystopia and presents the possibility of reading this texts in the tradition of 'feminist Science fiction.'

Given the wider geographical ambit of South Asia, neither the present book claims to cover the entire range of Muslim women's fiction in the region nor does it comprehensively list the works of all the important Muslim women writers from the late 19th century to the present. Instead, the book engages itself with certain gaps within the literary historiography in South Asia and initiates conversations between gender studies and genre studies. In doing so, the book departs from the current, limited but significant, scholarships available on the life narratives of Muslim women in South Asia[17] and explores a simultaneous tradition of fiction-writing by Muslim women from the late 19th century. Most of the fiction written by Muslim women are largely ignored by literary criticism, and also by much feminist criticism in South Asia. This book may be regarded as the first academic investigation of the tradition of Muslim women's fiction, focusing on both genre fiction and genre formation in Muslim South Asia.

Notes

1 For instance, the genre of *ghazal* is more often accused of depicting eroticized/romanticized images of women.
2 Scholars such as Gail Minault and Siobhan Lambert-Hurley have addressed the problems of invisibility of Muslim women in Indian historiography. For more details on their works, see the works cited.
3 Suhrawardy mentions Muhammadi Begum as the first Urdu woman novelist in her study of Urdu fiction. Begum published her first novel, *Sharif Beti*, in 1902. See Suhrawardy, p. 123. Suhrawardy was not acquainted with Rashid-un-Nisa's *Islahun nisa,* as the novel was lost for years and was discovered later. Syeda S. Hameed and Ṣughra Mahdi mention Rashid-un-Nisa's name in the introduction of their collection of translated Urdu stories. See *Parwaaz: a Flight of Words: Urdu Short Stories by Women,* Kali for Women, 1996, p vii. For more details on Rashid-un-Nisa and her novel, see *Khudā Bakhsh Library Journal,* Issue 153, 2008, p. 59.

4 In her seminal book on the emergence of the novel in India, Meenakshi Mukherjee regards *Yamuna Paryatan* (Marathi; 1857) and *Alaler Gharer Dulal* (Bengali; 1858) as the beginning go a 'new literary form in India.' See, Mukherjee, *Realism*, p. 21.

5 Scholars have disagreements on the question of the 'first Urdu' novel. See Asaduddin.

6 It is noteworthy to mention that Nazir Ahmad has not only written *Islahi adab* (advise literature) for women. His other books could also be classed under the same category. He wrote *Chand Pand* (1871) for his son, Bashiruddin. *Al-Huquq wa al-Faraiz* (1906) contains advice for all Muslims.

7 Some of these Urdu Women's magazine were: *Rafiq un nisa* (from Luckhnow, started in 1884), Sayyid Ahmed Delvi's *Akhbar un nisa* (started in 1884, Delhi), and *Sharif Bibiya* (started in 1893, Lahore). Mahua Sarkar notes various several women's magazines in colonial Bengal. See Mahua Sarkar (2008) and Gupta (2009).

8 Mernissi denounces the West's obsession with eroticization of bodies of Muslim women in paintings and cinema. She notes, 'The Westerners also referred primarily to pictorial images of harems, such as those seen in paintings or films, while I visualized actual palaces – harems built of high walls and real stones by powerful men such as caliphs, sultans, and rich merchants. My harem was associated with a historical reality. Theirs was associated with artistic images created by famous painters such as Ingres, Matisse, Delacroix, or Picasso – who reduced women to odalisques (a Turkish word for a female slave) – or by talented Hollywood moviemakers, who portrayed harem women as scantily clad belly-dancers happy to serve their captors.' See Mernissi (2001, 14).

9 From Mernissi's aforementioned comment, it appears that visual and print cultures in the West endorse stereotyped erotic-submissive images of Muslim women. However, it would be reductive and naive to come to this conclusion. Mohja Kahf's extensive reading of representations of Muslim women elucidates that there is nothing 'essential or time-less behind Western representations of Muslim woman; they are products of specific moments and developments in culture' (02). She studies canonical male-authored texts in the Western literary traditions from the Medieval Age to Romanticism and demonstrates how the image of Muslim women metamorphoses from 'a high-ranking noblewoman' ' of the Medieval Age to 'wanton queen' and 'helpless damsel' of Renaissance to 'veiled woman in harem' of the 17th century to the odalisque in the 18th century. See *Kahf* (1999).

10 For a detailed analysis of Sir Syed's views on female education, see Minault (2019).

11 Some of the fiction of Hijab Imtiaz Ali and Qurratulain Hyder depict the influence of *Dastaan* and *Qissa* tradition.

12 Gopal states that Premchand, the doyen of Urdu/Hindi novels, grew up reading Urdu translations of his favourite novels of Reynolds. See Gopal (2006).

13 C M Naim mentions the Urdu translations of Reynolds' novels, such as *The Mysteries of the Court Room of London* (translated and serialized in 'Navilist' by Ghulam Qadir Fasih) and *The Mystery of London*, and explains how Fasih's translations encouraged Urdu authors to write novels based on Reynolds' works: Naim documents at least 14 titles of novels based on Reynolds' mystery series. The mysteries were adapted for colonial urban spaces in South Asia, such as *Mistriz of Ludhiyana*, *Mistriz of Kabul*, *Misriz of Rawalpindi*, *Mistriz of Peshawar*, among others. For more details, see Naim (2018).

14 Siobhan Lambert-Hurley also discusses various 'missing links' in the historiography of Indian Muslim Women. Through her work on Sultan Jahan, she attempts to bridge the gap. See Lambert-Hurley (2007).

15 Some of the notable works by Muslim women authors on the partitions of Indian subcontinent are Khadija Mastur's *Aangan* (Women's Courtyard) and *Zameen* (Promised Land), Mumtaz Shahnawaz's *A Heart Divided*, Zahida Hina's *Junoon Raha Na Pari Rahi* (All Passion Spent), Begum Anis Kidwai's *Azaadi ki Chaawon mein* (In the Shadow of Freedom), Attia Hossain's *Sunlight on a Broken Column*, Ismat Chugtai's *Jadien* (Roots), and Qurratulain Hyder's *Akhiri Shab ke Humsafar* (Firefly in the Mist) and *Mere bhi Sanamkhaane* (My Temples, too).

16 For discussion on the New Women in public imagination, see Nelson (2001).
17 Siobhan Lambert-Hurley and Gail Minault have some pioneering works in the area. See Lambert-Hurley (2007), Lambert-Hurley (2018), and Gail Minault (1998). Ghazala Jamil's book explores Muslim women's narratives about their own situation. See Jamil (2018).

Works cited

Abu-Lughod, Lila. *Do Muslim Women Need Saving?* Harvard UP, 2013.

Aftab, Tahera. *Inscribing South Asian Muslim Women: An Annotated Bibliography & Research Guide.* Brill, 2008.

Ahmed, Leila. *Women and Gender in Islam: Historical Roots of a Modern Debate.* Yale UP, 1992.

Ali, Rabia Umar. "Muslim Women and the Partition of India: A Historiographical Silence." *Islamic Studies*, vol. 48, no. 3 (Autumn), 2009, pp. 425–36.

Amina Wadud. *Inside The Gender Jihad: Women's Reform in Islam.* One World Publications, 2006.

Asaduddin, M. "First Urdu Novel: Contesting Claims and Disclaimers." *Early Novels in India*, edited by Meenakshi Mukherjee, Sahitya Akademi, pp. 117–42.

Ashraf, Bibi. "How I Learned to Read and Write." Translated by C. M. Naim, *Urdu Text and Context: The Selected Essays of CM Naim.* Orient Blackswan, 2004.

Azeem, F., and P. Hasan. "Language, Literature, Education and Community: The Bengali Muslim Woman in the Early Twentieth Century." *Women's Studies International Forum*, vol. 45, July–Aug. 2013, pp. 105–11.

Bakhtin, Michael. *Problems in Dostoevsky's Poetics.* Translated by Carly Emerson, University of Minnesota Press, 1984.

Balabanlilar, Lisa. "The Begums of the Mystic Feast: Turco-Mongol Tradition in the Mughal Harem." *The Journal of Asian Studies*, vol. 69, no. 1, 2010, pp. 123–47.

Barbosa, Duarte. *A Description of the Coasts of East Africa and Malabar in the Beginning of the Sixteenth Century.* Hakluyt Society, 1866.

Bawarshi, Anis S. *Genre And The Invention Of The Writer: Reconsidering the Place of Invention in Composition.* Utah State UP, 2003.

Bokhari, Afshan. *Gendered Landscapes: Jahan Ara Begum's (1614–1681) Patronage, Piety and Self-Representation in 17th C Mughal India.* Universitat Wien, 2009.

Bynum, Caroline Walker. *The Holy Feast and Holy Fast: Women in the Medieval Period.* California UP, 2006.

Chattopadhyay, Bodhisattva, et al. *Indian Genre Fiction.* Routledge, 2018.

Clure, M. "Social Hindrances." *Daylight in the Harem: A New Era for Muslim Women*, edited by Annie Van Sommer and Samuel M. Zwemer, Anderson &Ferrier, 1911, pp. 91–102.

Cooke, Miriam. *Women Claim Islam: Creating Islamic Feminism Through Literature.* Routledge, 2001.

Coryat, Thomas. *Early Travels in India (1583–1619).* Oxford UP, 1921.

Culler, Jonathan. *Structuralist Poetics.* Cornell UP, 1975.

De Souza, Eunice. *Purdah: An Anthology.* Oxford UP, 2004.

Derrida, Jacques. "The Law of Genre." *Acts of Literature*, edited by Derek Attridge, Routledge, 1992, pp. 221–52.

Foucault, Michel. "Nietzsche, Genealogy, History." *Language, Counter-Memory, Practice: Selected Essays and Interviews*, edited by D. F. Bouchard, Cornell UP, 1977, pp. 139–64.

Frow, John. *Genre.* Routledge, 2006.

Fuller, Marcus B. *The Wrongs of Indian Womanhood.* Fleming H. Revell Company, 1900.

Gandhi, Supriya. *The Emperor Who Never Was: Dara Shukoh in Mughal India*. The Belknap Press of Harvard UP, 2020.

Gopal, Madan. *My Life and Times: Munshi Premchand*, Roli Books, 2006.

Gupta, Sarmishtha Dutta. "Saogat and the Reformed Bengali Muslim Woman." *Indian Journal of Gender Studies*, vol. 16, no. 3, 2009, pp. 329–58.

Harker, Jaime, and Cecilia Konchar Farr, *This Book Is an Action: Feminist Print Culture and Activist Aesthetics*. U of Illinois P, 2016.

Hirsch, E. D. *Validity in Interpretation*. Yale UP, 1967.

Holmes, Diana. *Romance and Readership in Twentieth-Century France*, Oxford Studies in Modern European Culture. Oxford UP, 2007, p. 04.

Jameson, Fredric. *The Political Unconscious*. Methuen, 1981.

Jamil, Ghazala. *Muslim Women Speak: Of Dreams and Shackles*. Sage Press, 2018.

Joshi, Priya. "Culture and Consumption: Fiction, the Reading Public, and the British Novel in Colonial India." *Book History*, vol. 1, 1998, pp. 196–220.

Kahf, Mohja. *Western Representations of the Muslim Woman: From Termagant to Odalisque*. University of Texas, 1999.

Khoja-Moolji, Shenila. *Forging the Ideal Educated Girl: The Production of Desirable Subjects in Muslim South Asia*. U of California P, 2018.

Lal, Ruby. *Empress: The Astonishing Reign of Nur Jahan*. W. W. Norton, 2018.

Lambert-Hurley, Siobhan. *Elusive Lives: Gender, Autobiography, and the Self in Muslim South Asia*. Stanford UP, 2018.

———. "Life/History/Archive: Identifying Autobiographical Writing by Muslim Women in South Asia." *Journal of Women's History*, vol. 25, no. 2, 2013, pp. 61–84.

———. *Muslim Women, Reform and Princely Patronage: Nawab Sultan Jahan Begam of Bhopal*. Routledge, 2007.

———. "Narrating Trauma, Constructing Binaries, Affirming Agency: Partition in Muslim Women's Autobiographical Writings." *Partition and Practice of Memory*, edited by Churnjeet Mahn and Anne Murphy, Palgrave Macmillan, 2018.

Latif, Bilkees. "Rare Visage of Moon." *The Untold Charminar: Writings on Hyderabad*, edited by Syeda Imam, Penguin Books, 2008, pp. 26–34.

Lawerence, Lipking. "Aristotles' Sister: A Poetics of Abandonment." *Critical Inquiry*, 1983, pp. 61–81.

Loomba, Ania. *Revolutionary Desires: Women, Communism, and Feminism in India*. Routledge, 2018.

Loomba, Ania, and Ritty A. Lukose. *South Asian Feminisms*. Duke UP, 2012.

Makien, Merja. *Feminist Popular Fiction*. Palgrave Macmillan, 2001.

Malhotra, Anshu, and Siobhan Lambert-Hurley. *Speaking of the Self: Gender, Performance, and Autobiography in South Asia*. Duke UP, 2015.

Mernissi, Fathima. *The Forgotten Queens of Islam*. U of Minnesota P, 1993.

———. *Scheherazade Goes West: Different Cultures, Different Harems*. Washington Square Press, 2001.

Metcalf, Barbara. *Perfecting Women: Maulana Ashraf Ali Thanawi's Bihishti Zewar, A Partial Translation*. Oxford UP, 1992.

Miller, Carolyn R. "Genre as Social Action." *Genre and the New Rhetoric*, edited by Aviva Freedman and Peter Medway, Taylor and Francis, 1994, pp. 23–42.

Minault, Gail. "Sayyid Mumtaz Ali and 'Huquq-un-Niswan': An Advocate of Women's Rights in Islam in the Late Nineteenth Century." *Modern Asian Studies*, vol. 24, no. 1, 1990, pp. 147–72.

————. *Secluded Scholars: Women's Education and Muslim Social Reforms in Colonial India.* Oxford UP, 1998.

————. "Sir Syed on 'The Present State of Education Among Muhammadan Female'." *Cambridge Companion to Sayyid Ahmad Khan*, Cambridge UP, 2019, pp. 55–68.

Moretti, Franco. "Conjectures on World Literature." *New Left Review*, Jan.–Feb. 2000, pp. 54–68.

Mukherjee, Meenakshi. *Early Novels in India.* Sahitya Akademi, 2002.

————. "The Epic and the Novel in India: A Tangled Genealogy." *The Novel: History, Geography, and Culture* edited by Franco Moretti, Princeton UP, 2006, pp. 596–631.

————. *Realism and Reality: The Novel and Society in India.* Oxford UP, India, 1985.

Naim, C. M. "Homage to a Magic Writer: The *Mistriz* and Asrar Novels of Urdu." *Indian Genre Fiction*, edited by Bodhisattva, et al, Routledge, 2018, pp. 38–56.

————. "Prize-Winning Adab: A Study of Five Books Written in Response to the Allahabad Government Gazette Notification." *Moral Conduct and Authority: The Place of Adab in South Asian Islam*, edited by Barbara D. Metcalf, U of California P, 1984, pp. 290–314.

Najmabadi, Afsaneh. *Women with Moustache and Men without Beard: Gender and Sexual Anxieties of Iranian Modernity.* U of California P, 2005.

Nelson, Carolyn Christensen. *A New Woman Reader: Fiction, Articles, and Drama of 1890s.* Broadview Press, 2001.

Oesterheld, Christina. "Nazir Ahmad and the Early Urdu Novel: Some Observations." *The Annals of Urdu Studies*, vol. 16, 2001, https://minds.wisconsin.edu/bitstream/handle/1793/18265/7_Oesterheld.pdf? Accessed 5 Jan. 2020.

————. "The Neglected Realm of Popular Writing: Ibne Safi's Novels." 2009, http://crossasia-repository.ub.uni-heidelberg.de/650/1/Oesterheld_IbneSafi_2009.pdf. Accessed 10 Dec. 2019.

Parker, Sarla. "Beyond Purdah: Sunlight on a Broken Column." *Margins of Erasure*, edited by Jasbir Jain and Amina Amin, Sterling Publisher, 1995, pp. 106–18.

Pelsaert, Francisco. *Jahangir's India* (The Remonstrantie). Translated by W. H. Moreland, W. Heffer & Sons Ltd, 1925.

Pernau, Margrit. "Asghari's Piety." *Learning How to Feel: Children's Literature and Emotional Socialization, 1870–1970*, edited by Ute Frevert, Oxford UP, 2014, pp. 57–73.

————. *Ashraf into Middle Class: Muslims in the Nineteenth-Century Delhi.* Oxford UP, 2013.

Pritchett, Frances W. "Afterword: The First Urdu Bestseller." *The Bride's Mirror: Mirat ul-Arus: A Tale of Life in Delhi in a Hundred Years Ago* by Maulvi Nazir Ahmad. Translated by G. E. Ward, with an afterword by Frances W. Prichett, Permanent Black, 2001, pp. 204–21.

Rashid-un-Nisa. *Islahunisa.* www.rekhta.org/ebooks/islah-un-nisa-rashid-un-nisa-ebooks. Accessed 25 July 2019.

Robinson, Francis. "Technology and Religious Change: Islam and the Impact of Print." *Modern Asian Studies*, vol. 27, no. 1, Feb., 1993, pp. 229–51.

Sarkar, Mahua. *Visible Histories, Disappearing Women: Producing Muslim Womanhood in Late Colonial Bengal.* Duke UP, 2008.

Sarkar, Tanika. *Words to Win: The Making of Amar Jiban: A Modern Autobiography.* Zubaan, 2013.

Scott, T. J. "Women in India, Intellectual Conditions." *Heathen Women's Friend*, 1869.

Shah, Hasan. *The Nautch Girl.* Translated by Qurratulain Hyder. Sterling Publications, 1992.

Showalter, Elaine. *A Literature of Their Own.* Princeton UP, 1977.

Sommer, Annie Van, and Samuel M. Zwemer. *Our Muslim Sisters, A Cry of Need from Lands of Darkness Interpreted by Those Who Heard it*. Fleming H. Revel, 1907.

Stevenson, Deborah. "History of Children's and Young Adult Literature." *Handbook of Research on Children's and Young Adult Literature*, edited by Shelby A. Wolf, et al., Routledge, 2011, pp. 179–92.

Suhrawardy, Shaista Akhtar B. *A Critical Survey of the Development of the Urdu Novel and Short Story*. Longmans, Green and Co., 1945.

Tharu, Susie J., and K. Lalita. *Women Writing in India: 600 B.C. to the Present: Vol. 1, 600 B.C. to the Early Twentieth Century*. The Feminist Press, 1991.

Woolf, Virginia. *A Room of One's Own*. Hardcourt Inc., 2005.

Yegenoglu, Meyda. *Colonial Fantasies: Towards a Feminist Reading of Orientalism*. Cambridge UP, 1998.

Zwemer, Samuel M. *Moslem Women*. Central Committee on the United Study of Foreign Missions, 1926.

SECTION I
Genres and early fiction

1

FRUITS OF FREEDOM

Rokeya Sakhawat Hossain's writings as genre fiction[1]

Barnita Bagchi

Rokeya Sakhawat Hossain's narrative writings are for the most part also pieces of genre fiction. Hossain published these writings in a variety of Bengali-language periodicals (such as *Mahila*, *Nabanoor*, *Bangiya Musalman Sahitya Patrika*, *Saogat*, and *Mohammadi*); she also wrote one, classic piece of genre fiction in English, 'Sultana's Dream,' in an Indian periodical edited by Indian Christians, *The Indian Ladies' Magazine*. Hossain hardly ever wrote long novels or short stories. Most of the time, she eschewed realistic writing, preferring instead the speculative mode in genre fiction. Her work is full of utopian novellas, parables with folk-tale- and fairy tale-like structures, sketches that play with mythology, and fiction that mixes romance, melodrama, and utopia. Hossain wrote as a transcultural and simultaneously South Asian and Bengali Muslim writer. She became a byword for Bengali women's activism and writing, dialoguing across religions, while maintaining a strong identity as a Muslim writer, activist, and woman. My chapter analyses two pieces of utopian fiction by Hossain, '*Sultana's Dream*' (1905) and *Padmarag* (The Ruby 1924); two fabular narratives, '*Srishtitattva*' or *The Story of Creation*, first published in 1920, and "*Narisrishti* or *The Creation of Woman*, first published in 1919, and the *rupaka* narratives (allegorical tales or parables), '*Jnanaphala*' (*The Fruit of Knowledge*, 1922) and *Muktiphala* (*The Fruit of Freedom*, 1921), in which Hossain combined critiques of colonialism and patriarchy. This chapter argues that Hossain needs to be analysed as a hybrid, speculative writer, adroitly and supply engaged in processes of translation and transculturation as much as in innovative creation. Gender justice, freedom from colonialism, and the rights of women, I argue, are ringing, recurring themes in her oeuvre. The chapter places Hossain's oeuvre in the context of genre fiction in Bengali, Indian, and global contexts. adventurous mobilities across cultural, historical, geographical, and literary knowledge, I argue, characterize Hossain's work.

DOI: 10.4324/9781003002062-3

Hossain is seen today, thanks largely to the work of feminist scholars such as Bagchi (2009), Amin (1996), and Ray (2002), as a major figure in the history of women's activism and education in South Asia. There were other women from the Bengali Muslim community who had written genre fiction before Hossain. Scholars such as Sonia Nishat Amin (1996) and Anisuzzaman (2000) have exploded the myth of the 'backward' Bengali Muslim writer, male or female: it is now evident that writings by this community had its own history and early achievements, which literary history simply forgot in its mainstream narratives, for a long time. Anthologies such as *Women in Concert* (Akhtar and Bhowmik 2008) have collected early writing by Bengali Muslim women. Nawab Faizunnesa (1834–1903) was a significant predecessor of Hossain in the field of Bengali Muslim genre fiction. Faizunnesa authored *Rupjalal* (1876), a fictional narrative recounted in Bengali mixed with Urdu and Persian, partly in poetry and partly in prose. Influenced by the medieval Bengali *Mangalkavya* tradition of writing eulogistic verse about a god or a goddess, the poem is also similar to the *Arabian Nights*. Bengali lyric poetry conventions and meters are blended with Muslim literary traditions of mixed-language writing (Hasanat 2017). Faizunnesa was a female upper-class landowner who founded schools, madrasas, and charitable institutions especially for women. The British empire conferred on her the honorary title of Nawab in 1889. While in the Preface to the book, Faizunnesa writes that one of the purposes of the work was to alleviate her sufferings with her bigamous husband Mohammad Gazi Chowdhury, the text itself has two fictional female protagonists, Rupbanu and Hurbanu, who accept bigamy and live happily with Prince Jalal, who in turn treats both wives equally (Hasanat 2008, 2017). Compared to Faizunnesa, Hossain's genre fiction is far more bold and uncompromising in its vision of women's rights and equity, but one can trace a common genealogy in which both can be placed, one in which philanthropy, educational opportunities, and the improvement of women's lot are all emphasized.

Hossain also needs to be placed in larger understandings of Bengali, Indian, and global genre fiction. Recent scholarship has elucidated how innovative and bold Hossain's utopian fictions are (Bagchi 2008, 2009). Utopias etymologically hinge on a pun in the meaning of the Greek word 'utopia,' at once 'no place' (ou-topos), and 'a good place' (eu-topos). Female utopias conjure up an idealized world where the wrongs of women are ameliorated by active, thoughtful women. *Sultana's Dream* is also a major example of South Asian science fiction, or *kalpavigyan*, a term 'coined as recently as 1962 by Adrish Bardhan to announce the first SF Magazine in Bangla, *Ascharja* [Wonder] of which he was the main editor' (Chattopadhyay 2018). For Bodhisattva Chattopadhyay, 'the central problem of *kalpavigyan*' is 'how to synchronize in aesthetic representation the supposedly universal nature of science with the particulars of the socio-cultural imaginary, especially when the relation between the two is often antagonistic or implicated in questions of cultural power' (Chattopadhyay 2016, 454). Chattopadhay, building on the work of Bagchi (Bagchi 2009) on the importance of utopia in Hossain's work, has called

Hossain's brand of *kalpavigyan* or science fiction 'speculative utopianism' (Chattopadhyay 2017).

Emerging scholarship sees Hossain as part of both global and local feminist literary and social experimentation and innovation, seeing her as a predecessor who has many resonances with later Bengali women writers such as Lila Majumdar and Nabaneeta Dev Sen, who use humour and wit to criticize social inequity and injustice (Bagchi 2013), and seeing her also in comparative perspective with white feminist writers of speculative fiction, such as Charlotte Perkins Gilman, whose *Herland* was published ten years after Hossain's *Sultana's Dream* (Bagchi 2020).

Hossain also shows continuities and resonances with contemporary feminist and socially engagée South Asian science fiction writers such as Vandana Singh (Bagchi 2016). Hossain's intertextual engagement with 19th-century British female writers of sensation fiction, such as Marie Corelli (Bhattacharya 2006), can now be mapped in synchrony with other South Asian adaptations of Victorian British genre fiction writers, such as Urdu adaptations of sensational 'urban mysteries' genre fiction by the British male writer G. M. Reynolds (Naim), reinforcing the argument made in this chapter about Hossain's engagement in the processes of transculturation or imagination across cultures.

Hossain's most memorable writing uses fairy tale and constructive parable, rather than dystopian apocalypse, as revelatory modes. She delights in writing speculative fiction, an umbrella term encompassing science fiction, fantasy, utopian, dystopian, and other primarily non-realist genres (REF). Positing a dual crisis posed by colonialism and patriarchy, Hossain writes about pacific, educative, female-ruled worlds (cf. the analysis of *Sultana's Dream* and *Padmarag* later in this chapter) and creates depictions of the plight of the nation, which are narratologically similar to a folk tale and fairy tale (cf. the analysis of *Jnanaphala* [The Fruit of Knowledge] and *Muktiphala* [The Fruit of Freedom] later in this chapter). An anti-colonial and anti-patriarchal consciousness permeates her writing. Even if there is deepest social, military or political crisis in the background in her narratives, Hossain's fables plead for a better future and for prolonged, processual change.

Born into a landholding family in east Bengal, Hossain (1880–1932) did not get formal schooling or higher education. Her conservative father discouraged Rokeya's hunger for learning, but a supportive elder sister and elder brother helped her pursue her study of English and Bengali, respectively. This elder brother also facilitated Hossain's marriage at the age of 16 to a much older man who respected Rokeya's intelligence, hunger for education, and talent for writing. After marriage, Hossain moved to a provincial town, Bhagalpur, in what would be a present-day province of Bihar in India, where her husband was a government official. Hossain wrote *Sultana's Dream* while living in Bhagalpur, and the fable was published in a magazine called *The Indian Ladies' Magazine* in 1905. The Indian Tamil Christian writer Kamala Satthianadhan (1879–1950) started this periodical in 1901. The magazine published major women writers, such as the poet and nationalist leader Sarojini Naidu.

Hossain became a regular and familiar writer in Bengali-language periodicals and reviews, such as *Nabanoor, Mahila*, and *Nabaprabha*, by 1904. Hossain was bequeathed a legacy of Rs. 10,000 by her husband to start a school for girls, and when she was widowed at the age of 29, she first attempted to start this school in her marital place of residence, Bhagalpur. However, relations with members of her marital family became sour, and Hossain moved alone to Kolkata. In 1911, she started the Sakhawat Hossain Memorial School for Muslim girls in a rented house in Kolkata, with eight students. The school was very successful, and kept on expanding: even today, the Sakhawat Hossain Memorial School is a well-regarded school in Kolkata. In 1916, Hossain started the Bengal branch of the Anjuman-e-Khwatin-e-Islam, an association for Muslim women, engaged in welfarist and developmental work, including literacy and vocational training classes in the slums of Calcutta.

Sultana's Dream

In Hossain's *Sultana's Dream* (1905), a utopian feminist fable, women's education, in the concrete shape of all-women universities, propels social change and progress in an imagined country where women rule public affairs, while men, in a tongue-in-cheek role reversal, remain confined to activities in the private sphere. Ladyland is the dream-vision of Sultana, a recognizably non-Occidental woman: the fact that the term signifies a female political ruler clearly points to how sweeping Rokeya's goals for Bengali, Indian, South Asian, and non-Occidental women's education were.

In 1905, when Hossain's husband read *Sultana's Dream*, he had commented, 'A terrible revenge!' *Sultana's Dream* is widely read and appreciated and retains its freshness and innovative status as one of the most successful pieces of Indian writing in English. In Ladyland, when a queen who 'liked science very much (Hossain 2005, 7) had all the women educated, early marriage was stopped, and two separate universities were built for women, strange things started happening, as any reader of *Sultana's Dream* will know. When the men's military self-aggrandizement leads the country to the brink of ruin, the Lady Principal of one of the universities uses the fruits of scientific research conducted in the women's universities to scare the enemy into running away by directing rays of concentrated heat and light at them. By this time, the women have placed the men in the mardana as a pre-condition for their help in the war, and the rest is herstory, a milestone in the lineage of feminist utopias. The ladies 'rule over the country and control all social matters, while gentlemen are kept in the mardanas to mind the babies, to cook, and to do all sorts of domestic work' (Hossain 2005, 15). In this science and technology-loving utopian fable, agriculture, transport, and many other activities are carried on by electricity, and there are other technological schemes for efficiency. *Sultana's Dream* is a short work, but it bears the twin signatures of most literary feminist utopias across space and time, namely the belief that female knowledge and leadership are the keys to human development and progress and that women do better at furthering such development if allowed to so untrammelled by patriarchy. Analysing *Sultana's Dream*, Chattopadhyay writes about the dream-framing of the work. Within the global context, psychoanalysis, oneirocriticism, and their many predecessors were central to modernist aesthetics. Dreams offered ways to imagine and live past the structures of daily life, lent fluidity to reason, and, above everything else, allowed a 'science' of unvoiced desires. While it was not until Girindrashekhar Bose's work and the Indian Psychoanalytic Society (founded 1922) that Freudianism came into wider cultural circulation in colonial Bengal, there were already other indigenous frameworks to work with, and dream revelations held a central place in many religious traditions, Christian, Islamic and Hindu. To employ dreams as a means of voicing desire may have been structurally available, but it is their use for women's education, scientific training, and ultimately emancipation that makes *Sultana's Dream* radically futuristic (Chattopadhyay 2017, 9–10).

This writer concurs and adds that it is evident from *Sultana's Dream* that the driving force behind the radical futurism of the utopian feminist country of Ladyland is women's education (Hossain 2005, xii), an education that does not turn out docile clones, but which rather facilitates innovation. Hossain lays particular emphasis on the importance of women familiarizing themselves with the world of science. In the unconventional, inverted world of *Sultana's Dream*, the men, whose advantage is brawn rather than brain, remain confined to the *mardana* and perform the daily mundane chores, while the women, headed by a queen who is ably supported by her deputies – the female principals of the two women's universities – use their superior intellectual ability to govern the country wisely and well.

In two universities in Ladyland, which are built exclusively for women, novel schemes are drawn up and subsequently implemented: one allows water to be drawn directly from the clouds, while the other enables solar heat to be collected, stored, and concentrated. When the male soldiers of the country prove themselves powerless to thwart the threat of invasion by an enemy nation, the female principals of the universities step into the breach, making the withdrawal of men into the mardana a pre-condition for agreeing to defend the country. Using concentrated solar heat, the enemy is defeated. The women continue to govern the country, now called Ladyland, creating a utopia where science, technology, and virtue work together. Air travel is the only mode of transport, land is cultivated by electrically driven motors, and weather is controlled. The utopian country is both garden-like and technophilic, both pastoral and futuristic.

Jnanaphala and *Muktiphala*

Hossain imagined women's education as the foundation of political freedom in her allegorical narratives *Jnanaphala* or The Fruit of Knowledge and *Muktiphala* or The Fruit of Freedom. Positing causal links between women's rights, women's education, women's agency, and political freedom, Hossain argued in the two *rupaka* or allegorical, parable-like tales that British colonialism de-industrialized India and concealed this and that it offered very few resources for furthering Indians' welfare, in areas such as education and healthcare. Generically, these works are hybrid: they can be seen as political allegories, as parables, as fairy tales, and as fables. In *Jnana-phala* [The Fruit of Knowledge] (1922), Hossain regards the eating of the fruit of knowledge in the garden of Eden, through the agency of Eve, in a positive light: Hossain thus reworks, from an anti-colonial South Asian perspective, a 'fortunate Fall' political paradigm.

> Eve requested him to eat the fruit which was in her hands. Adam too awoke to knowledge on eating the rest of the fruit from his wife. Then he began to feel his own deprived condition in every layer of his heart. – Was this paradise? This loveless, workless, lazy life – was this the pleasure of paradise? He also realised that he was a political prisoner; he had no ability to set foot outside the boundary of the garden of Eden! In place of a house made of bricks and mortar, he lived in a beautiful palace made of coral and crushed pearls, but he did not have a goat's worth of things he could call his 'own' – not even a piece of clothing to wear! What sort of royal pleasure was this? Now the happy dream of heavenly pleasure, which was in fact ignorance, was shattered – he clearly felt the wakeful condition of knowledge.
>
> (Hossain 2001, 175)

It is important to remember that the story of Adam and Eve is, though we have chosen to forget this, not a European story but an Asian one, found both in the *Bible* (a product of West Asia, lest we forget) and in the Koran. When a Muslim South Asian feminist creates a version of the story vindicating Adam and Eve's eating of the forbidden fruit of knowledge, she does not have to go through only European writers such as John Milton: the tale is also a part of her own heritage, and she uses it creatively and politically. In Hossain's parable, one fruit from the Tree of Knowledge falls onto the earth, and a tree is born from it, though human beings are by and large ignorant of the effects of this fruit. Inhabitants of a country called *Paristan* or Land of Fairies (allegory for Britain and other colonizing coun-tries) get to drink the juice of some of these fruits and gain knowledge. Becoming imperialist traders, they exploit the great wealth of *Kanakadvipa* or the Island of Gold (allegory for India and other colonized countries), which overflows with food crops, but whose inhabitants live in a state of innocence. Eventually recogniz-ing that their country is being drained of its wealth through unequal commerce with *Paristan*, some of the people of *Kanakadvipa* get to taste the juice of the Fruit of Knowledge. They then go in search of the original tree that bore the Fruit of Knowledge. To do this, they have to withstand opposition from the inhabitants of *Paristan*, an allegory of the opposition of imperialists to the colonized gaining emancipatory knowledge. After a long search, the search party finds the tree. It is withered and cannot be made to revive. In a dream, a sage appears to the *Kanakad-vipa* explorers and tells them:

> Two hundred years ago, the selfish, short-sighted, foolish wise men of that country forbade the women to eat the fruit of knowledge; in time, that order

became a social edict, and the men monopolized that fruit for themselves. Since they were stopped from picking and eating that fruit, the women did not tend or care for that tree. And since the Tree of Knowledge was deprived of the nurture and care of women's tender hands, it died. Go, return to your country; go and sow the seeds of those guavas. Let the jinns who want to cut down the guava tree do so; do not stop them – instead, save the eeds in secret. Tend the newly planted sapling, men and women, and you will get the results you hope for. Be careful! Do not deprive your daughters of guavas! Remember without fail that women have all rights to the fruit which they themselves brought to the earth!

(Hossain 2001, 175. Unpublished translation by Barnita Bagchi)

In The Fruit of Freedom (1921), Kangalini, the pauperess, erstwhile queen of the country of Bholapur, and an allegorical representation of the Indian nation, is shown to be dying under colonialism. The ablest of her various sons, Layek [The Capable One], dies; the rest are cowards, sycophants of the British, or corrupt (the allegorically named sons include Darpananda [One who Rejoices in His Vanity]; Kritaghna [The Traitor]; Ninduk [The Villifier]; and Matridrohi [Rebel against His Mother]). We are told that the reason for the mother's illness is a curse brought on by an ascetic, due to her treating her daughters as inferior to her sons. The ascetic says to her:

Child, it is very unjust that you love your sons far more, while you don't love or care at all for your daughters. As a result, you will suffer because of these spoilt sons . . . You will have to suffer the results of being the mother of unworthy sons and of being partial in showing love towards your children." I . . . asked him, touching his feet, "When will my curse end?" In answer to that, the ascetic said, "On Mount Kailasha there is a tree bearing he Fruit of Freedom; the day that someone brings you that fruit and feeds it to you, you will recover.

(Hossain 2001, 120. Unpublished translation by Barnita Bagchi)

When Kangalini's older sons, characterized by greed and cowardice, cannot bring back the fruit from the closely guarded gardens of Mayapur [Land of Illusion/ Fancy], which we may read as an allegory for the colonizing country, Kanagalini's daughters Srimati and Sumati, along with their younger brothers, decide that they will step outside the home, make the difficult journey to Mayapur, and get the Fruit of Freedom. In a symbolic gesture, Srimati unbinds her hair and says that she will keep it loose until she is successful in getting the fruit. This is a re-working of an episode in the Hindu epic *Mahabharata*, where Draupadi, the Pandava queen, decides not to bind or wash her hair until one of her husbands can bathe her hair in the blood of the enemy prince Duhshasana. In Hossain's story, the woman herself decides to act. Both The Fruit of Knowledge and The Fruit of Freedom are political narratives. They are also parables about men's and women's rights, agency, action, and freedom. The date of publication of the parables is significant.

The anti-colonial Non-Cooperation movement, led by Mohandas Karamchand Gandhi, was sweeping India in the period 1921–22: Hossain's narratives are part of that political mood and moment. The parables are about civic participation in a colonial country where the colonized inhabitants have almost no citizenship rights. Hossain, a powerful creative fabulist as much as a political one, writes these narratives as a South Asian woman, using topoi from the Koran as much as from South Asian fairy tales and myths.

Hossain's status as a witty, biting, creative writer gave her educational and civic work a sharpened edge, greater public visibility, and greater power to mould public opinion about women's education. Hossain argued that by imparting education to women and men, an emancipatory knowledge would be born.

Srishtitattva and *Narisrishti*

Hossain's essay *Srishtitattva* [The Story of Creation] (Hossain 2001, 109–11), first published in 1920, shows Hossain's biting wit, boldness, and playfulness. This essay complements an earlier essay by Hossain, *Narisrishti* [The Creation of Woman] (Hossain 2001, 135–39), published in 1919. In the earlier essay, *Narisrishti*, the Creator said that he combined many apparently contradictory qualities in creating the woman. This earlier essay, Hossain states, is a free translation of a piece she read in English, itself translated from Sanskrit: 'A Hindu Legend of the Creation of Woman':

> At the beginning of time, Twashtri – the Vulcan of the Hindu mythology – created the world. But when he wished to create a woman he found that he had employed all his materials in the creation of man. There did not remain one solid element. Then Twashtri, perplexed, fell into a profound meditation. He roused himself to do as follows: He took the roundness of the moon, the undulations of the serpent, the entwinement of climbing plants, the trembling of the grass, the slenderness of the rose-vine, and the velvet of the flower, the lightness of the leaf and the glance of the fawn, the gayety of the sun's rays and tears of the mist, the inconstancy of the wind and the timidity of the hare, the vanity of the peacock and the softness of the down on the throat of the swallow, the hardness of the diamond, the sweet flavour of honey and the cruelty of the tiger, the warmth of fire, the chill of snow, the chatter of the jay, and the cooing of the turtle dove. He united all this and formed a woman. Then he made a present of her to man. Eight days later the man came to Twashtri and said: 'My lord, the creature you gave me poisons my existence. She chatters without rest, she takes all my time, she laments for nothing at all, and is always ill.' And Twashtri received the woman again.
>
> But eight days later, the man came again to the god and said: 'My lord, my life is very solitary since I returned this creature. I remember she danced before me, singing. I recall how she glanced at me from the corner of her eye, that she played with me, clung to me.' And Twashtri returned the woman to him.

Three days only passed and Twashtri saw the man coming to him again. 'My lord,' said he, 'I do not understand exactly how, but I am sure that the woman causes me more annoyance than pleasure. I beg of you to relieve me of her.'

But Twashtri cried: 'Go your way and do your best.' And the man cried: 'I cannot live with her!' 'Neither can you live without her,' replied Twashtri.

And the man was sorrowful, murmuring: 'Woe is me, I can neither live with or without her.'

(Anon 642)

Hossain changed this story, adding, for example, many elements in her version: her list includes 33 elements in all, including the sourness of tamarind, the bitterness of quinine, the fiery taste of chillies, the absentmindedness of philosophers, the proneness to error of politicians: this shows the original story undergoing fascinating processes of transcreation, and the emergent female identity that Hossain represents is also seen in far more diverse, colourful light.

In *Srishtitattva* or The Story of Creation, a companion story, we find women belonging to various religions sitting together conversing amicably: many other works in Hossain's oeuvre depict the same scene (*Padmarag*, for example). The Hindu god Twashtri or Tvasti (the second word is the one Hossain uses) appears before the women. In Vedic Hinduism, Twashtri made tools and weapons for Gods, notably Indra's *vajra* or thunderbolt. The word Twastri means carpenter and 'chariot maker.' In a witty passage, Hossain combines an account of Gandhi's then-recent political non-cooperation movement of 'Satyagraha' (literally 'eagerness for truth' or civil disobedience) with Tvasti's revision of the original story of creation:

> Tvasti: It is this: she gave the article titled 'The Creation of Woman' to the monthly journal named *Saogat*. At that point the Editor was not in Kolkata; the fools in the office published it omitting two footnotes written by her. Without these footnotes, the essay has become difficult to understand in places. So discerning readers, not being able to comprehend it fully, cannot be fully satisfied. Then they say, "Call that blighter Tvasti, let him come and explain where and what the mistakes are!" See, at convenient and inconvenient times, if they find occasion for a planchette, they call me from heaven and bother me. Listen to today's incident: some young men have got caught up in the satyagraha movement. The ruling officials say, give up the eagerness for truth [satyagraha] and embrace the eagerness for lies [mithyagraha]. Two lawyers, who were harassed by the police since they did not embrace falsehood, have escaped to Ranchi. Their home is not far from yours. But you should know that robbers never listen to religious tales. Even in the unceasing rain and mud of Ranchi they have no respite. During the day, they devote themselves to the propagation of the attempt to embrace truth, against the embrace of falsehood, and spoil the peace of the country by

their lecturing! And at night the friends spoil the peace of heaven with their planchettes! Until midnight or one o' clock at night we are disturbed by the summons of the lawyers. At least in your mortal world there is the C.I.D. to punish young men for breaking the peace: but in heaven there are no measures to subdue them. That is why, you see, my chariot of vapour got caught on a pitcher on your roof while I was returning so late at night from the lawyers, and I too barely escaped from falling noisily. Being drenched by rain does not suit me in my old age, and so the moment the brave Bina opened the window, I entered the house.

(Hossain 2001, 136–37. Unpublished translation by Barnita Bagchi)

This passage is funny. Hossain, however, on a more serious underlying note, brings together anti-colonial politics in the public sphere and feminist and gender-related issues, often stereotypically seen as part of the private sphere: Hossain shows that anti-colonial and gender politics interweave and should not be viewed in isolation. Tvasti proposes the following revision to the story:

We saw that poor Lord Tvasti was overwhelmed by sleep. At times he was speaking in a low voice while yawning, with eyelids nearly closed; at yet other times he was rubbing his eyes and speaking in a loud voice, and was testing whether Bina had written things down correctly. If there were mistakes, he was making her cross them out and write again. It was as if he was trying to prove by the elaborateness of his words that he was not assailed by sleep. At one point he roared and said:

'Do you know, my children, when I was creating woman I had no objects in hand: I had to collect the smell of one substance, the taste of one, and the vapour of one. But during the creation of man I did not have to worry at all. I had many objects in my treasury – I took what came to me when I stretched out my hand. Such as, when I was creating teeth, I took the whole poison-fang of the snake; to prepare hands, feet, nails, etc. I took the whole claw of the tiger; at the time of filling the brain cells I used the whole brain of the donkey. ["Cells" in English in the original. – Translator.] At the time of the creation of woman, I took only the heat of fire. In the case of men I took a piece of burning coal. Child! Write this.'

Bina wrote, 'Burning coal.'

Tvasti: 'Children! Listen attentively, in the case of women I took only the cold of snow, while in the case of men I used pieces of ice, and even the whole Kanchenjungha peak. Have you written this, Bina?'

(Hossain 2001, 138. Unpublished translation by Barnita Bagchi)

This is bold feminism which makes devastatingly witty and negative comments about the male gender. We have in this sketch too, as in the other pieces I have analysed, no doomsday scenarios, though we have humorous playfulness as regards religious myths. Hossain makes us inhabit mythical and realistic temporalities, mixes gods and women, and creates fables and allegories discussing how female agency can bring solutions to the crises created by colonialism and patriarchy.

Padmarag

In her novel *Padmarag* (1924), Hossain delineates Tarini Bhavan, a community of women and a feminist utopia situated in the heart of Kolkata. In this institution, some women, led by a Brahmo widow named Tarini Sen, create a world of welfarist action. *Padmarag* describes a female-founded and female-administered community set in contemporary Bengal. Here, women from many religions, regions, and ethnicities, with histories of patriarchal and familial oppression, cooperate to found a community. Formal education, propagating crafts, caring for the sick and the destitute, Tarini Bhavan is the centre of many activities. The novella also offers a series of personal narratives of the women working in the institution. These tales recount and indict familial and marital oppression, to redress which the institution Tarini Bhavan is founded. Hossain shows that Hindus, Brahmos, Muslims, and Christians, black and white women, all suffer from patriarchal oppression and all need to receive refuge and education from communities of cooperative, competent women.

This work is very much a piece of genre fiction. It is a free-flowing narrative with liberal doses of melodrama, romance, disasters, and coincidences. However, cohabiting with the melodrama in the work is a contrasting mundane, workaday strand which is manifest above all in the depiction of a female-administered school and institution. Hossain, an educational leader and civil society actor in real life, has humorous descriptions of the trials faced by the administrators of a girls' school. She thus also gives us vignettes of pioneering working women typing, writing, teaching, or taking care of other duties, trying to create a utopia in an everyday, humdrum world.

While the mysterious young Muslim heroine Siddika/Zainab/ Padmarag (she is referred to by many names), who arrives under conditions of distress in the community, is regarded in the work as the epitome of pathos, Siddika comes to realize that other members of Tarini Bhavan also have led lives full of suffering and tragedy. Listening to these women's sad tales bonds Siddika with these other women. Helen Horace, for example, a white woman who teaches in Tarini Bhavan, is married to a criminal lunatic who is imprisoned in Broadmoor Criminal Lunatic Asylum and cannot be divorced from him according to English laws. Helen is tied for life to a lunatic. Sakina, another member of the community, fails in her marriage because her husband's mistress says on the wedding day that Sakina is not beautiful, so the husband discards his bride. Usha is not accepted by her in-laws after she is rescued from abduction by robbers – she is supposed to have lost her character. The redress for such injustices is the Society for the Alleviation of Female Suffering, which forms the core of Tarini Bhavan. Here, 'abandoned, destitute, neglected, helpless, oppressed women' 'declare war against society' (Hossain 2005, 104).

The philanthropic institution Tarini Bhavan is named after its founder Dina-Tarini Sen, a Brahmo woman. 'Dina-tarini' means 'saviour of the distressed.' Literally, 'tarini' is a boatsman, who in the metaphorical sense rows the distressed out of danger. It is a name infused with the spiritual, and many Bengali songs are addressed to God imaged as Dina-tarini. Tarini Sen is thus a saviour. Tarini is the second wife and then a widow of a much older barrister. She founds the institution at the age of 21, against the wishes of relatives. The autobiographical resonances with Hossain's life are evident.

Tarini Bhavan has a school for both day-scholars and boarders. It also has a workshop or training institute for adult women, a home for widows, and a home for the sick and refugeless. A Society for the Alleviation of Female Suffering forms the ethical core. Many of the inhabitants of Tarini Bhavan are called 'sisters of the poor,' wear a uniform of saffron or blue, and have no separate rooms: the monastic ideal of service and renunciation is palpable. Vocational training is given in Tarini Bhavan, in occupations such as bookbinding, spinning, sewing, making sweets, typing, nursing, and teacher training. The women also offer nursing and other kinds of care and relief during famine and flood. Some trainees help in running the home for the sick and distressed, where poor and handicapped people receive medical attention.

The pupils in the Tarini Bhavan school are given an education in all standard subjects, such as mathematics, geography, and the physical and life sciences. They are taught to be self-sufficient. The school accepts grants neither from the British colonial government nor from the princely states loyal to the colonial order. The students are taught history in such a way that they do not despise their own past and culture. The women who live in and run Tarini Bhavan engage in much humour and banter among themselves, giving *Padmarag* as a literary work a welcome tone of hope, that very utopian emotion (Bloch 1995) amidst all the pathos and tragedy of patriarchal injustices that the utopian community seeks to remedy.

Conclusion

Hossain combined pedagogic work with action in a more broadly defined social and public sphere. She used irony, wit, humour and satire with devastating effect, combining such witty, biting, funny polemics and feminism with a frontal presence as educator and civil society actor. The solution that Hossain offered for the negative forces of Indian patriarchy and British colonialism was women's and men's education. From this education, she argued, an emancipatory knowledge would be born. Through her polemical, witty, often humorous genre fiction, Hossain espouses freedom and the rights of women and colonial subjects. Hossain also ranges across religions, literatures, and cultures in her writing. Hossain's genre fiction, as this chapter has shown repeatedly, is transcultural, in the sense not only of moving supply across cultures but also in the sense of questioning stereotypical, monolithic notions of culture. Inventive and innovative, witty, satirical, passionate, and intellectual, Rokeya Sakhawat Hossain's fiction is driven by a constant, dynamic quest for justice that is mirrored in the aesthetic forms of genre fiction she wrote in, from the social-aesthetic dreaming of utopian narrative to parables using folk-tale and fairy tale.

Note

1 This chapter draws on Bagchi (2008) and Bagchi (2013) in its analysis of *Jnanaphala*, *Muktiphala*, *Srishtitattva*, and *Naritattva*.

Works cited

Akhtar, Shaheen, and Mousumi Bhowmik, editors. *Women in Concert: An Anthology of Bengali Muslim Women's Writings (1904–1938)*. Stree, 2008.

Amin, Sonia Nishat. *The World of Muslim Women in Colonial Bengal*. Brill, 1996.

Anisuzzaman. *Muslim Manas o Bangla Sahitya, 1757–1918*. Pustak Bipani, 2000.

Anon. "A Hindu Legend of the Creation of Woman." *The Literary Digest*, vol. 20, no. 21, 26 May 1900, p. 42. Accessed 7 July 2018.

Bagchi, Barnita. "Crooked Lines: Utopia, Human Rights and South Asian Women's Writing and Agency." *Australian Journal of Human Rights*, vol. 22, no. 2, 2016, pp. 103–22.

———. "Fruits of Knowledge: Polemics, Humour and Moral Education in the Writings of Rokeya Sakhawat Hossain, Lila Majumdar and Nabaneeta Dev Sen." *Asiatic: IIUM Journal of English Language and Literature*, vol. 7, no. 2, Dec. 2013, pp. 126–38.

———. "Hannah Arendt, Education, and Liberation: A Comparative South Asian Feminist Perspective." *Heidelberg Papers in South Asian and Comparative Politics*, vol. 35, 2008, https://doi.org/10.11588/hpsap.2008.35.2203.

———. "Speculating with Human Rights: Two South Asian Women Writers and Utopian Mobilities." *Mobilities*. Special Issue on "Mobile Utopia." vol. 15, no. 1, 2020, pp. 69–80.

———. "Towards Ladyland: Rokeya Sakhawat Hossain and the Movement for Women's Education in Bengal, c. 1900 – c. 1932." *Paedagogica Historica*, vol. 45, no. 6, 2009, pp. 743–55.

Bhattacharya, Prodosh. "Two Occidental Heroines Through Oriental Eyes." *Reorienting Orientalism*, edited by Chandreyee Niyogi, Sage, 2006, pp. 116–34.

Bloch, Ernest. *The Principle of Hope*. Translated by Neville Plaice, N. (3 vols.). MIT Press, 1995.

Chattopadhyay, Bodhisattva. "Bengal." *The Encyclopedia of Science Fiction*, edited by John Clute, David Langford, Peter Nicholls, and Graham Sleight. Gollancz, 31 Aug. 2018, www.sf-encyclopedia.com/entry/bengal. Accessed 5 Feb. 2019.

———. "On the Mythologerm: Kalpavigyan and the Question of Imperial Science." *Science Fiction Studies*, vol. 43, no. 3, 2016, pp. 435–58, www.jstor.org/stable/10.5621/sciefictstud.43.3.0435.

———. "Speculative Utopianism in Kalpavigyan: Mythologerm and Women's Science Fiction." *Foundation: The International Review of Science Fiction*, vol. 46, no. 127, 2017, pp. 6–19.

Hasanat, Fayeza. "The Burdens of Translation: Nawab Faizunnesa's Rupjalal." *The Daily Star*, 24 June 2017.

———. *Nawab Faizunnesa's Rupjalal*. Brill, 2008.

Hossain, Rokeya Sakhawat. *Rokeya Rachanasamgraha* [Collected Works of Rokeya Sakhwat Hossain]. Edited by Miratun Nahar. Vishwakosh Parishad, 2001.

———. "Srishti-tattva." Translated by Barnita Bagchi. Unpublished.

———. *Sultana's Dream and Padmarag.* Edited by and part-trans. Barnita Bagchi, Penguin Classics, 2005.

———. "The Worship of Women." *Talking of Power: Early Writings of Bengali Women from the Mid-Nineteenth Century to the Beginning of the Twentieth Century*, edited by Malini Bhattacharya and Abhijit Sen, Stree, 2003, pp. 105–15.

Naim, C. M. "Homage to a 'Magic-Writer': The Mistrīz and Asrār novels of Urdu." *Indian Genre Fiction: Pasts and Future Histories*, edited by Bodhisattva Chattopadhyay, Aakriti Mandhwani, and Anwesha Maity, Routledge, 2018.

Ray, Bharati. *Early Feminists of Colonial India: Sarala Devi Chaudhurani and Rokeya Sakhawat Hossain.* Oxford UP, 2002.

2

LOCATING ROMANCE AND WOMEN WRITERS IN URDU LITERATURE

Hijab Imtiaz Ali's genre fiction

Shweta Sachdeva Jha

Contextualizing Urdu romance and genre fiction has both its excitement and challenges, and it offers a great opportunity to explore issues of genre, agency, and histories of gender. Although there is research on women's magazines, women in education, and women's language (*begamati zuban*), studies on women authors of Urdu romance or mysteries rarely exist. Most contemporary studies of women's writing are confined to the Progressive Writers Movement and literary styles marked by social realism. Women authors such as Rashid Jahan (1905–1952) and Ismat Chughtai (1911–1991) became prominent in the Progressive Writer's Movement and both of them believed strongly in the political role that literature could play in social reform to challenge caste discrimination, class hierarchies, and women's oppression in a patriarchal society such as ours.

Interest in women novelists or short story writers before the mid-20th century has been marginal because of few women writers of Urdu fiction in the 19th century. This has two reasons, low numbers of literate women in *ashraf*[1] families and higher social status of poetry over prose. In the late 19th century, many women poets were *tawaif* or courtesans, and erasure of their poetic lives and compositions from histories of Urdu poetry was a consequence of social reform movements and fashioning of a 'modern' Urdu poetic sphere (Sachdeva 208–211).[2] The appearance of the first phase of writings by *ashraf* women in the late 19th century was directly related to reform movements, impetus towards women's education and a burgeoning Urdu publishing industry in colonial India (Lelyveld, Naim, Stark). Publication of reading material for young women, such as manuals on manners and morals like *Bihisti Zewar* (*Heavenly Ornaments*) published in 1905 by Maulana Ashraf Ali Thanawi (d. 1943) with their focus on women's education was accompanied by emergence of women editors and magazines (Metcalfe, Minault, Khoja-Moolji). Writing became a powerful act of agency and self-representation leading to experimentation with autobiographical forms by Muslim women (Lambert-Hurley).

DOI: 10.4324/9781003002062-4

Bibi Ashraf recalled her struggle to teach herself to read and write in her note, clearly revealing the limited access women had to basic education and books in 1899 (Naim 99). Bibi Ashraf's autobiographical piece first appeared in two instalments in the year 1899 in the journal *Tehzeeb-e-Niswan*, one of the first magazines for women to be published from Lahore. The magazine was started by Muhammadi Begum and her husband Sayyid Mumtaz Ali (1860–1935). Muhammadi Begum (1878–1908) was one of the first women to write novels in Urdu, and the subject of our chapter, Hijab Imtiaz Ali, (henceforth Hijab) was her daughter-in-law, married to her son, Syed Imtiaz Ali Taj (1900–1970). Muhammadi Begum and Hijab are both key figures in the development of Urdu fiction where the former also provided a literary space for women to write and was the author of didactic fiction (Khoja-Moolji). Hijab (1908–1999) went on to carve a niche as a popular writer of romance and horror fiction.

Since the late 19th century, texts read for pleasure and commercial publishing began to offer readers an immense range of options in Urdu in the form of tales, novels, plays, songbooks, *dastans*,[3] and novels which made for a 'highly intertextual world' (Orsini 105). However, 'reading matter for women was [largely] produced by men, voicing their concepts and ideals and/or serving their commercial interests' (Oesterheld 218). Women become more visible as authors in the early 20th century due to the rise of literacy levels among women from *ashraf* backgrounds, and as they begin to write for a rapidly transforming public sphere (Oesterheld 218). Hijab was an active participant in this transformation. Here is an introduction by her contemporary[4] Shaista Suhrawardy Ikramullah (1915–2000):

> Hijab Ismail, now Mrs. Imtiyaz Ali Taj, made her debut in the literary world ten years ago. In this short time she has gained for herself a very definite place in it and is ranked amongst the successful young short-story writers. Hijab Ismail's style of writing is entirely different from that of any other contemporary writer. It is a personal and intimate one, and she creates an atmosphere surcharged with romance as the background of her stories.
>
> (Suhrawardy 283)

Suharwardy was clearly intrigued by Hijab's fiction and found it entertaining and gripping, she was also impressed by the immense popularity of Hijab's romance narratives. Recently, Hijab has been called 'Pakistan's Barbara Cartland' (qtd in Hussein 12). An exceptional woman, Hijab Imtiaz Ali was fluent in many languages, including Urdu and English, and was the first Muslim woman to get a pilot's license in British India. A prolific writer, in her lifetime of 91 years, she wrote many short stories, novels such as *Meri Natamam Mohabbat* (My Unfulfilled Love, 1933), *Zalim Mohabbat* (Cruel Love, 1938), horror stories such as *Count Ilyas ki Maut* (Death of Count Ilyas, 1935), memoirs, plays, newspaper articles and much more.[5] In his study on Urdu fiction, *Urdu Afsana aur Afsana-nigar* (Urdu Novels and Novelists), the critic Farman Fatehpuri wrote of Hijab as a much-loved writer of the 20th century (1982).

Born in Hyderabad and raised in Madras (now Chennai) in India, Hijab wrote her first story *Meri Natamam Mohabbat* (My Unfulfilled Love 1933) at the young age of 11 and a half. She married Syed Imtiaz Ali Taj (1900–1970), the son of Muhammadi Begum and a well-known playwright in Urdu and moved to Lahore in the early 1930s. In her life span of 91 years, she witnessed the Partition of the Indian subcontinent, the emergence of two separate nations of India and Pakistan, the Indo-Pakistan War of 1965, and the emergence of the third nation of Bangladesh in 1971. Delving into her entire literary oeuvre over the long span of her career is beyond the scope of this chapter, but I explore two of her most popular texts, *Meri Natamam Mohabbat* (My Unfulfilled Love) and *Zalim Mohabbat* (Cruel Love), to address three specific questions: Does Hijab's fiction qualify as a 'romance' in the same vein as the Anglo-American women's romance? Does an Urdu 'romance' exhibit any cultural features specific to South Asia? Who read these stories, and what can its publication and reception reveal about the development of women's writing in Urdu? To begin with, I first explain my approach to genre fiction and romance in Urdu.

Approaching genre fiction in Urdu literature

In their recent edited volume on *Indian Genre Fiction*, the editors interpret 'genre fiction' as an umbrella term that encompasses popular fiction and also retains the literal meaning of the term 'genre' to classify texts into tragedy, poetry, drama, novel, etc. (Chattopadhyay, Mandhwani and Maity 1). But who makes the distinction between 'literary' and 'popular fiction'? In a polemical essay, Leslie A. Fiedler argues that librarians, publishers, publishing awards, and academics classify texts, songs, or any art form into categories of popular literature or culture, and in this attempt they are both illusive and unreal. Instead of terms such as literary and popular fiction, Fiedler proposes an approach to literature which will:

> . . . if not quite abandon, at least drastically downgrade both Ethics and Aesthetics in favour of 'Ecstatics'. Once we have *ekstasis* rather than instruction and delight the centre of critical analysis and evaluation, we will find ourselves speaking less of theme and purport, structure and texture, ideology, and significance, irony and symbolism and more of myth, fable, archetype, fantasy, magic and wonder.
>
> (Fiedler 41)

In the same vein, Joshua Rothman reiterates the problem of distinguishing 'genre fiction' from 'literary fiction' in his essay 'A Better Way to Think about the Genre Debate' to argue that:

> Genres themselves fall into genres: there are period genres (Victorian literature), subject genres (detective fiction), form genres (the short story), style genres (minimalism), market genres ("chick-lit"), mode genres (satire), and

so on. How are different kinds of genres supposed to be compared? ("Literary fiction" and "genre fiction," one senses, aren't really comparable categories.) What is it, exactly, about genre that is unliterary – and what is it in "the literary" that resists genre? The debate goes round and round, magnetic and circular – a lovers' quarrel among literati.

(Rothman 2014)

Rothman sees this debate only amongst the literati; however, it has a deeper significance and affect on critics and scholars who select texts, often 're-member' them, and forget others according to subjective models of 'literariness.' There are several histories of Urdu fiction, yet the non-Urdu-speaking reader is only familiar with some key women authors whose work has been translated into English. Among these women writers of prose fiction, the names of Rashid Jahan (1905–1952), Ismat Chughtai (1915–1991), Qurratulain Hyder (1927–2007) are the most well known. Even the enterprising two volume series on *Women's Writing in India* (1997, 2012), edited by Susie Tharu and K. Lalita, does not refer to Hijab Imtiaz Ali possibly because her work did not fit into literary fiction.

Romance or horror can be read as part of genre fiction to explore agency and voices of women as both readers and writers of fiction that lie beyond the prescribed standards of decorum and the literary ambit of realism. Studies in Urdu genre fiction in Urdu can help us trace the desires of women and their search for pleasure. These texts can also be read as challenges posed to patriarchal norms of behaviour and social protocol. In the contemporary world of e-books and writing on the internet, genres like romance and mystery are easily available, and Hijab's fiction continues to find a presence now in different Urdu blogs and websites such as the one by *Rekhta* Foundation which showcases scans of her fiction in early editions in the form of e-books.[6] Despite her publications in several editions, she remains ignored in the field of recent literary criticism and academic scholarship. In Urdu, Mujeeb Ahmad Khan (2008, 2010) was the first to compile excerpts from her essays, letters, short fiction, and plays.[7]

I found Khan's (2008) collection recently after I had read Hijab's short story in English translation by writer and critic Aamer Hussein, who called her the 'Queen of Romance' (Hussein 2005). Elsewhere I explore the gothic stories in Hijab's oeuvre to argue that her fiction marks a crucial moment in the history of Urdu fiction (Sachdeva Jha 2021). Analysis of her stories in a wider context of romance studies as well as women's writing is long overdue. A key question to begin this discussion would be: whether romance means the same to a woman reader in Urdu and English?

In his essay on genre and romance, the Marxist critic Frederic Jameson defines genres in two ways: the first as 'contracts between a writer and his readers; or . . . literary *institutions*, which like the other institutions of social life are based on tacit agreements or contracts' (Jameson 138). and the second as 'that literary phenomenon which may be articulated *either* in terms of a fixed form *or* in terms of a mode, and which *must* be susceptible of expression in *either* of these critical codes optionally' (Jameson 138). Hijab's romance is a genre in both these two ways. First is the expectation she creates and fulfils in the reader about a story where the love and relationship between a man and a woman becomes its central theme and second where she articulates desire, anxiety, and love using a range of modes familiar to the reader of Urdu storytelling and poetry, which comes close to the style of what Pasha Mohammad Khan has recently explored as Urdu romance (2019).

As a genre in English and European literature, romance has a long history of critical analysis ranging from W. P. Ker, Erich Auerbach, Northrop Frye, Patricia Parker, David Quint, to Jameson. Lee rightly argues that instead of being a genre, romance is more a *key word* using the vocabulary of Raymond Williams, because it is a term whose 'semantic shifts open a window on social and historical upheavals of a far greater scale' (2014). Thus, a slight pull at the key word 'romance' can unravel a web of critical commentaries and justifications on the use and meaning of the term. However for us, romance as a means of literary classification and as a genre in Urdu literature is of prime relevance.

Romance in the world of Urdu fiction

Ralph Russell traces romance in Urdu through the fantasy and adventure stories called *dastans* which were an oral form of storytelling and were first written down and published by the Nawal Kishore Press of Lucknow in the 19th century. The Urdu *dastan* followed a style similar to the Persian *dastan* of Amir Hamza, widely available as *Tilism-i-Hoshruba* both in Urdu earlier and now in English. Novelists like Abdul Halim Sharar (1860–1926) began to call their fiction *naval* or novel in 1899. Sharar's *Flora Florinda* was published in 1899 and Russell refers to him as a pioneer of historical romance in Urdu (127). He argued that Sharar's fiction had traces of the *dastan* tradition with stylized dialogues where:

> There is the same evocation of the heroic age of Islam, the same battle of unalloyed virtue against unalloyed voice, the same dependence on exciting episodes following one upon another to maintain the reader's interest, and the same spicing of the story with erotic detail.
>
> (Russell 128)

Khan (3) approaches romances as a performative 'verbal art' that were primarily oral forms of storytelling in the form of *qissah* and *tilism* (enchanted worlds) which were central to these tales of wonder. His analysis dives into the textured form of the *qissah* as well as locates it in its material context of Urdu print culture, tracing the role played by Naval Kishore Press and performers or *dastango*. He traces the epistemological roots of wonder or bewilderment as well as warns against taking the *qissah* as the same as an English or French romance (185–187). To engage with the deeper implications of the changing typology of *qissah* to *naval* (novel) as well as the ideological contexts of it (Khan 163–194) is beyond the scope of this chapter however it is a crucial debate that we need to address in the near future. Khan's recent work is a major contribution to this debate. Returning to this world of adventure, and wonder, how do we place the women writers of romance? Did they think of adventure, wonder, eroticism in the same way as men? In feminist studies of English fiction, women's romance stands as a genre within popular literature predominantly written and consumed by women. Merja Makinen defines this 'romance' as a genre based on a formula which:

> . . . concentrates on the emotional intensity of the experience of the protagonist falling in love and carefully prolongs the process of anticipation, bewilderment and desire that she experiences as she is pursued and/or played with by the 'hero'. (23–24)

Interestingly apart from the protagonist (woman) and the 'hero' who feel this sense of desire, Makinen also thinks of the reader and her 'vicarious participation in this heightened state of desire, this 'falling in love', the experience of being courted, as a feature that marks out the romance genre format (24). Romance therefore offers women a means to express 'repressed feminine desire' (Maniken 25). Her study focuses on a series of English romance novels based on paper backs published by Mills and Boon, Harlequin, and Silhouette Books, publishers explicitly associated with publishing affordable paperbacks. Drawing connections between the writing of romance fiction, commodity production and readership, Janice A Radway argues that 'book buying . . . cannot be reduced to a simple interaction between a book and a reader. It is an event that is affected and partially controlled by the material nature of book publishing and a socially organized technology of production and distribution' (Radway 20).

But can we locate Hijab's romances in this debate? No, Hijab's romances were different both in the stylistic aspect as well as in its material context from its Anglo-American counterpart. Although mine is a work in progress, it seems clear to me that unlike the paperback romance in the Anglo-American tradition, Hijab's romances were not marginal in their publication or circulation. Her stories were published in prestigious Urdu journals[8] such as *Saqi* and *Nuqoosh* which published a wide range of fiction by both men and women authors including contemporaries associated with Progressive Writers Movement (Fatehpuri 140) who later become central to feminist scholarship. Further these journals were read by both men and women even if women's readership might have been lower due to literacy levels. Hijab's romances are therefore culturally specific and further so in her use of landscape, vocabulary, and autobiographical elements from Urdu romanticism. This socio-cultural specificity of her romance fiction becomes visible as we delve deeper into her stories.

Plots, motifs, and style in Hijab's stories

Hijab wrote her first story before her marriage, therefore it was published under her maiden name, Miss Hijab Ismail. Subsequent to her marriage to author Imtiaz

Ali Taj, she moved to Lahore and her fiction was published under her married name, Hijab Imtiaz Ali (Fatehpuri 140). Her first novel, *Meri Natamam Mohabbat* (My Unfulfilled Love) tells the story of a young girl Ruhi who lives with her grandmother and her father. The mother is not mentioned. The name Ruhi is derived from the Urdu word 'ruh,' meaning soul, spirit, or life. Ruhi becomes a means for Hijab to explore female psyche, feminine desire and sexuality beyond normative models of prescribed behaviour for *sharif* girls from *ashraf* families (Sachdeva Jha 2021). Dubrow has shown how Urdu fiction was a site to fashion and create new ideas of *sharafat* both for men and women (2017). In most of Hijab's stories, Ruhi figures as the narrator and the protagonist, and readers consistently meet other characters like Dr. Gar, her family doctor, Zulfi, her friend and alter ego. This repetition of same characters through more than one story marks a brilliant narrative technique used by Hijab to build a regular readership who eagerly waited for the next story to be published in journals or as self-contained books. In her memoirs, *Kagazi Hai Pairahan* (The Paper Attire), the famous Urdu writer Ismat Chughtai (popularly called Ismat) remembered the time when their family had to leave Aligarh to stay in Sambhar, where her father was posted as a judge. A small town where she had no access to books, she recalled her feelings while reading Hijab's fiction:

> The greatest deprivation we suffered from was of books. Naiyer [her niece] had books that were in her course in the eighth grade; I had them for the ninth and tenth grades. I do not know what hope for the future made me hold them close to my heart, because there was none. We would receive *Tahzib-i-Niswan*, in which the romantic stories of Miss Hijab Ismail . . . were published. We read those stories together and got lost in the exotic world filled with the aroma of orange buds, the maddening music of the unearthly *arghanoon* (only later in life did I come to know that this was nothing but the ordinary organ), tapering fingers and heavenly dresses. lost, but I was disinterested and I would get jealous. The stench of salty streams, the peeling lime of old walls, leaking roofs, doors with thick nails and closed streets. Naiyer would really get lost in them. I was not one for such exotic stuff, it would leave me cold. The stench of the salt lakes, crumbly walls, leaking roofs, heavy nails—this was our world. There was no way out, not even for death.
>
> (Chughtai trans. Asaduddin 109)

Unlike the young Ismat, who was shocked by the contradiction between reality and Hijab's fictional romantic ambience, there were other women like her niece who loved reading her fiction. Repetition of characters make all her stories connected to each other, Suhrawardy aptly notes:

> All Hijab Ismail's short stories are links of a single chain, they are the different incidents and adventures that came the way of the wild, romantic and beautiful *Ruhi*. . . . The setting has all the voluptuous richness, romance and colour

that one associates with Oriental harems. It is also surcharged with the luxurious modernity of Fifth Avenue. By blending the two seemingly contradictory atmospheres Hijab Ismail has succeeded in conveying an impression of an extremely colourful and luxurious existence, but an utterly unreal one.

(Suhrawardy 283)

Suhrawardy and Ismat's critique of Hijab's romances defines another moment in the history of women's writing and readership patterns in Urdu. This shift towards social realism will be discussed later in the chapter, for a moment, let us ponder over Hijab's style and her use of certain formulae.

Hijab's central protagonist Ruhi is a young woman from a wealthy family. In all her stories, homes are full of fine upholstery, delicate gold curtains, breakfast table laden with fresh marmalades and varieties of juicy fruit, and a dedicated and faithful domestic servant *Zunash*, whose task is to wake her up to offer tea, cook her favourite meals, and accompany her on her many travels.[9] Hijab creates an ambience of luxury through use of possessions, like an expensive shawl, homes with fireplaces, lavish meals, continental cuisine and delicate cutlery. For example, in a story called *Havanshre ka Station* (The Station of Havanshre), Ruhi visits her friend Zulfi's home after many years. She gets drenched on the way to the house and has her black Siamese cat with her. While she sits down near the fire side, and pets the cat beside her, Zulfi, her friend laments that although she would have liked to offer her tea in Michelangelo cups, this time she can only manage with ordinary cups (Hijab 63). In all stories, Ruhi plays on the *arghanoon*, which is often described as producing delicate music. Hijab's meticulous detailing of possessions also marks the class and social status of the characters as *ashraf* men and women.

For instance, in the story *Nila Lifafa* (The Blue Envelope 1938), the character Sir Jafar is punctual about meal times and enjoys eating food the European way, using cutlery such as forks and knives on his dining table. These minute details in the setting, dining tables, marmalades, European cutlery, and the dapper suits worn by Sir Jafar make him the *ashraf* or modern man. Apart from wealth, these possessions are also a marker of European influence, which in turn was seen as a sign of modernity. But what does this modernity mean for women? Does modernity mean access to education or possession or choice to marry the man of your choice?

The title of the first story, *Meri Natamam Mohabbat* (My Unfulfilled Love) clearly hints towards a tragic love story. Ruhi is in love with the long-serving 40-year-old Captain Fakri, the ADC to her grandmother. Ruhi's father and grandmother are very fond of Fakri. The story moves slowly through long-winded conversations, has a strong undercurrent of passion, and Hijab deftly makes the reader aware of Ruhi's love for Fakri. He lovingly calls her *kamsin* Ruhi or *nanhi* Ruhi. The word *kamsin* can mean delicate, young, innocent, or allude to 'virgin' Ruhi, reaffirmed by the title *nanhi*, little or young girl. Ruhi's father and grandmother, old Zubeida Khanam, have arranged her marriage to Shahbaz, a wealthy young cousin.

Ruhi is young and of a delicate constitution; she has been complaining of fever and faints frequently. These fainting spells are psychosomatic outcomes of the conflict betwee her desire for Captain Fakri and the social expectations of being a dutiful and loyal *sharif* girl who does not defy parents. Being in Captain Fakri's company makes Ruhi feel better, so her parents inadvertently often encourage them to spend time together without realizing the affect it has on their young daughter. It is not a surprise why young women and men would love to read Hijab's stories about passionate and tender romantic associations in a society where marriages were based on decisions made by families. There are moments of physical intimacy, for example when Fakri touches Ruhi's forehead to ask her if she feels well or when he pulls her into an embrace; however, as a *sharif* girl, Ruhi never expresses her love directly to him. In *Meri Natamam Mohabbat*, she does not wish to marry Shahbaz, but a large part of the initial development of the plot is based on her attempt to indirectly make Fakri realize that she loves him. Later in the story, when Fakri realizes their feelings for each other, he decides to approach Ruhi's father. Hijab uses a delicate balance to express sexual desire which is bound within models of social decorum or *tahzib* that does not defy standards of manners and etiquette. *Meri Natamam Mohabbat* was an iconic story written by a young Hijab and has a young protagonist from an *ashraf* family who is in love with a mature man. Although conformist in comparison to the writings of later women writers, Hijab's stories ushered a change in Urdu literary tradition.

Hijab's narratives: reshaping earlier traditions

Hijab's stories mark a shift in the world of Urdu publishing. Authorship by a young woman at a time when prose or fiction writing was still dominated by men make her a remarkable figure. Her stories exhibit an influence of Urdu poetry and *dastan*, yet they also diversify from earlier traditions in her use elements of magic or fantasy with realistic descriptions of household objects, self-reflexive narrators and subtle hints towards hierarchies of class and gender. Her narratives lie at the cusp of earlier writing on romance as fantasy and an exploration of feminine desire, often a taboo in patriarchal societies. Sometimes when the reader expects anger or a dramatic twist or a passionate outburst, Hijab exercises subtle control and avoids melodrama to reveal the social anxieties and the dubious status of a young woman as a desiring subject.

In *Natamam Mohabbat*, Ruhi's father is surprised by Fakri's proposal as a suitor for his daughter. The lover is a much older man in comparison to his young, 'frail' daughter. In a calm conversation between the two men, the father mentions the huge age gap between the two. At moments, when we expect anger or possibly a dramatic twist, there is subtle control over excessive emotion. For instance, Ruhi's father is shocked by Fakri's proposal since he is a much older man. Fakri insists he is not old; Ruhi's father reassures him that a man of 50 is not an old man, yet the gap of 39 years is worrisome. Further, since Zubeida Khanam has already fixed a match for Hijab, challenging that would bring dishonour to his family. The conversation reveals the harsh truth of a woman's status as an object desired for possession and exchange in the marketplace of marriage. The refusal eventually ends in tragedy with Fakri's suicide, Ruhi is left heartbroken, while Shahbaz marries another girl of his own choice. While traversing the tropes of romance, one can see that there is no possibility for love in this marketplace. Hijab's romance thwarts readerly expectations and does not end in marriage. Fantasy does not provide a resolution.

However, Hijab's romances borrow from the adventure tales of *dastan* with Ruhi as the granddaughter of a Turkish princess and her lovers as inaccessible or unattainable like the beloved in the Urdu *ghazal*. Taking a familiar trope from the Urdu *ghazal*, Hijab creates what Annemarie Schimmel says in the context of Ghalib's *ghazals*, 'sensual pictures of fragile beauty [which] can be found side by side with sighs of utter despair' (221). In another common image borrowed from Urdu romanticism, Hijab uses the garden as a setting for intimate conversations between lovers. Dark clouds, fragrant flowers such as jasmine, the deep red rose and the melodies sung by birds, music played by Ruhi and images of the lover being carried in a boat into the turbulent sea show the inherited tradition of Urdu poetry. Husain's exploration of the relationship between cultural values, fragrance and garden poetry traces this back to Deccani Urdu in Hyderabad (2000). Here is an illustration from the *Zalim Mohabbat* (Cruel Love), where Ruhi narrates:

> The next day when I awoke, a beautiful morning had opened its eyes like a mischievous dawn. Facing the garden, the windows were open and the untouched ray of the sun was laughing at the turbulent blue sea. In the garden, birds were busy singing morning *ragas* but my heart was anxious, despite the charms of the alluring morning. I drew the gold window curtain beside my pillow and looked into the garden. Just underneath the window a big, bright, red rose was swaying in the fragrant breeze of the spring.
>
> (My translation, Hijab 271)

First published in the magazine *Saqi* (1938), *Zalim Mohabbat* told the story of Ruhi and her fiancé Muneer, who is indisposed. He is in love with her and often dreams of their marriage and their future thereafter. However, Ruhi is in love with Muneer's friend Chashmi. She loves going for walks in the garden and frequently meets him there. These meetings with the sunlight streaming into the afternoon make the day hot while the young lovers have conversations in the alcoves and corners. These cool shaded corners where the lovers meet are in direct contrast with the passion and conflict raging within Ruhi. Long passages describe Ruhi's feelings for Chashmi and the subtle ways in which she tries to express her love to him. Once she tells him that she is writing a story about a young girl who is in love with a man. The entire conversation takes place in the shade, in a garden on a hot June afternoon. Chashmi keeps warning Ruhi to be careful of the heat, a subtle warning to young women, the landscape mirrors inner feelings, passion needs to be controlled. Ruhi's behaviour can threaten the social fabric of *ashraf* society. Her love for an older man or the friend of her fiancé can destroy well-established hierarchies of class and defy rules of decorum set for women and men by their families and society at large. Hijab plays with conventions of Urdu romanticism, imagery and form which also makes visible a tussle between earlier values of *tahzib*, emerging social hierarchies and the changing milieu of colonial modernity.

This milieu of the late 1930s is created through visible material wealth of Ruhi's household; professions of characters such as a family doctor (Dr Gar), official (Sir Jafar), ADC (Captain Fakri), continental cuisine and use of cutlery (Sachdeva Jha 2021). References to French writers such as Guy De Maupassant (1850–1893), modern musical instruments like the *arghanoon* or *organon* exhibit the modernity and the cosmopolitanism of her fiction in late colonial India (Sachdeva Jha 2021). In *Zalim Mohabbat*, Ruhi's beloved Chashmi enjoys boating just as her father was shown to do in *Meri Natamam Mohabbat*. The sea and the lone sailor on a boat figure prominently in Maupassant's short fiction too. When Chashmi is surprised to find Ruhi waiting for her at the shore, he asks her why are you out in this hot sun? Ruhi laments that it is impossible to tell him the real cause. Instead she changes the topic and says, she is writing a novel and is stuck at a point. She asks him if he would listen to her plot and help her out, however she warns him that 'the novel is a little more colourful, you won't accuse me of nudity, will you?' (*afsana kuchh zyada rangin hai. Ap mujh par uryani ka ilzam to na lagayenge?*) Chashmi has read Maupassant's fiction and reassures her that he won't be scandalised. Ruhi says, 'Oh no, no. This novel is not like that. Even in its stark nakedness, the pain of life lies concealed here' (Hijab 227).

Romance is just one of the strands in Hijab's fiction, it puts emotions upfront however it also enfolds reality in the same vein. Further research on emotions and love in Hijab's writing can go a long way to chart literatures on love in South Asia as done by Orsini (2000) and feed into contemporary debates on histories of emotions in South Asia (Pernau 2021). Often Ruhi is advised to be in the real world, her forays into imaginary worlds are seen as dangerous and are the cause of her ailing health. Ruhi/Hijab constantly assert that 'poetry and fiction are my spirit and thinking about them is my life.' (Hijab 227) In this world fiction is interspersed with reality.

Hijab asserts her own individuality through her narrative style and directly addresses the reader as a strong authorial persona. Although the word 'hijab' literally means the veil, the author Hijab never shies away from asserting her identity as the creator of romance narratives. She intersperses fiction with snippets from her own life. For Fatehpuri (141), Hijab was a woman from (*asuda hal*) a wealthy background who did not have much experience of life's troubles. Although considering her popularity he has to concede that readers share a bond with her and he writes, 'studying the lives of commoners (*awam-i-mutale*) had made her empathetic towards them and their aspirations' (My translation, Fatehpuri 141). Fatehpuri failed to see the cleverly crafted persona of Hijab as a storyteller of romances.

In an interview with Yusuf Kamran in the programme *Dastango* (Performer of *dastaan*) telecast in the year 1978 on Pakistani television, Hijab consciously blurred the distinction between her characters and herself. She insisted that she was like them and recalled her young days surrounded by the beautiful gardens, sunsets, fragrances, and a fairy tale childhood in Hyderabad. She encouraged the audience to trace the semblance between the fiction she wrote and her real life. Her use of kajal and dreamy gestures make her seem theatrical like an actor. Hijab the person, Hijab the persona, and Ruhi the character all overlapped in a complex set of performances and the same holds true in her romance narratives.[10] In an issue of the Urdu journal *Nuqoosh*, Shaukat Thanavi (1904–1963), said that, 'Hijab describes a world where she takes the reader on a trip with her, the reader might think that this is a fictional world . . . even I thought the same. However, the more closely I got a chance to see Hijab I got to know that she writes what she actually feels' (my translation, cited in Fatehpuri 142). Like other critics, Thanavi could not also see through her clever and deft use of the autobiographical mode in her narratives.

In the introduction to her much published story *Meri Natamam Mohabbat*, Hijab wrote wrote that 'whenever someone praises *Natamam Mohabbat*, I feel shy and I keep trying to change the topic, which often baffles my addressee.' (My translation, Fatehpuri 142). She wrote the story when she was 11 years old and was not allowed to write as her family thought that writing without supervision would hamper her education. She got a chance to free herself from regular teaching as she fell ill and was sent away from home to recuperate. Once she reached there, she felt her 'spirit/soul blossom' as she could spend long hours in writing stories. 'At the age of eleven to write about a profound subject like love, without any experience, [she says,] could it have been anything except the madness of adolescence?' (Fatehpuri 143)

Drawing another close connection between her passion for flying airplanes and her heroine in *Zalim Mohabbat*, Ruhi is shown to have just returned after a short flight in her airplane. *Hawabazi* or flying was both Hijab and her character's cherished past time. It is difficult to separate the woman Hijab from the narrator/protagonist Ruhi or her fiction. Hijab/Ruhi constantly revel in the act of writing and reading stories, flying airplanes, and ruminating over love and beauty of nature in its sunsets and verdure. The self-reflexivity, and layered narratives of Hijab's stories accord her a special position in the literary history of Urdu fiction (Sachdeva Jha 2021). Recently Aamer Hussein has written of Hijab's unique style and how her fiction can be seen as an example of postmodernist fiction in early twentieth century fiction in South Asia. Tracing the influence of Sigmund Freud, he rightly points out that her fiction explores deep into the female psyche to engage with recurrent themes of fear, anxiety, desire and female sexuality. He describes Hijab as:

> a highly self-conscious novelist, a postmodernist *avant la lettre*, concerned with the self-reflexive narration of memory and desire and the slippages of language which involuntarily reveal repressions, evasions and lack.
>
> (Hussein 10)

Hijab's fiction was self-conscious and culturally specific. Published both in magazines like *Tehzeeb-e-Niswan* targeted at women readers as well as journals like *Saqi and Nuqoosh*, read both by men and by women. In the absence of specific studies on readership, it can still be suggested that Hijab's popularity might have been more amongst women readers on the basis of memoirs. In her memoirs, Ismat wrote that 'Miss Hijab Ismail was the queen of newspapers. It was a romantic name that evoked novelty, grace, and a glimpse of melancholic beauty' (Asaduddin 50). Ismat was intrigued by her as well as mocked her style as unrealistic and melodramatic. However, for Hijab the romance was imaginary as well as real.

To use Frederic Jameson's beautiful formulation, romance is 'that form in which the world-ness of world reveals itself . . . for romance as a literary form is that event in which world in the technical sense of the transcendental horizon of my experience becomes precisely visible as something like an inner worldly object in its own right' (Jameson 142). Hijab's romances also reveal this world-ness of the *ashraf* household in all its variegated detail, its opulent lifestyle, the dreams of young women, their authoritarian parents and grandmothers and forbidden love. These worlds also reveals the anxiety in men like Captain Fakri, who succumb to the hierarchical and oppressive world of *ashraf* patriarchy. To some, Hijab's romances may seem conformist or stereotypical but to me, the act of writing and reading romances offers possibilities of female agency and subversion.

I see Hijab in conversation with Urdu literary traditions, French short stories and at work to create a voice to express feminine consciousness that defies linear narration. Restraining herself to one particular genre either of romance or social realism would not have fit Hijab's persona. As Hussein (11) argues, it required the 'work of a fabulist, a romance writer and a dreamer like Hijab' to experiment with fiction. To understand this experimental mode, we must return to Hijab's contemporaries in the Progressive Writers Movement and locate her with other writers of the time.

History of Urdu fiction and Hijab's position

While Hijab explored the world of dream and anxieties, told stories about women from *ashraf* families, other women writers such as Rashid Jahan and Ismat Chughtai were forging their way into mainstream debates on women's education, same sex desire, poverty, social discrimination, and motherhood. These writers preferred to use realism and satire as modes of narration and were associated with the Progressive Writers' Association, which included male writers like Sajjad Zaheer (1905–1973), Ahmed Ali (1910–1994), and others. Just before Hijab published her first story, in December 1932, a collection of stories in Urdu titled *Angare* was published. Within a few months, this collection was banned in March 1933, and all the printed copies were confiscated. *Angare* consisted of five short stories by Sajjad Zaheer, two by Ahmed Ali, one short story by Mahmuduzzafar (1908–1956), and a short story and play by Rashid Jahan. All four of them were young men and women from *sharif* backgrounds. They were bilingual and had received an English education. Their work *Angare* was banned on charges of explicit sexuality, obscenity, and blasphemous writing. In an incisive and comprehensive history of the Progressive Writers Movement in Urdu, Jalil locates the publication of *Angare* has a significant moment which drew 'public anger verging on mass hysteria' (Jalil 147). The collection, 'was a self-conscious attempt to shock people out of their inertia, to show them how hypocrisy and sexual oppression had so crept into everyday life that it was accepted with blithe disregard for all norms of civilized society' (Jalil 151). Each story 'dealt with the lives of the most disenfranchised, disempowered and downtrodden. When not shabby and poor, these lives were certainly marked by decay and disintegration and in the case of women, marginalisation and exclusion.' (Jalil 152) Although in direct contrast to the Progressive Writers, Suhrawardy (258) regarded Hijab as 'amongst the first-rate writers of short-stories in Urdu'.

Unlike their attempt to speak in voices other than their own (Jalil 152), Hijab chose to create a character who is indistinguishable at times from her own literary persona and her life. If Rashid Jahan exposed the oppressed lives of Muslim women through the problem of second marriages, sexual abuse, and lack of contraceptives, Hijab displayed it through a lyrical form of the romance. Ruhi is trapped in a family from where there is no escape. Whether it is Hijab's depiction of her marriage being fixed to a man she doesn't love and the suicide of her lover, or Rashid Jahan's story on the sordid life of Muhammadi Begum, whose husband wants sex even when she is pregnant, both women wrote against patriarchy and repression of feminine desire and agency although in different styles. As a woman from a privileged family who could learn to fly an airplane, Hijab chose a style that was reminiscent of Urdu romances, but she reworked it to sharpen her own style in the Urdu literary world. Her stories reveal a shift from the world of magic, fantasy, and romance to show traces of *ashraf* households, which had assimilated European lifestyles by the 1930s and were well versed in European literature. Her stories were part of a global conversation of genres, practices of consumption and anxiety in the 20th century.

Real life encounters between Ismat and Hijab become symbolic moments in the history of women's writing in Urdu. Ismat kept iterating that she could not write like Hijab. When her family had shifted to Sambhar, where her father was employed, Ismat found it difficult to pass time in the small town and sought an escape through reading Hijab's stories and the life depicted in these stories often made her wonder. She recounts, 'I think I was jealous of the poetic ambience of Mrs. Imtiaz Ali. In our family romantic ambience could not have blossomed' (Asaduddin 40). Unlike Hijab, Ismat and Saadat Hasan Manto were the *terrible enfant* of Urdu writing (Jalil 152). They had to appear in court to answer charges of obscenity against their stories *Lihaf* and *Boo*. During this visit to Lahore, Ismat met Hijab for the first time at a dinner and later, she wrote:

> I met Hijab Imtiaz Ali. She was heavily made up, a thick lining of kajal in her eyes. She looked somewhat angry, somewhat melancholic. Whenever anyone asked her a question, she would gaze into space.
>
> 'A fraud.' Manto whispered into my ears, dilating his large eyes.
>
> 'No, she is lost in the world of her dreams created by her pen and prefers to stay int that multicoloured shell.'
>
> (Asaduddin 35)

They met a second time when Ismat had to go for another trip to Lahore. This time she found Hijab to be friendly, informal, and talkative. She wrote that it felt as if Hijab had had a second birth, and she dared to ask if she could see the *arghanoon*, often described in Hijab's stories.

> Ismat asked her, "Do you really have an *arghanoon*?"
> "Yes. Do you want to take a look at it?"
> "Of course. This word in your stories had an intoxicating effect on me. I also told her that at some point of time, I had written some prose verse in imitation of hers, which I had burnt later. At the sight of the *arghanoon*, all my zest and anticipation fizzled out. The instrument was the sort of baby piano that de Melo played in film songs! It was used as background to suggest the heroine's mental state when she was angry! The word 'organ'is so dull; the addition of the Urdu letter *ghain* made it sound like a lilting tune of Asavari."
>
> (Asaduddin 35)

Ismat's recollection of Hijab in her memoirs is a poignant moment of location and self-referentiality in the corpus of women's writing in Urdu. These memories relate conflict, difference and transition (Sachdeva Jha 2021). To Suhrawardy, Hijab's writing was escapist:

> In her style Hijab Ismail is regarded as amongst the first-rate writers of short-stories in Urdu, yet her work is in direct contrast to that of the young socialist writers, and it cannot be considered as good as theirs for though escapist literature has its uses, literature that has a criticism of life and which tries to deal with its complexities and problems is the better and the more enduring. Hijab Ismail's stories make one forget the realities of existence, but they cannot be forgotten for any length of time. Literature that can help us to face these realities or to understand them is the superior of the two.
>
> (Suhrawardy 284)

For Manto, Hijab was a fraud while to Ismat, her imaginary romances were far from reality. Despite the views of her contemporary literary scholars, Hijab was an astute observer. Hers was a search for meaning in a world of her own creation. Self-reflexivity and complex use of imagination and multiple narrative styles make Hijab's fiction a perfect example of what we call genre fiction today. Defying easy classification, her stories reveal a woman writer who did not shy away from re-thinking, re-shaping and creating new forms in Urdu fiction.

Conclusion

Amidst the growing influence of Marxism and Progressive Writers in Urdu fiction in the 20th century, there was a simultaneous world of Urdu genre fiction with its romances, detective fiction, mystery novels, and horror stories. Hijab was a regular contributor to this literary world, and although her fiction may not have appeared to be as radical or realist to some or later critics, she was a widely read author. On 15 August 1947, the subcontinent witnessed the emergence of two independent nations of India and Pakistan, but Hijab's fiction has continued to be part of the common history of Urdu genre fiction that was read on both sides of the historical divide and possibly even in the nation of Bangladesh whose birth she witnessed in 1971. This chapter is an attempt to draw our attention towards women as writers and readers of romance, a genre they shaped as well as challenged to address questions of sexuality, gender hierarchies and the world of Urdu literature.

Notes

1 The Urdu term *ashraf* has its origins in the word *sharafat*, which might be translated as nobility of behavior rather than nobility of birth. The period subsequent to the Rebellion of 1857 saw the gradual emergence of a Muslim middle class in the subcontinent. This new middle class was distinct from the class in Europe as it did not emerge out of an industrial context in Delhi. Rather, the *ashraf* class in the Indian subcontinent emerged from different educated, professional groups such as poets, scholars, religious elites, and traders, with a growth in public institutions such as universities, colleges, print media and the shaping of a new public sphere (Pernau 2013).
2 *Tawaif* is an Urdu word used for courtesans who were held in high esteem in princely courts such as Awadh and Hyderabad. These women were talented performers who were skilled in the arts of poetry and dance. Often called nautch girls by early 19th century European travelers, many lost their status and livelihoods after the Rebellion of 1857 and the implementation of Anti-Contagious Diseases Act, which led to their marginalization and victimization.
3 Ralph Russell argues that *Dastaan* is in the same tradition of storytelling as Cervantes' romances. The *Dastaan* is a widely spoken form of storytelling with long stories featuring picaresque plots, adventures, and elements of fantasy. The *Dastaan* also influenced novelists like Ratan Nath Sarshar (1847–1903).
4 Suhrawardy Ikramullah did her doctoral dissertation at the School of Oriental and African Studies, University of London, and wrote a meticulously researched history of Urdu fiction which continues to be a rich resource for most scholars of Urdu fiction.
5 Since mine is a work in progress, I cannot provide the exact number of her publications.
6 https://rekhta.org/authors/hijab-imtiyaz-ali
7 I am grateful to him for sending me details of his books and his support as I work through Hijab's work.
8 *Saqi* was edited by Shahid Ahmed Dehalvi, the grandson of Deputy Nazir Ahmed. *Nuqoosh* was edited by Muhammad Tufail, and its first issue was published in 1948 in Lahore.
9 *Meri Natamam Mohabbat* has Zubeida Dadi sitting on a soft, luxurious sofa while Ruhi rests often on a couch and wears soft, muslin dresses.
10 This interview was produced by Khwaja Najamul Hasan for Pakistan Television PTV in *Dastango* in 1978.

Works cited

Ali, Hijab Imtiaz. "Havanshre ka Station" cited in *Gulistan our bhi Hain*, edited by Mujeeb Ahmad Khan, Kitabi Duniya, 2008, pp. 58–71.
———. *Lash aur dusre Haibatnak Afsane*. Darul Ishaat Punjab, 1933.

———. *Meri Natamam Mohabbat aur Dusre Ruman.* Darul Ishat Punjab, 1933.

———. "Nila Lifafa." *Count Ilyas ki Maut aur Dusre Haibatnak Afsane.* Darul Ishaat Punjab, 1938.

———. "Zalim Mohabbat." *Gulistan aur Bhi Hain,* edited by Mujeeb Ahmad Khan, Kitabi Duniya, 2008, pp. 271–78.

Asaduddin, M. *Ismat Chughtai: A Life in Words, Memoirs.* Penguin Random House India, 2013.

_____ *Ismat Chughtai: Lifting the Veil.* Penguin Books India, 2001.

Chattopadhyay, Bodhisattva, Aakriti Mandhwani, and Anwesha Maity, editors. *Indian Genre Fiction: Pasts and Future Histories.* Routledge, 2019.

Chughtai, Ismat. *Kaghazi hai Pairahan.* Hindi translation, by Iftikar Anjum. Rajkamal Paperbacks, 1998.

Dubrow, Jennifer. "*Sharafat* and *Bhal Mansi*: A New Perspective on Respectability in *Fasana-e-Azad.*" *South Asian History and Culture,* Vol. 9, no. 2, 2017, pp. 181–193. Doi: 10.1080/19472498.2018.1446796.

Fatehpuri, Farman. *Urdu Afsana aur Afsana Nigar.* Urdu Academy Sindh, 1982.

Fielder, Leslie A. "Towards a Definition of Popular Culture." *Superculture: American Popular Culture and Europe,* edited by C. W. E. Bigsby, Bowling Green University, Popular Press, 1975, pp. 28–42.

Husain, Ali Akbar. *Scent in the Islamic Garden: A Study of Deccani Urdu Literary Sources,* Oxford UP, 2004.

Hussein, Aamer, editors. *Kahani: Short Stories by Pakistani Women.* Saqi Books, 2005.

Jalil, Rakshanda. *Liking Progress, Loving Change: A Literary History of the Progressive Writer's Movement in Urdu.* Oxford UP, 2014.

Jameson, Frederic. "Magical Narratives: Romance as Genre." *New Literary History, Critical Challenges: The Bellagio Symposium,* vol. 7, no. 1, 1975, pp. 135–63.

Kamran, Yusuf. Interview with Hijab Imtiaz Ali, *Dastango.* Producer, Khwaja Najamul Hasan, Pakistan Television, 1978. Youtu.be/PfFXZQc-5dg. Accessed 02 July 2020.

Khan, Mujeeb Ahmad. *Gulistan Our Bhi Hain: Hijab Imtiaz Ali ke Afsane.* Kitabi Duniya, 2008.

_____. *Hijab Imtiaz Ali: Fan aur Shakhsiyat.* Educational Publishing House, 2010.

Khan, Pasha M. *The Broken Spell: Indian Storytelling and the Romance Genre in Persian and Urdu.* Wayne State UP, 2019.

Khoja-Moolji, Shenila. *Forging the Ideal Educated Girl: The Production of Desirable Subjects in Muslim South Asia.* U. of California Press, 2018. Doi: https://doi.org/10.1525/luminos.52.

Lambert-Hurley, Siobhan. *Elusive Lives: Gender, Autobiography, and the Self in Muslim South Asia.* Stanford UP, 2018.

Lee, Christine S. "The Meanings of Romance: Rethinking Early Modern Fiction." *Modern Philology,* vol. 112, no. 2, Nov. 2014, pp. 287–311.

Lelyveld, David. *Aligarh's First Generation: Muslim Solidarity in British India.* Princeton UP, 1978.

Makinen, Merja. *Feminist Popular Fiction.* Palgrave Macmillan, 2001.

Metcalfe, Barbara Daly. *Perfecting Women: Maulana Ashraf Ali Thanawi's Bihishti Zewar.* U of California P, 1992.

Minault, Gail. *Secluded Scholars: Women's Education and Muslim Social Reform in Colonial India.* Oxford UP, 1998.

Naim, C. M. "How Did Bibi Ashraf Learn to Read and Write." *Annual of Urdu Studies,* vol. 6, 1967, p. 99.

_____ "Homage to a 'Magic Writer': The *Mistriz* and *Asrar* Novels of Urdu." *Indian Genre Fiction: Pasts and Future Histories* edited by Bodhisattva Chattopadhyay, Aakriti Mandhwani and Anwesha Maity, Routledge, 2019, pp. 38–56.

Oesterheld, Christina. "Islam in Contemporary South Asia: Urdu and Muslim Women." *Oriente Moderno*, vol. 23, no. 84, Nr. 1, 2004, pp. 217–43.

Orsini, Francesca. *Print and Pleasure: Popular Literature and Entertaining Fictions in Colonial North India*. Permanent Black, 2009.

_____Ed. *Love in South Asia: A Cultural History*. Cambridge UP, 2006.

Pernau, Margrit. *Ashraf into Middle Class: Muslims in Nineteenth-Century Delhi*. Oxford UP, 2013.

_____. "Studying Emotions in South Asia." *South Asian History and Culture*, vol. 12, no. 2–3, 2021, pp. 111–128. Doi: 10.1080/197472498.2021.1878788

Pritchett, Frances W. *Marvellous Encounters: Folk Romance in Urdu and Hindi*. Riverdale Company, 1985.

Radway, Janice A. *Reading the Romance: Women, Patriarchy and Popular Literature*. U of North Carolina P, 1984.

Rothman, Joshua. "A Better Way to Think About the Genre Debate." 6 Nov. 2014, www.newyorker.com, www.newyorker.com/books/joshua-rothman/better-way-think-genre-debate. Accessed 12 Dec. 2019.

Russell, Ralph. "The Development of the Modern Novel in Urdu." *The Novel in India, Its Birth and Development*, edited by T. W. Clark, George Alien & Unwin, 1970, pp. 122–32.

Sachdeva, Shweta. *In Search of the Tawaif in History: Courtesans, Nautch Girls and Celebrity Entertainers in India (1720s–1920s)* 2008. University of London, PhD dissertation.

Sachdeva Jha, Shweta. "Tracing Terror and the Uncanny in the Gothic Urdu Fiction of Hijab Imtiaz Ali." *South Asian Gothic: Haunted Cultures, Histories and Media*, edited by Katarzyna Ancuta and Deimantas Valanciunas. U of Wales Press, 2021 (forthcoming).

Suhrawardy, Shaista. *A Critical Survey of the Development of the Urdu Novel and Short Story*. Longmans Green and Co., 1945.

Stark, Ulrike. *An Empire of Books: The Naval Kishore Press and the Diffusion of the Printed Word in Colonial India*. Permanent Black, 2008.

Tharu, Susie J., and K. Lalitha, editors. *Women Writing in India Volume 1: From 600 BC to Early Twentieth Century*. Oxford UP, 1993.

3

'I'M NOBODY! WHO ARE YOU?'

Mrs. Abdul Qādir's horror fiction and the non-authorial[1]

Jaideep Pandey

> My art has had no influence from any other short story writer's language or expression. My art is only and only mine. No other gaze has fallen on it.
>
> (Qāsmī 397)

> I have made no deliberate efforts to acquire the present style of my art. I only write those revelations that appear to me, when I sit amidst broken ruins and old remains.
>
> (Qāsmī 406)

Mrs. Abdul Qādir (1898–1976) cuts a curious figure as a woman writer within Urdu literary history. Nadīm Ahmed Qāsmī, at the end of his 1989 anthology, *Delicate Impressions*, directs a questionnaire to the 24 short story writers whose works are anthologized in the volume. The questions are primarily about the nature of these author's craft, how they negotiate questions of influence, everyday experience and its relationship to art, and their opinions on contemporary Urdu literary trends. While other authors take the opportunity to considerably elaborate their understanding of literature (not consistently of course), Mrs. Abdul Qādir's responses are evasive and brusque at best, and absolute refusal to answer at worst. Cutting herself and her craft off from canon, influence, and, most interestingly, her subjectivity, Qādir instead insists on how 'ruins' and old buildings generate those stories within her.

In this chapter, I look at the horror fiction written by Mrs. Abdul Qādir, to locate how her oft-used term *māfauq al-fitrat* or the supernatural translates into a new generic aesthetic that provides a counterpoint to the push of modernity that one encounters in the dominant trends of early to mid-twentieth century Urdu writings. I hope to locate how the choice of a visceral, non–realist genre on the one hand and the strategy of erasing authorial identity on the other hand in

DOI: 10.4324/9781003002062-5

the works of Mrs. Abdul Qādir complicate normative expectations from Muslim women's writings (heavily hinged on realism). To this end, I attempt to draw the preliminary contours of the genre of horror fiction and how that allows for a deconstruction of modernity beyond the paradigm of life writing and self-narration that has been established as benchmark for Muslim women's literary writings (both within the Progressive Writers' Association and often by contemporary scholarship, which demands constant narration of subjectivity from the texts it labels as 'authored' by Muslim women). The larger attempt will be to use Mrs. Abdul Qādir's work as a starting point to think of a genealogy of literary attempts by Muslim women outside the overarching and dominant strand of realist writing, as well as the critical strain that *requires* the proverbially 'veiled' subjects to speak of themselves.

The self-imposed literary isolation of Mrs. Abdul Qādir and its positioning within a volume like *Delicate Impressions* itself bespeaks of certain tensions between post-facto critical attempts to relate a history of women's literary endeavours in Urdu prose. *Delicate Impressions* curiously sits somewhere between a *majmu'a* (collection) and a *tazkirah* (biographical memoirs) in generic terms, i.e. to say, it both collates examples of short stories by women writers and appends them with brief life histories of the authors. At the end of the volume is a section titled '*Mere Khayāl Mein – Sawālnāma*' ['In My Opinion – Questionnaire'], where the responses of the women authors to a set of eight broad questions are recorded. The attempt then is to form a cohesive history of women writers in Urdu, their literary techniques ('*fan*'/'skill/art' as the book says), now linked to the short biographies. This persistence of what might be perceived as an outdated form of biographical criticism is quite common when it comes to women writers of Urdu and, I would argue, is a legacy from the formative period of Islamic Reform and literary modernity in Urdu, to which I now briefly turn.

Urdu literary modernity and the injunction to narrate

The rubric of colonial modernity is often heavily emphasized within the study of Indian literary cultures in general, and Urdu literary trends in particular. The year 1857 is a watershed moment post which the Muslim *shurafā* reorganized themselves not just in socio-economic sense, but also in the sense of cultural vocabulary. This trend is not merely externally imposed, as Frances Pritchett has demonstrated, but formed an important component of the self-identification of the 'new' generation of literary writers. Further, this shift into newness, what one might dare to call 'modernity,' was also enacted through a shift in literary genres, particularly the arrival of the novel form (Dubrow 41–3). The central nexus of writers to emerge from this was the *Anjuman Tarraqi Pasand Mussanifin-e Hind*, or the Progressive Writers' Association (not, of course, restricted only to Urdu or Hindi). The PWA embraced both a set of literary principles, as well as analogous principles of socio-economic critique. Further, the PWA also had particular kinds of literary and intellectual roots.

As Carlo Coppola notes, the PWA had its roots in earlier reform movement across the Indian subcontinent, produced by a need to inhabit a cultural and socio-economic colonial modernity. Frances Pritchett on the other hand argues that the also necessitated a severing away from an older literary tradition now deemed as apolitical, ineffectual and fabular. Consider, for example, Munshi Premchand's landmark speech delivered on the first meeting of the PWA in Lucknow, 1936:

> The standard of passion was desire-nourishment and the adornment of beauty. In expressing these sensual emotions, poets used to show off miracles of inventiveness and acumen. In poetry some new artifice, or new simile, or new flight of fancy, was sufficient to earn praise − no matter how remote from reality it might be. . . . He writes a story, but he fleshes it out with reality − but in such a way that there would be movement and power of expression as well; he views human nature with a subtle scrutiny. He examines psychology, and tries to make his 'characters' such that in every situation, on every occasion, he would make their behavior like that of flesh-and-blood people.
>
> (Rahbar 235)

Premchand (echoed by others such as Ali Sardar Jafri and Sajjad Zaheer, to name a few) makes a critical distinction between the past, soaked in sensuality, mysticism, and religion, and the modern moment of 'literature,' where it is weaving a fabric with verisimilitude that produces a connection with the real, and therefore the potential for political action.[2] What then gets excluded? It is the older world of poetry, with its anthropomorphism, obsession with love and sexuality, decadence of poetry, and obfuscating of historicity. Faisal Fatehali Devji draws an explicit link between this and the exclusion of the world of 'za'if.' The word za'if means weak and ineffective but, as Devji indicates, takes on definitions of the gendered world of women and effeminate men (segregated from the outside world) that need to be excluded from what he calls the 'public-discursive' world of modernity (143–44).

While a comprehensive survey of PWA is neither possible nor necessary here, I would conclude by saying that while realism activated certain kinds of political thought, action, and interrogation in Urdu, it also, at the same time, occluded other registers of writing. Further, this occlusion was enacted in gendered terms. Women writers thus were particularly *coerced* in a way to narrate lives, within reformist discourse, within the PWA's emphasis on realism as a way of political action, as well as within contemporary 'liberal-secular' critical circles. All these, particularly the last, are even truer in the case of those placed under the category of 'Muslim Women.' Even if belatedly, recent work on Muslim women's writings has begun to problematize this seemingly neat equation between author, text, and history, with the sum being carried to the critic.[3] However, this enquiry has still pretty much centred on the genre of life writings. In this context, it is important to ask − is it possible to read other(ed) genres, to think of political practices grounded in embodied knowledge, visceral materiality, and potentially radical a-temporality?

Mrs. Abdul Qādir and critical reputation

There seems to be very little on the writings of Mrs. Abdul Qādir, even though as Aamer Hussein notes, Qurratulain Hyder placed her pretty much in the mainstream of Urdu writers. She is missing, for instance, from Shaista Ikramullah Suhrawardy's magisterial study of Urdu prose, where she goes to the length of discussing every major and minor prose writer and dedicates a special chapter to women short story writers (Suhrawardy 123–66, 233–42). Her collections, however, give indication of being immensely popular, as the editor of her collection, *Sadā-e Jars wa Dīgar Afsāne* [The Sound of the Bell and Other Stories], notes: '*Mrs. Abdul Qādir apne haibatnāk aur pur asrār afsānoṇ kī wajah se duniyā-e adab mein kāfī ma'rūf ho chukī haiṇ*'/'Mrs. Abdul Qādir has become quite famous in the world of literature, because of her terrifying and mysterious short stories' (Qādir 7). He further offers proof for this by pointing out that the first edition of her collection *Lāshoṇ kā Shehr aur Dīgar Afsāne* [City of Corpses and Other Stories] sold out in a record time of one and a half year. Even at the level of a sales pitch, Mrs. Abdul Qādir seems to be claiming a recognizable name for herself, as the paratextual material of her early editions point out. Her '*hairatnāk afsāne*'/'shocking stories' are regularly advertised on the back cover of each of her collections, pointing to a market which associated her with a specific type of readerly expectation and experience. In this sense, Mrs. Abdul Qādir seems to be carrying pretty much the name and stature of the author of a genre fiction with a specific market.

Her editors seem to place her completely apart from reformist strains of writing, which were immensely popular, or even expected from women writers, as the previous section indicates. Rather, she seems to be placed most firmly within a certain sensational ethos. The editor of *Sadā-e Jars wa Dīgar Afsāne*, for example, says there is no '*islāhī-e lā'ehā-e'amal*'/'clarity of corrective actions' to be found in her stories, but a certainty of '*zehnī tafrīh*'/'mental pleasure' for any '*sāhib-e zauq*'/'possessor of taste.' This identification of her stories with a certain affective, pleasure-driven principle of taste, which is simultaneously '*haibatnāk*'/'terrifying' as well as possesses '*jāzbiyyat*'/'attractiveness' and, in the words of the editor to her novel *Takht Bagh*, '*aish-o-masarrat*'/'pleasure and happiness' seems to be the hallmark of her writing. This combination of fascination and repulsion, as we will see, marks several of her stories as well.

Rather than using the self-explanatory term 'horror,' it would perhaps be more productive to see the Urdu words that recur through Mrs. Abdul Qādir's stories that indicate the preponderance of a certain kind of mood and ethos. The first is the landscape itself, which is given the central position within the creative process of Mrs. Abdul Qādir. As I pointed out in the beginning, Mrs. Abdul Qādir categorically disconnects herself from any canon, the dominant literary tendencies, such as the PWA, and own subjectivity. Instead, she projects creative power onto a landscape fashioned as a kind of gothic sublime. The landscape, with ruins, old buildings, ancient temples, and lush natural vistas becomes the author or creator, which are, in a sense, writing *through* Qādir. The landscape is also deeply de-historicized (except for an occasional year or so), and even depopulated. The emphasis rather is on sensual perception or what is a key term in her stories and the description of her own artistic process – '*ilhām*' or 'epiphanies'/'revelations.' It is within this uplifting moment of epiphany that is shared between the author, the text, and the reader that the genre consolidates itself.

This visceral nature of the creative process can be traced through some other frequently used terms, such as '*haulnāk*'/'terrible,' '*haibatnāk*'/'terrifying,' '*hairatnāk*'/'shocking,' '*riqqat*'/'frenzy,' and '*hasrat-āmez*'/'desire-inspiring.' These are all terms of affect, as opposed to any purported rationality, and it is within these that Mrs. Abdul Qādir's fiction is grounded. Thinking in terms of generic debates contemporaneous to her (outlined in the previous section), this would be anathema. This can be seen in some confusion surrounding her work, both in her own time and outside it. Aamer Hussein looks at a mixed jumble of genres in Mrs. Abdul Qādir's work- romance, *dāstān* tradition, old wives' tales, and of course gothic. One could also think of the 'sublime' in this connection, which wouldn't be a new observation. One of the earliest commentators on Mrs. Abdul Qādir, Shaukat Thānvi had observed that when he first read one of her stories, titled *Rakshash* or Monster, he thought it was a translation from a European story, because it seemed too unfamiliar and unprecedented in the world of Urdu prose. Thus, Mrs. Abdul Qādir seems to be both out of sync with time and place in her own milieu. The editor to *Takht Bagh* summarizes this adequately in the terms – '*anokhī*'/'unique,' '*nirālī*'/'quaint,' '*judāgāna*'/'different.' (15)

It is this dislocation that is central to how Mrs. Abdul Qādir employs and delineates the term '*māfauq al-fitrat.*' The term literally means above and beyond nature, i.e. a term corresponding to the supernatural. The word '*māfauq*' carries interesting connotations vis-à-vis the task of the genre. Derived from the Arabic root (*fe-vāv-qāf*) meaning 'above,' the term seems to imply something that rises above the everyday. This dislocation is a crucial element to the readerly experience that Mrs. Abdul Qādir seeks to produce. Her stories always put in contrast a stark, materialistic reality, with a deeply evocative, 'un-real' one. *Mu'allim kā Rāz* [The Secret of the Tutor], for example, takes place in a well-to-do, seemingly reformist household. The woman of the house has employed a tutor for the children of the house, clearly doesn't follow purdah, and chides the superstitions of her *mulāzims* or servants. She is thus an immediately recognizable figure, as is the household, partly located between a forward moving present and troubling remnants of the past. The dislocation is through the figure of the tutor, who plunges the story suddenly away from this warm familiarity of a reformist house into the deep, rural recesses of Kashmir's de-populated landscape. The tortured tutor, lying between his experience of modern education and job in bustling Lahore, and the depopulated backwaters of Kashmir's mysterious landscape signify the fruition of this.

Similarly, in *Kāsa-e Sar* [Skull], the narrator and his friend have finished their college education and are actively looking for modern, bureaucratic jobs (the kind that Pritchett describes for a modern educated Muslim male). Both of them end up working in a Bank in colonial Assam (now Meghalaya). It is here that the rift appears, and the narrator is plunged into a landscape of complete unfamiliarity and dislocation. Similarly, in *Sadā-e Jars* [The Sound of the Bell], the narrator Mumtaz and his friend Khalil are friends from college, who drift apart after the former is married. They are reunited in a rundown bungalow in Calcutta, over some long-shared interest in ancient Egypt and its '*ajīb-o-gharīb ashiā*'/'strange and foreign things.' These fault lines between a rationally knowable, forward moving world of modern jobs, education and a well-to-do upwardly mobile lifestyle, and an ahistorical landscape, located almost as it were in a civilizational deep history, are crucial to the enactment of a sensational horror in Mrs. Abdul Qādir's work.

Beyond this, there is a sense in which māfauq-al fitrat also connotes an exit from the realm of humanity itself. At one level, the world of horror of Mrs. Abdul Qādir is haunted by close encounters with entities such as '*jinn*'/'spirit,' '*bhūt*'/'ghost,' '*malik-ul maut*'/'angel of death,' and '*farishta-e ajal*'/'angel of death.' However, at another level, the shift is also into a world which is non-human, which is a very important way in which the genre seems to depart from dominant trends of realist writing in Urdu around this period, which offer a more anthropocentric world. In *Kāsa-e Sar* [Skull], for example, the narrator arrives in Shillong, devastated by the death of his mother. His pain and loneliness are further exacerbated by what he perceives as the ill-will of his friend's wife towards him. It is at this point that he turns to the world of nature:

> However, I would often get scared of the house becoming a battleground, and would go far away from the city to take my mind off things, where I would take pleasure in the beauty of nature's green vistas, among the happy loneliness of the fertile sloping hills, mysterious silences and carefree dawns. I would desperately search for a soulful calm in the beautiful wild shrubs laden with betel creepers. Tapioca stumps and vibrant areca palm trees would be my companions, and I would experience real calmness, lying down in the smooth embrace of the green grass.

The shift in *Kāsa-e Sar*/'Skull' is symptomatic of the larger trend in Mrs. Abdul Qādir's tales, where humans venture out into the non-human world, whether accidentally (in *Rākshas*/'Monster,' for example, where two girls encounter a ghost while playing in an abandoned temple) or in order to process some kind of loss or trauma (as in this example). In *Kāsa-e Sar*/'Skull,' this world of nature is initially bucolic and exists in a very simple sense of pathetic fallacy, i.e. it simply replicates the inner mood of the narrator. However, soon, the world of nature takes a life of its own and pulls the narrator into its terrifying affect. It is here that the term '*jāzbiyyat*'/'attractiveness' becomes crucial to understanding the non-human. The narrator in *Kāsa-e Sar*/'Skull' develops an unhealthy obsession with being outside in the seemingly bucolic vistas of nature in general, and with the skulls that lie scattered around the riverbank that he frequents in particular. This powerful attraction, expressed through an overflow of emotion and an obsessive contemplation, culminates in this scene reminiscent of *memento mori* traditions:

> But once I was done with this task and took out the feathers from the skull, I realized that this too was a human skull, much like mine. Who knows how high he must have helped up his head while walking, and the jewels that must have been inside his head? My head started spinning when I realized the instability of this world's existence. Ah, such a painful culmination to human life! With my heart heavy with these thoughts, I sat there for a while with the skull in my hand, contemplating existence and death.

The human subject here appears stripped of its humanity, and only as subject to the vagaries of nature and time. This terrifying encounter with what one is tempted to think of as Freud's 'uncanny' also forms the core of the story's progress in *Mua'llim kā Rāz*/'The Secret of the Tutor' as well. Husnat Ahmed, who hails from a village named Akhnūr in the province of Jammu, returns to find that his beloved cousin, Sakina's attitude towards him has changed, and her love seems to have cooled off. One night, Husnat follows her in one of her mysterious nightly walks:

> The person was walking very slowly. When I reached closer the person, I realized it was Sakina. She walked to the edge of the bamboo thicket and then stopped, and I hid behind a tree to look at her. By this time, the bamboo trees were separated a little and a young man emerged, whose beauty would have made the moon look insipid.

The bamboo thicket, which forms the edge of the magisterial hereditary estate of Husnat's family, as the site of this romantic rendezvous is significant. The household is painted as the very picture of idyllic domesticity. The bamboo thicket lies at the edge of it, and almost seems to connote in the text the edge of the human world. The young man, who is later identified by the name Rafiq, emerges from this bamboo thicket, and is a man of exquisite beauty. Sakina ends up marrying Rafiq, and when Husnat visits them after his return from Lahore, he finds the same titillating, intoxicating beauty in their household, which sits in the middle of a lush, secluded garden. One evening, as a local snake charmer comes to entertain the members of the household, Rafiq's ire is provoked. What follows is an interesting exchange, in which Rafiq chides both Sakina and Husnat for their indulgence in such entertainments:

> Rafiq- "My dear! These people are very dangerous- they steal the beauty of beautiful ones, make a young person old, suck off the blood of the brave, and ruin the lives of lovers. What do you know? Their magic is bewitching." Saying all this, he kept looking at both of us intently. Suddenly, I felt that my

heart on its own was succumbing to him. Sakina too began to feel ashamed at her own behavior. She helpless swayed into his control. Rafiq took her in his arms with deep affection, and then took us both inside, where he continued offering advice to us very softly.

. . .

In the evening, when I set out to go back home, I felt as if I was recovering from the hangover of some intoxication. My body felt drained with deadening exhaustion. I crashed on my bed and began thinking of my predicament- of how inflamed Sakina seemed at Rafiq's untimely strictness, and how I myself was irritated. But when he gazed at us with that intensity, our hearts melted as if made of wax. Perhaps he knew some strange sorcery. Or his gaze has some satanic power.

It is of course finally revealed that Rafiq is a snake who can transform himself into the shape of a human being (not an inspired original twist, as anyone who grew up in the Hindi-Urdu speaking world would have already guessed, given the deep association between bamboo forests, snakes, and the bewitching beauty often associated with them). However, it is the set of contrasts that Mrs. Abdul Qādir establishes between two colliding worlds that is most compelling. In fact, this passage perhaps would be representative of both the generic features of horror, as well as the characteristic style of writing for Mrs. Abdul Qādir. Story after story reveals an educative, rational, and thinking individual drawn into a world of *tilism,* or enchantment. This world is often associated with non-human nature and striking beauty and inspires unsettling desire in the seemingly rational protagonist. The primary tension that the stories seem to stage is through the collision between these two polarities of 'rationality' and 'modernity' on the one hand and chaotic desire on the other hand.

This category of desire, I would argue, forms the fundamental fulcrum along which *māfauq al-fitrat* pivots in the textual world of Mrs. Abdul Qādir. The word *fitrat,* much like the corresponding English word 'nature,' is associated both with the world of nature and human disposition or character. The horizon above *fitrat* then is also one outside 'natural' human disposition. This unnaturalness is encapsulated best in the rubric of desire. The world of horror in Mrs. Abdul Qādir's oeuvre is one which is cast in terms of an uncontrollable and dangerous desire. Quite apart from supernatural beings (i.e. the first level of *māfauq al-fitrat* that I identified), this threatening desire is the perhaps the most fundamental aspect of the *haibat/*terror, *hairat/*shock, and *haul/*dread that the stories are supposed to inspire in the readers.

This threatening desire is directed at various things. First and foremost, of course, is the past. As mentioned earlier, Mrs. Abdul Qādir explicitly locates this as a source of her own creativity. Terms such as *āsār/*relics and *khandar/*ruins are the locations where the author experienced various sorts of *Ilhām/*epiphanies, and subsequently proceeded to write them out. Even within the stories, the past is the object of deep, erotic fascination. Faisal Fatehali Devji, in his discussion on *Umrao Jan Ada*, points out that the reformist approach to the past was almost pornographic and the world of the past was often made into the receptacle of unabashed eroticism. One can see the free exercise of this in Mrs. Abdul Qādir's works (Devji 4–6). In *Kāsa-e Sar*/'Skull,' for instance, the skulls take the narrator back to an ancient (almost ahistorical) world of occult practices of burial that stands in sharp contrast to his own experience of burying his mother. In *Sadā-e Jars*/'Sound of the Bell,' the obsession with the ancient past of Egypt is pretty explicit and forms the basis of an unhealthy obsession and the untimely death of the narrator's friend, Khalil. This desire for the past is deeply tied to three aspects. The first is an obsession with '*ashiā*' or 'things.' Objects overpopulate the world of Mrs. Abdul Qādir's fiction. The obsessive contemplation over objects from the past often proves to be the trigger for horror. The second is dead languages. The fascination with dead, ancient languages is a running trope in several of the texts. In *Kāsa-e Sar*/'Skull,' the skulls that the narrator obsesses over carry markings that the narrator thinks are dead languages. He even sends a sample to an 'expert of dead languages,' who however is unable decipher them. In *Rākshas*/'Monster,' it is a professor of dead languages who is finally able to pierce through the mystery and solve the possession that occurs when the two girls play in an abandoned temple. In *Sadā-e Jars*, both the narrator, Mumtaz, and his friend Khalil are obsessed over ancient languages, particularly those associated with Egypt.

This dual fixation with languages and objects links it into the third terrain, which is that of religion. As several authors have argued, with the spread of a variety of reformist movements across post-1857 British India, there was a move towards establishing formalized, purified, religious practices. In Islam too, *tajaddud*, or renewal, was an important trend, and even though several differences existed across a host of reformist trends, there was a general consensus that there needed to be a return to the Islam of Prophet Muhammad.[4] What does Mrs. Abdul Qādir's horror fiction offer in this regard? Mrs. Abdul Qādir's fiction is populated by several kinds of non-'Islamic' practices, whether it is the incantations of the snake charmer in *Mua'llim kā Rāz*/'The Secret of the Tutor,' the pre-Islamic world of Egyptian mummification in *Sadā-e Jars*/'Sound of the Bell,' or the vaguely 'tribal' practices of burial of the dead in *Kāsa-e Sar*/'Skull.' In fact, Mrs. Abdul Qādir's only novel, *Takht Bagh*, is introduced by the editor with the following words:

> *Mrs. Abdul Qādir ek musalmān khātūn haiṇ, lekin unhone is kitāb meiṇ hinduānā tarīq-e zindagī, aur un kī andarūnī kharābīyoṇ kī jis tarah qalaī kholī hai, un ko paṛhne ke ba'd mosūfa ke kamāl muta'le kī dād denī paṛtī hai.*
>
> (Mrs. Abdul Qādir is a Muslim woman, but after reading the way she has unraveled the coating of Hindu style of life, and its inner flaws, one has to praise the excellent study that the author has done.)

(5)

There is then an overrepresentation of occult 'Hindu' practices in Mrs. Abdul Qādir's fiction. While the editor of *Takht Bagh* frames this is as a patently 'critical' reformist project, the rest of the paratextual material that I have discussed earlier strongly undercuts this claim. Apart from the fact that the editor of *Sadā-e Jars wa Dīgar Afsāne*/ [Sound of the Bell and Other Stories] categorically denies the possibility of any *islāh*/reforming from Mrs. Abdul Qādir's fiction, the general advertisement and packaging of the book seems to completely forgo any claim or reform or teaching. The texts too seem to be offering singularly immersive reading experience, rather than any instructive or heuristic dimension. There is then a new kind of textuality at what work here, one that is different from the explicitly pedagogic purposes of reformist texts, or of the realist orientation of the Progressive Writers' Association. There is an eroticism in the act of reading, one that doesn't lead to moralistic conclusions, but rather contemplates too deeply the possibility of desire within reading practices. The overrepresentation of occult 'Hindu' practices in my opinion then is also thrown into confusion through this contradiction between moralizing on the one hand and erotic reading on the other hand.

This desire, in my reading, is manifest most clearly in a range of sexual desires that are hinted at in her stories. In her response to the place of sexuality in Urdu prose, which Ahmad Nadeem Qāsmī asks in his questionnaire, Mrs. Abdul Qādir classifies it as an affront to the very idea of the craft of writing. This may lead one to think that there is a certain kind of prudery at work in her fiction, as opposed to, for example, the more explicit sexual dimensions of authors like Ismat Chughtai. However, I would argue that Mrs. Abdul Qādir rather eschews diagnostic and psychologized assessment of sexuality and desire and rather builds it into the sensational experience of the text itself. Chughtai, for example, in her preface to *The Crooked Line* says the following:

> *Magar jahāñ tak mere mutāla'e kā t'āluq hai, Ṭeṛhī Lakīr kī heroine nā zehnī bimār hai aur nā jinsī. Jaise har zindā insān ko ande māhaul aur ās-pās kī ghalāzat se haizā, tā'ūn ho saktā hai, isī tarah ek bilkul tandurust zehniyat kā mālik bachā bhī a ar halat māhaul mein phañs jāye to bimār ho jāta hai aur maut bhi vāqe' ho saktī hai.*

(Chughtai 6)

(However, as far as my study is concerned, the heroine of Ṭeṛhī Lakīr is neither mentally sick, nor sexually. Just like any alive human can catch plague or cholera because of bad atmosphere and surrounding filth, a child who possesses a healthy mind, if trapped in the wrong atmosphere, can fall sick and even death can occur.)

Overtly, Chughtai's novel is more open and direct in its approach towards sexuality and discusses desire in visceral detail (often built up into her image of a progressive author). However, as one can see here, there is also a prescriptive, normative lens through which sexuality is viewed and framed. The language she employs is a resolutely modern one – 'zehnī bimār'/'mentally ill,' 'tandurust'/'healthy,' 'haiza'/'cholera,' 'ta'un'/'plague' etc.[5] Mrs. Abdul Qādir's fiction does not employ this vocabulary. In fact, there is almost an absence of any prescriptive framework for assessment, and what the reader might experience is space of suspension. This allows the text to place before the reader a titillating set of submerged erotic possibilities.

One instance of this is language of desire for objects and even more outrageous, dead bodies that one sees in '*Sadā-e Jars*/'Sound of the Bell.' Khalil's obsession with the mummies from Egypt is expressed in an explicit moment of declaring love for the dead body of a young woman, who even the narrator identifies as full of '*husn-o-shabāb*'/'beauty and youth.' The moment reaches a fever pitch when Khalil, crouched next to the mummy, makes a declaration of love: '*us kī hālat ab ek afsosnāk had tak pahunch gayi thi- woh lāsh se izhār-e mohabbat kar rahā thā*'/ 'his condition had now reached a saddening limit- he was declaring his love to the dead body' (16–17). This unsettling moment becomes even more disturbing when an explicit comparison is drawn between Nasima (Mumtaz's wife) and the dead body of the young beautiful woman. This moment culminates with Mumtaz and Nasima leaving the house the very next day, and days later, receiving the news that Khalil has died, and left all his possessions to Mumtaz.

Beyond the dead, the non-human too is an object of desire. Sakina's husband, Jamil, who is half human, half snake in *Mua'llim kā Rāz*/'The Secret of the Tutor,' is an object of intense desire and beauty not just for Sakina but, as the previously cited passage indicates, even for Husnat himself. In fact, homoerotic desire too is a powerfully recurring motif, often submerged in the more ambiguous term '*muhabbat*.' '*Muhabbat*' in Urdu is not necessarily sexual, like 'ishq, nor however is it as tame as the more common '*pyār*.' 'Muhabbat,' carrying connotations of intense liking and attachment, recurs across stories to indicate bonds between men. In *Sadā-e Jars*/'Sound of the Bell,' the bond between Khalil and Mumtaz is deep and intense; however, they drift apart with the marriage of Mumtaz to Nasima. A similar pattern can be seen in *Kāsa-e Sar*/'Skull,' where the narrator and Jamil share an unbreakable bond, strong enough apparently to inspire the jealousy and anger of Jamil's Assamese wife, Hana. In fact, beyond the death of his mother, the narrator is pulled towards spending time in the empty hills because of his estrangement with Jamil, engineered apparently by Hana. The short story has another such homoerotic bond, that between the narrator and Faiz. The narrator encounters a weak and ailing Faiz during his solitary trysts with the forest and develops an intense bond. Faiz, in the end, is revealed to have died a while back and comes back as a spirit only to help the narrator out of a terrible predicament. Homoerotic bonds are thus a crucial component of the way desire moves within these texts.

Urdu horror and its genealogies

The framework of *māfauq-al fitrat* in particular, and the wide range of affective terminology that Mrs. Abdul Qādir uses in general, allows her to create a textual space which can speak of dangerous, forbidden desires, associations, fetishes and obsessions beyond the rational, and centrality of human subjectivity, which often structures the contemporaneous realist text. Alongside this, the suspension of authorial responsibility and agency allows for a deeply visceral text, with no explicit agenda or even structure. Subjectivity in fact then only exists in Mrs. Qādir's texts to be threatened and unsettled, its boundaries blurred by the presence of a much larger, menacing world. What can then one conclude from a such a body of texts?

My argument here is not to add to the list of genres within which Muslim women wrote. There is a perceived necessity to prove that Muslim women in colonial India and beyond wrote and spoke and lived, and this creates a persistent demand of a diversity of texts that they wrote. However, this is a point that needs to be proven only to the wilfully ignorant. The sheer range of writing in Urdu, widely available for those who wish to look, cancels even the need to ask this question. Further, I do not seek to prove that there is anything unique or revolutionary about the horror fiction of Mrs. Abdul Qādir in particular, and in Urdu in general.

Rather, I offer two sets of tentative conclusions. The first is vis-à-vis precisely the demand one places on Muslim women's writings. The demand, particularly from 'liberal' sections under the current climate of growing Islamophobia, is to validate the 'active' and 'agential' lives of Muslim women, where they can be shown performing as diverse a set of tasks as possible. However, the reading of all such diverse tasks boils down to the biography and lives of these women. Thus, so far as the category of Muslim women's writings is an externally ascribed one (as opposed to when it is claimed by the author, which makes for an altogether different claim), it always demands life narratives and historical proofs of existence. Apart from being a parochial and moot question, this approach also flattens the complex textual spaces that such authors create, all of which may not be hinged on what externally appears to be a tiringly all-consuming identity. In other words, one must attempt to create a more complex and multifaceted set of terrains for women-authored texts in Urdu, rather than a set of self-fulfilling questions, to give a fuller account of a text's constitution and life within a literary world.

If one looks at the example of Mrs. Abdul Qādir, there are multiple more streams and questions within which her work needs to be placed, as opposed to simply 'Muslim Woman Writer.' What Shaukat Thanvi had said in exaggeration, i.e. he thought that her work was a translation of a European tale, points to a potentially important trajectory of literary circulation. C. M. Naim, in a recent article on the translations of sensational fiction of George William MacArthur Reynolds into Urdu talks of how it was a booming business in its own right, spanning translations, adaptations, literary comparisons, and even one *Savānih-i'Umri* or biography from 1910 Lahore. Reynolds, as Naim points out, is an almost forgotten name in English Literature and is excluded from the hallowed halls of the English novel. There is evidence then of alternate currents of literary transmissions across English and Urdu print of late 19th and early 20th centuries, one that wasn't guided by syllabi or intellectual prescriptions, but instead by a pleasure of voracious and affective reading.

Mrs. Abdul Qādir's fiction seems to be pointing to the possibility of a similar trend. Her *'judāgāna'*/'different' attitude, if one thinks about it, isn't that different or unique. In fact, from the themes that I have analysed earlier, it would be very valid to make a comparison between her work, and the penny dreadfuls and sensational novels of the English print sphere of the 19th century. The privilege of realist fiction and the history of the Progressive Writers' Association obscures these other potential histories of reading, writing, and circulation practices. Further, it places women authors in the unbreakable trap of having to narrate their experience over and over again, even when that might be at stake at all. Works like those of Mrs. Abdul Qādir then can form the starting point for alternate webs of literary transmission in the colonial Urdu print sphere, as well as allow a different set of questions to be posed to women-authored texts, apart from those that simply call for the endless validation of the existence of Muslim women as subjects, when they were doing so much more than simply exist as historical proof.

Notes

1 All translations from Urdu are mine.
2 See Ali Sardar Jafri. *Taraqqi Pasand Tehreek ki Nisfi Sadi.* [Half Century of Progressive Writers' Movement]. Educational Publishing House, 1976, and Sajjad Zahir, "Adab aur Zindagi" [Literature and Life] in *Mazamin-i Sajjad Zahir.* Uttar Pradesh Urdu Academy Lucknow, 1979, pp. 36–46, for articulation of similar views.
3 See, for instance, Anshu Malhotra and Siobhan Lambert-Hurley, editors. *Speaking of the Self: Gender, Performance and Autobiography in South Asia.* Zubaan Books, 2017; Siobhan Lambert Hurley, "Life/History/Archive: Identifying Autobiographical Writing by Muslim Women in South Asia," *Journal of Women's History,* vol. 25, no. 2, pp. 61–84; S. Lambert-Hurley. *Elusive Lives: Gender, Autobiography and the Self in Muslim South Asia.* Stanford UP, 2018.
4 For a detailed discussion on the semantics and practice of the term *tajaddud* within Islamic reformism discourse, see Barbara Metcalf.
5 Of course, it is an entirely different matter if the text of Chughtai's novel in fact serve this pedagogic purpose. I say this so as not to create a stark binary between the realist and the non-realist. Tropes and elements from the latter often make their way into the former.

Works cited

Chughtai, Ismat. *Ṭeṛhī Lakīr.* Kitāb Kār, 1990.
Coppola, Carlo. "Premchand's Address to the First Meeting of the All-India Progressive Writers Association: Some Speculations." *Journal of South Asian Literature,* vol. 21, no. 2, 1986, pp. 21–39.
Devji, Faisal Fatehali. "Apologetic Modernity." *Modern Intellectual History,* vol. 4, no. 1, 2007, pp. 61–76.
———. "The Equivocal History of Muslim Reformation." *Islamic Reform in South Asia,* edited by Filippo Osella and Caroline Osella, Cambridge UP, 2013, pp. 3–26.
———. "Gender and the Politics of Space: The Movement for Women's Reform in Muslim India, 1857–1900." *South Asia: Journal of South Asian Studies,* vol. 14, no. 1, 1991, pp. 141–53.
Dubrow, Jennifer. "Cosmopolitan Dreams: The Making of Modern Urdu Literary Culture in Colonial South Asia." University of Hawai'i Press, 2018.
Hussein, Aamer. "Forgotten Stories." *DAWN.COM,* 13 Mar. 2016, www.dawn.com/news/1245286. Accessed 25 Aug. 2019.

Naim, C. M. "The 'Magic-Making' Mr. Reynolds." www.dawn.com/news/1194870. Accessed 30 Aug. 2019.

Pritchett, Frances W. *Nets of awareness: Urdu poetry and its critics*. U of California P, 1994.

Qādir, Mrs. Abdul. *Lāshoṇ kā Shehr* [City of Corpses]. Shāhi Press, 1956.

———. *Sadā-e Jars wa Dīgar Afsāne* [Sound of the Bell and Other Stories]. Urdu Book Stall, 1939.

———. *Takht Bāgh*. Khwāja Press, 1963.

Qāsmī, Ahmed Nadīm, editor. *Nuqqūsh-e Latīf: 24 Afsānā Nigār Khawātīn ke Afsāne aur Adbī wa fanī nazariyāt*. Track and Tie Printers, 1989.

Rahbar, Hans Raj. *Premchand, His Life and Work*. Atma Ram and Sons, 1957.

Suhrawardy, Shaista Akhtar Banu. *A Critical Survey of the Development of the Urdu Novel and Short Story*. Longmans Green and Co. Ltd., 1945.

4

GENDERING THE URDU DOMESTIC NOVEL

Muhammadi Begum, Abbasi Begum, and the women question

Mohammed Afzal

Introduction

Muslim women often appeared as passive objects of reform in the early Urdu novels written by men in late 19th century North India. Male reformers infused heavy doses of didacticism in the genre of the Urdu domestic novel to re-cast women. The use of the epistolary technique in these novels served the purpose of a conduct book. The dominance of the patriarch is established in these novels as they elaborate and dictate the rules of behaviour in their letters and lectures of guidance. The prescriptive literature of the age contains a portrait of the ideal woman as viewed by men in Indian society. In these manuals of family life, the household is conceived of as a distinct spatial entity whose boundaries are redefined by the responsibilities assigned to its female inhabitants, especially the housewife. The evolution of the Urdu domestic novel in late 19th century was inseparably tied to the emergence and institutionalization of home as a distinct private sphere. This conceptualization of household was accompanied by a recasting of woman, who was projected as an efficient manager of the household and an intelligent companion of her husband. In its approximation of the British ideal of wife as the mistress of the household, 19th century reformist discourse on womanhood restricted the exercise of woman's agency within the narrow boundaries of marriage and domesticity. The reconfiguration of the domestic space, which was a response by the Indian intelligentsia to the exigencies of the colonial regime, contributed to the reconstitution of patriarchy in colonial North India.

However, women writers contested the patriarchal discourse of Indian reformers by appropriating the genre of the Urdu domestic novel. After entering the male-dominated world of literature, they engaged in recasting themselves through literary portrayals. In *The Emergence of Feminism in India, 1850–1920* (2005), Padma Anagol observed that Indian women in the 19th century challenged reformist

DOI: 10.4324/9781003002062-6

discourse on the roles of women and articulated aspirations that did not conform to male perceptions (Anagol 06). The proliferation of women's journals in India from the 1880s and 1890s as a result of print revolution provided Indian women a platform where they could articulate their opinion on a whole range of issues. The collaboration of Muhammadi Begum (1878–1908) with her husband Mumtaz Ali (1860–1935) as the editor of the weekly newspaper *Tehzeeb-e-Niswan* demonstrates that Muslim women actively engaged in redefining their roles in society. The pioneering work of Muhammadi as the first women editor of *Tehzeeb* included in her portrayal of an ideal Muslim woman not only the concept of women's paid work but also the practice of modern medicine, showing that the sphere of women's activities is not limited to the management of home. The fiction that originated from the pages of this journal, which had close proximity to women's organizations in the second decade of the 20th century, bore the indelible marks of contestations over gender roles. Abbasi Begum's heroine is an embodiment of Muslim women's aspirations for a modern lifestyle marked by the influence of British culture and an increased social interaction with British women. The fictional protagonist of Abbasi's novel is a departure from the nationalist construction of the image of an authentically Indian woman in the 1890s. Women novelists' accounts of the untold sufferings of women within marriage undercut the 19th-century Urdu novelists' valorization of this institution and their depictions of domestic felicity.

Muhammadi Begum and *Tehzeeb-e-Niswan*

Muhammadi Begum was the daughter of Syed Ahmed Shafi, who worked as Assistant Commissioner in the Punjab government in 19th century colonial India (Tahir 26). She was married to Mumtaz Ali, whose treatise on women's legal rights in Islam *Huquq-e-Niswan* (Women's Rights 1898) focused on the glaring discrepancy between the legal status of Muslim women in Islamic law and their miserable plight in Indian society caused by the prevalence of social customs. In partnership with his second wife Muhammadi, Mumtaz founded *Tehzeeb* in Lahore in 1898. The 1880s and 1890s witnessed the spate of women's periodicals in India: *Rafiq-e-Niswan* (A Woman's Friend), a bi-monthly and multilingual journal founded in 1884 by Methodists, *Akhbar-e-Nisa*, the first Urdu magazine for women published in 1884 from Delhi by Syed Ahmad Dehalvi (1846–1918), and *Sharif Bibiyan* in 1893. *Tehzeeb* was a product of this wave of periodical literature directed at women readers, and Mumtaz as the founder of the renowned publication house "Darul Ashat Punjab" in Lahore knew how to utilise the power of print for advocating women's rights (Tahir 27). *Tehzeeb* was originally conceived of as a paper in which only women's articles would be published. In *Huquq-e-Niswan*, Mumtaz announced that he would encourage his female relatives to contribute articles to the journal without any fear of ridicule from the world. He also declared his intention of finding an editor from within his family circle (M. Ali 56). However, men's contributions were also accepted after the establishment of the paper, and the couple penned articles for it and solicited contributions from relatives, acquaintances, and literary figures. Muhammadi's position as the sole editor of the magazine encouraged women to publish their creative and critical output in the journal. Its use of simple Urdu language enabled it to reach out to women with basic literacy levels. The conversational tone of the weekly facilitated a dialogue between the journal and its readers. Letters to the editor provided an additional avenue for an exchange between literary sisters. The magazine sought to broaden the horizons of its women readers by enabling communication with a larger world. From 1898 till her death in 1908, Muhammadi's hard-work and intellectual calibre established *Tehzeeb* as an important vehicle of women's voices. Her exercise of complete editorial authority over the selection of articles reflects the part played by women writers in the creation of literary tastes and the forging of women's identities at the turn of the century. This journal is an example of how the growth of Urdu periodical press in India was enlisted in the advancement of Muslim women's education and progress.

Economic precarity and the ideal of domesticity

One of the earliest women's narratives published in *Tehzeeb* was an autobiographical account of the challenges a widow named Ashrafunnisa (1840–1903) encountered in learning to read and write in a patriarchal society (Naim 99). The story was originally published in two instalments on 23 and 30 March, 1899. Later Muhammadi also compiled her biography, which was published as *Hayat-e-Ashraf* (The Life of Ashrafunnisa). Ashrafunnisa was married to Syed Alamdar Husain, who worked as Deputy Inspector of School in Jalandhar district in Punjab and later as Assistant Professor of Arabic and Persian at Government College Lahore. After his death in 1870, his widowed wife was offered a teaching job by W. R. M. Holroyd, Director of Public Instruction in Punjab. But she declined the offer because of the stigma attached to women's paid work in her time. The fact that Ashrafunnisa had to work at Victoria Girls' School, Lahore, in order to support her family (when it was offered to her second time) exposed the elitism of the male reformist agenda that restricted women to the interior of the house. Ashrafunnisa's rise to the position of headteacher and her improvement of the reputation of the school she served till her death in 1903 are the material for a female bildungsroman. Muhammadi's compilation of *Hayat-e-Ashraf* is an alternative representation of the life of a Muslim woman, whose economic independence and determination is held up for emulation. The life of a widow who earned her livelihood as a teacher and headmistress served as a role model for the editor of *Tehzeeb*, who was buried next to her grave as per her wishes (Tahir 28).

The legacy of writing and work left behind by Ashrafunnisa reappears in Muhammadi's oeuvre. Muhammadi's exploration of the theme of work in her novel *Sharif Beti* (1908) is a radical departure from the portrayal of female characters in the Urdu domestic novels written by men. In Nazir Ahmad's *Mirat ul-Arus* (1869), Asghari's refusal to accept wages for teaching girls in her home is an assertion of her *sharafat*. On the contrary, the title page of *Sharif Beti* declares that it is the story of a poor Muslim girl, who uses education and her skill to earn respectability and prosperity

(M. Begum *Sharif Beti* i). This fictional work is addressed to the girls from the lower echelons of society. In the 'Introduction' to the third edition of *Sharif Beti* (1918), Mumtaz Ali criticized contemporary authors for their portrayal of affluent families in their stories, arguing that the depiction of luxurious lifestyle in these tales instils in the poor girls a sense of contempt for their own life. He emphasized the need for writing stories about the girls from low-income families (ii). Unlike Nazir's fictional heroine Asghari, the protagonist of *Sharif Beti* does not belong to a prosperous Muslim family. After the death of her father, Abdul Ghani, and her mother's mental illness, the entire burden of supporting the family and household responsibilities fall on the shoulders of the 11-year-old Sharifun. Her combat with poverty is rendered more difficult by the limitations imposed on the mobility of women by the burden of *sharafat* and honour (03, 07).

In this book, Muhammadi borrows the theme of girls' school from Nazir's *Mirat ul-Arus* to depict the journey of its protagonist, who adopts the profession of teaching to battle adversity. Because of the disgrace associated with the very idea of women's contribution to family income, the heroine declines the offer of teaching girls in her neighbourhood. Badi Bi, a woman of the barber caste who often visits Sharifun's family, succeeds in convincing her to open a school for the affluent girls in her own house. The centrality of Badi Bi (a maid) to Sahrifun's rise to prosperity indicates the respect accorded to women's paid work in Muhammadi's story. The character of Bi contrasts starkly with Nazir's presentation of Azmat (a maid) as the cause of financial mismanagement in Asghari's household. Muhammadi's selection of the narrative of an impoverished girl introduces the element of economic compulsion that illustrates the unsustainability of the doctrine of separate spheres in the lower strata of society, extending the scope of women's activities. The author dramatizes the female protagonist's negotiations with the contending demands of respectability and deprivation to re-define the concept of *sharafat* in the changing economic conditions of *ashraf* families in North India. Shenila Khoja-Moolji observed that Muhammadi Begum seems to be 'playing a role in destigmatising both works undertaken at home so that families did not have to hire servants as well as income generation by *sharif* women' (Khoja-Moolji 45).

Incompatible marriages and the question of consent

Muhammadi Begum's novel *Safiya Begum* (1902) deals with the calamitous consequences of childhood engagements. The eponymous protagonist of the novel is a young Muslim girl born in a prosperous family. She is engaged from childhood to her consumptive cousin named Safdar. The theme of incompatibility governs the delineation of this unsuitable pair in the story. Safdar's lack of interest in education is contrasted with Safiya's contributions to women's journal and her domestic skills (M. Begum *Safiya Begum* 38, 46). The fiancé's awareness of his fatal illness propels him to break this engagement. The heroine's father Asghar, who is a government employee, does not approve of this betrothal and expresses a sense of relief at its termination. However, Safiya's unhappiness is not the reason for Asghar's disapproval of this engagement. On the contrary, Asghar holds that girls should have no say in the selection of their husband and it should be left to parents to settle the issue of marriage (40). After the end of this childhood promise, search for a suitable match begins and Hamid Ali's name is proposed by Nasir, who invokes the Prophet's command to consult girls in matters of their marriage (43). Hamid, who is a civil surgeon and referred to as a 'gentleman' because of his education in London, is an embodiment of this modern outlook (49, 70). He not only communicates his desire to marry Safiya by writing a letter to her father but also arranges the formalities of his own marriage (51). A twist in the tale comes when the machinations of Safdar's mother and his father Akbar prevent the solemnization of this marriage. Safdar's mother instigates her son to declare his claim over Safiya as his fiancé. How Safdar's consent is engineered by his parents is shown as a travesty of the contractual character of Islamic marriage. Akbar Husain's emotional blackmail of his younger brother, Asghar, results in the latter's half-hearted acceptance of Safdar as his son-in-law. This episode reveals that the pressure created by relatives is a real determinant of marriages rather than the choice of boys and girls.

The determination of the heroine's fate by her parents and relatives highlights her helplessness. The author shows how patriarchy uses the concept of modesty as a tool to deprive women of their agency, voice, and rights (57, 85–86). A false code of honour and a strong feeling of filial duty impose limits on Safiya's choices, and the only escape from this moral dilemma in Muhammadi's fictional universe is death. Safiya's preparations for her final exit from the stage of this world on her wedding night highlights the poignant story of her marriage authored by the gender norms of her society. By transforming the scene of wedding into a funeral procession, the author protests against the custom of early engagements that is opposed to the ideal of companionate marriage. The protagonist's decision to end her life can be interpreted as a refusal to submit to the humiliations of a forced marriage. How education can be utilized as a tool of women's empowerment is illustrated in the episode in which Safiya inks her grievances in the form of a letter, as opposed to the representation of educated women as ideal wives and efficient managers of the household in 19th century reformist novels. The author's employment of the epistolary technique to draw readers' sympathy for the heroine shows how women novelists appropriated this literary device often used by male novelists as an instructional tool. The influence of the moving testimony penned by a dying widow in Nazir Ahmad's *Ayama* (1891) is detectable in Safiya's last will, which is an impassioned plea for consulting girls in the decisions affecting their entire life (99).

The literary depiction of the fatal consequences of childhood engagement in *Safiya* can be understood in the background of the debate that raged after the enactment of the Age of Consent Act in 1891, an act that raised the age of consent for all married and unmarried girls from ten to 12 years and made its violation a criminal offence. A catalyst for the passage of this bill was provided by the rape and death of an 11-year-old girl, Phulmoni Dasi, by her husband Hari Mohan Maitee in 1889 in Bengal. The act, viewed by many reformers as an interference by colonial government into the domestic sphere and Hindu religion, received support from women reformers like Pandita Ramabai (1858–1922), who insisted on a complete ban on child marriages. Muhammadi's story of protest against the custom of childhood betrothal can be termed as a clear precursor of the feminist movement in Urdu fiction. Gail Minault drew attention to the 'distinctly feminine perspective' of the novel (Minault 114). New scholarship on Muhammadi Begum has stressed her message of 'female emancipation' (Hussein 78). Dismissing the view that Muhammadi was a mere imitator of Nazir Ahmad, Aamer Hussein noted that the female novelist articulated an independent voice by appropriating a patriarchal literary tradition that posed the threat of relegating her to the margins of Urdu fiction (79). Safiya's death created 'a cast of brides' in Urdu novels, who would rather commit suicide than submit to the humiliation of a forced marriage (80). In *Safiya*, the threat of a daughter's sinful suicide is used as an outcry against her marginalisation in the transactions of marriage (81). Referring to Safiya's last will addressed to the editor of *Tehzeeb-e-Niswan*, Hussein declared that it is for the 'first' time that a 'woman's I resounds in Urdu fiction' (80).

Purdah, women's health, and medical profession

Like Nazir Ahmad, Muhammadi Begum uses the device of itemized domestic description in order to develop female characters. Nazir's praise for the order and cleanliness of an English household in *Banat-un-Nash* (1872) re-appears in Safiya's hygienic, simple, and English-style room, which is decorated with nice and delicate shelves, a flower vase, a mirror, towels, a beautiful foreign casket, postal stamps, stationary, a pen case, a small bed, a couple of tables, and almirahs. A paraphernalia of paintings and a sewing machine are also in her possession. One of the two almirahs in her room contains bottles of medicine and tools for surgery, while the other has excellent and very expensive books (M. Begum *Safiya Begum* 07–08). The graphic description of Safiya's room serves to demonstrate not only her knowledge of domestic science but also the intrusion of colonial modernity into her existence. In *Safiya*, the benefits of education are not limited to the good management of household affairs. The study and practice of modern medicine is included in the portrayal of an ideal Muslim girl, extending the boundaries of work permissible to women. The presence of allopathic medicines, syringes, thermometer, and surgical tools in her room reflects the aspiration of a Muslim girl for the modern profession of a doctor. Safiya writes prescription and performs surgery on the boils of female patients from the confines of purdah (04). Her interest in medicine generated by a 'firangi' lady doctor has bearings on the boundaries of the domestic sphere (22). The contradictions created in the heroine's life by the conservatism of her family and the new opportunities offered by a contact with the West manifest in her visit to Nawab's house. Safiya's decision to treat the daughter of Nawab is disapproved by her mother, who protests that leaving the chaperoned space of home can endanger the honour of a girl. The elaborate arrangements made to escort her to the Nawab's house indicates how the delicate subject of women's seclusion is handled with great sensitivity in the novel (11). Muhammadi takes pains to show that the protagonist of the novel is taught at home (03). Whenever Safiya needs to discuss the complex nature of a disease or its prescription, the lady doctor (her teacher) is called at home (18). The heroine's observance of purdah inhibits her practice of medicine.

This dilemma confronted by Muslim women at the turn of the century can be explained by tracing the history of the Islamic reform movement in India and the changing fortunes and identity of Muslim community in late 19th century colonial India. The denunciation of customs and traditions in the writings of the 18th and 19th century Muslim reformers with a view to restoring sharia in Indian society initially helped in improving the condition of Muslim women, for the authority of scriptures was cited to advocate widow remarriage, education of women, inheritance of property by daughters, and the girl's consent in her marriage. However, numerous political and social changes brought about in the second half of the 19th century led to a consolidation of Muslim community. An emphasis on the numerical strength of the community and its unity was considered key to deriving political advantages from the colonial dispensation. The limitations imposed by the need for solidarity subordinated the women's question to the interests of the larger community. One of the implications of this communalization of Indian politics was the emergence of a consensus within the community on certain social issues, which tended to conserve certain customs and practices for maintaining community cohesion. This identity politics created a dilemma for women whose agitation for their rights was entangled in the symbols and practices perceived as the essence of the Muslim community (Lateef 16–18, 80).

The inextricable link between the women's question and colonialism is demonstrated in Safiya's interaction with a 'firangi' female doctor. The extension of medical aid to Indian women in late 19th century colonial India can explain this episode in the novel. Supply of medical help to India began with Christian missionaries' penetration of the secluded space of *zenana* with the motive of curing women's ailments (A. A. Ali 94). The Dufferin Fund was started in 1885 under the patronage of Queen Victoria to focus on the health of Indian women (Billington 88). The principal objective of Lady Dufferin's efforts was 'to carry help and alleviation into the remote chambers of *zenana* and *bibi-ghars*, behind whose jealously closed doors no men, save those of the family, might pass, and to which, if such assistance were to be taken, it must be at the hands of trained women' (90). The simplistic assumption underlying the Dufferin Fund was that Indian women's access to medical care was restricted only by purdah and no other socio-economic factors. Despite an implicit acknowledgement of the victimization of Indian women by patriarchal norms, advocates of *zenana* medical care under the Dufferin Fund were content 'to work within the parameters of purdah' (Lal 41). Even though extension of medical care to Indian women provided the British women opportunities of medical employment, an integral part of the Dufferin scheme was to train the educated Indian women (Billington 94). The titular protagonist of *Safiya* receives training from a 'firangi' lady doctor, who visits her home quite often (M. Begum *Safiya Begum* 18–19). Safiya's treatment of Nawab's daughter in *zenana* and other women reflects her concern for the health of Indian women, a concern reflective of a feeling of global sisterhood in India despite national, racial, and religious differences.

Antoinette Burton observed that the agitation for women's entry into the male-dominated medical work led the early Victorian feminist struggle and the extension of medical care to Indian women justified British women's access to medical employment (Burton *Burdens of History* 112). In the 1880s, British women doctors' work in India coincided with a concern expressed by social reformers for social maladies affecting women, such as polygamy, widowhood, and child marriage. Edith Pechey (1845–1908), who campaigned for women's entry into the field of medical profession, also advocated women's freedom of choice in marriage during the age of consent controversy in India. She supported Rukhmabai (1864–1955) in her resistance to a forced married life and raised funds for her medical studies at the London School of Medicine through a British suffragist, Eva McLaren (Jayawardena 82–87). Burton contended that the institutions associated with women's movement in the Victorian age contributed to the support of several bodies dedicated to women's medical care in India, including the National Association for Supplying Female Medical Aid to the Women of India (Burton Contesting the Zenana 374–75). In this sense, Safiya's training under a 'firangi' doctor is a literary representation of global sisterhood that emerged in the field of medicine (M. Begum *Safiya Begum* 17).

Magazine fiction, colonial modernity, and the Muslim professional class

The paper established by Muhammadi contributed to the growth of women writers, who played a key role in the development of a nascent feeling of Muslim sisterhood in South Asia (A. A. Ali 25). The novel *Zohra Begum* by Abbasi Begum (d. 1924) was serialized in the pages of *Tehzeeb* from 1914 to 1916. Very little biographical information is available about Abbasi. The title page of the 1929 edition of *Zohra* describes her as the wife of Syed Muhammad Ismail, Undersecretary, His Highness Nizam Government, PWD. She is the mother of a famous Urdu writer and editor, Hijab Imtiyaz Ali (1903–1999), who was married to Muhammadi Begum's son, Imtiyaz Ali Taj (1900–1970), a renowned Urdu dramatist. Abbasi's daughter earned the distinction of being the first Muslim woman pilot in 1939 in undivided India (Anwar Ahmad 267). Abbasi contributed many articles and short stories to the Urdu periodicals *Tehzeeb-e-Niswan*, *Ismat*, and *Tamaddun*. The central theme of her stories is the subjection of women. Her short story titled *Giraftar-e-Qafas* (1915, Incarcerated in a Cage) took up the subject of women's seclusion. The comparison of a veiled woman to a caged bird in the story is a critique of the system of purdah. *Zulm-e-Bekasan* (Victimization of the Friendless) is an account of the exploitation of women by men (Khaki 254). Her novel *Zohra* began to appear in instalments the same year the All India Muslim Ladies' Conference was established with the efforts of Shaikh Abdullah (1874–1965) and the Begum of Bhopal (1858–1930). The spread of women's organizations in Punjab began in the first decade of the 20th century. The women of the Shafi family in Punjab founded the Anjuman-e Khatunan-e Islam in Lahore in 1907. Nazr Sajjad Hyder (1894-1967), who contributed articles to *Tehzeeb*, was also on the committee of the All-India Muslim Ladies' Conference. Wahida Begum Yaqub, Mumtaz Ali's daughter from his first marriage and the editor of *Tehzeeb-e-Niswan* (1908–1913), was elected the vice-president of the All-India Muslim Ladies' Conference (Minault 121, 286). By publishing the reports, programme, and criticism of the Ladies Conference, the journal assumed the role of an unofficial organ of the emergent feminist movement in Punjab (Saiyid 56). This close association between women's organizations and *Tehzeeb* must have influenced selection of articles for the periodical. The message of gender equality that the paper sought to deliver also impacted the fiction published for the consumption of Tehzeebi sisters. My analysis of Abbasi's novel takes into account the conversation that goes on between *Zohra* and the articles that were published in the magazine in the years in which the novel was serialised.

The fictional representation of the theme of incompatibility in *Zohra* was supplemented by the journalistic pieces. The article titled 'Khud-Pasand Larkiyan' (Narcissistic Girls, 10 April 1915) complained against the self-centredness of modern girls. It urged parents to exercise control over the sartorial choices of their daughters so that they do not encounter difficulties if married into a conservative family. The writer concluded with an appeal to parents to keep their daughters away from 'new fashion' so that any possibility of conflict of lifestyles after marriage is eliminated (Hakim 173). 'Bar ka Intekhab' (The Selection of Bridegroom, 30 September 1916) emphasized that compatibility of temperaments should also be a determining factor in the selection of husband. The author opined that the marriage of an educated and accomplished girl with an illiterate man causes her unmeasurable miseries and calamities. An uneducated husband prevents his wife from the perusal of books and newspapers owing to his inability to understand the benefits of education. Wife's subordination to her husband in the institution of marriage produces enormous difficulties if she wants to reform her husband. If husband's family does not understand the value of education, they will also disapprove of women's reading and writing. The contributor concluded by asserting that even a wealthy husband cannot provide happiness if there is incompatibility in the two parties concerned (S. F. 420–422).

Abbasi's novel is a story of two marriages in which characterization is linked to an illustration of the theme of conjugal adjustment. In its depiction of ideal conjugality through the pair of Saghir and Khujista, Abbasi participates with her literary predecessors in the construction of home as an emotional space, the novels in which domestic bliss was often linked with the family settings of the service class in North India. The early Urdu and Hindi domestic novels that are set in the kachahri milieu often embraced the ideal of companionate marriage (*Mirat ul-Arus* and *Devrani Jethani ki Kahani*). The marriage proposals of a barrister and a surgeon are considered desirable for an educated girl in *Safiya*. The marriage of Husnara's daughter to a barrister in Jamila Begum's Urdu short-story *Husnara Begum* (December, 1915, *Tehzeeb-e-Niswan*) is a reward for the hard work of an abandoned wife (J. Begum

612–616). In Abbasi's fictional work, conjugal happiness is tied to the 'modern' outlook of the new bureaucratic and professional class that was the product of Macaulayan educational policies in India. This English educated professional class among Indian Muslims also owed its existence to Syed Ahmad Khan's advocacy of foreign education. The Muslim social reformer encouraged students from North Western Provinces to go to Britain in order to become barristers and civil servants (Hali 364). In *Zohra*, Saghir's pursuit of law in Britain makes him a representative of the growth of independent professions in colonial India (Misra 45). Khujista's brother Salim is a barrister and her father Shaukat a schoolteacher. Her education and command over English language make her a suitable match for barrister Saghir (Abbasi Begum 70).

The physical proximity of fiction to the articles on social problems in magazines led to an overlap between the concerns of fiction and that of society. The growth of realism in South Asian fiction can be attributed to the publication of the novel in the periodical. A number of articles describing the virtues of an ideal housewife appeared in *Tehzeeb*. The list of the desirable qualities of a bride were expanded to include knowledge of English language. Mumtaz Ali's 20 February 1915 article 'Larkiyon ke Liye Angrezi' (English for Girls) was a reply to the objections raised against the teaching of English to girls. The contributor pointed out that there are households where parents talk to their children only in English and it would be preposterous if their daughters are deprived of this opportunity. He argued that if women know English, they can write a telegram and help their children in studies. Basic knowledge of English was identified as an essential requirement of house-keeping in such households (M. Ali Larkiyon ke Liye Angrezi 87–88). An article published in the 25 September 1915 issue of *Tehzeeb* reiterated the same point, adding that Muslim women's ignorance of the knowledge available in English language hinders them from engaging in an intellectual discussion in English parties. Because of this disadvantage, they are held in contempt in modern societies. Moreover, those men who graduate from prestigious universities search for brides, who possess knowledge of English language (R. Begum Angrezi Taleem Niswan 465–466). The journalistic pieces written in support of imparting the knowledge of English language to Muslim women embraced the position taken by the Begum of Bhopal and Fatima Begum, the editor of *Sharif Bibi*, in their speeches delivered at the time of the founding of the All-India Muslim Ladies' Conference in 1914 (Saiyid 58–60). This was a step taken for the modernization of Indian Muslim women. However, this emerging model of an educated wife familiar with English language in *Tehzeeb* is attributable to the demand by a bureaucratic class for English-knowing brides. In *Sarala Devi Chaudhurani and Rokeya Sakhawat Hossain: Early Feminists of Colonial India* (2002), Bharati Ray argued that the men of this class needed a suitable match capable of fulfilling family obligations in the 'modern' context (Ray 34). These articles have echoes of the views expressed by the male reformers of the 19th century, whose goal was not the establishment of the equality of women with men in the family unit but cultivation of qualities required by a professional class in the colonial settings.

Zohra articulates the values and assumptions of this class in its treatment of the subject of compatibility. Abbasi employs the popular device of descriptive detail to indicate the social position of the Shaukat family. The extent of the Anglicization of this class is demonstrated in the portrayal of Shaukat Lodge in the novel. The structure and design of the house (a bedroom and drawing room) and its furniture (table and chairs) are indicative of the western outlook of its inhabitants. A precise account of the daily routine and social engagements of the members of the Shaukat family is provided to show their acculturation to British civilization. Mr. and Mrs. Shaukat go for an evening walk; their son Salim is member of a 'club'; their daughter Khujista attends 'tea parties' and interacts with English women, such as Mrs. Hope and Mrs. Nelson (Abbasi Begum 42–43). The elitism of the Shaukats is reflected in their purchases for Khujista's wedding. Jewellery is ordered from P. R. & Sons and furniture from an English company called Robert in Bombay. However, their Anglomania is peppered with doses of swadeshi as they also buy some furniture and clothes from Indian artisans. The Shaukats' purchase of Indian goods, which comfortably coexists with their Anglomania, perhaps reflects Abbasi's awareness of Nazir Ahmad's condemnation of lavish expenditure on the imported items of luxuries with its ruinous effects on the growth of native industry (Nazir Ahmad *Ibn-ul Vaqt* 102–104). The presence of British cultural values is perceptible in the titles Mr. and Mrs. that are prefixed to the names of Shaukat and his wife. The conversation of the residents of Shaukat Lodge is sprinkled with English words. The women in Shaukat Lodge have the demeanour of memsahibs and wear night gowns, blouse, sarees, socks, and shoes. Khujista has learnt to play piano and possesses knowledge of both Indian and European cuisines (Abbasi Begum 67). The realistic bent of the Urdu domestic novel is exploited in *Zohra* to portray the family life of the emerging Muslim professional class, which included a growing familiarity with British culture facilitated by the growth of female clubs and towns in urban areas. *Zohra* is one of those novels published in the first quarter of the 20th century that reflected 'the effect of Western influence on Muslim homes' and 'the intense admiration that was felt for things English at this period' (Suhrawardy 720).

In the portrait of Zohra, Abbasi reconceptualized the ideal of the new Muslim womanhood. Zohra steps out of the confines of her home to study in a school. Her social interaction with European ladies has also broadened her horizons. To celebrate her success in examination, she throws a tea party in which biscuits, cake, cola, ice-cream, and fruits are served. Zohra's mother, Kabiruddola, complains that she remains obsessed with books and is always busy writing articles for English newspapers and magazines. Zohra is also interested in medicine (Abbasi Begum 09). The protagonist's break with traditions is shown in her rejection of traditional jewellery in favour of plain clothes. She is teased for her memsahib-like appearance and criticized for her refusal to wear heavy ornaments and a nose ring at the wedding ceremony (108).

Women's jewellery, attires, and the related question of colonial modernity were often discussed in *Tehzeeb*. Ahlia Khwaja Husain Ali Chinar's 'Zebar' (Jewellery, 25 March 1916) was a disapproval of women's waste of money on conventional jewellery for the vulgar display of their wealth and status. The article also highlighted the folly of educated women who are equally guilty of spending huge sums on foreign-made ornaments, with the only difference that they have ceased using the jewellery of conventional style (Chinar 147–148). 'Zebar aur Libas' (Jewellery and Attire, 11 November 1916) advised moderation in costumes and ornaments. It offered a criticism of old-fashioned women who prefer heavy clothes and jewellery and do not allow any modification in their costumes. The author was equally critical of the Anglomania of the new women, whose adoption of 'European' manners and white dress and their refusal to wear even a ring was symptomatic of their desire to become more English than the English (Ahmad Begum 510–511). The article 'Naye Fashion' (New Fashions, 25 November 1916) by Nazr Sajjad Hyder is a scathing indictment of the shallow understanding of British culture. Hyder pointed out that Indian women have been denied English education, but a section of this sex have aspirations to become 'fashionable.' Admitting that mixing of Western and Eastern lifestyles would only result in an improvement of the old and reform-worthy Indian customs and traditions, the author advised that it is possible only if we have a comprehensive understanding of British life, which is unimaginable without a complete English education. She cited the example of a 50-year-old woman, who is wearing white kurta, dupatta, skirt, boots, with an English hairstyle. Emphasizing the awkwardness of her ordinary bangles, ear pins, and the ornament worn in the septum of her nose (bulaq), Hyder ironically pointed out that this woman holds on to her 'bulaq' and husband because of her lack of education. The writer also criticized the elitism of educated Indian women, who refuse to interact with Hindustani women and have a tendency to socialise only with English ladies. The contributor drew attention to the aspirations of these women to live in the houses decorated with English furniture, without adopting the desirable qualities of English civilization, such as cleanliness, housekeeping, childcare, and thriftiness. Hyder also satirized Indian women's use of English words such as ayah, cook, baby, aunty, papa to address their servants, family and relatives. This is a criticism of the peculiarities of Indian modernity, especially its selective adoption of European modernity (Hyder 533–535). Contributors to *Tehzeeb* debated the influence of British lifestyle on Indians and its desirability or harmful consequences. Their attempts at coping with colonial modernity included discussions of women's sartorial choices. Many articles appeared in the journal on the propriety and impropriety of modern dress. 'Libason par Beja Aitraz' (Unreasonable Objections to Attire, 6 March 1915) drew attention to the tendency of raising senseless objections to women's dress made in a 'purdah party.' The author of the article lamented that women waste their time commenting on each other's attires instead of refining their manners and civility through social interaction for which these parties are arranged. Stressing the diversity of Indian cultures and individual preferences, the writer pleaded for the need for flexibility with regard to dress as long as it is not a violation of sharia. The contributor's acknowledgement that she has modified her own traditional dress in accordance with new fashion and has learnt a couple of things from European ladies is tied up with the inference of the article that there is no harm in borrowing good things from other cultures (Arif 115–117).

The journal's receptivity to other cultures, especially the British, also influenced the fiction published from its platform. The pronounced features of a modernized woman in the character of Zohra marks a departure from the nationalist construction of an authentically Indian woman in the 1890s. This imaginary figure was uncorrupted by any influence of the West and was distinguishable from memsahibs. But *Tehzeeb* drew a comparison between the status of Indian women with the women of other nationalities, listing achievements of famous public figures such as Florence Nightingale. It eulogized the hard work of European women and also celebrated their entry in the fields of trade, commerce, industry, mining, construction, bureaucracy, handicraft, literature, editorship, and legal professions (European Aurton ki Jafakashi 13–15). The editor's scathing review of Rabindranath Tagore's 'Aurton ke Haalat Mashriq aur Maghrib Mein' (Comparison of the Condition of Women in the East and the West) reveals that any hint of the glorification of the status of contemporary Indian women was unacceptable by the editor (Our Thoughts 34). The magazine's emphasis on the desirability of changes in the gender norms of Indian society made it amenable to Western influences. Indian women's interaction with European women and their joint struggle for women's rights in early 20th century disseminated the ideology of global sisterhood that also informed the fiction published in the periodical.

A dissolute nawab and a modern wife

In the 19th century Urdu reformist novels, illiterate wives were often blamed for conjugal unhappiness. But Abbasi's novel is a gendering of the theme of incompatible marriage from the viewpoint of its titular protagonist Zohra, whose dreams of domestic felicity are shattered by an old-fashioned, pleasure-loving husband, Qaisar Jung. The essence of suitability and unsuitability is defined by Abbasi's contrast between the lifestyles of the decrepit Muslim nobility and the new emergent professional class in early 20th century India. The worldviews of these two classes are symbolized by the buildings in which the representatives of these social groups reside. If Shaukat Lodge is an embodiment of the social and cultural values of the new Muslim professional class, Qaisar Mahal stands for what was viewed as the decadence and lethargy of a *nawabi* life in the aftermath of 1857. The spatial arrangement of Shaukat Lodge with its emphasis on fresh air is explanatory of the more relaxed gender norms constructed as per the social requirements of the professional class. If the modernity of this newly emergent class holds out a promise of domestic felicity, the constricted space of Qaisar's closed palace represents the confinement and entanglement of women in a close-knit family circle of nobility. Zohra's inability to meet her parents a day after her wedding highlights the curtailment of her freedom in such an environment. A feeling of immurement issues from the high walls of Qaisar Mahal. A contrast is drawn in the novel between Zohra's freedom to interact with European ladies at her home and the oppressive environment of the aristocratic mansion. Abbasi's short story *Giraftar-e-Qafas* also dealt with the theme of captivity. In *Zohra*, it is suggested that Kabiruddola has exchanged her daughter's freedom for the wealth of the Qaisar family. The suspense surrounding the entry of a mysterious woman (who turns out to be Mughlani) into the palace creates an atmosphere of intrigues. The bride's struggles to adapt to an obsolete lifestyle and her alienation from the gossip of old servants in the mansion are stressed in the novel.

The recurrent theme of *nawabi* dissipation is exploited by Abbasi to draw the portrait of Qaisar Jung. The word 'Qaisar' is a general title for the Greek or Turkish emperor and it signifies an exercise of despotic authority over the inmates of the palace. Evocation of the scenes of aristocratic indulgence serves to bring out Qaisar's dissolute lifestyle. The descriptive power of the novelist is displayed in her portrayal of the sumptuousness of the nawab's rooms. The expensive furniture of aristocratic taste adorns the palace. The floor is covered with Persian carpets, and the air of the whole mansion is perfumed. The writer paints a picture of aristocratic lethargy and indulgence. The old nawab is resting on a luxurious and costly bedstead with the support of a cushion. Servants are continuously serving him glasses of sherbet mixed with rose water and kewda (Abbasi Begum 81–82). Qaisar's endless leisure is shown in the pomp and elegance of his room of retirement. Servants on both sides are cooling him with fans, while the meritorious singers of the time are waiting for his orders to sing in a melodious voice in order to recreate the environment of Inder Sabha (Abbasi Begum 87). The literary reference to the celestial court of the Hindu god Indra in the Urdu play *Inder Sabha* penned by Agha Hasan Amanat (1815–1858) and possibly commissioned by Wajid Ali Shah (1822–1887) evokes the memories of the twilight of Awadh kingdom. The use of Wajid Ali's nick-name Qaisar is reminiscent of the last nawab's lavish patronage of and contribution to music, dance and literature (Sharar 138, 141). However, this episode furthers the plot of the novel by creating a milieu of sensuality with an ominous suggestion that Zohra's marriage with Qaisar would result in her subjection to the nawab's sexual pleasures. Qaisar's lust for her is depicted in the scene in which he bribes Mughlani to influence Kabiruddola's consideration of his marriage proposal for Zohra. Later in the novel, Qaisar's insistence on watching mujra in spite of his wife's objections demonstrates his pursuit of pleasures that ends in his death (Abbasi Begum 202).

The figure of a profligate nawab was very common in the early Urdu novels. These satirical portrayals of Muslim aristocracy were intended to urge the Indian youth to adapt to the changed political conditions of North India after 1857. In *Taubat-al-Nasuh*, Nazir's description of Kalim's palace of delight and place of retirement highlighted the extravagance and immorality of *nawabi* lifestyle (Nazir Ahmad *Taubat* 188–189). In *Fasana-e-Azad* (serialized between 1887 and 1883) by Ratan Nath Sarshar (1847–1903), description of the feminized body and attire of a nawab, and his indulgence into music are used to reduce the sophistication of old Lucknow culture to the caricature of an effeminate and lethargic Muslim aristocrat (Sarshar, vol. I, 13–21). If *Taubat* highlighted the obsolescence of the old *nawabi* way of life, *Zohra* indicts the despotism of aristocratic masculinity.

This condemnation of the so-called profligacy of Muslim aristocracy was part of the project of middle-class respectability, which had no place for the world of courtesans and their patron, elite nawabs. Historians have studied the expulsion of the subversive figure of courtesan from the respectable world of the Indian middle-class in the early 20th century, because her presence constituted a threat to the new moral regime in which companionate marriage was a norm (Gupta 111–112). Sanjay Joshi has discussed that the new service communities of North India as the 'new arbiters of appropriate social conduct' sought to redefine respectability, which included a new construction of womanhood (Joshi 02, 61). What was implicit in the banishment of courtesan in the newly defined respectability of the middle-class was a censure of the 'dissolute' behaviour of the Muslim aristocrats, who were promoters of this immoral and wasteful system of patronage. Abbasi's criticism of the gender norms of *nawabi* worldview assumes the norm of companionate marriage.

Aesthetics of sorrow and woman's agency

After Kabiruddola's acceptance of Qaisar Jung's marriage offer, Zohra looks depressed and grief-stricken (Abbasi Begum 93). At the time of marriage ceremony, the novelist offers an insight into the heroine's mind and highlights her miserable condition. She faints; her heart sinks with grief; her body gets numb; but she does not utter a single word against her mother's wish (107). The tragic aspect of her character derives from her entanglement in the conflict between her filial obligations and her secret desire to wed a compatible life partner. The tragic protagonist's duty to her mother deprives her of agency in the proceedings of her marriage. This episode portrays the hollowness of *nikah*, in which the consent of the bride is emptied of its real purpose. The novelist protests against the determination of Zohra's fate by her mother's greed and Mughlani's manipulations (100). Zohra's silent submission to the dictates of her mother is reminiscent of Rashidul Khairi's depiction of Saleha's patient endurance of her step-mother's tortures and her sufferings in marriage in *Hayat-e-Saleha* (Khairi 128, 152). Abbasi's advocacy of the restoration of women's agency in the hallowed contract of marriage is articulated by Saghir, who laments that those girls who are educated, intelligent, and whose intellect is superior than their parents are not permitted to have a say in the decision affecting their entire life (Abbasi Begum 75). The novelist invokes the authority of scriptures to reclaim women's rights in the institution of marriage. The representation of the injustice of forced marriage is Abbasi's expression of an outcry against gender oppression and is a contribution to the emergence of feminist consciousness in Urdu literature.

The elements of implausibility in the plot of *Zohra* betray the limitations imposed on the literary imagination of a Muslim woman writer by the pressures of a conservative society in the second decade of the 20th century. Despite highlighting Zohra's unwillingness to marry Qaisar, the ending of the novel emphasizes her unwavering devotion to her husband and unbearable grief after his demise. Her second marriage with Salim, presented as a suitable match, could have been a happy resolution of the problem. Given the advocacy of widow remarriage by Muslim reformers, Zohra's rejection of *nikah* with Salim appears strange. However, it must have been difficult for an Indian Muslim woman novelist in the early 20th century to create a plot in which a female protagonist is united with a man of her choice, especially after her widowhood. This insistence on Zohra's unwillingness to live after Qaisar's death is intended to augment the cruelty of her fate so that a strong feeling of pity could be evoked. The author refuses to dilute Zohra's miseries by not permitting her to re-marry as an escape from her sufferings. In Abbasi's fictional universe, only the funeral of the heroine can bring an end to the wretchedness of widowhood. Zohra's heart-rending cries and mental agony owes something to his predecessor Rashidul Khairi (1868–1936), who is referred to as *musawwir-e-gham* for his consistent depiction of the sorrows of women. The pathos created by Zohra's relentless lamentations and death brings out the disappointment of a modern woman's quest for fulfilment within the institution of marriage. However, this aesthetics of sorrow is as much a protest against women's oppression in a patriarchal society as it is a glorification of women's silent submission to an unjust social order.

Conclusion

The theme of incompatibility in *Safiya* and *Zohra* raised the question of women's agency in the age of feminism. The investigation of the institution of marriage from women's viewpoint in these novels is attributable to the entry of women in the male-dominated field of Urdu literature. These narratives of self-sacrifice and unfulfillment questioned the male novelists' idealization of marriage in their literary works. The subject of incompatibility in these novels is tied up with a demand for the restitution of Muslim women's rights. However, the adoption of the framework of religious rights and obligations for the exploration of this theme exhibits the constraints imposed by the identarian politics of the Muslim community on women's articulation of these issues.

The note of dirge in the last sections of the aforementioned novels the unmitigated sorrows and funerals of heroines the unmitigated sorrows and funerals of heroines introduce melodramatic elements in these novels. It appears that Safiya and Zohra are resigned to their fate and lack courage to confront the insurmountable difficulties presented by social conventions. This surrender dilutes the dignity bestowed upon the heroine of a tragedy. Zohra's protracted lamentations after the death of her husband, intended to draw pity from readers, ends up portraying her as a mere victim of patriarchy. This insistence on victimhood deprives her of agency, raising questions about the capability of women to act on their own. The record of Safiya's sufferings left behind in her letter verges on the idealization of self-sacrifice celebrated by patriarchy. The depiction of women's silent endurance of miseries as a protest against injustices is also fraught with dangers, for in a male-chauvinist society the degree of sufferings a woman undergoes is directly proportional to the virtuousness, dignity, and strength of their characters. However, if the deafening silences of Safiya and Zohra are intended to highlight the denial of voices to women in the transactions of Indian society, it will not be incorrect to pronounce that early Muslim women novelists sought to exploit the representational possibilities of silence to forge women's narratives.

The element of economic compulsion in *Sharif Beti* demonstrates that adherence to the gendered division of labour is unviable in the lower strata of society. *Safiya* shows that an accommodation of the Muslim heroine's aspirations for the vocation of medicine required a rewriting of gender roles in an age which subordinated the women's question to identity politics. Abbasi's criticism of women's incarceration in an aristocratic family is tied up with a search for nuptial fulfilment in the lifestyle of the new Muslim professional class. How Muslim women's exposure to the British civilization impacted the formation of their identity in early 20th century colonial India is investigated in *Zohra*. However, the dialogue between Abbasi's novel and the articles in *Tehzeeb* exhibits a complex engagement with the entanglement of women's question with the issue of colonial modernity. Both *Safiya* and *Zohra* show the influence of the British culture on Indian homes in early 20th century and how it enabled the cultural dialogue between the Indian and British women, forging a zone of contact that facilitated a scrutiny of Indian attitude towards women in a universalist paradigm.

If the predominance of dialogues in *Safiya* are signs of the inadequate development of Urdu novel at the beginning of the 20th century, the novelist's detailed description of Safiya's room shows her attention to material detail. The use of the epistolary technique to unfold the consciousness of the heroine reflects Muhammadi's contribution to the growth and gendering of the Urdu domestic novel. Abbasi's use of the device of descriptive detail to portray the milieu in which her characters move is a testimony to the evolution of domestic realism by women novelists. An inventory of the furnishings of the Qaisar Mahal and the Shaukat Lodge not only symbolise the social positions and values of the Qaisar and Shaukat families but also serve as a tool of characterization. Moreover, the presence of a female perspective in the glimpses of domestic life offered in these novels marks a significant departure.

Works cited

Ahmad, Anwar. *Urdu Afsana: Ek Sadi ka Qissa*. Kitab Nagar, n.d.
Ahmad, Nazir. *Ayama*. Matba Shamsi, n.d.
———. *Banat-un Nash*. Kitabi Duniya, 2003.
———. *Ibn-ul Vaqt*. Jayyad Barqi Press, 1937.
———. *Mirat ul-Arus*. Kitabi Duniya, 2003.
———. *Taubat-al-Nasuh*. Maktaba Jamia, 2018.
Ali, Azra Asghar. *The Emergence of Feminism Among Indian Muslim Women, 1920–1947*. Oxford UP, 2000.
Ali, Mumtaz. *Huquq-e-Niswan*. Matba-e Rifah Aam, 1898.
———. "Larkiyon ke Liye Angrezi". *Tehzeeb-e-Niswan*, 20 Feb. 1915, pp. 87–88.
Anagol, Padma. *The Emergence of Feminism in India, 1850–1920*. Ashgate, 2005.
Arif, S. J. "Libason par Beja Aitraz". *Tehzeeb-e-Niswan*, 06 Mar. 1915, pp. 115–117.

Bailey, T. Grahame. *A History of Urdu Literature*. Oxford UP, 2008.

Begum, Abbasi. *Zohra Begum*. Daarul Ashaat Punjab, 1934.

Begum, Ahmad. "Zebar aur Libas". *Tehzeeb-e-Niswan*, 11 Nov. 1916, pp. 510–511.

Begum, Jamila. "Husnara Begum." *Tehzeeb-e-Niswan*, 18 Dec. 1915, pp. 612–616.

Begum, Muhammadi. *Safiya Begum*. 4th ed. Daarul Ashaat Punjab, 1926.

———. *Sharif Beti*. 3rd ed. Union Steam Press, 1918.

Begum, Rafia. "Angrezi Taleem Niswan." *Tehzeeb-e-Niswan*, 25 Sep. 1915, pp. 465–466.

Billington, Mary Francis. *Woman in India*. Chapman and Hall, 1895.

Burton, Antoinette. *Burdens of History: British Feminists, Indian Women, and Imperial Culture, 1865–1915*. U of California P, 1994.

———. "Contesting the Zenana: The Mission to Make 'Lady Doctors for India', 1874–1885." *Journal of British Studies*, vol. 35, no. 3, July 1996, pp. 368–397.

Chinar, Ahlia Khwaja Husain Ali. "Zebar." *Tehzeeb-e-Niswan*, 25 Mar. 1916, pp. 147–148.

"European Aurton ki Jafakashi." *Tehzeeb-e-Niswan*, 8 Jan. 1916, pp. 13–15.

Gupta, Charu. *Sexuality, Obscenity, Community: Women, Muslims, and the Hindu Public in Colonial India*. Permanent Black, 2005.

Hakim, Ahliya Abdul. "Khud-Pasand Larkiyan." *Tehzeeb-e-Niswan*, 10 Apr. 1915, p. 173.

Hali, Altaf Husain. *Hayat-e-Javed*. National Council for the Promotion of Urdu Language, 2004.

Hussein, Aamer. "Forcing Silence to Speak: Muhammadi Begum, *Mirat ul-Arus*, and the Urdu Novel." *The Annual of Urdu Studies*, vol. 11, 1996, pp. 71–86.

Hyder, Nazr Sajjad. "Naye Fashion." *Tehzeeb-e-Niswan*, 25 Nov. 1916, pp. 533–535.

———. "Is Par Hamare Khayalat". *Tehzeeb-e-Niswan*, 15 Jan. 1916, p. 34.

Jayawardena, Kumari. *The White Woman's Other Burden: Western Women and South Asia During British Rule*. Routledge, 2016.

Joshi, Sanjay. *Fractured Modernity: Making of a Middle Class in Colonial North India*. Oxford UP, 2001.

Khaki, Masud Raza. *Urdu Afsane ka Irtaqa*. Maqtaba Khayal, 1987.

Khairi, Rashidul. *Hayat-e-Saleha*. Alhumya Press, n.d.

Khoja-Moolji, Shenila. *Forging the Ideal Educated Girl: The Production of Desirable Subjects in Muslim South Asia*. U of California P, 2018.

Lal, Maneesha. "The Politics of Gender and Medicine in Colonial India: The Countess of Dufferin's Fund, 1885-1888", *Bulletin of the History of Medicine*, vol. 68, no 01, Spring 1994, pp. 29–66.

Lateef, Shahida. *Muslim Women in India: Political and Private Realities, 1890s-1980s*. Kali for Women, 1990.

Minault, Gail. *Secluded Scholars: Women's Education and Muslim Social Reform in Colonial India*. Oxford UP, 1998.

Misra, B. B. "The Middle Class of Colonial India: A Product of British Benevolence." *The Middle Class in Colonial India*, edited by Sanjay Joshi, Oxford UP, 2011, pp. 33–46.

Naim, C. M. "How Bibi Ashraf Learned to Read and Write." *Annual of Urdu Studies*, vol. 6, 1987, pp. 99–115.

Ray, Bharati. *Sarala Devi Chaudhurani and Rokeya Sakhawat Hossain: Early Feminists of Colonial India*. Oxford UP, 2012.

S. F. "Bar ka Intekhab." *Tehzeeb-e-Niswan*, 30 Sep. 1916, pp. 420–422.

Saiyid, Dushka. *Muslim Women of the British Punjab: From Seclusion to Politics*. Macmillan Press Limited, 1998.

Sarshar, Ratannath. *Fasana-e-Azad*. 4 Vols. National Council for the Promotion of Urdu Language, 2002.

Sharar, Abdul Halim. *Lucknow: The Last Phase of an Oriental Culture.* Translated and edited by E. S. Harcourt and Fakhir Hussain, *The Lucknow Omnibus.* 4th ed. Oxford UP, 2010.

Suhrawardy, Shaista Akbar Bano Ikramullah. "The Role of Women in the Life and Literature of Pakistan." *Journal of the Royal Society of Arts,* vol. 106, no. 5025, Aug. 1958, pp. 713–726.

Tahir, Naim. "Syed Muhammadi Begum: Bhulaya na Jayega." *Syed Muhammadi Begum aur unka Khandan,* edited by Naim Tahir, Sang-e Mil Publications, 2018, pp. 25-31.

SECTION II
Genres and modernity

5

WOMEN WHO WIELDED PENS

Khadija Mastur

Mehr Afshan Farooqi

> *Only women who wielded a pen could express the desires, thoughts and ideas of their gender.*
>
> Akhtar Husain Raipuri[1]

What are the common motivations that prompt women to write? Do men and women write differently in given political, social, and cultural circumstances? How did Urdu literary culture enable women to explore new forms of writing? This chapter is an attempt to take a more complex approach to women's history and the relationship between gender, history, and the self through the writing of Khadija Mastur.[2]

Educating Muslim women; the role of men

Historically and politically, the aftermath of the rebellion of 1857 signaled an almost complete abolition of the old culture and its values. The Muslim elite and service gentry who had served the Mughal rulers had to come to terms with the realities of British rule, its ideas and institutions. One of the most evident examples of the reaction among Muslims was the emergence of educational, social, and literary modernism, a movement led by Sir Syed Ahmad Khan (1817–98). Among the points at issue in the context of change, the status of women gained increasing importance. Although Sir Syed himself cannot be considered a staunch advocate of female education, some of his supporters felt a deep urge to challenge the old values and make an argument for literature to become socially responsible and responsive. Among these intellectuals, Saiyyid Mumtaz Ali holds a special position.

Saiyyid Mumtaz Ali (1860–1935) authored a somewhat radical treatise in defense of women's rights in Islamic law, *Huquq un-Niswan* (Women's Rights).[3] When he

DOI: 10.4324/9781003002062-8

showed it to Syed Ahmad Khan on a visit to Aligarh in the 1890s, Sir Syed was shocked. He tore the manuscript and threw it into the wastepaper basket. Fortunately, lunch was announced at this moment and Mumtaz Ali quickly retrieved his manuscript when Sir Syed left the room. In deference to Sir Syed, Mumtaz Ali waited until the former's death before publishing it in 1898. The most pressing argument that Mumtaz Ali made in his book was in favour of women's education. He argued that educated women will know their rights and duties as true Muslims and not be slaves to custom and superstition.

According to Gail Minault, *Huquq un-Niswan* is an impressive volume because of its careful organization; logical, debate-style arguments; and its rationality in dealing with a subject that is close to people's intimate lives and emotions. Mumtaz Ali wished to equip Muslim women with a re-affirmation of their equality with men as human souls and with a reformulation of the fundamentals of their rights in Islamic law. He stated that keeping women in ignorance and isolation was not a requirement of Islam.[4] On the question of women's education, he discussed what kind of education was appropriate for women and proposed a broad, humanistic one, instead of a narrow, household-centred one. His views on purdah are open-minded. He does not argue for abolishing purdah, but for a pattern of behaviour and dress that embodies *shari'at* inspired modesty. Mumtaz Ali recommended a burqa, for outdoor activities. Unfortunately, *Huquq un-Niswan* was too advanced for the times. The slim volume was mostly treated with apathy and quickly forgotten. Nonetheless, Mumtaz Ali had great success in disseminating his ideas through his weekly newspaper, *Tehzeeb-e-Niswan* (Women's Culture, Lahore 1898), founded in partnership with his wife, the talented Muhammadi Begum (1878–1908).[5]

Although *Huquq un-Niswan* was not a success, Maulana Ashraf Ali Thanvi's monumental compendium of useful knowledge for women *Bihisti Zevar* (Ornaments of Paradise 1905) was very popular and soon became an integral part of every Muslim bride's dowry. Maulana Ashraf Ali Thanvi (1864–1943) was a scholar and a Sufi, one of the most prominent mystics of his time. *Bihishti Zevar's* premise was the *hadith*: It is a duty incumbent on every Muslim man and every Muslim woman to acquire knowledge. Maulana Thanvi emphasized individual piety over public ritual as the core of religious life. The phenomenal success of *Bihisti Zevar* lies in perpetuating a 'feminine' ideal that applies to all believers.[6]

To Nazir Ahmad (1833–1912) goes the credit of producing fictional heroines as role models. A younger contemporary of Syed Ahmad Khan, Nazir Ahmad was one of the brightest students of Delhi College and one of its most renowned graduates. He became a Deputy Inspector of Schools at Allahabad in the 1860s and eventually became a Deputy Collector in the Revenue Service. Deputy Nazir Ahmad's first novel, *Mirat ul-Arus* (The Bride's Mirror), was originally written as a guide for his daughters. In 1869, Deputy Nazir Ahmad entered the book for a competition for useful works in the vernacular, especially suitable for women of India. *Mirat ul-Arus* won the prize; the government bought two thousand copies of the book and recommended it for adoption as a textbook for girls.

The Deputy wrote many more prize-winning novels.[7] His interest in women's education went beyond the conventional misogynistic views of his senior contemporary Sir Syed Ahmad. He felt that women might be physically weaker to men, but their minds were equal. Education was more important for women than for men because women could educate the children before they started school and provide them with moral guidance. The stories of his fictional heroines, Akbari and Asghari, became very popular. The awareness of the powerful influence of the zenana in men's lives was acknowledged by Nazir Ahmad and Muslim reformers. Within this reformist trend, Nazir Ahmad had many imitators, among them his son Bashiruddin Ahmad and his nephew Rashidul Khairi, but his merit, in comparison with the others, lies in his greater ability to combine didactic intentions with literary quality.[8]

Poet-critic-reformer Altaf Husain Hali's (1837–1914) *Majalis un Nissa* (Assemblies of Women 1874) created another fictional heroine, the paradigmatic Zubaida Khatun.[9] She was educated at home by her parents and triumphed over adversity because of her virtues. The book unfolds through a series of fictional conversations among women in a prosperous Muslim household narrated by an old governess who is an outspoken advocate of women's education. *Majalis un Nissa*, like *Mirat ul-Arus*, won a prize and was adopted as a textbook for girls' schools. Maulana Hali, as his pen name 'Hali' denotes, was consciously 'up to date.' There was a pronounced influence of Western (English) ways of thinking, especially about literature, on Hali. His ideas on women's education written in his exemplary prose style had great appeal. His women characters reflect on the need of girls to be educated. Hali's reformist vision was not extreme but it was tinged with Victorian attitudes such as the importance of emotional restraint.

Urdu as the language of modernity: women novelists

With all the excitement about social reform for women, and the launch of journals, such as *Tehzeeb-e-Niswan* (a weekly that lasted from 1898 to 1949), that were especially for women writers and readers, it doesn't come as a surprise that women novelists emerge in this period. Muhammadi Begum (d. 1908), the first woman to edit a journal, began by writing manuals on subjects of domestic interest. She branched into full-fledged novels, leading the way for other women writers. Her early death from influenza at age 30 was a big loss to the genre. Noteworthy among those who followed Muhammadi Begum's lead are Nazr Sajjad Hyder (1894–1967), Abbasi Begum, and Akbari Begum, who chose to be known through her son's name, Valida Afzal Ali. Akbari Begum was the author of a three-volume saga titled *Gudar ka Lal*, (The Ruby among Rags).[10] As Aamer Hussein has pointed in his illuminating essay on Muhammadi Begum, 'the pioneering presence of women in the Urdu novel's evolution is remarkable and worthy of canonization. These women's contribution to fiction had a tinge of feminist colors at a time when such a practice could not even be conceived of in Europe.'[11] Though Nazr Sajjad Hyder's novels are now forgotten, her fame lives on through her daughter Qurratulain Hyder, one of contemporary India's most acclaimed novelists. Hijab Ismail, the daughter of Abbasi Begum, a budding writer herself, was married to Muhammadi Begum's writer-dramatist, filmmaker son, Imtiaz Ali Taj. Hijab's work has recently received the renewed attention that it deserves.

The publication of *Angare* (Embers), a collection of short stories, in 1932 was the precursor of the Progressive Writers Association, which was officially launched in Lucknow in 1936. Rashid Jahan, (1905–52) a woman medical doctor, was among the contributors of *Angare*. She was the eldest daughter of Shaikh Abdullah, a pioneer of women's education and founder of Aligarh Zenana Madrasah (Aligarh Girls' School) in 1906. His wife, Begum Waheed Jahan, supervised the school with exemplary dedication and was responsible for its unprecedented success. The school became a boarding school when the residence hall opened in 1914. It went on to become an intermediate college in 1925 and started degree classes in 1937. Rashid Jahan graduated from Aligarh Women's College, then went on for medical degrees. Her work inspired one of the greatest fiction writers in Urdu, Ismat Chughtai (1915–91).

The models of writing presented by the Muslim reformers, be they scholars, novelists, or journalists, informed and guided a second wave of women writers in Urdu. The role of popular Urdu fiction in Urdu impacted the young Muslim girl's sense of self as she grew up in the 1930s. Middle-class girls who became avid readers were encouraged to read didactic literature. However, it is easy to imagine that they were drawn to novels such as those by Rashidul Khairi, which were romantic sagas tinged with a message for social reform. It was in the 1930s that we find women expressing themselves in Urdu literature in a big way.

Khadija Mastur (1927–82) was prolific in that she published five collections of short stories and two novels in the space of a tumultuous life riven by the scarring ordeal of losing her father at a tender age and the upheaval of Partition.[12] She started writing at a very early age, and her work was noted by Urdu's stalwart Marxist-Progressive critics such as Ehtesham Husain, Akhtar Husain Raipuri, and eminent poet Faiz Ahmad Faiz. In Pakistan, Mastur's mentor Ahmad Nadim Qasmi (1916–2006) was the influential editor of the journal *Funoon* (Arts). Qasmi helped the fledgling writer find her feet in the new nation's literary surroundings.[13] Mastur served as the secretary for the Progressive Writer's Association at Lahore (1950–?) Yet, Mastur's name is seldom mentioned in the same breath as her senior contemporary Ismat Chughtai. In fact, her fictional voice pales in comparison to Ismat Chughtai's strident, trenchant critique of patriarchy and the claustrophobic life in the zenana. Mastur's unadorned, matter-of -fact style does not match with her peer Qurratulain Hyder's (1927–2007) sublime, historically rich, nostalgia-filled prose either. Although Mastur's affiliation with Progressive ideology becomes a given because of her association with Qasmi, I will argue that her work transcends ideology. She reflects on women's lives with a symbiotic lens that imbricates the relationship between gender, history, and the self.

Akhtar Husain Raipuri's foreword to Mastur's second collection *Bochchar* is on point. Raipuri, an eminent Urdu literary critic, proved to be the theoretical anchor of the Progressive Writer's Movement.[14] In his foreword to Mastur's collection, Raipuri sums up the literary debate on women in literature in bold strokes and goes on to make an incisive statement:

> Thus far, the writing on women's issues were the triumph of men. They were gazing at the subject of woman that had evolved from an imagined, idealized topic to a novel one [*jins-e latif*]. Still, it was impossible for them to understand how a woman views the challenges of life, what she thinks, what she really feels. Only women who wielded a pen could express the desires, thoughts and ideas of their gender.
>
> (Raipuri 258)

Raipuri endorsed Khadija Mastur's promising style even at this early stage of her writing. He describes her style to be unaffected but sharp:

> I am convinced that readers will find a uniqueness in her writing that is rare in men fiction writers who focus on gender. In her stories we see the sketches of middle-class and lower-class women. Her writing is imbued with reality; it is not couched in fancy. She knows how to describe ordinary events in an evocative manner.
>
> (259)

Khadija Mastur in Hajira Masrur's memory

Khadija Mastur's diminutive physique enfolded a fiery personality that is described by her sister Hajira Masrur in a refreshing introduction to Mastur's short story collection *Thake Hare* (Tired, Defeated).[15] Hajira lovingly reminisces the childhood memories of her sister, only a year and five days older, who she describes was both sensitive and hot-headed. I think Khadija may have felt neglected at the arrival of her younger sibling. A vignette described by Hajira illustrates her sister's sensitivity. That Hajira chose to share this goes on to show its deep impact on the sister's psyche.

> My mother [ammi] told us: 'Khadija was not jealous of her new sister like the other siblings. Ayesha, the eldest often showed her possessiveness towards me and would scratch the new baby when she got a chance. One day, when Hajira was nearly a year old, I washed her face and loving remarked, 'See, my moon has appeared." Khadija was standing nearby but I didn't pay her any attention. She slipped away quietly. After a few minutes she returned, her face was dripping with water and she rubbed it against the loose end of my sari. After I wiped it, she lifted her innocent face and said, 'ammi, look Khadija has appeared.' This was her strong, genuine response to my exaggerated remark about Hajira's face being moon-like.'[16]
>
> (Masrur 11)

Hajira chooses to interpret this evocative episode as an assertion of Khadija's strong idea of self. She preferred to proclaim her self-Khadija, instead of a sentimental, metaphorical moon-like creature. I disagree with Hajira's reading of this episode. Khadija needed her mother's attention. She was reminding her mother of Khadija, the neglected child. She went on to pour the angst of neglected childhood in many of her fictive characters.[17]

In Hajira's recollection, Khadija emerges as an energetic, enterprising child, with long hair braided into two tight plaits, who resisted fitting into the model of a 'good' girl. Her braids looked awkward with the frock she wore and marked her out from other children at the 'country-club' who wore their hair fashionably short. Khadija had a sharp tongue that earned her the nickname, 'Khadija *Qainchi*' (scissor-tongue), which didn't seem to bother her (Masrur 13). She would threaten to snip the ears of children who teased her. According to Hajira, her sister was happiest when playing with street children instead of the well-heeled ones who came to the 'country-club' where games and other activities were organized. She was generous to a fault; sneaking goodies from the kitchen to share with friends whose parents were poor. The sisters were encouraged to excel in the small, secure world located in the outskirts of Lucknow, where her father, Tahur Ahmad Khan, was a local official and the mother an educated, literary woman who wrote for women's journals.[18] Books lined the shelves in their living room. Khadija had picked the word 'plot' from her parent's literary discussions and held on to the 'plots' that she wanted to write about. All of this when she was only eight years old (Masrur 19). The daughters were not burdened with housework or pushed into learning culinary skills; they were inspired to study and do well in school. Hajira describes Khadija's admirable interest in everything, including cooking!

Their father's sudden death in 1936 upturned the comforts of childhood. One can only imagine how the family survived without a steady income. The family of five sisters and two brothers were plunged into a harrowing period of adversity.[19] The genteel impoverishment of their family must have deeply affected the susceptible Khadija because she draws on the experience of severe hardship in many of her stories. There was no possibility of a college education. Hajira's narrative mentions dates very sparingly. One milestone mentioned is 1942 was when she joined her sister in writing fiction. At this point they were in their teens. Khadija's writing was getting published in journals and getting noticed. In 1946, the sisters were volunteering at the polling station for Muslim League. After partition, the family made their way to Lahore. It was in Lahore that the sisters became closely connected with the Progressive Writers Association.

The political, cultural, and the personal world

How much of a role do life histories and the cultural milieu play in the fashioning of the woman's self in South Asia? What narrative choices do women prefer? These questions have been asked in the context of autobiographical writing by South Asian women.[20] The line between fiction and autobiography is not sharply defined, in fact fiction and autobiography bleed into each other. The fictional form can disguise a deeply autobiographical sentiment. Uma Chakravarty makes the point that the fictional form allows the female author to speak for a larger feminine self beyond the personal experience, thus amalgamating the individual self with the history of South Asian women.[21]

It is almost axiomatic that South Asian societies privilege the social and the communal over the individual. It would, however, be exaggerating to assume that social and cultural constraints stifle individual expression. I will show that fiction was a cathartic medium for women to release congealed emotions of their inner lives; pain, suffering, and humiliation. Personal and political histories of the protagonist can overlap. By anchoring her fiction in her own temporal, geographical, and cultural world, the author complicates the relationship between the fiction and the personal. I will examine Khadija Mastur's symbiotic rapport with her heroines, particularly in *Panchvi Barsi* (Fifth Anniversary) and *Lalah-e Sahrai* (Tulip of the Desert).[22] I will connect the voices from the aforementioned stories to the powerful characters in her most representative work, the novel *Aangan*. I argue that Mastur's orphaned childhood, her empathy with the underclass, her progressive politics all combine in her fictional voice.

Panchvi Barsi is narrated in the voice of Aliya, the much-loved daughter of middle-class parents who was relieved to give up school after the sixth grade because her heart wasn't in learning. Her elder brother was in the last year of college, and her parents' hopes were pinned on their son's success. Aliya herself was lost in daydreams, such as when she would have a beautiful home of her own with that yet unknown partner. The thought filled her with warm, melting sensations. Almost every day, neighbourhood women would drop by to help her mother in preparing beautiful, richly embroidered clothes for her trousseau.[23] Aliya even tried one set of clothes secretly. How exquisite was the gold and silver work and how heavy! She could barely walk in those clothes. Then one day her elder brother returned home with a fever. The fever was persistent. Months of treatment ate into the family's financial reserves. Items from her trousseau were sold one by one at throw away prices to pay medical bills. Even the pure air of the sanatorium could not revive her brother. His death left the family shattered and deep in debt. Their father's pension barely covered day-to-day expenses.

A year passed somehow. On her brother's first death anniversary, Aliya prepared his favourite dishes with care; the group of indigents who were served the meal licked their fingers with appreciation. Time went by. Aliya's youth was at its peak but there were no proposals for her marriage:

> Time can be like a sharp needle; it can repair rents by darning them. Sorrows began to hide their face in corners. When emotions buried under the weight of sorrows raised their head, her heart stopped. Her youthfulness had become as formidable as a dense forest. No wayfarer would want to stop there for a moment's breath.
>
> (Mastur 234)

Aliya's world was as empty as the boxes that once held her trousseau. Desires crawled in her body making her restless. A sweet ache filled her limbs and made her edgy. Then she overheard her mother saying that no one wanted an aging girl with no trousseau. Aliya became dry-eyed as the fourth death anniversary of her brother came and went.

> The tumult of emotions ultimately cooled and ceased. Streaks of gray were showing above her temples. Moonlight became like the dull light of the lamp in a niche.
>
> (Mastur 234)

On the fifth anniversary of her brother's death when she heard her mother's tearful voice call out, she could bear it no more. The story ends with an emotional crescendo as Aliya cries:

> "Your son has been dying for five years but isn't quite dead yet – is he waiting to kill me before he dies?" Aliya screamed at the top of her lungs and left for her room. Her mother looked after her with eyes wide with shock and collapsed on the floor with a thud as if someone had given her a hard push.
>
> (Mastur 239)

Lalah-e Sahrai's heroine is Shamim, who steps up to shoulder the burden of running the house upon her father's sudden death from heart failure. Shamim was finishing her masters and dreaming of a happy future with a life partner. Now, she finds a teaching job and courageously supports the education of her younger siblings. Times are hard because of the war. The family adjusts to their impoverished circumstances. Years begin to go slowly by, while Shamim's life is tied to the drudgery of work. The war ends and the freedom movement gains momentum. Partition follows in the wake of violence. Shamim and her family leave their home for Pakistan.

> In Pakistan, Hindu homes stuffed with abandoned goods had become houses of mourning. People grabbed whatever they could. Hearths were lit. Chimneys spewed smoke. Some were weeping for the bygone days. Eyes searched for missing dear ones. Valuable furniture was used as wood for stoves. Expensive curtains became bedsheets It seemed as though the forlorn homes were asking what all this was about.
>
> (Mastur 249)

Shamim's family settled into a large bungalow that contained nothing but broken furniture and some odd and ends. She found a job at the local college. The large bungalow with empty rooms was depressing for her. Shamim wished they could have an apartment in the city where the bustle of daily life would be a comfort. Eventually, rehabilitation services split the bungalow into two residences, and a prosperous family with young adults moved in. They hired domestic help and spruced up their side of the bungalow. The young ladies enjoyed balmy evenings sitting in the lawn on expensive wicker chairs; music floated in the air. In due course of time, they were married off amid celebrations and fanfare.

Shamim became more irritable and short-tempered as time went by:

> She would quarrel and cry at every little provocation just like uneducated women. She would blame her mother and sisters for ruining her life. Their lips were sewn because they were intimidated. But behind her back, they spoke ill of her. Everyone except her mother. Amma would say: her youth has been wasted for your sake. She is going to be thirty-six soon. If she were married, she would be the mother of two children with a home of her own; my girl's looks have been ruined.
>
> (Mastur 254)

One day on her way to college she was caught in a heavy downpour. As she tried to take shelter from the rain, a car pulled up and a gentleman offered her a ride; he introduced himself as her neighbour. For days after the incident, Shamim dreamed about every moment with him in the car. How elegant his hands looked at the steering wheel, the little mole on his chin, the pleasing manner of his speech. She was lost in sweet memories that grew more explicit as she dreamed on. Every evening she walked on her side of the lawn hoping to catch a glimpse of the man of her dreams.

One evening she was walking restlessly:

> The garden, glowing in the night's soft light was making her burn slowly, gently. Her heart was calling out silently, she was yearning for him. She wanted to become his, kiss him, fall at his feet, she felt that if she didn't see him now, she would die –
>
> (Mastur 254)

Shamim crossed the lawn to the neighbour's side and knocked on the door. The door was opened by the man, and she stood there gazing at him with love-sick eyes. She was steeped in love from head to toe

> "How can I help you?" The man asked seriously. "No, nothing! Thank you." She turned around quickly and did not look back to see the baffled look on the man's face as he stood stupefied seeing her in this state.
>
> (Mastur 239)

Mastur's heroines: of mothers and daughters

Mastur fashions her heroines as strong women whose conflicts are with their mother and with the culture that instils internalized constraints of gender roles.

Mothers perpetuate gender ethics that entail crushing responsibilities for women and impose cultivation of virtues such as sweetness, innocence, simplicity, and bashfulness. A classic example is her novel *Aangan's* unforgiving portrait of the role women play in preserving the rigid bonds of patriarchy and class hierarchy.[24] Internalized gendering is the hardest roadblock faced by women all over the world.[25] The dynamics of class and gender are etched sharply in *Aangan*, set in a small town in North India where feudal values are being stripped of its material base through the declining fortunes of the Muslim family. With the patriarchal and social power stripped of its material base, the traditional family's women are in the throes of bitterness and anger. The patriarchs are largely absent because of their involvement in the freedom movement.

In the afterword to her translation of *Aangan*, Daisy Rockwell perceptively remarks that Aliya's mother and grandmother play active roles in destroying the lives of those who dare step outside the boundaries of tradition. The behaviour of these women is so brutal at times that they end up looking far worse than the actual patriarchs of the family (Rockwell 373). Aliya's mother is by far the most toxic character in the novel. Her class consciousness is so rigid that it almost sounds that she supports honour killing when she critiques her mother-in-law for failing to poison her daughter when she was discovered in a romantic liaison with a man from a lower status. Aliya's father and Bade Chacha (father's older brother) pale in contrast with the fury of Aliya's mother and the venom she pours against the more vulnerable members of the family who are tied to the household through servitude or through the assertion of feudal patriarchal paternalisms.

Mastur has created memorable, paradigmatic younger women characters. Tahmina, Aliya's older sister, is an archetype of the female who doesn't complete her education because of 'delicate' health and is daydreaming of marriage on the lines of romantic fiction she reads. She commits suicide when her overbearing mother refuses to accept her romantic longing for her cousin Safdar because he is low-class. Aliya is the studious type who has been scarred so badly by her sister's suicide and her mother's dictatorial attitude that she finds the idea of romance repulsive. Chammi, their motherless cousin who has been abandoned by her father is a feisty rebel who refuses to be cowed down.

Mastur turns the courtyard into a space for privileging women's voices. I would argue that Aliya's deep discomfort with, and her gradual awareness of, the hierarchies of power within the household is the dominant theme of the novel. It is no coincidence that Mastur's stories feature fatherless heroines. The death of a father or an elder brother plunges the family into unforeseen hardships. These hardships push women to take on the role of the breadwinner albeit at the cost of their emotional well being. At the same time, hardship gives these women power and agency.

Shamim steps into her father's shoes and takes care of her mother and siblings (*Lalah-e Sahra'i*). She does everything a man would do to provide but she is unhappy. Aliya in *Panchvi Barsi* finds her voice. She talks back at her mother. Yet these women are not free from the shackles of romance. Mastur is skeptical of romance and knows that tales of true love and romantic bliss help to perpetuate the patriarchal system. It is *Aangan's* heroine Aliya who claims the liberty of choice when she rejects the advances of Jamil, the offer of marriage from the doctor at the rehabilitation camp, and in the end, her cousin Safdar. She survives the trauma of partition and overrides her dominating mother, who becomes dependent on her.

> Although the novel's prose is spare, even inelegant, Mastur succeeds in her purpose of producing an intellectual heroine who does not believe in class hierarchy. Throughout the novel Mastur has refrained from giving a physical description of the women characters. At the end, a widowed Chammi is happily married to Jamil while Aliya has a buffet of unromantic, realistic choices. She chooses independence from the imprisoning influence of patriarchy but has not found the path to emotional contentment through companionship or friendship.
>
> (Rockwell 387)

To what extent does Mastur's fiction based on familial relationships fit into the genre of domestic fiction? Nancy Armstrong's pathbreaking *Desire in Domestic Fiction* (1987), a historical study of British novels by women, formulated a domestic household that acted as a metaphor of a collective of families something akin to what we call ' "society."[26] Armstrong spoke essentially to a Western readership and not a global one. Revisiting *Desire in Domestic Fiction* some 30 years later in a special issue of *Modern Language Quarterly* (March 2019), Armstrong responds to an 'obvious silence' in her work – the gap between epistemology and political philosophy, that is, the question of domestic fiction's relationship to Marxism.[27] How does the British domestic novel manipulate the gap between the discourse of economics and human consciousness. One way is to set up a conversation with novels from other regions and languages. Mikhail Bakhtin postulated that the dialogic style of the novel helps differentiate the 'national traditions' of the novel (259–422). The Urdu novel in the period leading to partition and beyond builds on the discourse of social power, political philosophy, and history. The Marxist-Progressive Writer's Movement had a stronghold on literary imagination especially in Urdu, and its subscribers imparted large doses of ' "social realism' in their fiction. Mastur's novels are tied to the personal and political self-cultivation of her female protagonists. Her biggest and most important novel *Aangan* (1956), which won Mastur the prestigious Adamji award, has been conceived as a 'Progressive' text that incorporates dominant leanings of the doctrine of Marxist socialism as a new approach towards life.[28] Mastur recasts woman and womanhood, with an eye on the political history of the subcontinent. The novel emphasizes conflict in both the public and personal spheres; it is a confluence of a larger, complex, external struggle embodied in the conflict between the colonizer and the colonized and a series of domestic, familial, and personal conflicts. National and familial prospects become intertwined – the breakdown of the one, heralding the breakdown of the other (Rizvi 142).

To get back to the question of the authorial self and its resonance in women's writing. Mastur's depiction of the battle between emotions, constraints of tradition, internalized gendering, and intellect are filtered through her inner self. Her characters are imagined through the prisms of her past and continue to evolve. The extent to which women's writing represent the ' "truth' about women is relative to what we perceive as truth. Apparently, in the novel *Angan*, Aliya rejects Safdar's proposal immediately when she learns that he has moved away from his leftist-Marxist ideals and wants to earn money to live comfortably:

> 'I will look after you. I've changed the direction of my life – if the world is destroyed, so be it, it has nothing to do with me. I will just earn money now, enjoy myself; now I will fulfil the dreams of owning a car and a house. I cannot go to jail now. Right now, I'm trying to get an import – export license. I'll get it very soon. Aunty, I'm going to become an important man now, please do accept me.'
> 'What?' Aliya stared at Safdar as though he were a stranger.
> What, is this now your life's goal, such a tiny thing? Aliya felt as though she had travelled here from far off, through desert lands. Flat-out exhausted. Thirsty for many lifetimes.
> Please, could someone pour just a few drops of water down her throat?
>
> (Rockwell 368)

Aliya's rejection of Safdar makes a strong, artful statement of Khadija Mastur's progressive ideological stance. But it seems more an extension of fantasy than truth:

> 'I'm not getting married, Amma. You listen too, Safdar, I'm not getting married.' Aliya stood up from her chair. 'Now when you come here, please keep in mind that I still miss my sister, Tahmina. I wish to be released from that memory!'
> She ran quickly to her room. 'Goodbye!' she called.
>
> (Rockwell 369)

Notes

1 Akhtar Husain Raipuri, "Dibachah," to 'Bochchar', in *Majmua' Khadija Mastur*, Sang-e Meel Publications, Lahore, 2006, p. 258.
2 I am grateful to Najeeba Arif, Asif Aslam Farrukhi, and Daisy Rockwell for helping me find materials for writing this chapter.
3 Gail Minault remarks that Syed Ahmad's reaction might let one to assume that Mumtaz Ali was 'Western-educated,'. On the contrary, he was a Deobandi with a solid education in Islamic sciences as well as English. His family was closely associated with the founders of Deoband and with the intellectual legacy of Shah Waliullah of Delhi. The path he followed as a reformer was reflective of the times but also unique in some respects. See Gail Minault, *Secluded Scholars*, pp. 72–98.
4 *Huquq un-Niswan* offers illuminating arguments on matters of men's authority over women, the strength of women's testimonies, matters of inheritance. He subjects the polygyny argument to careful scrutiny. See Gail Minault, "Women, Legal Reform and Muslim Identity," p. 4.

5 In starting a journal too, Mumtaz Ali sought Sir Syed's advice. Sir Syed was not very convinced that such a publication would succeed. He suggested that having a name similar to his own journal, *Tehzibul Akhlaq* (The Social Reform), might blunt the opprobrium.

6 See Barbara Metcalf, "Islamic Reform and Islamic Women: Maulana Thanvi's Jewelry of Paradise," p. 190.

7 See C. M. Naim, "Prize-Winning Adab, A Study of Five Books Written in Response to the Allahabad Government Gazette Notification," pp. 292–93. See also the English translation, *The Bride's Mirror: Mirat ul-Arus: A Tale of Life in Delhi a 100 Years Ago*, translated by G. E. Ward. Permanent Black, 2001.

8 Rashid ul Khairi (1868–1936) was the most prolific of the Urdu novelists. He authored some 80 books including novels, collections of short stories, and essays. He founded the women's journal *Ismat* in 1908. Bashiruddin Ahmad's most well-known work is the novel, *Iqbal Dulhan* (1914).

9 See Gail Minault, *Voices of Silence* (1986).

10 *Gudar ka Lal: Khavatin aur Ladkiyon ke liye ek Nasihatkhez Navil* (The Ruby Among Rags: An Instructive Novel for Women and Girls) published in 1907 deals with women's education, incompatible marriage, and polygamy.

11 'Hussein raises another important question based on his study of the writings of Muhammadi Begum and her successors: that is, the extent to which the oppression of peoples by regimes imperial, colonial or neocolonial parallels the subjection of women by society, and of the discontinuous coincidence of the rise of women's movements and those of national liberation. All too often the latter appropriates the former and, in the aftermath of independence, dismisses it as a secondary agenda. Then the demand for gender equality rises again, to be faced with fresh hostilities, political, social, religious; it is reformulated with ever more radical words of resistance, for which the documents of self-determination are essential material'. See Hussein, *"Forcing Silence to Speak: Muhammadi Begum, Mirat ul-Arus and the Urdu Novel"*, pp. 71–86.

12 The short story collections are as follows: *Khel* (Game 1944), *Bochchar* (Heavy Rain 1946), *Ek Roz aur* (One More Day 1951), *Thake Hare* (Tired, Defeated 1962), and *Thanda Mitha Pani* (Cool, Sweet Water). Her first novel *Aangan* (Courtyard) was published in 1962. The second novel *Zamin* (Land) was published in 1987. *Aangan* was translated as *The Inner Courtyard* by Neelam Hussein, New Delhi, Kali for Women, 2001 and more recently by Daisy Rockwell as *The Women's Courtyard*, New Delhi, Penguin, 2018. Rockwell has a perceptive afterword Noted Progressive-Marxist literary critic Akhtar Husain Raipuri wrote the foreword to *Bochchar*, and Faiz Ahmad Faiz wrote for her third collection, *Ek Roz Aur*. Her sister Hajira Masrur wrote an introduction to the fourth collection, *Thake Hare* (1962).

13 Editor, poet, and fiction writer Ahmad Nadim Qasmi was a formidable force in Pakistan. Qasmi was elected Secretary General of the Progressive Writer's Association of Panjab in 1948; the following year he was elected the Secretary General of the Association for Pakistan. But since their activities were curtailed, he resigned within a year. Nonetheless, he was incarcerated twice for his affiliation with Communist ideology. After General Ayub's military coup in 1958, all left-leaning organizations were banned in Pakistan. In 1962, Qasmi launched the journal *Funoon*. Apparently, Qasmi was a controversial figure. Fateh Muhammad Malik's controversial book *Nadim Shinasi*, published from Lahore, Sang-e Meel, 2011, tarnished Qasmi's reputation by exposing his high-handed behaviour and intolerance of eminent peers such as Faiz Ahmad Faiz. Mastur was married to Qasmi's nephew, journalist Zaheer Babar in 1950. Mastur was frail, her health was poor. She was taken to London for treatment in her last days and died there on July 26, 1982. Her body was brought back to Pakistan and buried in Lahore.

14 Akhtar Husain Raipuri (1912–92) was the firebrand leftist intellectual whose essay 'Adab aur Zindagi' became the cornerstone of the Progressive Writers' Movement. Raipuri was a polyglot: a scholar, journalist, lexicographer, literary critic, and creative writer. His trenchant essays examined searing questions about the objectives of art and literature and offered new ways of thinking on the purpose and aesthetics of

literature. See my column on Raipuri in *Dawn*: www.dawn.com/news/770008/column-stars-from-the-past-akhtar-husain-raipuri-1912-1992-by-mehr-afshan-farooqi

15 Khadija Mastur, *Thake Hare* (Tired, Defeated), Lahore, Guild Publishing House, 1962. I found it incredibly difficult to piece together biographical details of her life and dates of publication for her work. The name of the suburb in Lucknow where the family lived or their father's profession is not mentioned by Hajira. Fortunately, Rashida Qazi's thesis, *Urdu ke Afsnanavi Adab men Khadija Mastur ka Maqam*, published by the Idarah-e Furogh-e Qaumi Zaban, Islamabad, Pakistan, 2012, provides important details. I am grateful to Najeeba Arif for sending me a copy of relevant chapters.

16 Comparing the face of a child or a beloved to the moon is a common term of affection.

17 For example, Chammi, a memorable character in the novel *Aangan*.

18 Tahur Khan was a veterinarian. Raipuri mentions 'Jhawai Tola,' as the neighborhood in Lucknow where Khadija's family lived perhaps after the demise of their father.

19 Apparently, their mother married again and the relationship of the sisters with their stepfather was cordial. Maulana Mustafa Khan Maddah, Khadija's stepfather, wrote humorous under the pen name of Ahmaq Phaphundvi. I want to thank Asif Farrukhi for sharing his tribute to Hajira with me. See 'Hajira Masrur ki yad men' (In memory of Hajira Masrur) in *HamSab*, March 2019, www.humsub.com.pk; Farrukhi recalls his interactions with Hajira Masrur in her last years with sympathy and respect for her reticence in sharing the memories of their past. Apparently, Hajira was writing a memoir but could not complete it because of ill health.

20 See Anshu Malhotra and Siobhan Lambert-Hurley, editors, *Speaking of the Self: Gender, Performance and Autobiography in South Asia*.

21 Uma Chakravarty, "Betrayal, Anger and Loss, Women Write the Partition in Pakistan," in Malhotra and Lambert-Hurley, p. 123. Chakravarty offers a reading of three novels, Mumtaz Shah Nawaz's *The Heart Divided* (1948), Khadija Mastur's *Aangan* (The Women's Courtyard 1962) and Zahida Hina's *Na Junun Raha na Pari Rahi* (All Passion Spent, 1996).

22 Both stories are from the collection *Thake Hare*, Guild publishing House, Lahore, Karachi and Dacca, 1962.

23 Mastur tellingly uses the term '*mashshatah*.' That is women whose job is to adorn brides and arrange marriages.

24 Daisy Rockwell, Afterword in *The Women's Courtyard*, New Delhi, Penguin, 2018. I am grateful to Daisy Rockwell for sharing her Afterword with me while the book was still in press. It is unusual to have two contemporary English translations of an Urdu novel. Neelam Hussain's translation of *Aangan* as *The Inner Courtyard* was first published by Simorgh and then by Kali for Women in 2001. A small number of Mastur's short stories were translated by Tahira Naqvi as *Cool, Sweet Water*, Karachi, Oxford UP, 1999.

25 See Mahashweta Devi, *Imaginary Maps*.

26 See Nancy Armstrong, *Desire and Domestic Fiction: A Political History of the Novel*.

27 See Nancy Armstrong, "Afterword: Waiting for Foucault," pp. 37–49.

28 See Carlo Coppola, editor. *Marxist Influences and South Asian Literature*.

Works cited

Armstrong, Nancy. "Afterword: Waiting for Foucault." *MLQ*, Mar. 2019, pp. 37–49.
———. *Desire and Domestic Fiction: A Political History of the Novel*. Oxford UP, 1987.
Bakhtin, Mikhail. "Discourse in the Novel." *Dialogic Imagination: Four Essays*, edited by Michael Holquist, translated by Caryl Emerson and Michael Holquist, U of Texas P, 1981.
Chakravarty, Uma. "Betrayal, Anger and Loss, Women Write the Partition in Pakistan." *Speaking of the Self: Gender, Performance and Autobiography in South Asia*, edited by A. Malhotra and S. Lambert-Hurley, Duke UP, 2015, pp. 121–40.

Coppola, Carlo. *Marxist Influences and South Asian Literature.* Chanakya Press, 1988.

Devi, Mahashweta. *Imaginary Maps.* Translated and introduced by Gayatri Chakravarty Spivak. Routledge, 1995.

Hali, Maulana. *Majalis un Nissa,* and *Chup ki Dad* (In Praise of Silence; long poem) translated into English by Gail Minault *Voices of Silence.* South Asia Books, 1986.

Hussein, Aamer. "Forcing Silence to Speak: Muhammadi Begum, *Mirat ul-Arus* and the Urdu Novel." *Annual of Urdu Studies,* no. 11, 1996, pp. 71–86.

Masrur, Hajira. "Introduction." *Thake Hare* by Khadija Mastur. Guild Publishing House, 1962, pp. 1–20.

Mastur, Khadija. *Thake Hare.* Guild Publishing House, 1962.

———. *The Women's Courtyard.* Translated by Daisy Rockwell. Penguin, 2018.

Metcalf, Barbara. "Islamic Reform and Islamic Women: Maulana Thanvi's Jewelry of Paradise." *Moral Conduct and Authority: The Place of Adab in South Asian Islam,* edited by Barbara Metcalf, U of California P, 1984, pp. 184–95.

Minault, Gail. *Secluded Scholars, Women's Education and Muslim Social Reform in Colonial India.* Oxford UP, 1998.

———. "Women, Legal Reform and Muslim Identity." *Comparative Studies of South Asia, Africa and the Middle-East,* vol. XVII, no. 2, 1997, pp. 1–10.

Naim, C. M. "Prize-Winning Adab, A Study of Five Books Written in Response to the Allaha bad Government Gazette Notification." *Moral Conduct and Authority: The Place of Adab in South Asian Islam,* edited by Barabara Metcalf, U of California P, 1984, pp. 290–314.

Raipuri, Akhtar Husain. "Dibachah, to *Bochchar.*" *Majmua Khadija Mastur,* Sang-e Meel Publications, 2006.

Rizvi, Fatima. "Politicizing Literature: Progressive Nationalism and Feminism in Khadija Mastur's Inner Courtyard (*Aangan*)." *South Asian Review,* vol. 31, no. 1, 2010. pp. 141–61.

6

'STUDIES IN [] DYING CULTURE[S]'

Qurratulain Hyder and Urdu Fantasy Fiction in Self-translation

Fatima Rizvi

Qurratulain Hyder (1927–2007) was a singular voice in experimental Urdu fiction. She began writing at a fairly young age. Her long fiction and non-fiction explore historical, political, cultural, and sociological themes realistically. Her short stories are thematically diverse. Taken together, Hyder's fictions syndicate her lived experiences and imaginings in narrative styles and expressions concomitant with them. In essence, her texts, wistfully looking back at, and longing for the multiculturalism of a bygone era, claim the romantic, and because, among other things, they employ various narrative techniques and casually blur boundaries that compartmentalize form, they are experimental. Writing during a time radicalized by Marxist and socialist ideals, she kept her own, drawing disdain from her senior contemporaries and members of the Progressive Writers' Association.[1] The realistic, utilitarian, *adab bar āye zindagi* or art for life mode of the Progressive writers was straightforward and unadorned. Believed to be cut off from the reality of the masses, Hyder was perceived as a writer preoccupied by and large with socio-culturally non-curative issues. Her subjects and style, new to Urdu fiction, were debated. However, like the intellectually inclined Progressive writers Ahmed Ali and Sa'adat Hasan Manto, Hyder was an individualist asserting self-determination over political dogmas and employing styles and techniques that ensured hybridity.[2] Though she often wrote in the *adab bar āye adab* or art for art's sake mode and gave precedence to the imaginative spirit, her intent was serious and rooted in her socio-cultural milieu. A few of Hyder's stories qualify as romantic fantasies. They transport the reader into a carnivalesque historical past by some means or other and include horror, suspense, and adventure. Women occupy centrality in all of these. These stories, essentially entertaining, are not entirely escapist or cut off from reality, for they cradle concerns with which she has had a longstanding affiliation – a desire for conservation of dying cultures and a deep-seated interest in political and social histories across civilizations and across time. This chapter analyzes select fantasies as willing suspension

DOI: 10.4324/9781003002062-9

of disbelief, their serious end being conservation of ancient cultures it analyzes their association with the real or the normative, and their hybrid sensibility.

Introduction

Before analyzing Qurratulain Hyder's engagement with elements or aspects that constitute the fantastic, this paper looks at a few definitions of the fantastic and/or of fantasy literature. Andrew Raymen gives that any text which has elements that would usually be considered outside the bounds of 'normal' experience, in other words, any text with fantastic elements, can fall under the category of 'Fantasy.' He adds that there is no consensus among critics as to whether Fantasy is a genre, mode or stance ("The Problem . . ."). Todorov notes that in fantastic texts, a writer describes events that are not likely to occur in everyday life, and these very likely involve the supernatural. However, this is a very wide category, its extension is 'much too great'. He qualifies that yet another attempt to locate the fantastic would be to identify the reactions of the reader – not the implicit reader, but 'the actual person holding the book in his hand.' Citing H. P. Lovecraft, Todorov notes that 'the criterion of the fantastic is not situated within the work but in the reader's individual experience – and this experience must be fear (34).' Brian Attebury contends in *The Fantasy Tradition in American Literature* that 'any narrative that includes as a significant part of its make-up any violation of what the author clearly believes to be natural law – that is fantasy' (Morse 1). George P. Landow observes that our view of fantasy and the fantastic is contingent upon our view of reality – probability and improbability following from what we conceive as the probable or the likely (Morse 1). These views demonstrate that the fantastic is, broadly speaking, constituted of the supernatural; it involves an experience of fear and a violation of the reader's sense of reality or the laws of probability. The stories in this study involve any one or some of these interpretations or principles regarding fantasy. Hyder was familiar with the indigenous, oral tradition of the *dastān*, replete with the fantastic, which she had inherited as a constituent of her literary heritage. In the *dastān* cycles of the romantic, open-ended, escapist, heroic stories, far removed from reality, there are neither disturbing or frightening visions nor sinister dreams, neither dread of encounters with the supernatural nor threat to life posed by them. The protagonists are valorous heroes, kings, generals, warriors, *parīs* (fairies), *deos* (trolls), *ayyārs* (magicians), damsels in distress, and tricksters. The action involves great acts of valour and gallantry, honour, romance, joviality, deceit, and spacio-temporal magical transportation. These *dastān*s contributed perhaps to the cheerful ease with which Hyder juxtaposes the supernatural against the realistic to transcend limitations imposed by plausibility and by linear, chronological time. Though an aura of make-believe, the illusory, and the chimerical qualifies the purely entertaining *dastān*, Hyder's stories are neither purely entertaining nor entirely thrilling. In them, she employs the fantastic as a vehicle to project a larger, essentially bourgeois concern – that of recreation of cultural ambience and/or the historical past along with a will for preservation of endangered and/or dying languages – a fact evinced by her Urdu language texts. Hyder's fantasy stories evolve by means of a suspension of disbelief, most of the time, on the part of the reader and at times on the part of the protagonists as well. Aware of Hyder's interest in recreating cultural and historical ambience, from readings of her realistic fiction, we do not look further 'for ulterior meanings and concealed mysteries' and 'suppose[] [her] situations to be real and respond to their dramatic truth with appropriate emotions' (Bowra 65).

Hyder had imbibed her Indo-Muslim cultural heritage, enriched with Persian, Turkish, and English linguistic and literary cultures, owing to an erudite, progressive ancestry, a bourgeois socio-cultural milieu, and her readings in a well-stocked library at home. Through a profound comprehension of these, an exceptional capacity for recall, and experiences gained by extensive travel, she steadfastly articulated this multi-cultural legacy. Hyder refers to her oeuvre largely comprising realistic fiction and centring the landed and capitalist classes as 'a tongue-in-cheek "Studies in a Dying Culture"' (*The Sound* . . . xiv). She also asserts, 'History is my base. [] I can't write about things in mid-air.' (Das 112). Hyder's disposition to conserve culture by means of her fiction and/or follow historical facts as a 'base' may be perceived as the motivational factor behind her fantasies as well. These short stories centring historical, political, social, and cultural features of ancient Egyptian, Byzantine, Sassanian, Zoroastrian, medieval Indian, and renaissance British cultures are her effort at conservation. She believed that several ancient and rich cultures or at least elements of these cultures were gradually fading into oblivion even among people who professed to own or belong to them. She expresses concern that languages like Coptic, Syriac, and Zend have lost their speakers, their usage confined to religious texts or the clergy (Akhtar 71). Like most intellectually inclined Indian language writers and poets, Hyder was keenly interested in and influenced by the political and literary goings on in her own country as well as in the West, and this manifests in most of her fiction, her fantasies – historical, scientific, and speculative, included.

This study conducts close, textual readings of four self-translated short stories, *A Night on Pali Hill* ("Palī Hill kī ek Rāt"), *Confessions of Saint Flora of Georgia* ("Saint Flora Georgia kē Aitrafāt"), *My God, Veer, Doesn't that Lady in Mauve Look like Bette Davis?* ("Do Sāēh"), and *Beyond the Speed of Light* ("Raushni kī Raftār").[3] In these stories, Hyder employs fantasy, horror, 'pastiche and brittle humour, rough juxtapositions, historical vignettes, fragmented chronologies and multiple voices' (Hussein; quoted in Menon 205), thereby 'mak[ing] transitions that we did not know the narrative was capable of (Amit Chaudhuri; quoted in Hussein; "That Little Bird . . ." xxiv).'. Anthropologically speaking, Hyder mostly adopts an emic or insider approach to elucidate cultural patterns in these narratives, letting her protagonists, partial outsiders to, or descendants of the culture in focus, interact with insiders/members, with a view to empathetic reception. However, an etic approach, achieved by means of reliance on historical fact and records is perceivable in some of the texts as well. Hyder believed that 'innovative writing can encompass "fact, reportage, imagination, documentary presentation, the epistolary form" and so on' (Menon 205). According to Amit Chaudhuri, Hyder is 'detached, quirky, fragile, nervous, by turns melancholy and extremely funny, . . . an emigrant and gypsy of *narrative* structure, which for her is always a point of departure rather than a resting place.' This disposition enables 'experimentalism that crosses the conventional boundaries of the term. . .' (Hussein; "That Little Bird . . ." *xxiv*). The stories analyzed in this paper testify to these observations.

'A Night on Pali Hill'

Todorov explains the fantastic as a supernatural event that would be inexplicable by the laws of the familiar world. The person experiencing it would have to concede that either he is a victim of an illusion of the senses, a product of the imagination – and the laws of the world remain what they are; or else the event has indeed taken place, it is an integral part of reality – but then this reality is controlled by laws unknown to us. The fantastic occupies this duration of uncertainty. It is a hesitation that is experienced by a person who knows only the laws of nature, confronting an apparently supernatural event (25). This view holds true for *A Night on Pali Hill*, a horror drama in which Hyder gets closest to sinister gothic imagination. The play could have been the outcome of hearsay, tagging old, dilapidated, abandoned, sinister looking villas as haunted houses, in suburban Bandra, and nearby suburbs in Bombay, especially before hyper-commercialism coupled with scarcity of space, led to their demolition to make way for high-rises.

Embedded in Parsi tradition, *A Night . . .* is conceived as a performance that plays out on a rainy night in July 1976, inside a decrepit looking but luxuriously furnished neo-Georgian villa, in the plush locality of 'Pali Hill.' An atmosphere of eeriness pervades as dated and contemporary cultural allusions are juxtaposed by bringing together Iranian diaspora under one roof. The elderly, resident sisters of the villa, Homai and Rodaba Junkwalla and Aunt Feroza are decedents of the earliest diasporic Zoroastrians. Wealthy, Europeanized Parsis who have fallen into bad times, the sisters, particularly Homai, are caught in a time freeze. They strike the reader as relics of a glorious past, locked out of the present and deprecatory of anything Indian, particularly of the change that has come about in their contemporary environment. In stark contrast with them is the young, tourist couple, Gulchehr Isfandiari and Dara Kazimsadeh, studying abroad and engaged to be married. Muslims from contemporary Iran, they are polite, progressive, and unprejudiced, even empathetic towards the decedents of their ancient fire worshiping ancestors who were driven out of their homeland by Islamic invaders. Also brought into play is the popular appeal of the Bombay film industry – Gulchehr excitedly articulates her knowledge and love of Hindi cinema, and this is contrasted with the stiff upper lip reserve of Homai and Rodaba, and their affinity with all that is British, ranging from popular musical numbers to comportment and etiquette, education and materiality.

As Rodaba and Homai, in particular, delve on their glorious past with melancholia, a carnivalistic scenario makes the play verge on the bizarre and the surreal. Gulchehr and Dara, seeking refuge from the torrential downpour, become increasingly uncomfortable, as do the readers or the audience, as the seemingly realistic scene gradually and increasingly becomes phantasmal. As the love-story of Homai and Hoshang unfolds, the apparently ordinary meets with the dated and grotesque. A sense of expectancy rivets the readers or the audience. As they speculate on the experiences of Gulchehr and Dara, or, as Gulchehr and Dara, unwilling guests, are compelled to remain inside the villa by the torrential rain, despite their growing unease, much remains enigmatic and inexplicable. The ambiance is entirely suited to create horror and dread. The reader is informed that Sir Ardeshir Kaikaous Junkwalla, Homai, and Rodaba's father shot himself in the head, on a similar rainy night, in that very room.

Robert F. Geary quotes Rudolf Otto to observe that the gothic novel is a literary manifestation, 'that the numinous may break free of an inherited doctrinal context, returning now as a pleasing shiver, now as primitive dread' (Morse 9). Though 'A Night. . .' does not qualify as gothic fiction, owing to the absence of stock gothic constituents, the spectral ancient lady (Aunt Feroza), first, tapping on the floor upstairs, then coming down, dressed in a white, lace blouse, and white, China silk sari, with brooch, court shoes and accoutrements, mouthing portentous, numinous proclamations, is Hyder's response to the ghosts and vampires of gothic fiction. Her esoteric, saturnine raspings on life after death and the hereafter leave the protagonists horror-struck:

> All is Barzakh or Hell. There is no Paradise. I have come down at midnight to inform you that he has reached the bridge and has faced Mehr Davar, and now my case is about to be presented before Mehr Yazd
>
> (*The Street Singers* . . . 166).

The erectly seated wax figure of Hoshang Saroshyar Mirza, Homai's fiancé, wearing the death-mask Aunt Feroza commissioned on his death by burning in the fire, (started in all likelihood by him) and the howling cats provide the final touch to the ghoulish atmosphere that pervades. In the world of the dead,[4] Aunt Feroza would belong to the category of the 'living dead' – those who have died but who haunt the earth for evil or other purposes. Hoshang is doomed to 'common death' (Calabrese 40–41) because his mortal life is terminated unnaturally by the fire, his body is put to rest, but his continued existence in the lives of the Junkwalla sisters is apparent in the shape of the wax figure. The actual existence of Homai and Rodaba may also be speculated. In his essay 'From Providence to Terror: The Supernatural in Gothic Fantasy,' Geary notes that a free-floating sense of the numinous was an 'awkwardness and confusion' that kept the gothic a subgenre whose supernatural elements seemed clumsy 'trappings' not grounded in a coherent belief, and hence easily absorbed into the romantic mode (Morse 9). Throughout the performance, discomposure arises from the challenge posed by the eerie and ghostly to the real or the normative. The neo-Georgian villa on the dark, rainy night provides the perfect setting for the paranormal experiences of the unsuspecting, Iranian couple, who represent the normative or the real in the play. The apparent disappearance/invisibility and reappearance/visibility of the taxi, is another disturbing feature. Aware only the laws of nature, Dara and Gulchehr experience 'hesitation' or 'uncertainty' while they are confronted by what seems like the supernatural, in the Junkwalla household. They rush out of the villa to escape the extreme discomfiture occasioned by the bizarre goings-on, but they as well as the audience and readers know that their experiences have no logical explanation.

From a psychoanalytic point of view, if Homai is a flesh and blood presence, she would constitute a 'self,' existing in relative isolation in the world she has constructed around herself. Her belief in the living reality of Aunt Feroza, or her handling of the wax figure of Hoshang, as though it were alive, is an outcome of this. Dara and Gulchehr would constitute the 'others' or the outsiders infringing upon Homai and Rodaba's world. As such, they experience increasing discomfort first, when they hear Aunt Feroza's tapping on the roof every now and again, then see her apparition and shudder. When Homai wheels the wax figure of Hoshang wearing a death-mask in the wheel-chair, for a romantic, candle-light dinner the young couple rush out, horrified. In all likelihood, Homai's treatment of the wax figure has been occasioned by psychosis resultant of her unstated sexual desires. Todorov notes that 'psychoanalysis has replaced (and thereby made useless) the literature of the fantastic' but goes on to add that 'the themes of fantastic literature have become the very themes of the psychological investigations . . .' (160–61). So, while psychoanalysis would render a fantastic reading of the play inoperable, reading it from a fantastic point of view would perhaps give that the living are haunted, or perhaps, Homai and Rodaba are also apparitions.

The menacing uneasiness in the play recalls Henry James' *The Turn of the Screw*. Long after James' story has ended, the reader is not sure whether ghosts haunt the old estate or whether the goings-on are the hallucinations of a governess coerced by a disturbing environment. In both these texts, the mystery and the ambiguity persist, the hesitation characteristic of the 'true fantastic' sustains for a long period (Todorov 44). Louis Vax's remark that 'an ideal art of the fantastic must keep to indecision' holds true (Todorov 44). Hyder's play develops with the hurriedness of a suspense thriller – the suspense remains unresolved because the young Iranian couple rushes out of the house in alarm. It is possible that Hyder was influenced by Ibne Safi's detective fiction of the *Jasoosi Duniya* (*Detective World*) series, comprising horror, mystery, speculation, thrilling suspense, humour, and political consciousness and enjoying a huge cult following. In *A Night . . .*, all of these features co-exist. The audience and the young couple bear up to the chilling atmosphere throughout the performance, till the wax figure of Hoshang wearing the death-mask is wheeled in.

Hyder was impressed with the Parsi community's belief in and observation of customary prayer, ritual, and tradition, despite their erudite advancement, education, and Westernization. At a marriage ceremony of one of her Parsi friends, Hyder notes that the priests, reciting verses from the ancient Avesta, struck her as belonging to a by-gone era. It seemed to her that in voices full of strange mystery they intoned prayers recited three thousand years ago in the temples of Iran (Akhtar 72). Hyder adds to the mysterious by making Homai recite prayers in Avesta and by making Aunt Feroza reflect on life, death, and life after death.

Hyder's connect with international affairs is preserved in her reference to the crash of the New York Stock Exchange as directly affecting trade and commerce by the business magnate. She also projects the culture-rich Junkwalla sisters as harking back to a vanished but glorious past while in the midst of a corroded present. Throughout the play, Hyder's sense of wry humour is unmistakable, whether in the Junkwalla' sisters' mistaking the Iranian couple for hippies, in Gulchehr's comments regarding their fascination for Hindi films, or in the various contrasts projected in the interactions between the two pairs of protagonists.

'Confessions of Saint Flora of Georgia'

In *Confessions of Saint Flora of Georgia*, Hyder quite literally makes dry bones come alive. *Confessions* . . . is a historical fantasy that transports the reader into the magnificent Byzantine Empire, now unstable and decadent, verging on collapse, by means of reportage and vignettes. Two skeletons that come alive are Hyder's means of transportation into the carnivalesque past. The manner of their coming to life recalls the prophet Ezekiel's dream vision of the valley of dry bones from the Hebrew Bible. Saint Flora picks up her skull and adjusts it upon her shoulders in a manner similar to that of the dry bones that connect into human shape in the biblical narrative. Now dead for over a thousand years, Saint Flora's skeleton awakes in its centuries old monastic crypt in present-day Georgia, when it is accidently touched by the wing of a 'forgetful angel' condemned to remain 'for the last seventy thousand years' a 'trainee cherub,' looking for his lost rosary. Finding it for him, she requests a lease of life for one year to freely roam the world, because having spent 25 years confined in various nunneries, she 'want[s] to see a bit of the world, and crave[s] to wear pretty clothes' (*Street Singers* . . . 84). She goes on to request the revival of 'an interesting corpse' (*Street Singers* . . . 84) to make her lease an exciting one. So, the skeleton of Father Gregory Orbiliani is raised. Despite the fact that the narrative is a confessional grounded in Christian numinous belief, and the action unfolds rationally and realistically in the recognizable, contemporary world, the non-rational opening of the story classifies it as a fantasy. The narrative wills the reader to suspend disbelief in the possibility of the skeletons' coming to life. He/she continually negotiates with the goings-on, which evoke wonder and astonishment and suspend disbelief also in the implausibility of two globe-trotting skeletons failing to be noticed. The reader is aware of their reality from the very beginning and accepts them as intrinsic or germane to the narrative. Since the narrative is a historical fantasy, involving faith and piety, conjectures can be made about the historic or devout notables who may have served as originals for the two protagonists. Perhaps Saint Flora of Cordova, one of the earliest female Christian martyrs in Islamic Spain, served as an inspiration for Saint Flora and Father Gregory Orbiliani, may have been inspired by a prince of the House of Orbeliani of Tiflis, Georgia. However, there is no authenticating this, and at least in the case of Saint Flora, the parallel does not extend beyond the name. This story then 'intertwines [Hyder's] fascination with history and religion with [a] blend of whimsicality, playfulness and tragedy that characterized her later fiction.' (Hussein; quoted in Hyder 2009).

Hyder historicizes her text by means of continual references to conquest and displacement. Greek Orthodox Christians of Constantinople are caught in a state of flux during the period when Islamic rulers were fast becoming 'the new World Power and Time was siding with them . . .' (*Street Singers . . .* 88); Ottoman Turks are about to overthrow the Christian Byzantine kingdom; and the Zoroastrian Sassanian, Persian Empire, is about to be overthrown by the Arab Muslims. Byzantium, synonymous with artistic, literary, cultural and architectural sophistication, and magnificence and grandeur, is now draining of economic resources and overridden by monarchical conspiracy, intrigue and rebellion; so is Ctesiphon, the capital city of the equally culture-rich Sassanian Persian Empire. The dominant histories, interwoven as backdrop, are brought up as they are perceived or experienced by Lady Flora Sabina.

Foregrounded is the confessional made by the skeleton of the eponymous Saint Flora Sabina of Georgia, daughter of Stephen Honorius, Minister in the court of the Byzantine emperor, analeptically narrating her personal history, to Father Gregory Orbiliani, of Georgia, son of the Grand Duke of Tiflis. Her confession navigates the reader spacio-temporally to Ctesiphon, where her father has been, for all practical purposes, exiled, as ambassador and to Georgia, where she is cloistered in a Greek Orthodox Christian monastery. As she falls in love in quick succession, quite insensibly, with three young men professing different spiritual orders, Lady Flora experiences disappointment three times over and is subjugated and stifled on account of political, cultural, and religious constraints before being forced into a cloistered existence. As the daughter of a nobleman, who incurs the displeasure of the monarch, Lady Flora is forced to make compromises. She is controlled by the masculine world of power and conquest, she inhabits. Father Orbiliani articulates little, prompting her to articulate her route to sainthood, instead. So, the narrative unfolds as herstory[5] rather than as a history of conquest and empire building. The foregrounding of the story of Saint Flora's path to sainthood, though fictional, may be read as Hyder's attempt to contravene devaluation or negation of women in standard histories and ensure that the marginalized and subjugated are given voice. However, the element of fantasy strengthens the view that as a historical study, the narrative may instead, impede women's progress.[6] Moreover, Lady Flora Sabina's title turns out to be a partial truth, for sainthood hasn't been formally conferred on her – she reveals in her confession that a week before the official canonization 'the Reds closed down this convent' (*Street Singers . . .* 97).

In Russian Georgia, the two skeletons acquaint themselves with the here and now of the contemporary world. Father Orbiliani, who was intellectually inclined while he lived, participating in hair-splitting debates regarding academic matters and questions of religious and spiritual dogmas in self-imposed seclusion, seems to have awoken, furnished with knowledge of the contemporary world, but Saint Flora is as light-hearted as she was before being cloistered, ever as keen to dress gorgeously and make merry. They are mistaken alternately for Russian fugitives and as spies contemplating asylum, and they are welcomed in contemporary America, in the days of the Cold War. However, just before they are about to be taken into custody for theft, they call the bluff as they slowly take of their gloves, safety glasses and masks. The narrative is open-ended, leaving the reader with his/her imagination.

Hyder's recreation of the historical past reads like a pastiche or a burlesque, despite her serious intent to recreate the opulence and cultural sophistication of the Byzantine and Sassanian Empires. With the two fossilized skeletons clothed in stolen habits, roaming freely in the contemporary, living world without being made out, ludicrousness, humour, romance, and suspense take over as in an amusing yarn. Horror eludes the narrative. Implausible action, witty repartee, and comical observations and references to scientific progress take over. There are ample instances of ludicrousness in both action and dialogue. During the course of the narrative, Lady Flora mistakes the siren of a ship ready to sail as the trumpet heralding Dooms Day and falls in a faint. As Father Orbiliani smokes expensive cigarettes and as smoke is seen coming out of his skeleton's nostrils, she is very perturbed because 'only the Devil and his brood spit fire and smoke' (*Street Singers* . . . 86), and hurriedly she makes the sign of the cross and begins to pray. Father Orbiliani shows a propensity for petty larceny, and every time he succeeds, he comments that God is on their side. As Saint Flora probes Father Orbiliani about his love life, he sharply responds: 'why must you dig up old skeletons?' Or when he smokes too much, Saint Flora responds: 'Father, too much smoking would be injurious to your lungs,' then comments immediately after that both these comments are instances of 'black humour' (*Street Singers* . . . 98).

Hyder's narrative juxtaposes ancient history with contemporary world politics in the days of the cold war between Russia and America, in an attempt to specify that war games and empire building practices of the past have been replaced by political manoeuvrings and neo-colonialisms of the present. Characteristically, Hyder employs W. B. Yeats's poem *Sailing to Byzantium* in the text to raise the idea, mouthed by Father Orbiliani, that Byzantium is no place for the old (*Street Singers* . . . 107). In a story where 'the British are semi-barbarians' (*Street Singers* . . . 91), the Western world comes into the narrative only as the skeletons' foray into ultra-modernity. Perhaps, Hyder is saying that the earliest advancements of sophistication, culture, and learning lie in the east. Contributing to the tragic in the story is Saint Flora's longing for love – a desire denied to her while she lived and an impossibility looming large, despite her proximity with Father Orbiliani after being raised from the dead.

'My God, Veer, Doesn't that Lady in Mauve Look Like Bette Davis?'

My God, Veer, Doesn't that Lady in Mauve look like Bette Davis? is also a historical fantasy that unfolds in the city of Agra, home to some of the most magnificent monuments of the medieval, Mughal era. It juxtaposes 16th-century India with her contemporary self (September 1965) by making two ghosts walk the earth. At the centre of the story is melancholia – loss of secular ideals, war between India and Pakistan, the idea that independent India hasn't been able to cope with her freedom, and nostalgia for an era that exemplified syncretic culture. Highlighted here through the wistful ghost of Akbar, these are ideals Hyder takes up over and over again in her long fiction. Elizabeth I's ghost is exponential of renaissance England. Hyder notes that she wrote 'Do Sāēh' after her return from a sight-seeing tour of Agra. The story is 'about two travelers – Akbar the Great and Queen Elizabeth – who disguise themselves and come to modern-day Agra' (Akhtar 141). However, Hyder's idea of 'disguise' goes no further than the contemporary attire worn by her distinguished looking shades – a white, silk suit, and a mauve cardigan and slacks.

The two travellers, an elderly Indian gentleman, Shri M. A. Mirza, and a middle-aged British lady, Miss. Betty Henry, arrive at a posh hotel in a Rolls Royce and seek to check into two single rooms. Without their passports, the two, particularly the gentleman, are visibly ill at ease with the formalities of the check-in. On their visits to various monumental sights, the gentleman is seen lost in contemplative reverie. Owing to her white skin and attractive looks, the lady attracts the attention of several guides and Indian and American tourists, even the comment My God, Veer, doesn't that lady in mauve look like Bette Davis? ("*My God . . .*" 175). While the gentleman sinks in a trance, the lady expresses awe and admiration at the monumental grandeur of Agra and Fatehpur Sikri. The Taj Mahal is at the centre of controversy, with people conjecturing its origins – a young lecturer proclaiming emphatically to his students that it is a Rajput palace – 'It's about time we rewrote our history . . .' (173) or a white tourist announcing that going by the inefficiency around him, he was 'inclined to believe the theory about the Taj being designed by an Italian' (175). Contemporary India baffles and saddens the gentleman, but the lady is patronizing – 'My dear . . . they aren't even a nation yet, the poor dears' (173). Somewhat dismissive of the 'dust and grime' of her companion's 'dearly loved *India*' ("*My God . . .*" 172), she provides the reality check, commenting upon the current political scenario over-ridden with fanaticism and communal hatred; an economy in shambles and dismissive about the poverty. She busies herself with touristy things like admiring silks and purchasing gifts and collectables.

Menon notes that Hyder's own 'political convictions – her lived politics . . . [is] a politics of absolute integrity and . . . an uncompromised secularism (205),' and this story may be read as a response to the communal hatred that was fast destroying the syncretism and tolerance envisioned by an emperor who had started a religion on these underlying principles in Islam and Hinduism – the *Dīn-i Ilāhī*. The 1965 war with Pakistan figures prominently as a religious war, with threats of bombing and fear of destruction of the material ruins of a glorious past. The threat of nuclear warfare, the right-wing politics of the *Jan Sangh*, unemployment and poverty, rapid and thoughtless industrialization, and the defeat of Nehruvian positivism feature in the story as the shadows explore the historically rich cities. The idea that lucre attracted British traders to India and the fact that Agra remains an ever attractive city for tourists and academics across the globe is also touched upon. Hyder's approach is impressionistic. Many ideas are introduced, but none of them are developed to make pertinent comment. The contrasts between medieval and contemporary India are by and large sketchy – caught by means of snatches of conversation, or brief comments made by the shadows.

Hyder is also minimalist in her description of the shadows – the white moustache and limp are symptomatic of Emperor Akbar and the fine, arched eyebrows and thin lips suggestive of Queen Elizabeth I. The two are also distinguishable by means of certain personal preferences or aspects – Akbar is an aficionado of music but incompetent at writing, and Elizabeth is tight-lipped about her suitors and condescending in her acceptance of a free India. The initial signatures made by the lady indicate their identity – M. A., stands for Mohammad Akbar and Mirza, indicates ancestry; Betty is short for Elizabeth and Henry refers to her farther, King Henry VIII. Hyder misses that Elizabeth was known as Bess and not Betty or that Betty was a name often used for girls of ordinary lineage, birth, and/or background. The checkout signatures suffix 'Emperor of India' and 'Queen of England' ('*My God* . . .' 179) to names that are reproduced only in part. At the crack of dawn, when the cock crows, their limousine melts into the moonlight.

Carlo Coppola notes that when she asked him for comment on this text, he 'had the temerity to suggest' that she should not specifically identify the two protagonists at the end of the story as Queen Elizabeth I, and Emperor Akbar. Instead '(i)t would make a better short story, . . . by allowing for ambiguity and for imaginative play in the reader's mind' (Afterword 195).[7]

The point as to why Hyder paired these two monarchs, belonging to two dissenting cultural backgrounds, is not touched upon in the text. The reader may conjecture that it is perhaps because both sovereigns were iconic of imperialistic expansion; resolute on literary and cultural advancement and commanded popular appeal. Moreover, their reigns matched approximately in terms of duration and period. Queen Elizabeth I reigned from 1558 till her death in 1603 and Jalaluddin Mohommad Akbar from 1556 till his death in 1605. Perhaps, the reference in the contemporary guide book, read out aloud by the lady in mauve, ' . . . *three unknown Englishmen – Leeds, Finch and Newberry* . . .' ('*My God* . . .' 177) arriving in Fatehpur Sikri with a letter from their sovereign, explains the pairing – that it was to the court of Akbar that the Queen of England sent her emissaries and traders, requesting genteel comportment and the permission to trade.

'Beyond the Speed of Light'

Beyond the Speed of Light may be read as science fiction, speculating cultural, historical, and spiritual issues by transporting the reader back and forth in time-present and time-past by means of a machine owing its existence to techno-scientific advancement. Unlike the New Wave science fiction writers who used their fiction to warn against evils, chaos, and despair caused by technological development and converted it into a literature of serious social comment (Tymn 47),

Hyder is content to travel into the past with a view to exploring the colourful and exotic, ethnic past of a lost race in ancient Egypt. The story develops on the opportunity provided by 'contemporary transportation technologies to show how humans (rather than aliens) might travel to exotic locales on the Earth' (Mambrol) – in this case, ancient Egypt. Unlike science fiction that burgeoned in the days of the industrial revolution in the 18th century, a period when steam-powered technologies provided greater promise of development, Hyder is not concerned with the idea that scientific learning 'might bring a better world' nor projects the idea that by means of new science 'mankind might learn to control its own destiny' (Tymn 42). However, while scientific research was generally considered a masculine profession, in Hyder's story, a female scientist is employed in an institute offering space research. Thus, she employs two archetypal models – an educated woman and futuristic technology, both of which were 'central to the speculative stories' in the 19th century (Mambrol). The young Syrian Christian scientist Dr. (Miss.) Padma Mary Abraham Kurien from Kerela, employed in the Space Research Centre in South India, is the archetypal scientist-explorer who shares her (spiritual) knowledge with her Hebrew ancestors. This story, propelled by means of a scientific device, may be perceived as advancement on the traditional fantastic machinery in some of her stories and may be read as a scientific fantasy.

Tymn notes that the most popular early 20th-century motif of Science Fiction was the 'lost race' and that 'escape' was its keynote. He adds that tales of lost lands and lost races provided readers with a temporary release from the cares of the mundane (44–45). The most popular writer of this mode was Edgar Rice Burroughs, in whose work, science was 'almost non-existent' and characterization superficial, but the 'striking settings and spell-binding adventures offered readers an escape from the gloom of industrialized cities and the realities of World War I.' A series of novels depicted the remnants of a once mighty civilization on Mars 'with great colour and vigour and exotic splendour' (45). *Beyond the Speed* . . . draws on these modes of the lost race, and escape. Hyder explores notions of civilizational and cultural evolution by catapulting her contemporary protagonist into time-past, then flying her ancient Egyptian protagonist into time-present.

Hyder conceives the story like a frame narrative. The introductory narrative centres Padma, leading a seemingly ordinary life. Guardian to her younger brothers, she hopes to settle down to a comfortable married life before it is too late (*Street Singers* . . . 125). The second narrative centres Padma's accidental travel to ancient Egypt of 1315 BC in a time machine, presumably stationed in the compound of her residence by her colleagues. The two narratives seem to converge at the point when Padma's mother brings up the idea of Padma's marriage with her 'Coptic Christian friend,' Monsieur Hermez, flash-forwarded into contemporary Bombay from ancient Egypt (*Street Singers* . . . 148). Padma's downheartedness at being a 'plain Jane' leads her to seek succour in the over-generalization that men would remain always unreliable, whether they belonged to 1315 BC or to 1966 AD (*Street Singers* . . . 148).

Padma's travel experiences, catapulting her several centuries back in time, are activated by a seemingly ordinary trigger in her routine activities. The time warp provides Hyder opportunities to explore the mystique of ancient Cairo or Memphis, Egypt – a world of libraries, learning, hieroglyphs, philosophies, and age-old beliefs and practices. Also, of bustling marketplaces, slave driving and lecherous pharaohs, their empire building urges and their harassment of the Hebrews or the Aprus, of pyramids and mummies, and of temples and pagan worship. Hyder explores the art and culture of ancient Egypt, where frescoes are painted on palace walls, where mythic beliefs are dramatized for the stage, fashionable citizens enjoy concerts, and extravagance is a way of life. Padma's host, the handsome, charismatic, artistically inclined, and good-natured Thoth, who has to explain to Padma what the play they are watching is all about, has remained in Egypt to prepare a new edition of *The Book of the Dead*, while his family accompanies royalty on expeditions abroad. His quote from the text, a hymn of the dead man's praise of the sun god Ra, sums up the essence of the story:

> As thou rose in Thy radiant glory, Thy priests came out laughing. Thy Boat of the Dawn came alongside The Barge of Night. And Annu's halls resounded with voices. Ages shall pass. Time shall keep blowing up its dust under Thee, Thou that art yesterday and today and tomorrow, O Ra! . . .
>
> (*Street Singers . . .* 134)

Padma is mistaken for a sky-maiden, a 'daughter of the high heavens', (*Street Singers . . .* 140), whom the pharaoh, whose mummy she has seen in The British Museum, becomes desperate to marry. In a frantic bid to escape her fate as his queen, Padma flees, meets with the Hebrews, her spiritual ancestors and informs them of the coming of Moses or Moshe, their persecution by the pharaoh, their deliverance, and the Great Exodus. She runs into trouble but just about manages to fly back into 1966 AD in her time machine, along with Thoth, also anxious to save himself from the pharaoh's wrath. In Bombay, the dashing Thoth goes on to become a most coveted artist, living for seven years in a plush apartment on Cumballa Hill before becoming depressed and 'time-sick' rather than 'home-sick' (*Street Singers . . .* 150) and pleading with Padma to take him back to Egypt of 1315 BC. While she's still there, one of her Hebrew acquaintances, overwhelmed with suffering, and too impatient to wait for the Exodus, takes off in the spaceship into safe future, leaving behind a promissory note for Padma, that he will fly her into her own time as soon as he returns. However, a proviso entails that the spaceship will blow up once it has completed its fourth journey.

Beyond the Speed . . . is an imaginative text, evidently developing on the idea that 'science has progressed so much that [Padma] has flown faster than the speed of light and returned into the past' (*Street Singers . . .* 144) or that she belongs to the age of scientists not prophets (*Street Singers . . .* 145). Hyder fuses science with religion, philosophy, art, culture, and the basic needs of ordinary human nature to elucidate ideas elaborated amply in her longer, realistic fiction – that abundance and perfection in philosophy, art, literature, and culture, and not war and war games, are the determiners of great civilizations; that time and history move in a cyclical order in repeated patterns of formation, development, disorder, and destruction or that the old order changes, making way for new, and these patterns constitute the civilizational advancement of man. The time machine enables the story's backward and forward propulsion, but Hyder has an eye continually focused on realistic, normative aspects related to language and dress, ideas related to love and marriage and her protagonists, aware of the time warp in which they are catapulted long to return to their own worlds. Hyder also explores ideas related to time past, present and future, notions of ephemerality, and the transience of temporal life posited against eternity. In a classic twist, characteristic of Hyder's ingenious narrative style, the story concludes inconclusively, leaving the reader to wonder at the fate of Padma.

Beyond the Speed . . . may reminiscence Rokeya Sakhawat Hossein's essentially feminist, English language text *Sultana's Dream* (1920), which also qualifies as science fiction. In a dream sequence, Hossein's protagonist applauds matriarchal society, which warrants education and scientific advancement with the help of technological apparatuses. Like most science fiction, utilitarian and serviceable development is the bottom-line in Hossein, despite the fact that her machinery is, in fact, quite rudimentary. Writing near about 50 years later, the most significant departure Hyder makes from Hossein is the omission of utilitarianism. Her female scientist and time machine are deployed to celebrate the once flourishing ancient art, culture, and philosophy of Egypt. This probably has to do with both the passage of time and shifting sociological concerns. It also reflects the contrasting inclinations of the two writers.

Conclusion

The four fantasies analyzed in this study are only occasional pieces in Qurratulain Hyder's essentially realistic oeuvre – engaging diversions or departures from a fundamentally serious, and thought-provoking corpus. As the mainstay in the Todorovian sense, the fantastic is not the crux of the stories. Though they are imaginative and deal with the supernatural, they do not generate spine-chilling fear or thrilling suspense characteristic of fantasy or speculative fiction. As a subsidiary component propelling a larger scheme, the supernatural machinery in Hyder is a means to transport the reader in both time and space into ancient realms. Unlike the gothic novels of 18th-century England, Hyder's stories augur no evil, and at times, her ghosts, spectres, and skeletons appear harmless, even ludicrous and facetious. However, they perform the function they are created to perform – they transport the reader into time past and bring in the nostalgic romance of a long-gone era. Therefore, Hyder is not entirely immersed in the genre of the fantastic for its own sake; she subordinates it to a larger intent.

By means of the fantastical devices – skeletons and apparitions and a machine that enables time travel, she is able to transcend spacio-temporal limitations, the ephemerality of time, and the restrictions imposed by actual horizontal travel. Hyder's treatment of the strange, and the bizarre, is with an eye ever focused on the normative. She engages the reader by fictionalizing and telescoping history; pastiche, burlesque, suspense, and speculation are thrown in for diverse effects. The fantasies commemorate the resplendence of ancient Oriental and Egyptian civilizations by exploring art, literature, philosophy, and lifestyle. They affirm that though these civilizations have faded out, they are foundational to the contemporary world. Hyder also explores spiritual and transcendental monotheistic and pagan beliefs, particularly those surrounding death and dying. She also has an eye on contemporary politics and current affairs such as the Cold War, the Indo-Pak war of 1965, communal bigotry and preceding these, the crash of the New York Stock Exchange.

By and large, Hyder's women represent bourgeoisie womanhood in relation to the socio-cultural and intellectual environment, with all the permutations and combinations of power and inadequacy which contribute to the formation of its textured fabric. The women central to the stories analysed in this study – Homai, Saint Flora, Queen Elizabeth I and Padma, are, owing to some compelling circumstance, single, either pining for romantic love or stoically acquiescent of their spinsterhood. They are quite unlike the female models proliferating Progressive literature, who believe in modernizing and living by Marxist and socialist ideals. Unlike her Progressive contemporaries, Hyder is not crafting the quintessential new woman who will make all manner of sacrifices to serve as a role model of social and educational advancement.

By translating herself, Hyder offers another variety of the fantastic in the English language. These stories may be read as Hyder's experiments merging elements from diverse literary traditions, conveniently borrowing or overlooking aspects of genre with a view to foreground and celebrate her studies in dying or archaic cultures. Perhaps the unwieldiness of the almost interminable *dastān* cycles led her to rethink form. The short story was the popular literary genre of the era and her ghosts and apparitions were harmless, even amusing rather than menacing or ominous. Covering horror, history, and scientific fantasy, Hyder's fantasy fiction ratifies that she is a subversive, individualistic, and experimental writer who endorses that contemporary society is but of ancient cultures and civilizations.

Notes

1 Ismat Chughtai's essay "Pompom Darling" is a scathing critique of the young Hyder's style and subjects. Chughtai parodies her as Pompom Darling, a character in the story 'Dajla ba Dajla Yam ba Yam' from *Shīshē kē Ghar* (*Glass Houses*). With regard to the Progressive's criticism against her, Hyder writes that 'first [she] was called a giggly schoolgirl, and then a bourgeoisie reactionary. [She] found it all very saddening' (*Narrative* 209).
2 For a study of these ideas, please refer to my papers: 1) "The Progressive Urdu Afsana: Towards a New Aesthetic" *South Asian Review*, Special Topic Issue "South Asian Modernism", Vol. 33, Number 1, 2012. (guest edited by Alpana Sharma) and 2) "Urdu Fiction: Celebrating Hybridity and Pluralism" *The IACLALS Journal* Vol. 1, 2015.

3 The Urdu stories appear together in the collection *Raushni kī Raftār* (1982, Educational Book House, Aligarh). Hyder self-translates in English and comments upon her stories without making reference to the original Urdu language texts, treating the self-translated ones as originals. While translating, she takes liberties, abridging, appropriating, and rewriting.

4 In his essay on Tolkein's *The Lord of the Rings*, Calabrese notes that the world of the dead contributes to the underlying presence of mythic continuity with the past. He mentions four manifestations of death in the epic: 1) common death, 2) the living dead, 3) those who pass through death to a resurrected state or changed state on earth, and 4) those who part peacefully, passing over the sea to the Blessed Realm (41).

5 A feminist term coined by Robin Morgan in her anthology *Sisterhood is Powerful* (1970), for history written from women's perspective, to foreground women's roles in history or bring them out of obscurity.

6 The idea is borrowed from Christina Hoff Sommers' *Who Stole Feminism? How Women have betrayed Women*. She argues that gender feminists in their enthusiasm to counter historical inequalities based on gender try to make historical studies more inclusive of women's roles, but these are artificial and impede progress.

7 Carlo Coppola's interview with Qurratulain Hyder will appear in a volume of interviews/essays he did over the years with/on various writers.

Works cited

Akhtar, Jameel. *A Singular Voice: Conversation with Qurratulain Hyder*. Translated by Durdana Soomro. Oxford UP, 2017.

Bowra, C. Maurice. *The Romantic Imagination*. Oxford UP, 2002.

Calabrese, John A. "Continuity with the Past: Mythic Time in Tolkien's The Lord of the Rings" *The Fantastic in World Literature and the Arts: Selected Essays from the Fifth International Conference on the Fantastic in the Arts*. Editor Donald E. Morse Greenwood Press, 1987, pp. 30–45.

Coppola, Carlo. "Afterword." *Journal of South Asian Literature*, vol. 31/32, no. 1/2, 1996/1997, Asian Studies Center, Michigan State University Stable 182–96. 31:1–2/32:1–2, 1997.

Das, Chaity. "Two or Three Things I Know about Qurratulain Hyder." *Journal of the School of Language, Literature and Cultural Studies*, edited by G. J. V. Prasad, Jawaharlal University, New Series 8 (Autumn) 2007, pp. 110–14.

Geary, Robert F. "From Providence to Terror: The Supernatural in Gothic Fantasy." *The Fantastic in World Literature and the Arts: Selected Essays from the Fifth International Conference on the Fantastic in the Arts*. Editor Donald E. Morse Greenwood Press, 1987, pp. 7–19.

Hussein, Aamer. "That Little Bird: Remembering Qurratulain Hyder." *Fireflies in the Mist: A Novel*, Qurratulain Hyder and Women Unlimited, 2008, pp. vii–xxvii.

Hyder, Qurratulain. "Confessions of Saint Flora Sabina of Georgia." *Wasafiri*, introduction by Aamer Hussein, Routledge and Taylor & Francis, vol. 24, no. 2 June 2009, pp. 8–17. (To cite this article: Qurratulain Hyder (2009) Confessions of Saint Flora of Georgia, Wasafiri, 24:2, 8–17, DOI: 10.1080/02690050902771563)

———. "My God, Veer, Doesn't That Lady in Mauve Look Like Bette Davis?" *Journal of South Asian Literature*, vol. 31/32, no. 1/2, 1996/1997, pp. 169–81.

———. "Novel and Short Story: Modern Narratives." *Narrative: A Seminar*, edited by Amiya Dev, Sahitya Akademi, 1994, pp. 207–14.

———. "Preface." *The Sound of Falling Leaves: Award Winning Short Stories*. Sahitya Akademi, 1994, 2016, pp. v–xv.

————. *Street Singers of Lucknow and Other Stories*. Introduction by Aamer Hussein. Women Unlimited, 2008.

Mambrol, Nasrullah. "Introduction to Science Fiction." *Literary Theory and Criticism*, https://literariness.org/2018/07/26/introduction-to-science-fiction/. Accessed 18 July 2019.

Menon, Ritu. "Endearing Iconoclast." *The Annual of Urdu Studies*. University of Wisconsin, vol. 23, 2008, pp. 202–5.

Morse, Donald, E., editor. *Introduction: The Fantastic in World Literature and the Arts: Selected Essays from the Fifth International Conference on the Fantastic in the Arts*. Greenwood Press, 1987, pp. 1–7.

Raymen, Andrew. "The Problem of Defining Fantasy Literature." *Fantasy, Politics, Postmodernity: Pratchett, Pullman Mieville and Stories of the Eye*. Rodopi, 2014.

Todorov, Tzvetan. *The Fantastic: A Structural Approach to a Literary Genre*. Cornell UP, 1975.

Tymn, Marshall B. "Science Fiction: A Brief History and Review of Criticism." *American Studies International*, vol. 23, no. 1, Apr. 1985, pp. 41–66.

7

'THE FORBIDDEN CITY'[1]

An exploration of Wajida Tabassum's magazine fiction[2]

Wafa Hamid

> Notions of the subject, individualism, freedom, agency, change, and history . . .
> have come to cluster around the figure of the Muslim woman (for whom the
> metonym is increasingly the veil). The Muslim woman is the object of imperial
> rescue, justification for imperial warfare, Orientalist cipher, target of jihadist vio-
> lence, and, increasingly, the discursive site upon which the central preoccupation
> of our time – how do you free yourself from freedom? – is worked out.
>
> (Abbas 2013)

While Islam is the second largest religious demographic in the world,[3] much of
the political debate on the subject of Muslim practice and life revolves around the
rhetoric of 'liberating' 'Muslim women,' secularizing 'Muslim culture,' and 'saving' the 'Muslim world' (Abbas 158). Wrapped in such rhetoric, the 'Muslim-
ness' of a Muslim woman is seen as enough evidence of her victimization and
oppression through the 'double tyranny' of her religion as well as patriarchy, thus
eliciting responses of horror, pity, anger, and even hate against the community
by and large and Muslim men in particular. More often than not, the Muslim
woman herself has little or no say in such a characterization which yokes together
women of diverse regions, cultures, class, and linguistic demographic as a homogenous lump. In spite of the multifarious and well-reasoned efforts to counter such
essentialist constructions, the stereotype of Muslim women as 'absolute victims'
in a 'backward'/'conservative' community largely persists (Najmabadi 1993; Abu-
Lughod 2000; Kidwai 2005; Mahmood 2004; Aftab 2008; Abbas 2013). As a result
of such persisting constructs, the image of 'The Muslim Woman' is largely perceived as one that resists modernity. This view, on the one hand, Schneider (2009)
remarks, overlooks ways in which 'as members of Indian society, Indian Muslims
are naturally involved in processes of economic change, nation-building and secu-
larization just like any other section of the population. On the other hand, the role

DOI: 10.4324/9781003002062-10

of the state is often neglected, especially with regard to the relationship between the state and patriarchal structures in society' (60). Such biases, along with various kinds of silences surrounding women, make it an especially difficult undertaking to engage with the role of Muslim women as social actors in their diversified and heterogeneous existence.

While there are many epistemological and methodological problems that ail research on Muslims in India, there have been attempts to historicize the voices and movements of Muslim women and men alike by the likes of Christina Oesterheld (1994, 2004), Vrinda Narain (1998, 2001), Gail Minault (1998), Azra Asghar Ali (2000), Sylvia Vatuk (2008, 2009), Nadja-Christina Schneider (2009), Nida Kirmani (2011), and Margrit Pernau (2012, 2013), to name a few. Muslim women's voices on the one hand have to negotiate with patriarchy within the Muslim society all the while struggling against the impulse of being excluded by dominant discourses within the nation and many a times even liberal feminism. The chapter, through its exploration of the short story genre and magazine fiction of Wajida Tabassum, tries to deconstruct and dismantle the stereotypical identity of Muslim women, produced in dominant discourses, as 'frail' and 'submissive'. I propose to analyse her stories under the genre of magazine fiction and erotica, while also investigating how Wajida Tabassum's writings expand the scope and validity of such categories. By delving deep into the portrayal of the psyche of her characters, the genre, and form of her stories, I intend to unfold layers of sexual attitudes which are also expressions of social conditioning of Muslim men and women in a decadent feudal set-up presented through the perspective of women.

> We should learn to read in various local and everyday resistances the existence of a range of specific strategies and structures of power. Attention to the forms of resistance in particular societies can help us become critical of partial or reductionist theories of power. The problem has been that those of us who have sensed that there is something admirable about resistance have tended to look to it for hopeful confirmation of the failure-or partial failure-of systems of oppression. Yet it seems to me that we respect everyday resistance not just by arguing for the dignity or heroism of the resistors but by letting their practices teach us about the complex interworkings of historically changing structures of power.
>
> (Abu-Lughod 53)

The chapter through its engagement with the multi-layered concept of agency and resistance also tries to envisage how Wajida Tabassum's writing, not only through its content but also through its circulation, negotiates the terrain of power and representation. Tabassum not only delegitimizes old taboos but also questions male dominance and prescribed gender roles through her intimate knowledge of life in traditional women's quarters, the *zenānā*. In reading her work, the chapter also looks at the importance of genres like domestic fiction and magazine fiction in Urdu literature and the way these forms not only fashioned the reading public but provided an outlet where Muslim women writers vocalized themselves against the double bind of patriarchy. The genre and the form are thus invested with an agency where the tropes of the silenced and 'veiled' lives of Muslim women in India (post-independence Hyderabad in particular) are challenged and resisted.

The Urdu short story and domestic fiction

The Urdu short story as it exists today is a literary phenomenon of recent origin. Although narrating anecdotes, tales, and stories are an age-old tradition of orality in Urdu, the short story as a genre owes much to Premchand (1880–1936), one of the most prolific fiction writers of modern India. It was Premchand who introduced Urdu and Hindi fiction 'to the living truth of human existence' by shedding its obsession with medieval romance and nostalgia and slowly adding the texture of realism through his pioneering works (Narang 113). By infusing the short story with characters from everyday life and their daily negotiations with hierarchies and struggles of existence, he introduced the Urdu short story to the realities of contemporary life. From these early beginnings, the genre moved to a sociological impetus and the psychological fascination in the 1940s, with writers like Saadat Hasan Manto, Mumtaz Mufti, and Ismat Chughtai's frank and outspoken stories exposing and displaying the 'emptiness of Indian religious life and the hollowness of Indian sectarian beliefs' (Narang 115). However, the partition of the subcontinent on the eve of Independence in 1947 marked a violent break from ancestral homes and histories, along with the destruction of roots and routes of being and identities. In relation, the short story genre moved away from the initial nationalistic and patriotic fervour exhibited during the early days of the Independence movement (as well as the initial exhilaration of freedom) to an unsettled nostalgia exploring silences that permeated the very fabric of contemporary society.

The narrative in the wake of Partition carried a charge and an urgency that spoke to the spirit and impulse of the time. Thus, literature in indigenous languages such as Urdu around this time was far less concerned with the nation as a category of reverence and much more with class structures, familial ideologies and the management of bodies, sexualities, idealisms, and silences (Ahmed 118). After the Partition, Urdu, which was a product of the composite culture of the subcontinent, began to be looked upon as the 'language of Muslims,' and the writer had to overcome yet another bias besides an already proliferating pile of prejudices. This, along with the declining socio-economic conditions of Muslims, as evidenced by the Sachar Committee Report (2006), gradually led to the weakening of Muslim women's voices in the literary sphere in post-independence India. However, reformers such as Rokeya Sakhawat Hossain, Mumtaz Ali, Zakaullah Waheeda Begum, Maulvi Chirag Ali, and Muhammadi Begum among others, continued to strive for social and religious reforms highlighting the role of Muslim women during the first part of the 20th century. As such the print medium became an important and popular site of not only instruction but contribution of Muslim women. The rise of many journals which saw contributions by women as well as readership of women became markers for the emergence of Muslim women in the public sphere. The study of such journals, even though relatively scarce, by the likes of Gail Minault (1998), Asra Asghar Ali (1998), and Christina Oesterheld (2004) makes it apparent how the journals transformed into mediums of change for the Muslim women: a site of participation in the public space while still reaching out to the private and domestic arenas.

It was around this post-partition period that the Urdu romantic/domestic digest emerged and increased in popularity among other genres. Such digests and magazines held an especially important position in the society as they were con- sumed largely – though not exclusively – by a female readership from a wide vari- ety of economic backgrounds. Urdu bookshops boasted of a proliferation of such digests where writings by women were both varied and abundant. There were titles such as *Shamā* (The Candle or Flame), *Bāno* (Lady), *Khwātēn* (Women), *Ustani* (Lady Teacher), and *Sacchi Kahāniān* (True Stories) which were household names and an extremely popular category of fiction. The high circulation of novels of manners, instructive stories, and domestic fiction can be credited to not only families but the women readers who many of these journals catered to (Minault 109). Having access to stories contributed by other women, they would devour every detail and description in the stories and wait with bated breath for the next issue. Whereas there is a tendency to marginalize such fiction as a local equivalent of the British Mills & Boons or the Barbara Cartland romance in an effort to trivialize the experiences and perspectives of women by equating domes- tic life and family relationships with banality, it was in such writing that the line between what constitutes the nation and other 'larger' concerns and domestic fiction was more often than not blurred. Many of these stories are literary expres- sions of women's lives.

> While these writings help us to understand the minds of Muslim women, at the same time, it also compels us to think, rethink and question our under- stating and popular notions about Muslim women, their thinking, choices, dreams and contributions.
>
> (quoted in Alam 2013)[4]

Rather than being silent and homogeneous, these Muslim women authors in their stories vocalized themselves through their bodies, sexualities and language to push the boundaries of the '*zenānā*.'[5]

The writer and her canvas

A bold voice with a deep insight into the male and female psyche, Wajida Tabas- sum (1935–2011) was an immensely popular writer of short stories, poetry, and songs. Born in Amravati, Maharashtra in 1935, she graduated from Osmania University with a Master's in Urdu language. In 1947, her family moved to Hyderabad, with this 'City of Nizams[6]' becoming the canvas for many of her short stories. First published in the magazine *Bīswīñ Sadī* (Twentieth Century), the Urdu monthly *Shamā* used to pay her a handsome sum for a single story in the 1970s (Khan 2011). At the time, there existed a dichotomy where women were taught to speak and write in *'begumāti zubān,'*[7] 'a chaste, civilized Urdu' as opposed to the more colloquial and conversational language found among 'ignorant or street people' (Minault 109). This is evident in references to 'good writing' by women where 'usually, they do not employ the speech which is common in the Deccan, and particularly the variety spoken by women, but write elegant standard Urdu' (Hashmi 55).[8]

It was in the backdrop of these reflections on taste and language that Tabassum's work first appeared in the monthly magazine *Bīswīñ Sadī*, where she chose to write in the Deccan or *Dakhini* dialect, setting aside the 'good,' 'standard' Urdu. *Bīswīñ Sadī* was one of the oldest Urdu magazines published since 1937 by Ramrakha Mal alias Khushtar Girami, which was later managed by Z. Rahman Nayyar, who took over the magazine in 1977.[9] The magazine published articles, political satire, cartoons, and short stories. In 1960, Wajida Tabassum's collection of stories was published under the name of *Shahr-e Mamnu* (The Forbidden City). The collection was widely appreciated and received critical enquiry and comparisons with Ismat Chughtai. Eminent Urdu critic Mujtaba Husain called her the first storywriter after Ismat Chughtai who could be called '*Sahib-e-asloob*' (a writer with a distinct style). In the late 1960s and 1970s, Tabassum started publishing for the digest *Shamā*, which was run by Yousuf Dehlvi along with his three sons. Shamā Publications was founded in 1947 in Delhi[10] and catered to the growing educated class in both India and Pakistan. It had an office in London through which it reached out to readers of Urdu and Hindi in Europe. Shamā Publications brought out three monthlies in Urdu: *Shamā*, a film and literary magazine with Urdu short stories and poems; *Bāno* which targeted the educated woman; and *Khilonā*, for children. Of these, *Shamā*, which was one of the most popular magazines of the time, provided a platform to many writers, who owe the beginning of their career to the magazine. It had a wide and committed readership in the Urdu-speaking families in both India and Pakistan, a necessary supplement for the reading class.

Wajida Tabassum's stories bring into practice the motto of the personal being vested with political significance, with the 'home' being both a space for oppression and confinement and yet teeming with a potential of agency. Most of her stories are set in the domestic spaces of the *havelī* or the *deolī*, in which she uses the space to symbolize the conflict and blur the boundaries between the inner/outer, subjective/objective, or private/public worlds and selves. *Havelī* derives from the old Arabic word '*haola,*' meaning partition. In modern Arabic, however, '*hawaleh*' means 'all around' or 'roundabout.' In Persian, the word '*havali*' means the same, and it probably travelled to India with the Mughals. Subsequently, the word '*havelī*' was derived from this Persian root. It originally described a piece of land belonging to the army, with the Mughals using the word to mean 'province.' It eventually came to mean 'the ground and the buildings on it like an estate' and finally came to denote 'the ample house of a wealthy family' (Prasad 3.1).

Shikha Jain (2004) problematizes this definition and argues that courtyards, scale of structure, or the façade are not the characteristics on the basis of which a *havelī* is defined. She instead argues in favour of a more social definition citing the one deployed by the exhibition catalogue at the Prince of Wales Museum in Mumbai in 1989, which describes the *havelī* as being symbolic of the generations who spent their life in the pursuit of architecture, customs, manner, arts, crafts, and music. These *havelīs* were the residences of *umraos*,[11] princes, *thakurs*,[12] *rājpurohits*,[13] as well as the *seths*.[14] Although the architecture of the *havelī* was conceived around a life of segregation for women, where their rooms were cut off from the rest of the world (Wacziarg & Nath 22), the *havelī* is both an enclosed space and an open space, in its design and symbolism, which further creates a dialectic in the conception of a 'home.'[15] As T. S Randhawa points out, 'the courtyard house architecture in India was not just an architectural style. It was a way of life' (1999, 29). The *havelī's* varied topography with its archetypal three levels connects the microcosm to the macrocosm. With its central courtyard open to the skies, the *havelī* 'breathes' ('*hawā*' means air) and lends itself to the multiple modes of living that lie within. It offers an ambivalent space in that it is 'enclosed' in nostalgia and tradition, the customs and rituals of a patriarchal social tradition, and yet is filtered through the social, political, and economic changes rooted in the 'public' sphere that permeate through the borders between the two.[16]

It is in such a space that Wajida Tabassum foregrounds her stories, facilitating a flexible relation between the inhabitants and the spaces of their 'home.' She is a writer situated both before and after India's independence from the British rule in 1947. This backdrop of ferment in Hyderabad's history, which was the effect of Independence and a subsequent Partition, is also reflected in the everyday interactions that constitute and transform the notion of 'home' in Tabassum's stories. Her stories are thus not only narratives but a palimpsest of history that depicts Hyderabad not through its lanes and markets, the beauty of the Chārminar, or the mystique that surrounds the 'City of Nizams' but through a quaint and curious mix of lived experiences and of bodies in motion that makes Hyderabad a consistent presence in Tabassum's stories. The domestic space in the process also assumes a new vitality where the everyday becomes a medium of the revelation of human character. Its interplay with external forces reflects the diversity of its inhabitants and the prevailing social mores of that time. The action of her stories thus takes place in the most intimate of spaces, like the *hammām* (communal bathhouse) of the story *Hal*,[17] the bedroom on the wedding night in *Chutney*,[18] or the inner quarters in *Zara Hor Upar* (A Little Higher). And it is these intimate spaces and the bodies inhabiting them where the everyday transactions of power and hierarchy are negotiated.

Wajida Tabassum wrote about male privilege, injustices, sexuality, and the struggles that women have to face in the society on a daily basis. Although depicting the aristocratic social life of Hyderabad, her stories can be approached through multiple perspectives lending themselves to many ways of reading. It is fascinating how Tabassum's stories, in spite of being confined to the four walls of the domestic space and inscribed within private lives, bring into sharp focus the deep-rooted structural hierarchies and inequalities of the society. Breaking away from the tradition of long narratives and male-centric didactic fiction, Tabassum's stories invest these seemingly mundane and trivial spaces with an immediacy and urgency rarely seen before. Her stories, told from a woman's point of view, rather than stereotyping or romanticizing their lives, make the domestic space an arena where power and agency is sought. Lila Abu-Lughod in her *Veiled Sentiments: Honor and Poetry in a Bedouin Society* (2000) foregrounds the importance of being sensitive and open to viewing of multiple and differentiated ways of resisting by women:

> First, how might we develop theories that give these women credit for resisting in a variety of creative ways the power of those who control so much of their lives, without either misattributing to them forms of consciousness or politics that are not part of their experience – something like a feminist consciousness or feminist politics – or devaluing their practices as prepolitical, primitive, or even misguided? Second, how might we account for the fact that Bedouin women both resist and support the existing system of power (they support it through practices like veiling, for example), without resorting to analytical concepts like false consciousness, which dismisses their own understanding of their situation, or impression management, which makes of them cynical manipulators? Third, how might we acknowledge that their forms of resistance, such as folktales and poetry, may be culturally provided without immediately assuming that even though we cannot therefore call them cathartic personal expressions, they must somehow be safety valves?
>
> (47)

It is thus, important to keep in mind that even though the setting of the stories is situated 'behind the veil,' in the inner most spaces of the house and *haveli*, these spaces can be equally important as spaces and sites for the negotiation of agency. As Saba Mahmood in her work *The Politics of Piety* (2005) on grassroot struggles through The Women's Mosque Movement in Cairo suggests, the modalities of agency with their meanings and effects aren't fully captured through the logic of subversion of hegemonic discourse only. There is a need to uncouple such notions of agency from the politically prescriptive project of a kind of feminism which equates the understanding of agency with radical resistance, while lacking a vocabulary sensitive to local strategies and negotiations of power.

The veil, following Mahmood's analysis, as well as the logic of Abu-Lughod and Najmabadi, among others, reveals the numerous struggles of power that are hidden behind it and have to be understood before formulating our thoughts around the idea of agency. The women in Tabassum's stories, although hidden behind 'the veil' of the private quarters and intimate spaces, nonetheless possess agency in their negotiations of power in these spaces. Their bodies also become a canvas for painting such forms and processes of navigating agency, as is clear in the story '*Uttran*' (Hand-Me-Downs), where the protagonist Chamki, who for the initial part of the story is constantly made aware of her identity as inferior and below in class to

Shehzadi Pasha,[19] her 'friend' as well as her mistress, refuses to reconcile herself to the unequal social conditions. Instead, on Shehzadi Pasha's wedding night, Chamki 'gives herself up' to the embrace of Shehzadi Pasha's groom: 'To rob him of his purity, to lose her own, and to plunder everyone' (121). In the story 'Pesh Bandi,'[20] a scene with the protagonist Gul Chaman,[21] who is the 'gift' from the bride's family to the groom, is described thus as she returns a necklace to the groom, the Nawab, which he had gifted her:

> Ye haar mere ko akeli ko zindagi bhar kafi ho jayinga . . . magar Hyderabad mein kitti sari gharib chokaryan hain nawab sahib, jin ko kabhi na kabhi pet ke wastey pesh bandhi ban ko, paisa kamaney ko dulhan par chana hor sej sajana padeinga
> (This necklace will be enough for me for my whole life . . . but Hyderabad has so many poor girls Nawab Sahib, who at some point have to become *pesh bandhi*, they will have to decorate the way to the bride's bed by warming it.)

> Nawab sahib aap badey aadmi hain, aap mere ko aaj ye vada deoki Hyderabad se is laanat ko aap khatm kar ke ich dam lenge. . . . dulhan ke wastey kaam kaaj ke wastey jayengi bhi to koi budhdhi aurat . . . mere jaisi jawan ladki nain, jis ke dil mein pyar to uske miyan ke wastey ho
> (Nawab Sahib, you are a big man. You have to promise me today that you will breathe easy only after you end this custom from Hyderabad. . . . Even if someone needs to go to help the bride and work for her in her new home it has to be an older woman . . . and not a young one like me who still loves her husband and is separated from him.)

(148)

Thus, the women in the stories use their bodies to negotiate with power, and though their actions cannot be read as radical resistance, it is important to note that within the structures of power and society, their bodies become indispensable sites for re-writing agency to negotiate with power, and this embodiment itself cannot be dismissed.

Although Tabassum's bold and distinctive literary style gained her critical acclaim with an ever-growing reader base, it also exposed her to criticism for its 'erotic' content and depiction of female sexuality. Many critics labelled her writing as 'light fiction,' 'sensational,' 'obscene,' and 'trivial,' which was considered inappropriate for a Muslim woman, while others decried the themes as not worthy of 'serious' literary production. Challenging similar commentary and attitudes about her own writing, the novelist Maggie Gee had this to say in response, 'Those of my books which deal with war or murder, which can be crudely categorized as male topics, receive far more attention and literary respect than those which deal with family or children or love or sex. Yet for me these are all great themes, themes from which you can make serious literary work'(173). Tabassum experimented with different styles of literary writing, yet she maintained a delicate and fine balance between the conversational and literary, the intimate and political, and the carefree yet serious in her writings. Her imaginative portrayal of the worlds of her stories reflects class, caste, gender, and many other social hierarchies in the most intimate of actions of the characters. Her stories are always told with clarity and simplicity in diction and with an economy, which gives only the essentials of character or situation heightened by sharp and vivid details.

Erotic lives and body politic

Anaïs Nin defines erotica as primarily dealing with the dialectics of desire: desire as the articulation of the tension that exists between a lover's emotions and the cravings of his body and desire as the tendency to give aesthetic form to sexual experience.[22] 'Erotics and aesthetics, then, depend on each other: as desire gives shape to man's life so does language enact or amplify the semantics of his sensual gestures. The sexual act in erotica is not an end in itself; it is only one of the forms that eroticism takes' (Kamboureli 144). Further, Foucault's definition of *ars erotica* notes it as a discourse where the notion of identity is subordinated to pleasure. 'If identity is only a game, if it is only a procedure to have relations, social and sexual – pleasure relationships that create new friendships, it is useful. . . . The relationships we have to have with ourselves are not ones of identity; rather, they must be relationships of differentiation, of creation, of innovation. . . . We must not exclude identity if people find their pleasure through this identity, but we must not think of this identity as an ethical universal rule' (Foucault 166).

I contend that Wajida Tabassum's stories with their constant interplay of power and hierarchies with the body as her canvas defy a simplistic categorization of her stories as erotica. While her writings do engage as an aesthetic form with the sexual experience, they do so by making this sexual experience a form of negotiating agency. Her stories, rather than making identity subordinated to pleasure, strike a fine yet fragile balance between pleasure, desire, and identity. Due to the imagination of the female body as a traditional passive object of pleasure, the sexual act, as well as the assertion of desire, becomes an assertion of the self. Tabassum's characters (re)define and (re)imagine themselves by embodying their desires. The visceral by exposing the body in its nakedness becomes a space for reclamation of the self.

Her stories can largely be divided into two categories or axes, though often crisscrossing and blurring such distinctions. Whereas some stories largely expose the everyday exploitation of women, their oppression and confinement by patriarchal social norms, revealing the hypocrisy of the so-called progressive society, a majority of her stories depict women, Muslim women in particular, as embodied, sexual beings with desires and needs. They challenge the notion of Muslim women as silent absolute victims, veiled and self-sacrificing, enshrouded and enclosed in the *purdah*, both literally and metaphorically. Her stories instead depict how 'it is in the riotous self-abandonment of their sexual expression that women are shown breaking the moulds of age, class, and social propriety to fully extend themselves as human beings who live in the light of their own conscience' (Choonara 145). From a confrontation between a husband and wife or a question from a woman to another – Tabassum makes the most seemingly innocent of situations charged with a potential to question and transform through her insightful depiction of each struggle and every feeling and emotion. 'he tales echoing from nooks and crannies of *havelīs* were as labyrinthine as the lives of those living there. Post sundown, the tales tumbling between seduction and exploitation would open their eyes' (Afreen 2018).

In her story *Thikānā* (Destination), Tabassum depicts the selfishness and the false pride of Nawab Iqtidar Jung. On catching Masood, the groom, on the wedding day trying to peep into his daughter (and the bride) Razia Bano's room through a *roshandān* (small window) he, in his anger, calls off the wedding. Having spent every penny he had in making the now called-off wedding a lavish affair,[23] he lives a life of penury with Razia. But even though he receives many proposals for her hand in marriage, he rejects them on some pretext or another just so he isn't left feeling lonely. The story ends with the Nawab later pimping Razia Bano to rich men for his needs, thanking God and calling this state his daughter's final *thikana* or destinationThe scene perfectly captures the dark irony of the situation where the father himself pimps his daughter for money:

> *Dono hathon mein dher sarey note uthae jab wo Panchi Baraq ke badnaam mohal-ley waley ik chotey se makaan mein apne baap ke saamne pahuchi to pehle baap ko soojha hi nahi wo kya karey.*
> (Holding many heavy bills in her hands when she reached her tiny apart-ment via Panchi Baraq's (the bird's cage) infamous locality, her father was too shocked to respond.)

> *Phir jab wo rupae baap ke saamne daal kar kamrey mein wapas chali gayi to. . . . do din ke bhukey pet ne khush ho kar parwardigaar ke saamne haath utha diye.*
> (Then, when she goes inside her room after leaving the money in front of her father . . . the two day long hunger made him raise his hands in prayer to God to say,)

> *Shukr hai mere mālik ke meri beti ko ik thikānā mil gayā.*
> (Thank you, my lord that my daughter has finally found her destination.)
> (131)

The story highlights the changes in the fortunes of the aristocracy post inde-pendence with the *wazifa* (pension) not meeting the lavish lifestyles the Nawabs[24] were used to, leading to many of them finding it difficult to make ends meet, even mortgaging their *havelīs* to continue living their older lifestyle. Another story, *Pesh Bandhi,* highlights the custom of taking a *mushtari*, a female domestic help along with the bride as a gift to the groom. In one such instance, Nawab Mumtaz is eager to meet his *Pesh Bandhi* more than the bride, and on seeing him, the *Pesh Bandhi* immediately takes off her clothes for a mere 20 rupees, which she laments is more than her husband's one-year salary. The story highlights the commodification and sexual exploitation of women who belonged to the dispossessed classes of the society and the appalling way in which women (wives as well as domestic help) were treated by the aristocracy. The story ends with the *Pesh bandi*, who remains unnamed throughout the narrative, thereby further bringing into stark contrast the de-humanization of women, strongly claiming her due by asking to end this custom of *Pesh bandhi* to alleviate the suffering of women.

Yet another story, *Jhoothan* (Leftover) exposes the debauchery of Nawab Iqtidar Yaar Jung, also called *Bade Sarkar*, who compares women to food, where just like food one is content only by trying a new woman every day.

> *Eikich khana khaatey aapka dil bhar jaata aap bol kar dusri haandi pakwa kar kha lete, koi kuch nahi bolta . . . pan aap zara biwi se ukta jatey hor chokri baandi se dil behlana chahtey toh sari duniya naman rakhti..ye duniya badi ajeeb o gharib hai* (When you get bored of eating the same food, you ask for a different pot full of food, no one says a thing . . . but if you get weary of your wife and want a little distraction through another girl, the entire world is after your life! It's a strange world.)
>
> (187)

He makes his servant, Kallu[25] pimp women to him every night only to discover later that Kallu has been pimping his own wife, Sakku (Sakina), to him, claiming she is a virgin. The Nawab thereby asserts his class and masculinity by decreeing that he would sleep with Kallu's wife for a month without giving Kallu any dues, while Kallu will sit at the door of the room listening through the night. The story depicts that in between the competition of the wits of the two men, the true victim is the woman, Sakku, who is disregarded by her husband as well as the Nawab as only a sex object and a way to gain money and status. The story further unfurls the many layers of hierarchy and satirizes the lifestyle of the Nawabs by also depicting the levels of hierarchy present within the household of the domestic helps, starting from the *Anna* (wet nurse) for breastfeeding, the *Mamaein* (to taste food and make sure it is well prepared before it is served to the Nawabs), to the *Mushtari* and *Choriyan*[26] (women for massages, etc.), and the *Chokras* (for routine odd jobs).

It is through stories like these that Tabassum exposes the structural hierarchies engrained within the aristocracy and the society enlarge, which for its maintenance relies on a continued exploitation of gender, class, and caste differences. What also makes her an important voice is the subtle way her stories emphasize the intersections of exploitation, where different levels of socializations, including class, caste, etc., interact with gender to create double bind in many cases. What sets Tabassum apart in such stories is that she maintains a delicate yet fine balance between the narrator's voice, which many a times merges into that of the characters,' making every character, each moment, seem deceptively simple, only to lead to a gradual peeling away of the complexity in its depth. This comes not only through the content of the stories but also through the very language used. Even though there was an expectation of using 'civil,' 'standard' Urdu, Tabassum writes in the local Deccan/Dakhini idiom of conversation.[27]

The second category of stories I divide Tabassum's writing into consists of those that explore how women experience and express themselves through their bodies. It is through such stories, I contend, that Tabassum presented a different way of writing, especially for women in the field of Urdu literature. The characters in such stories traverse a variety of emotions, carefully walking a tight rope between the personal and the collective. Among these I include, *Zara Hor Upar* (A Little Higher), which portrays the strife between Nawab Riyasat Yaar Jung and his wife, Pasha Dulhan.[28] One night, on seeing Nawab Riyasat Yaar Jung return to his room smelling of jasmine oil, with his clothes spoilt with kohl and tired of his illicit affairs with the *Mushtaris* and *Chokris*, Pasha Dulhan takes matters into her own hands. She asks a 15-year-old *chokra*, aptly named Rehmat, to be fed with dry fruits and rich food for more strength so he can massage her. The sensual tension between Pasha Dulhan and the young Rehmat, employed as a masseur, finds its climax in her seducing him, asking him to tactfully massage her a little higher each time till he can't control his urge.[29] When one night, on catching them in the act, the Nawab threatens to give her *talaq* (divorce), she says with élan, 'Then do it!' and 'I will tell the whole of Hyderabad that the children we have are not yours' (281). Thus implying he is impotent.

In two other similar stories, *Tiya Paancha* (Three to Five pieces) and *Naagin* (she-snake), Tabassum explores the frothing anger of a wife who publicly declares her husband an impotent. Whereas in '*Naagin*,' this reaction is elicited by Bade Sarkar's – who is married to Meher Aara – lack of courage in accepting his actions of consummating their marriage before the custom of *Ruqsati* (the ceremony of the bride leaving her house for the groom's after marriage). While in *Tiya Paancha*, it is a response to the Nawab cheating on her. The women in these stories so strongly rebel against the system that they are ready to accept the ignominy of being considered unwed mothers or having children out of wedlock rather than giving in to such partners, brutally hurting the royal ego of the men as well as the hollow system in question. In the story *Chutney*, one reads the sensual tension between the young Nawab and a ravishing beauty employed as a domestic help, which climaxes in her being raped on a rainy night. It is in the act of tearing open her dress in the gathering on the Nawab's wedding day that she makes her naked body, which is associated with shame and a marker of weakness for women, a medium of protest.

Another example is the story *Nath ka Gurur* (The pride of the Nose-ring[30]), where Shakoma, nicknamed Sharafat Dulhan by her husband, is shocked when her husband, Wajahat Nawab, claims he has become impotent after having sex with another woman and has married her only under family pressure. He instead asks her to keep the façade of their marriage intact to keep the '*izzat*' (honour) of the family. On return from one of his longer trips to look after his land and property, which has stretched to months, he discovers his household celebrating the birth of 'his' baby boy. On confronting the 'Innocent' bride, she justifies her act by saying that her mother-in-law had started looking for a second wife for him to have an heir to the property. 'Can there ever be more innocent a wife as me!' (33) Thus, I ate the *gandum* (wheat, considered as forbidden fruit) and have kept the '*Nath ka Gurur*' or your honour intact. A similar story, *Hal* depicts Nawab Daulat Yaar Jung, who married for a fourth time in hope of getting an heir (a boy). On their wedding night, he rejects his fourth wife, Sabira, comparing women to fields that a man might plough whenever he feels like it. Even though the Nawab sleeps around with other women, Sabira remains waiting for him every Friday, as she is given a bath and decked like a bride only to be left unfulfilled. On demanding sex from him, he dismisses her as not the subject of desire but only an object that is to please him, the man:

> *aurat mard ki kheti hoti, jab chahe aa le sakta . . . jab mera ji chahenga aa jaun ga.*
> (A woman is a man's field, he can come and take whatever he wants . . . I will come when I want.)
>
> (139)

Tabassum describes the erotic details of the female anatomy as Sabira takes off her clothes, and in her nakedness, on seeing the muscular *mashq* (water-bearer), Shamsu, who comes to fill the *hammam*, Sabira like the *sookhi zameen* (parched earth) absorbs his 'water' with a hiss. Tabassum stops at the point of being brash and ostentatious and with her signature witty, dark sarcasm shows the pregnant Sabira, on being questioned by the Nawab, later retorting, 'If I am a field, I also found a way to get ploughed. Did I do anything wrong?' (". . . aich boley na aurat to kheti hoti! bas mai bhi hal chalwa li") (140).

Her best-known piece *Uttran* (Hand-Me-Down), published in 1977, explores the relationship between two young girls, one the darling daughter of the aristocratic household and the other, her playmate, the daughter of her *Anna*. It shows the multiple times Chamki, the daughter of Shahzadi Pasha's wet nurse, is humiliated by years of wearing Shahzadi Pasha's hand-me-downs. And finally, on the rich girl's wedding night, she takes the first turn with her mistress' eager bridegroom, this time, in turn, giving her mistress a hand-me-down groom for life. There are countless other examples of Tabassum's frank portrayals of the relationship women have with their bodies and the subversions of their sexual experience. Such stories like *Nath Utarwai* (Deflowering Ceremony), *Phul Khilne Do* (Let the flowers bloom), *Mahak* (Fragrance), and many more created a heated discussion among Urdu writers about erotic content and obscenity, which was chiefly responsible for denying her a prominent place in Urdu literature which she rightfully deserved. In Tabassum's writing although characters don't necessarily completely rebel against their surroundings and the fragile balance, this fragile balance is continuously threatened by instability, with the periphery and the margins always ready to erupt. Her stories defy any attempt at a reductive reading and continuously challenge the reader to think and question one's reading, keeping one glued to the work till the very end with the transformative potential of the stories. Set against the backdrop of the decadent Hyderabad aristocracy, her stories delineate the feudal space, society, and manners.

Wajida Tabassum's stories occupy not only a place of aesthetic importance through the writer's perspective but also as a site reimagining the contours of agency, resistance and transgression. Her writing stands on its own as representation of women that pushes the confines of the private sphere. It is not just the details and content of the stories but also the form, with its substantial reading audience comprising of women, that provides a voice to otherwise silenced lives represented in popular narratives. This representation breaks away from the depiction of Muslim women as passive victims and instead engages with them as living, multifaceted beings who cannot be reduced to their religious or gendered identity. Her characters map the struggles, aspirations, and selfhoods of Muslim women of her time as they navigate the everyday challenges of society. Women in her stories are not only those who only nurture men and children, limited to the enclosed 'zenānā,' but ones who strongly claim their due. Wajida Tabassum played a seminal role in the development of the genre of magazine digest and domestic fiction in South Asia, locating the domestic space and the everyday as the subject of 'serious' fiction. She dealt with her characters with a candour and vitality rarely seen in contemporary Urdu literature, not only portraying their lives lived through the minutiae of rituals and domestic routine but also making this very domestic a distinctive arena where larger inequalities and structural hierarchies of the societies are played out. Wajida Tabassum broke through stereotypes as her characters come to life enriched with a sense of history weaving fact with fiction to write a history of lived experience and silences. Her short stories questioning the morality of the aristocratic Hyderabad blur the boundaries between the public and private, making the domestic and the body a city of forbidden agency and expression.

Notes

1 *Shaher-e-Mamnu,* roughly translated to 'The Forbidden City,' was the title of Wajida Tabassum's first collection of short stories.
2 Unless otherwise mentioned, all translations are done by the author from the original Urdu stories collected in the volume *Wajida Tabassum ke Bees Shahkaar Afsane,* edited by M. Irfan Ali.
3 As estimated by a study on "The Global Religious Landscape," *The Pew Forum on Religious and Public Life.* The Pew Research Center, 18 Dec. 2018.
4 This was part of an article, 'Women's World,' by Mahtab Alam, which consisted of an interview of Purwa Bhardwaj, one of the editors of *Kalam-e-Niswan,* carried out and published by *Nirantar: A Centre for Gender and Education,* which consisted of transliterations of stories and articles by women in Urdu journals. The interview and article was published in *The Hindu* on 12 Oct. 2013. www.thehindu.com/news/cities/Delhi/Women's-world/article11813689.ece.
5 *Zenānā* literally means 'of women.' The term referred to the inner quarters of the house, which were typically reserved for the women of the household. Thus, it refers to the domestic sphere, which used to be occupied by women.
6 Hyderabad is also known as 'the city of nizams' since the aristocracy of the princely state were called Nizams.

7 *'Begum'* was a way of referring to women, typically of higher class, and *'zubān'* or 'tongue' in this case also stands for language. Thus, *'Begumāti zubān'* refers to supposed refined women's language or women's idiom.

8 As quoted in Christina Oesterheld, "Urdu and Muslim Women," *Islam in South Asia*, edited by Daniela Bredi, Oriente Modern, no. 1, 2004, pp. 217–43.

9 The Evolution of *Bīswīñ Sadī* has been discussed in more detail in the article 'Remembering Z Rahman Naiyar and Bīswīñ Sadī,' *The World of Urdu Poetry, Literature & News*, 17 Jan. 2010. Accessed 6 Jan. 2019.

10 For more detailed discussion on the publication, see 'Of days gone by' By Nikhat Sattar, 1 July 2013, www.zubeidamustafa.com/of-days-gone-by. Accessed 14 Dec. 2018.

11 *Umrao* means 'noble' and usually refers to queens and princesses.

12 *Thakur* means 'lord,' 'god,' or 'master' and was a title used by the rulers of many princely states as landowners.

13 *Rājpurohit*. *Purohit* comes from Sanskrit: *Rāj* is 'rule,' *purás* is 'before,' and *hitá* is 'sent.' The word *purohita* meaning 'placed in front or before' and is used to refer to priests. *Rājpurohit* thus refers to the headpriest.

14 *Seth* usually refers to the moneylender or merchant.

15 See T. S. Randhawa, *The Indian Courtyard House*. Prakash, 1999.

16 Also see Sarah Tillotson, *Indian Mansions: A Social History of the Haveli*. 1st ed. 1994. Orient BlackSwan, 1998.

17 The term *'hal'* is a pun on the word, which literally means 'solution' as well as 'plough.' The story also plays with this duality in the meaning of the word.

18 *Chutney* means a mix of different elements together and is usually referred to a condiment made from mixing various spices and herbs. The word in the case of the title is again a play on the meaning, which also signals a chaotic mixing together.

19 *Shehzadi* means 'princess' and *Pasha* was a title given to a high rank official. The name *Shehzadi Pasha* thus means a princess of a higher class/ aristocracy, thus hinting at the larger preoccupation of the story, which involves class as well as gender.

20 The title, like many others used by Tabassum, is a play on the word, which while referring to the practice of sending another woman as a 'gift/present' with the bride for the groom also literally refers to a way of defending yourself. The word *pesh bandi* also doubles up on itself to give a sense of time, the one who is prisoner only for the time being or the present.

21 The name in true Wajida Tabassum style is a combination of *gul* (flower) and *chaman* (flowerbed). Thus, *gul chaman* is the flower as well as the flowerbed that is the foundation and strength of the flower.

22 Quoted by Smaro Kamboureli, 'Discourse and Intercourse, Design and Desire in the Erotica of Anaïs Nin,' *Journal of Modern Literature*, vol. 11, no. 1, Mar. 1984, pp. 143–58.

23 The excessive spending on the wedding to the point of eventually becoming a pauper at the end is also a reflection on the feudal society and the precarious position gender played in them. The daughter's wedding was and still is, in many ways, seen as an occasion to assert the family's status and honour, which was equated with how grand the wedding was itself. Even if the feudal society after Independence and Partition is itself in crisis with a drastic reversal of fortunes, it is the public image and family honour that is seen as paramount, even by the father, Nawab Iqtidar Jung, in the story.

24 Nawab was the title given to the native governors of the erstwhile Mughal empire.

25 *Kallu* literally means 'black.' The name itself highlights the way caste and class functioned in the society where people belonging to a 'lower' caste or class were giving names mocking their appearance or equating them to being dark or dirty and thus impure.

26 *Chokri* is also a colloquial way of referring to a girl, and *chokra* a boy.

27 The *Dakhini* idiom, apart from being much more ambiguous and suggestive, also plays with the gender of pronouns, since the pronouns are gendered masculine in the language, thereby further adding to the complexity od depiction of gender.

28 *Pasha Dulhan* means the bride (*dulhan*) of the Pasha, thus also pointing towards how women in the society were not only seen as sex objects but on marriage lost what little agency they had by only being referred to their husband's wife.
29 The scene with its tone and situation immediately brings to mind Ismat Chugtai's 1942 short story *Lihaaf* (The Quilt). Chugtai was a contemporary of Wajida Tabassum, who had made a name of her own in the literary world. Chugtai was charged with obscenity for her story *Lihaaf* and was the center of much controversy due to its content and references to homoeroticism. Chugtai never apologized and also went on to win the case.
30 The *nath* or the 'nose ring' is considered a symbol of marriage and the honour of the family, and thus the nose ring the bride wears during the wedding ceremony is usually heavy and big to reflect this responsibility.

Works cited

Abbas, Sadia. "The Echo Chamber of Freedom: The Muslim Women and the Pretext of Agency." *Boundary 2*, vol. 40, no. 1, 2013, pp. 155–89.
Abu-Lughod, Lila. *Veiled Sentiments: Honor and Poetry in a Bedouin Society*. U of California P, 2000.
Afreen, Saima. "Raconteur of a Forbidden City." *The New Indian Express*, 2018, www.newindianexpress.com/lifestyle/books/2018/mar/16/raconteur-of-a-forbidden-city-1788282.html. Accessed 14 Dec. 2018.
Aftab, Tahera. *Inscribing South Asian Muslim Women: An Annotated Bibliography & Research Guide*. Brill, 2008.
Ahmed, Aijaz. *In Theory: Nations, Classes and Literatures*. Oxford UP, 1991.
Alam, Mahtab. "Women's World." *The Hindu*, 12 Oct. 2013, www.thehindu.com/news/cities/Delhi/Women's-world/article11813689.ece. Accessed 10 Jan. 2020.
Alavi, Shams Ur Rehman. "Remembering Z Rahman Naiyar and Biswin Sadi." *The World of Urdu Poetry, Literature & News*, vol. 17, 2010.
Azra, Asghar Ali. "Recovery of Female Voice Through Women's Journals in Urdu in British India 1898–1947." *South Asia: Journal of South Asian Studies*, vol. 21, no. 2, 1998, pp. 61–86.
Choonara, Sameena. "A Review of *Parwaaz: A Flight of Words* (Urdu Short Stories by Women)." *The Herald (Karachi)*, 1997, pp. 145–46.
Foucault, Michel. *Ethics: Subjectivity and Truth*. New Press, 1997.
Gee, Maggie, and Lisa Appingnanesi. "The Contemporary Writer: 'Gender and Genre'." *Women, Writing and Marketplace*, edited by Judy Simons and Kate Fullbrook, Manchester UP, 1998, pp. 172–82.
Hashmi, Nasiruddin. *Khavatin-i Dakin ki Urdu khidmau Hyderabad*, 1940.
Jain, Shikha. *Havelis: A Living Tradition of Rajasthan*. Shubhi Publications, 2004.
Kamboureli, Smaro. "Discourse and Intercourse, Design and Desire in the Erotica of Anaïs Nin." *Journal of Modern Literature*, vol. 11, no. 1, 1984, pp. 143–58.
Khan, A. G. "Wajida Tabassum: A Defiant Writer." *The Milli Gazette*, 19 Feb. 2011, www.milligazette.com/news/441-wajida-tabassum-a-defiant-writer-urdu. Accessed 14 Dec. 2018.
Kidwai, Sabina. "Images and Representations of Muslim Women in the Media, 1990–2001." *In a Minority: Essays on Muslim Women in India*, edited by Zoya Hasan and Ritu Menon, Oxford UP, 2005, pp. 370–98.
Kirmani, N. "Beyond the Impasse: 'Muslim Feminism(s)' and the Indian Women's Movement." *Contributions to Indian Sociology*, vol. 45, no. 1, 2011, pp. 1–26, Doi: 10.1177/006996671004500101.

Mahmood, Saba. *Politics of Piety: The Islamic Revival and the Feminist Subject.* Princeton UP, 2005.

Minault, Gail. *Secluded Scholars: Women's Education and Muslim Social Reforms in Colonial India.* Oxford UP, 1998.

Najmabadi, Afsaneh. "Veiled Discouse-Unvelied Bodies." *Feminist Studies,* vol. 19, no. 3, 1993, pp. 487–518. DOI: 10.2307/3178098.

Narain, Vrinda. "Muslim Women's Rights and the Accommodation of Difference." *University of Southern California Review of Law and Women's Studies,* vol. 1, Fall 1998, pp. 43–72.

———. *Gender and Community: Muslim Women's Rights in India.* University of Toronto Press, 2001.

Narang, G. C. "Major Trends in the Urdu Short Story." *Indian Literature,* vol. 16, no. 1&2, Sahitya Akademi, 1973, pp. 113–32.

Oesterheld, Christina. "Voices from the Inner Courtyard: On Early Women Poets of Urdu." *Tender Ironies: A Tribute to Lothar Lutze,* edited by Dilip Chitre et al., Manohar, 1994.

———. "Islam in Contemporary South Asia: Urdu and Muslim Women." *Islam in South Asia,* edited by Daniela Bredi, Orient Modern, no. 1, 2004, pp. 217–43.

Pernau, Margrit. "Male Anger and Female Malice: Emotions in Indo-Muslim Advice Literature." *History Compass,* vol. 10, no. 2, 2012, pp. 119–28.

———. *Ashraf into Middle Classes: Muslims in Nineteenth-Century Delhi.* Oxford UP, 2013.

Prasad, Sunand. *The Havelis of North Indian Cities.* Unpublished study for the Royal College of Art, 1987.

Randhawa, T. S. *The Indian Courtyard House.* Prakash, 1999.

Sattar, Nikhat. "Of Days Gone by." 1 July 2013, www.zubeidamustafa.com/of-days-gone-by. Accessed 14 Dec. 2018.

Schneider, Nadja-Christina. "Islamic Feminism and Muslim Women's Rights Activism in India: From Transnational Discourse to Local Movement – or Vice Versa?" *Journal of International Women's Studies,* vol. 11, no. 1, 2009, pp. 56–71.

Tabassum, Wajida. *Wajida Tabassum ke 20 Shahkaar Afsane,* edited by M. Irfan Ali, https://archive.org/details/WajidaTabassumAfsanay/page/n1/mode/2up. Accessed 20 Mar. 2020.

Tillotson, Sarah. *Indian Mansions: A Social History of the Haveli.* 1st ed. 1994. Orient BlackSwan, 1998.

Vatuk, Sylvia. "Islamic Feminism in India? Indian Muslim Women Activists and the Reform of Muslim Person Law." *Islamic Reform in India,* Special Issue, edited by F. Osella and C. Osella, *Modern Asian Studies,* vol. 42, nos. 2 & 3, 2008, pp. 489–518.

———. "A Rallying Cry for Muslim Personal Law: The Shah Bano Case and its Aftermath." *Islam in India in Practice,* edited by B. D. Metcalf, pp. 352–67. Princeton U P, 2009.

Wacziarg, Francis, and Aman Nath. *Rajasthan: The Painted Walls of Shekhavati.* Vikas Publication, 1982.

8

'1971 NOVELS' IN BANGLADESH

Women's writing between the popular and the literary

Mosarrap Hossain Khan

Introduction

Do '1971 Novels' written by Bangladeshi women easily fit into an already created genre of fiction documenting the Bangladesh Liberation War in 1971? How do these novels negotiate between remembering a significant moment of national history and the popular demand of the market post 1992, when memory of the Liberation War re-emerges in Bangladeshi public consciousness? As the compartmentalization between 'literary fiction' and 'genre fiction' breaks down gradually, the '1971 Novels' pose a conundrum about the transformation of the novel form from its early novelty to early 20th-century commercial manifestation, what Joshua Rothman calls the genre novels' tendency to represent 'social facts rather than individual experiences' ('A better way'). In the case of novels on the Bangladesh Liberation War, this tension between social facts and individual experiences is particularly striking because these novels, at least the less literary ones, often narrate the sociological experience of the birth of a new nation, Bangladesh from (East) Pakistan, or try to recreate an authentic history, in which the individual experience gets subsumed within the larger political project. Thus, '1971 Novels' – as I would like to call them – complicate the official historiography of the Bangladesh Liberation War as one of triumph and glory. While Selina Hossain's *Hangor Nodi Grenade* (A Shark, A River, A Grenade 1976) fictionalizes the tale of an old mother sacrificing her disabled son during the war in a remote village, Shaheen Akhtar's *Talaash* (The Search 2004), narrates the journey of a raped woman during the war. By focusing their attention on the dispossessed and the marginal figures of history, these novels combine elements of serious historical introspection with the everyday life (or the suspension of it) of ordinary people. Through an analysis of these two novels, this chapter would attempt to theorize how the genre of '1971 Novels' complicates our understanding of popular and literary fiction.

DOI: 10.4324/9781003002062-11

'1971 Novels' as genre fiction

While it will be premature to delineate '1971 Novels' as genre fiction because national sentiment, incomplete mourning, political contingency, and the demands of market produce no definite template for what could be termed '1971 Novels.' Men's direct physical engagement in the war at the frontline and their literary production in the realm of serious historical and national concerns stand in sharp contrast to women's early literary production and consumption of popular genre fiction. Contrary to fiction written by male writers such as Shoukat Ousmane's *Jahannam Hoite Bidai* (1971), Anwar Pasha's *Rifle, Roti, Aurat* (1973), Syed Shamsul Haq's *Nishiddho Loban* (1981), and Anisul Hoque's *Maa* (2003), to name a few, women's fiction on the Bangladesh Liberation War depicts a distinctly gendered concern both in the domestic space and in the war zone. How do women writers of '1971 Novels' appropriate and expand the possibilities of the genre? If we were to employ the term 'genre fiction' to these novels as "an interpretative label" (Chattopadhyay et al. 2), we must first determine the recurrent motifs that operate in these novels. While there are certain formulaic similarities in tropes, motifs, and plot construction in the way these novels focus on the struggle for the emergence of a nation, their production and distribution, while appealing to a mass readership, still cannot be slotted into the comfortable logic of the market. This chapter argues for an understanding of the genre as certain thematic similarities, lending themselves to the task of remembering, consolidating, and fashioning a national identity. Unlike other popular genre fiction, such as science fiction, detective fiction, mystery, and romance, it would be impossible to slot these novels as entertaining. Yet, here our focus must be on the word 'popular' because post-1992, the Bangladesh Liberation War has occupied the centre stage in Bangladeshi consciousness, owing largely to the task of national healing by bringing the war criminals or Razakars (non-Bengali and Bengali collaborators of the Pakistani army during the war) to justice. A spate of memoirs, diaries, fiction, and anthropological work has emerged within a complex network of market and national reconstruction, lending these fictions a popular appeal. These novels fulfil both the requisites of generic specificities and at the same time provide insight into human condition caught in conflict, what author Anita Mason calls their openness to 'the universal' ("Genre fiction"). This popularity of the genre, as what Chattopadhyay et al. write in another context, "can make genre fiction a fecund site for articulation of mass resistance and disillusionment with the status quo" (7). This resistance is crucial if we consider how the spirit of the Liberation War has been appropriated by different regimes in Bangladesh. While the Awami League, the party of Sheikh Mujibur Rahman, hanged his killers and instituted the International Crimes Tribunal in 2009 to prosecute the collaborators of war crimes, the Bangladesh Nationalist Party (BNP) often points to Awami League's surrender to Indian interests during the Liberation War. In the contested and contesting terrain of national identity, these novels offer 'a veritable space where memory and history are written, edited, rewritten, and contested' (Das xii), where the victims and the witnesses provide a non-essentialized experience. These fictions act as a counter-discourse to the celebratory spirit of the Liberation War by dwelling on the unresolved fissures the war generated in the everyday life of people. The popularity of '1971 Novels' is, thus, an ambiguous legacy, where a renewed interest in the genre's retrieval of the past with identifiable tropes is undercut by its questioning of the celebratory narrative of national identity. Tahmima Anam's trilogy, comprising of *A Golden Age*, *The Good Muslim* (2011), and *Bones of Grace* (2016), which has brought the Liberation War back to the attention of Anglophone reading public and academia, is an important attempt at documenting the complex place of Islam in Bangladeshi national imaginary and how national reconciliation may still be possible once the role of religion is properly understood. Anam's attempt is part of a burgeoning body of literature in Bangladesh which could be termed 'war literature' (Das 8), in which the Liberation War continues to cast a shadow. Instead of 'war literature,' I prefer the term '1971 Novels' because a focus on the temporality of the event denotes a complex network of motivations, processes, exclusions, and subversions, which moves beyond the centrality of masculine violence coded in the term 'war literature.' This chapter analyses Selina Hossain's *Hangor Nodi Grenade* (A Shark, A River, A Grenade 1976) and Shaheen Akhtar's *Talaash* (The Search 2004), set almost three decades apart, to argue that the genre of '1971 Novels' operates within an imbricated discursive field of the popular and the literary.

Selina Hossain's *Hangor Nodi Grenade*

The '1971 Novels' bear a close relation to testimony or eyewitness accounts and work as an 'interpretative site' (Das 2017) or as a site of reflection for decoding the memory/trauma of the Liberation War. One of the major generic conventions in much of fiction around 1971 is its documentary impulse, the desire to represent an authentic experience of suffering during the war, 'a feel of being present at a particular event through the perspective of characters' (Waheed, 'The art of recreating the past'). Selina Hossain's *Hangor Nodi Grenade*, covering a span between 1947 and 1971, depicts a tender romantic relation between a middle-aged man and his young wife, Buri, who is fiercely independent and given to bouts of imagination. The novel is based on a story, which Hossain heard from her teacher (Waheed, 'The art of recreating the past'), of a rural woman who sacrificed her disabled son to Pakistani soldiers to save two freedom fighters during the Liberation War. While remaining true to this incident, Hossain fictionalizes the past of her protagonist by delving into Buri's mind to reveal the complexities of a contained life in a Bengal village. Buri as a barren mother with the desperate craving for a child and later giving birth to a disabled child becomes a metaphor for the impotence and 'dysfunctionality' of Bangladesh coming into being in a violent manner. A peasant woman, Buri's circumscribed life in Haldigram and her nascent political consciousness are framed as her 'sensuous apprehension of the world outside, her physical response to phenomena' (Das 231). In her childhood, her sole window to the world is Jaleel, who takes her to the railway station, where the receding train becomes a metaphor for mobility and journey into the unknown. Buri's world in Haldigram is lonely and limited in its spatial scope, unlike many of her friends and neighbours, especially men, including her two step sons, who are active participants in political events. As opportunity for physical mobility further decreases after her marriage to her own cousin, her consciousness expands exponentially, making the novel an exploration of Buri's ideas of freedom and independence, both individual and national.

The onset of the war is introduced in the novel through Buri's consciousness, which undergoes a change from relative stability to destabilization of the ordinary:

> Buri's thoughts become sharper. . . . Buri roams around Haldigram. She feels a new surge of energy in the calm, eternal flow of activity in the village. The people who used to endure without speaking up and whose heads used to hang low, talk in a different tone now. The shape of their jaws appears different.
>
> (Hossain 53)[1]

Her small circumscribed existence in her mind explodes into a restlessness that reflects the changes that occur in the village and the country. The sense of a political doom further intensifies when Jalil returns from Dhaka after losing his family in the conflict. Watching the lean, hungry village boys play, Buri wishes that her son Raees was physically able so she could send him to war along with those boys: 'Buri's heart felt heavy when she thought of her disabled son, along with these restless strong boys. No, he won't be useful. He can't be employed for anything. In the wave of new possibilities in Haldigram, Raees remains useless' (Hossain 55). At the end, Buri sacrifices her son in order to save two freedom fighters, Kader and Hafiz, from the Pakistani army. In delineating women's role during the Bangladesh Liberation War, Hossain's novel presents Buri as a militant woman, who, despite being confined to the domestic space, takes part in the war through the sacrifice of her son. Women's active militant participation in the war, as Nayanika Mookherjee writes, has been mostly silenced in the national discourse after being deified as *birangonas* or war heroines in post-war Bangladesh, which metaphorically represent them as a defilement of the idealized mother figure ("Gendered Embodiments"). Recent ethnographic and literary studies about survivor women (Mookherjee 2015; Harrington 2013; Saikia 2011) indicate a more complex story of their role both in the domestic sphere and at the war front fighting alongside their male counterparts. As Nahid Khan writes, Hossain's effort as a writer has been to rescue women from the stereotype of a victim and to represent them as heroic figures actively involved in the war alongside their male counterparts ('The writer, the warrior'). Hossain's representation of a heroic yet heartless mother destabilizes the distinction between the domestic and the public, between the housewife and the male guerilla. As Hossain says in an interview: 'In terms of emancipation – in this instance, anticolonial liberation war – the female figure by no means remains passive, but rather active on more levels than men can afford to imagine' (qtd. in

Fallwell 140). However, Buri's role as a militant woman still limits her within 'the image of the nurturing and sacrificing woman, as mother, wife or nurse that is authorized by the discourse of Muktijuddho' (Mookherjee 45), part of a popular conflation of nature, mother, and nation in Bangladesh.

Shaheen Akhtar's *Talaash*

Contrary to Selina Hossain's narration of an ideologically suffused nationalistic tale of sacrifice, Shaheen Akhtar's novel *Talaash* revisits the archive of the Bangladesh Liberation War to foreground the plight of *birangonas* or the war heroines in a way that 'gives them a voice they were always denied; it gives them a power that enables them to view and judge the War and the society as a whole' (Munim, "As the dead awakened"). Like Hossain's novel, *Talaash* is imbued with a documentary impulse, narrated by a reluctant researcher on the Bangladesh Liberation War, symbolically named Mukti (freedom), born on the day after the Operation Searchlight in 1971. Akhtar had earlier written *Ferdousi Priyobhashini: Ekok Nari* (2001) recounting the sexual violation of Priyabhashini by the Pakistani army men and collaborators. In the 1990s, Priyabhashini was the first woman to publically speak out against the rape and violation of women during the war. Her unapologetic public recounting followed in the context of Jahanara Imam-led Gono Adalat (Public Court) in March 1992 for the mock trial of Pakistani army and their non-Bengali and Bengali collaborators during 1971. Imam's role in mobilizing the younger generation made her 'the embodiment of motherhood in the national discourse' (Mookherjee 46). Following this mock trial and the publication of a photo in major Bangladeshi newspapers of three women raped during the war, *birangoans* returned to national consciousness after almost three decades. Akhtar's complex narrative technique adopts the form of an ethnographic research project on *birangoans* in which Mukti interviews Mariam, alias Mary, the protagonist, who in turn connects her own story to those of other women who are kept captive by the Pakistani army in camps. Chaity Das writes,

> In the manner of most researchers [Mukti] is compelled by her need to construct an account of the past that does not leak, an account that shall reinstate the 'birangona' at the core of the war, coax the inheritors of the legacy of independent Bangladesh into recognizing *how it is that freedom was achieved* and at what cost the war was fought and won (emphasis original).
>
> (218)

Mariam's account of her life during and after the war, narrated in a non-linear fashion as that of a survivor, of a *birangona*, counters 'the prevalent stereotype that all *birangonas* are ashamed and invisible as a result of their rape' (Mookherjee, 'Lessons').

At the very outset of *Talaash*, Akhtar's narration anticipates the fate of women such as Mariam who dare to transgress patriarchal social norms even in times of peace. Mariam and her brother Mantu's journey at night along Sundari's Lake on their way back from Dhaka is presented as a metaphor for women's helplessness since Sundari was forced to take her own life by drowning because of pregnancy outside wedlock. This foreshadows Mariam's own life as she is first banished to Dhaka from her village for spending three days with a boy, Jaseem, on the road. Akhtar writes, 'Not only during war, even during times of peace, a woman's life is a four-wheeled car in which the body is the driver. If she deviates a bit from the concrete path of rules, the car crashes into a garbage-filled ditch. Her life comes to an end. The woman becomes fallen' (Akhtar 7). Mariam is impregnated by a student leader Abed at the University of Dhaka and abandoned when the Pakistan army attacks Dhaka on 25 March. Abed's pre-marital physical relation with Mariam is coded as an anxiety over failed masculinity, which tries to gain control over a woman's body because it is difficult to wrest the nation-space from West Pakistani control – a woman's body fulfils his desire for territorial occupation. While Abed's political ideal for an emergent Bangladesh is premised on bravery and masculinity, he refuses to take responsibility for his unborn child. In Mariam's dilemma about her unborn baby, the novel intertwines the personal with the political. As in *Hangor Nodi Grenade*, the unborn child in *Talaash* functions as a metaphor for the nation and an attempt to conflate the feminine concern for motherhood with the larger concern for the birth of the nation. On the night Dhaka is occupied by the Pakistani army, Mariam induces a miscarriage by consuming a handful of sleeping pills, thereby merging personal tragedy with the national, anticipating that the birth of the nation would be futile like that of her child: 'The flow of blood crosses the drain and the gate, flooding the road, reaching the Paltan ground. Abed walks up to the stage. The audience claps. Mary gives birth to her baby. Faceless blob of blood, fatherless' (Akhtar 26). Once the war breaks out, Mariam returns to her village and is subsequently abducted by the collaborators who hand her over to the Pakistani army. In the camps, she meets other women from diverse social classes, both Muslim and Hindu, who are pressed into the service of providing sexual pleasure to army men and their collaborators. The rape of these women becomes a tool of humiliation, a way of violating the sanctity of women's body and patriarchal honour, as Mukti contemplates during her research: '[Women's sexual] organ becomes insecure during the war. The enemy's male organ penetrates it. The semen reaches the egg. The embryo starts growing soon. Despite initiating abortion through a special ordinance, the sanctity of a woman's body could never be recovered' (Akhtar 47).

On 23 December 1971, A. H. M. Kamruzzaman announced that all women raped during the war would be addressed as *birangonas* or war heroines, in an attempt to rehabilitate them in society with honour. Sheikh Mujib tells Mariam and other women at the rehabilitation centre: 'You are my mother. You are Birangonas' (Akhtar 215). In 1972, the independent Bangladesh government announced mass abortion of women like Mariam impregnated by enemy army during the war. The title of *birangona* evokes momentary interest among men who agree to marry these women as part of the national rehabilitation project. As the initial enthusiasm turns into contempt and shame, something that Mariam's incarcerated companion Anuradha anticipates in the Pakistani army camp – 'After victory is won in the war, men are hailed as heroes, while women are termed as sinful. They will turn us into prostitutes – you see!' (Akhtar 104) – the violated women take on the task of relocating themselves as the society and country fail them. As many of the so-called male freedom fighters, including Abed, enjoy the fruits of independence in the form of lucrative government contracts and posts, these women take to the streets in an effort to acquaint themselves with newly empowered men who frequent sex-workers. Mariam marries one such man, Mumtaz, who treats her like a prostitute and humiliates her with her past sexual violation, plunging women like her to destitution. Drawing on the three-decade-long silence and contemporary inter-est in *birangonas*,[2] Akhtar's novel recuperates their agency as unattached women, working either in urban offices or in brothels, divested of the ambiguous honour bestowed on them. As Mariam tells Mukti, 'The title of the Birangona felt like a poisonous insect or a contagious disease' (Akhtar 145). By fictionally reminiscing the traumatic memory of a gendered war, Akhtar creates a community of women who pull away from a masculine notion of nationalism and imagines the possibil-ity of a resilient sisterhood, unshackled by 'notions of respectability, embodied and circumscribed in domesticity' (Mookherjee 46). While Das reads the novel as one that 'replaces the predominant motif of sacrifice in post-war fiction with what it means to have experienced victimhood in its depths' (225), I shall argue that Akhtar complicates the binary of heroism and victimhood in emphasizing agency in post-war ordinary life. The narrative technique of ethnographic research coded within a fictional text destabilizes the boundary between fact and fiction, lending the novel a literary quality that rejects popular appeal to nationalistic sentiments.

Between the popular and the literary

The founding moment of the Bangladesh Liberation War has moved into the pop-ular domain with a renewed demand for the trial of war criminals, initiated with a mock trial by writer and activist Jahanara Imam in 1992. As Naeem Mohaiemen argues in the case of initial Western media interest in the Bangladesh Liberation War in 1971, the 24/7 TV cycle has also significantly contributed to an understanding of women's plight during the Liberation War in contemporary Bangladesh ('Accel-erated Media'). While the initial representation of the Liberation War is drawn as a masculine effort, the renewal of interest has been essentially centred on the 'woman question,' the violation and subsequent erasure of women from the narrative of the war. As we have seen in our analysis of two women's narratives, '1971 Novels' oper-ate within a changed discursive field, from celebration to reminiscence: Hossain's fiction is premised on heroic action, whereas Akhtar's novel excavates a shame-ful chapter of forgetting. In this, the novels seem to foreground memory of the war contingent on temporality at certain critical junctures of the nation's history, corroborating Bina D'Costa's claim, 'each generation is influenced by social and political changes that cause the reshaping of a shared historical discourse' (160). In this context, it is pertinent to remember Christopher Coker's argument that 'war novels' tend to be less ideological unlike history because of their focus on existential reality instead of a wider meaning:

> The historian judges a soldier's death allegorically, as the expression of patriotism, perhaps, or belief in a cause. The novelist will judge it in existential terms, as something unique to the character concerned. His task is not necessarily to make sense of the event, but to make sense of the experience, including for some, its apparent 'senselessness.'
>
> (6)

This seemingly easy distinction gets blurred in the case of '1971 Novels' as the early novels tend to be overtly ideological in the way they emphasize on courage and valour. The later novels like those of Akhtar's tend to be more focused on the existential reality, premised on the question of self-exploration in the way the masculine war erases women's sufferings and agency during the war. Such a distinction between Hossain and Akhtar's novels is also primarily about the difference between popular and literary representation of the Liberation War in fiction.

In 'war fiction,' the difference between the literary and the popular is not so much about the plot and the writing, as Milan Kundera notes, as it is about characterization, an exploration of the complexity of an 'existential code' (29). In a grim situation like war, the broad sweeping canvas provides the characters with the scope of figuring themselves out, going on an unexplored journey. Buri in Hossain's novel turns out to be a brave mother who sacrifices her son, while Mariam in Akhtar's novel is a survivor who finally discovers herself as a woman unfettered by traditional gender roles. The genre of '1971 novels' accounts for these two opposing poles of human experience during the war – the victorious celebratory womanhood and the exploratory reflective interiority which takes a critical look at the triumphal narratives. We could call those '1971 novels' popular which operate at the surface level, offering a visceral, sensational experience of the war and provide an ideological perspective by explicitly taking a stance. In contrast, the literary '1971 novels' eschew an overt political-ideological stance in favour of mundane existential code, embedded in the larger ethos of conflict. However, both the popular and the literary novels draw on tropes of heroism, cowardice, villainy, a well-marked enemy, the collaborators, and a utopic future, which is underpinned by a national imaginary of promise and resolution. In this, the elements of plot and storyline have a tendency to cater to popular sentiment, given to the work of mobilization of popular feeling at different historical moments, either to win the war or to demand a trial of the war criminals. This appeal to an explicit popular-national sentiment makes characterization contingent on the demands of the market, rendering both the popular and the literary form of '1971 novels' a site of mass resistance and disillusionment.

In her collection of essays, *Prisons We Choose to Live Inside*, Doris Lessing writes, 'People who have lived through a war know that as it approaches, an at first secret, unacknowledged elation begins, as if an almost inaudible drum is beating . . . an awful, illicit, violent excitement is abroad. Then the elation becomes too strong to be ignored or overlooked: then everyone is possessed by it' (910). '1971 Novels' as a genre is permeated with a secret unacknowledged elation too, cutting across the literary and the popular divide, as Lynn Hanley writes in the context of western war writing, 'both our popular and our highbrow representations of war sizzle with these keyed up emotions' (5). Fiction documenting the Bangladesh Liberation War, much like war writing in the West, privileges men's experience at the war front and as policy makers, leaving out women's experience either at home or as survivors of the war. Hossain and Akhtar's fiction seek to plug this gap, despite their contrasting approach: Hossain's novel depicts a sense of elation at the beginning of the war; Akhtar's novel distances itself from 'the patriarchal culture which inspires, fosters, and celebrates war' (Hanley 55), instead proposing a community of women, much like Virginia Woolf had envisaged in the *Three Guineas* (Hanley 58).

Notes

1 All translations from Selina Hossain and Shaheen Akhtar's Bengali novels are mine, unless otherwise mentioned.
2 Bina D'Costa offers three reasons for the possible silence surrounding *birangonas* after the war. First, the immediate focus of the independent Bangladesh government was integration of these women into society, because of which rape as a sexual crime received no significant attention. Second, the post-war diplomacy between India, Pakistan, and Bangladesh compromised the trial of war criminals and their collaborators. Third, the gradual rehabilitation of Bengali collaborators into Bangladesh politics both at the local and state level. See *Women and Genocide: Survivors, Victims, Perpetrators* (2018), p. 171. Nayanika Mookherjee posits that silencing of raped women results from a gendered construction of nationhood and the significance of class aesthetics, 'both of which limit the spaces available for "rescuing" the birangonas' (40).

Works cited

Akhtar, Shaheen. *Talaash. 2004.* Mowla Brothers, 2008.
Chattopadhyay, Bodhisattva, et al. *Indian Genre Fiction: Pasts and Future Histories.* Routledge, 2019.
Coker, Christopher. *Men at War: What Fiction Tells Us about Conflict, from the Illiad to Catch-22.* Oxford UP, 2014.
Das, Chaity. *In the Land of Buried Tongues: Testimonies and Literary Narratives of the War of Liberation of Bangladesh.* Oxford UP, 2017.
D'costa, Bina. "*Birangona*: Rape Survivors Bearing Witness in War and Peace in Bangladesh." *Women and Genocide: Survivors, Victims, Perpetrators*, edited by Elissa Bemporad and Joyce W. Warren, Indiana UP, 2018, pp. 159–90.
Fallwell, Lynne. "Bangladesh: The Forgotten Genocide." *The History of Genocide in Cinema: Atrocities on Screen*, edited by Jonathan C. Friedman and William L. Hewitt, I. B. Tauris, 2017, pp. 130–42.
Hanley, Lynn. *Writing War: Fiction, Gender, and Memory.* U of Massachusetts P, 1991.
Harrington, Louise. "Women and Resistance in West Bengal and Bangladesh: 1967–71." *The Journal of Postcolonial Cultures and Societies*, vol. 4, no. 2, 2013, pp. 47–79.

Hossain, Selina. *Hangor Nodi Grenade. 2003.* Ananya, 2010.

Khan, Nahid. "The Writer, the Warrior." *The Daily Observer,* 8 Mar. 2015, www.observerbd.com/2015/03/08/76597.php. Accessed 18 Aug. 2019.

Kundera, Milan. *The Art of the Novel.* Translated by Linda Asher. Grove Press, Inc. 1988.

Lessing, Doris. *Prisons We Choose to Live Inside.* Cornelia and Michael Bessie Books, 1987.

Mason, Anita. "Genre Fiction Radiates from a Literary Center." *The Guardian,* 22 Apr. 2014, www.theguardian.com/books/booksblog/2014/apr/22/genre-fiction-literary-centre-anita-mason. Accessed 10 Aug. 2019.

Mohaiemen, Naeem. "Accelerated Media and the 1971 Civil War in Bangladesh." *Economic and Political Weekly,* vol. 43, no. 4, 26 Jan.–1 Feb. 2008, pp. 36–40.

Mookherjee, Nayanika. "Gendered Embodiments: Mapping the Body-Politic of the Raped Woman and the Nation in Bangladesh." *Feminist Review,* vol. 88 (War) 2008, pp. 36–53.

———. "Lessons of Consent and Critique from Ferdousi Priyabhashini." *The Daily Star,* 15 Mar. 2018, www.thedailystar.net/opinion/tribute/lessons-consent-and-critique-ferdousi-priyabhashini-1548142. Accessed 25 Aug. 2019.

———. *The Spectral Wound: Sexual Violence, Public Memories, and the Bangladesh War of 1971.* Duke UP, 2015.

Munim, Rifat. "As the Dead Awakened." *Dhaka Tribune,* 2 Mar. 2017, www.dhakatribune.com/magazine/arts-letters/2017/03/02/as-the-dead-awakened. Accessed 25 Aug. 2019.

Rothman, Joshua. "A Better Way to Think about the Genre Debate." *The New Yorker,* 6 Nov. 2014, www.newyorker.com/books/joshua-rothman/better-way-think-genre-debate. Accessed 10 July 2019.

Saikia, Yasmin. *Women, War, and the Making of Bangladesh: Remembering 1971.* Duke UP, 2011.

Waheed, Karim. "The Art of Recreating the Past: In Conversation with Selina Hossain." *The Daily Star,* 26 Mar. 2009, www.thedailystar.net/news-detail-81322. Accessed 12 July 2019.

9

SUNLIGHT ON A BROKEN COLUMN AND *THE HEART DIVIDED* AS AUTOBIOGRAPHICALLY INSPIRED REALIST TEXTS

Navigating gendered socio-political identities in genre fiction

Mobeen Hussain

> Every first novel or any novel will have to be part of oneself and people one knows, but it is not the people and it is not actually the events but it is at the same time.
>
> – Attia Hossain[1]

Introduction

While autobiographical writings by Indian Muslim women during the late colonial period are rare,[2] two novels by Indian Muslim women narrate this era: *Sunlight on a Broken Column* (1961) by Attia Hosain and *The Heart Divided* (1957) by Mumtaz Shah Nawaz. Autobiographical narratives by non–Muslim Indian women have also received little attention – a recent book titled *Speaking of the Self: Gender, Performance, and Autobiography in South Asia* (2015) has addressed this lacuna by reconfiguring the definitions of 'autobiography' and 'life writing' to include other types of writing, ranging from periodical literature and devotional tracts to fiction.[3] Both novels fit within this wider framework of writing the self (Malhotra and Lambert-Hurley). Jasbir Jain insists that it would be unfair to Hosain to treat her novel's protagonist as her "alter ego" ('Attia Hosain' 95), and Mulk Raj Anand has attempted to retrieve her novel from autobiographical account by situating it within the post-modernist genre, like the works of Virginia Woolf and James Joyce (Burton, *Dwelling in the Archive* 117).[4] It is important not to conflate Hosain and Nawaz with their protagonists. However, I do not think that examining the ways in which they imbue their first and only novels with their own experiences is a fruitless endeavour. Born a year apart, in 1913 and 1912, respectively, Hosain and Nawaz came-of-age in the urban, modernising cities of Lucknow and Lahore and were educated in English and vernacular languages; their protagonists embody similar cosmopolitan trajectories.

DOI: 10.4324/9781003002062-12

By reading their English-language novels as belonging to two popular subcontinental fiction genres, partition fiction and the social realist novel, this chapter expands the parameters of genre fiction as a literary category to argue that both texts can be read as autobiographically inspired realist fiction. This symbiotic classification, rather than autobiographical novel, encompasses how both authors use their own lives as mirrors to illuminate parts of their societies – coalescing family ties with complex networks of kinship and dependency in the decades before and immediately after Partition. As such, these novels fit into the liminal space between autobiography, social critique and historical account.[5] As women from elite families, both authors reflect on changes in ancestral social power and deteriorating Muslim-Hindu relations; Nawaz's novel is more idealistic about a separate Muslim state than Hosain's work.[6] Both writers borrow from indigenous storytelling traditions, mining songs and poetry to inscribe rich detail about their gendered cultural worlds into English-language narratives, similar to writing practices of other Indian genre fiction writers (Chattopadhyay et al. 5–6). Nawaz, for instance, uses popular Punjabi folksongs in the depiction of wedding scenes (78–80). By writing in English, one can assume that the writers had their potential readers in mind, providing intimate accounts of Indian life to Western literary audiences. They employ a realist mode of writing, one that 'gives the impression of recording . . . a way of life' and close attention is given to 'details of physical setting and to the complexities of social life' (Baldick, 'Realism'). In doing so, both authors articulate expressions of Muslim and gendered selfhoods in their narratives; narratives which can be located within slippages between fixed literary genres and traditions (Chattopadhyay et al. 14). In repositioning the boundaries of popular genre fiction, this chapter takes a cue from Merja Makinen who argues that all popular genres, far from being conservative and parochial in form, are 'potentially transformable' (4). Popular genres are not static and are culturally transmuted. This chapter unpacks the emergence of partition fiction and social realist narratives in its analysis of *Sunlight on a Broken Column* and *The Heart Divided* to show how both genre forms find expression within these autobiographically inspired realist texts.

Astonishingly, *Sunlight on a Broken Column* (henceforth *Sunlight*) and *The Heart Divided* (henceforth *Heart*) have rarely been considered together, yet there are many similarities between the two. Both depict the cities the authors grew up in: Lahore for Nawaz and Lucknow for Hosain. These North Indian cities had large Muslim populations – the latter a city in decline and the former on the move but to be torn apart by Partition.[7] Their narratives include female protagonists who negotiate their identities as young female, colonial, Muslim subjects within varying temporalities and modernities, in both public and private spaces and through conflicting notions of how to be 'modern.' By employing self-representation as a literary tool, both novels depict the lives of *sharif* (respectable), elite, educated Muslim women in various ways. I consider the parallels between the authors and their works by comparatively exploring their narratives through two veins: first, gendered navigations in the making of identities amongst elite upper-class women and second, Pakistan as an idea within Muslim experiences of Partition. Within gendered navigations,

I will consider how three themes pervade the texts: the negotiation of *purdah* (the practice of sartorial and spatial segregation), education and mobility in political life, and negotiations of the marriage framework.

Within colonial, post-colonial, and literary studies, Hosain's *Sunlight* has received more attention than any other Indian Muslim female-authored book. The theme of *purdah* and its mental and physical restrictions have been examined in relation to patriarchal norms in pre-colonial and colonial India, often alongside Zeenuth Fatuhally's *Zohra* (1951) and Ahmad Ali's *Twilight in Delhi* (1940) (Jain and Amin). Others have focused on the descriptions of domestic interiors and architecture and conceived of *Ashiana*, the ancestral home in *Sunlight*, as a metaphor for nation and Indian womanhood (Burton 'Life Histories'; Jain 'Attia Hosain'; Kabir). It has discretely been categorized as 'partition novel,' 'resistance narrative,' and 'domestic fiction.'[8] Elizabeth Jackson has situated the writings of Indian Muslim women, including Hosain's *Sunlight* and Fatuhally's *Zohra*, into the genre of Anglophone social realism in the way they write about their domestic worlds (Jackson "Muslim Indian women writing" 5).

Heart, in comparison, has been largely absent from academic scholarship because its publication has been limited to the subcontinent. It is mentioned in a number of articles on Partition (Chakravarti), the representation of Pakistan and nationalist consciousness (Willmer; Saeed), and briefly within scholarship on memories of Partition (Saint; Zaman), but has been largely ignored within literary criticism. *Sunlight* has often been hailed as the first early novel on Partition by Muslim woman. However, *Heart* fits this categorization more accurately through its discussion of cross-party politics and the conception of Pakistan as an ideal. There has been considerable debate amongst critics about the designation of these texts as 'partition novels' as Hossain's novel jumps from the 1930s to 1952 and Nawaz's novel ends in 1942. Jill Didur notes that *Sunlight* 'investigates the way memory shapes, translates, and unsettles received notions about the past' and Uma Chakravarti has discussed how *Heart* enriches the parameters of the written memory of the Partition by women (Didur 100; Chakravarti 138). Such discussions foreground Partition as a much longer, enduring event. Thus, even as *Sunlight* and *Heart* do fit into the partition narrative framework, have these narratives ever been read as popular genre fiction? Rituparna Roy argues that Partition continues to serve as a compelling literary theme, engendering a substantially diverse body of fiction (13). Literary critics have also noted that early post-Partition Urdu literature in Pakistan was dominated by the single theme of Partition (Hasan 108). Partition narratives, then, have been a compelling theme for writers since the 1950s and join the annals of works that enjoy popular readerships.

The texts

Sunlight on a Broken Column tells the story of young upper-class Muslim woman, Laila, who relates her coming of age in a *taluqdari* (landowning) family in Lucknow. The novel is split into four parts; the first part intimately describes customs in the family's mansion *Ashiana* (40–41). It ends with the funeral of her paternal grandfather, Baba Jan. For Laila, the death of a patriarch sets in motion a transition from relative *purdah* to a more varied society. She lives with her uncle Hamid, who is described as 'more a Sahib than the English' (22). The second part plunges the reader into a sequence of events that leave *taluqdari* society in flux, including provincial elections and land reforms. Laila's personal struggles against colonialism and tradition become indistinguishable from the wider struggle for independence (Kabir 185). The third part ends in 1938 when the romance between Laila and Ameer, a poor friend of her cousin, becomes known to the family. The last section skips forward to 1952 and follows a widowed Laila as she visits *Ashiana* and reflects on the past 14 years; this part mirrors Hosain's own ambivalence towards Partition.

The Heart Divided was written between 1943 and 1948 and published posthumously, with limited editing, in 1957 (Nawaz 1957 Preface).[9] As such, the language is contrived at times and does leave readers wondering what the final version would have looked like. However, its form adds authenticity to the narrative as an immediate socio-political reflection.[10] The novel starts in 1930 and describes the friendship between the Muslim Jamaluddin family with the Kaul family, a Hindu Brahmin household, which becomes strained by personal and political developments (18). It follows the Muslim family closely, especially the siblings Habib, Zohra, and Sughra, as they navigate public life. The first part grounds a reader in Muslim North Indian culture through detailing Sughra's wedding to a cousin. Tensions are established early on through a fateful Muslim-Hindu romance between Habib and Mohini of the Kaul family. Part one culminates in Zohra out of *purdah*, Sughra's pregnancy, and Mohini dying. Part two starts amidst election fever in 1936, and, like *Sunlight*, political developments are interspersed throughout the text. This part follows the sisters' divergent paths from their natal home into various spheres of activity; Sughra becomes involved in social and political work through the Muslim League, whereas Zohra initially supports the Congress and pursues various personal and professional goals.

Both authors open their novels with retrospection: 'in later years Zohra often wondered when the change in her life began' (1) and 'the day my aunt Abida moved from the zenana into the guest-room . . . we knew Baba Jan had not much longer to live' (14). In anchoring their protagonists at the start, both novels follow the journeys of Zohra and Laila, although *Heart* has a wider narrative framework than *Sunlight* as events do occur without Zohra's presence. They also skilfully illustrate the interplay between traditions. Decorations of homes in Western and Eastern styles, either in separate male and female spaces or transformations of interiors, are often changes initiated by Westernising men. In *Heart*, Sheikh Jamaluddin's admirations for the West is transported into domestic interiors: 'his desire for a western way of life had been confined to furnishing a sitting-room and dining-room in the ladies' part as well as 'magnificent drawing room and dining room in the men's part of the house' (5). In *Ashiana*, Hamid's patriarchal rule of the home, after his father's death, represents a spatial transition from old to new through a literal stripping of tradition. For Laila, the drawing-room 'looked naked' and the rooms remind her of 'English homes I had visited . . . yet they were as different as copies of a painting from the original' (120–21). This mediation of emerging tastes by a generation growing up in 1930s and 1940s India is expressed as an 'abortion,' rather than a product, of two cultures in the novel (211). The 'abortion' between older traditions, often maintained by some elite families as markers of status, and conflicting 'modern' practices are intimately explored in both novels as layers of self-fashioning; layers which are familiar to audiences navigating the 'modern' within 20th- and 21st-century subcontinental lives.

Gendered navigations in the making of identities 'New Patriarchy' and the negotiation of purdah

Both *Sunlight* and *Heart* interrogate the functions of *purdah* as multi-layered, self-fashioning practices. The state of being 'in' *purdah* commonly refers to the *zenana*, a female space which separated elite Indian women from non-related males and certain women.[11] In *Sunlight*, Baba Jan is the harbinger of *purdah* (Palkar 109); both of his daughters, Aunt Majida and Aunt Abida, live in *purdah*. The space functions through a mobile, indispensable retinue of servants who bring news and safeguard the modesty of their mistresses. Nawaz's novel also includes servants as go-betweens in providing gossip for women (12). Women in/out of *purdah* signify status, custom, and one's political leanings, and it involves men policing the behaviour of women with help from older women as sustainers (Jackson, 'Muslim Indian women writing' 135). R. K. Kaul chides Hosain for having 'known better than to invest such an institution [harem] with an aura of romance' (34). This assessment is simplistic; Hosain critiques these institutions through the characters who inhibit cloistered feudal spaces. Laila's cousin, Zahra, dresses differently when married to an Indian Civil Service officer to suit his need for a modern wife: 'her blouse was tight across her breasts . . . no more loose, shapeless clothes, no more stooping and hunching of shoulders to conceal or deny one's body' (141). Here, she illustrates a clear binary in the sartorial practice of women as dictated by the demands of male figures. Nawaz, in contrast, illustrates a gradual shift away from the traditional aesthetics of *purdah* through sartorial choice. Zohra adopts a two-piece veil because of the comparisons her school friends made between different kinds of *burqahs* (long, loose garments covering the whole body); one is mocked as a 'shuttlecock' due to its 'single piece' design (8–9).

Critics have also noted that *purdah* goes beyond demarcations of space and dress; indeed, Hosain and Nawaz depict how mental barriers of *purdah* operate in the lives of men as well as women in contradictory modes of male domination as part of a 'new patriarchy.' New patriarchy emerged in the late 19th century as a preservation strategy to changes in public life propelled by British imperialism (Chatterjee 6). This articulation or mutation of patriarchy re-structured sources of authority from kinship networks and joint family systems to colonial models of conjugal relationships (Majumdar 161). For instance, Judith Walsh has shown how the spirituality of Bengali women was marked by their dress, eating habits, religiosity, and deference to husbands as opposed to older women in the family (52). Such markers of new patriarchy also emerged among elite Muslim groups and included educational reform (Minault 248). Aunt Majida of *Sunlight* states that Zahra 'has read the Quran, she knows her religious duties; she can sew and cook, and at the Muslim school she has learned a little English, which is what young men want now' (24). Here 'what young men want now' is crucial; the educated modern wife now needed to socialize in public life. Aunt Saria also states that 'young men want their wives to be educated enough to meet their friends and to entertain' (110). This remark is similar to Aunt Majida's summation but denotes different markers of 'modern' and 'educated.' In response, Uncle Hamid admonishes 'stop interrupting with your irrelevant remarks, Saira. I wasn't even thinking of marriage' (110). Hamid's remark indicates a liberal attitude, however; he simultaneously exercises authority in determining Laila's future (and that of his other dependents). All three characters subscribe to different kinds of modernities, proscribing different levels of training to young women in line with men wanting educated wives. Hosain's contribution in *Our Cause: A Symposium by Indian Women* (1938) and Mumtaz's mother's, Jahanara Shah Nawaz, autobiography also evoke these new desires of European-educated men from the late 19th century (Hosain, 'Seclusion of Women' 210; J. Nawaz 12).

Tensions within new patriarchy also involved deciding who decision-makers were: husbands, fathers, older women, or the younger female protagonists. In *Heart*, Sughra's father urges Mansur, Sughra's husband, that allowing her out of *purdah* 'might do her a world of good,' and Mansur worries about his mother's reaction, indicating that although women were often patriarchal enablers, the wishes of husbands took precedent within the bounds of new patriarchy (323). Jahanara Nawaz, for instance, mentions how her mother's (Mumtaz's grandmother) transition from *purdah* into society was met with her father's initial disapproval and was countered by stating that it was her husband's wish (J. Nawaz 59). In this way, *purdah* became an extension of male spousal expectation. As Palkar notes, 'marriage, like the joint family, contributes to the perpetuation of purdah' (110). Uncle Hamid of *Sunlight* shows his dislike for the 'unreasonable demands' and 'unreasoning restrictions' of the joint family system (167). The emphasis on 'unreasonable' intonates his perception of Eastern familial traditions as backward yet he continues to dictate patriarchal expectations.[12] Laila narrates how 'Aunt Saira was Uncle Hamid's echo' and that 'he had her groomed by a succession of English 'lady-companions.' Before she was married, she had lived strictly in purdah, in an orthodox, middle-class household. Sometimes her smart saris, discreet make-up, waved hair, cigarette-holder and high-heeled shoes seemed to me like fancy dress' (87). Saira has adapted to the demands of modern social spaces. Similarly, Zahra transforms to play the 'part of the perfect modern wife as she had once played the dutiful purdah girl' (140). She has not 'changed within herself' but changed 'her appearance, speech and mannerisms' with a 'Western gloss' and was 'all her husband wished her to be' (140). Saira and Zahra engage in exercises of self-fashioning by exchanging one mask for another; their masks are invisible sartorial and behavioural markers of *purdah* and, as Didur puts it, exchange 'one set of patriarchal expectations for another' (Didur 115). They move in circles proscribed by their husbands and their patterns of life compliment their husbands including involvement in women's organizations (123).

Nawaz and Hosain, like other women of their social milieu, critiqued *purdah* as an unhealthy practice for the body and mind. The *zenana* had been 'patholo-gised as unsanitary' in twentieth-century medical discourse (Chaudhuri 87).[13] In *Heart*, Nawaz's disapproval of physical *purdah* is demonstrated through Sughra who admonishes the lack of exercise perpetuated by it (371). They also show how *pur-dah* continued to be bound up with notions of class and status despite much tex-tual production which attempted to re-evaluate its usefulness in society.[14] A *purdah* lady in *Heart* remarks that ladies out of *purdah* in Delhi 'don't come from the old families' (368) in which *purdah* is maintained as a feudal status symbol. Whereas, in *Sunlight*, Abida and Majida 'no longer observed purdah' from Mushtari Bai, an old courtesan who has renounced her profession (66); this exception to convention, as indicated by the female servants who shun her, indicate contradictions within the practice (Amin 123).

Alongside critiquing the internal contradictions of *purdah*, Nawaz and Hosain also depict how navigating *purdah* was a gradual negotiation of self-fashioning and value reconfiguration for young women like their protagonists. There is a transi-tion in patriarchal control, from Baba Jan to Hamid in *Sunlight* and from Zohra's paternal grandfather to Jamaluddin in *Heart*, who are more compliant to changing customs. When Laila's cousins return from England her life changes: 'It has been restricted by invisible barrier almost as effectively as the physically restricted lives of my aunts in the *zenana*. A window had opened here, a door there, a curtain had been drawn aside; but outside lay a world narrowed by one's field of vision' (173). Curtains, doors, and windows denote restricted barriers but also lead towards new modes of being, such as opening up unsegregated social spaces. *Purdah* moves beyond the tangible to re-articulations of spaces from strictly segregated social 'invisible barrier[s]' to a more mixed society. This depiction of negotiating *purdah* as a *process* also reflects on the complexities of individual notions of respectability. Jahanara Nawaz asserts that hers 'was a liberal family' who did not observe *purdah* from the family circle (12). Similarly, Attia Hosain reflected that although she and her sisters 'were not in pardha in the sense that we were wearing burqas when we went out . . . we had a confined kind of a life' ('Harappa interview'). Her own journey from a limited social space to attending college and the All-Indian Wom-en's Conference is translated into the novel through Laila's expanding social circle.

In Nawaz's novel, Zohra's first navigation of *purdah* is depicted within the first few chapters. She forgets to 'put on the cape of her burqah' when shopping and concedes that it would be 'great fun going along the Mall in tonga with no cum-bersome veil to hamper her' (7–9). Zohra interprets her father's words of 'it doesn't really matter, since no one recognized you' as 'tactic permission' (17). This focus on recognition shows how, for many, the restrictions of *purdah* were circumstantial.[15] Zohra's gradual navigation of *purdah* is depicted throughout the novel; she goes shopping, visits the cinema, entertains with her father (180), and eventually moves to a new city to work (409). One cyclical example epitomises this journey; she is permitted to participate in a mixed inter-college debate (241) after being prohibited from doing so when her grandfather was alive earlier in the novel (73). Nawaz seems to have been inspired by the navigations of *purdah* in her own family, many of whom were part of Muslim women organizations (J. Nawaz 33). Mumtaz herself navigated a gendered discourse of respectability in undertaking higher education and political work.

Nawaz also portrays *purdah* in more nuanced ways. The story of Zohra's friend Najma's forced marriage to an older man is a cautionary tale. Her husband takes 'her to Europe' and 'she came out of purdah and met lots of people' but is subjected to domestic abuse (258–59). Nawaz's examples sermonize how moving out of *purdah* did not solve other problems women faced. Unlike Hosain, who primarily focuses on segregation, Nawaz also unpacks sartorial choices further. She shows how the *burqah* allows anonymity, which can function as strategy to mobility (Chakravarti 125). Wearing the *burqah* allows Zohra to contact and travel with a friend to help publish a letter on behalf of an arrested protestor: 'how it got to the press was a great mystery' (53). Antoinette Burton comments on this circumstantial fluidity in *Sunlight* when Uncle Hamid's *purdah* relatives are mobilized to cast votes for him in the elections (Burton, *Dwelling in the Archive* 119). Even Aunt Abida takes care of the estate under the secure confines of *purdah* (60). Indeed, reformers like Rokeya Shakawat Hussain believed that progress could be made without abandoning *purdah*.[16] This exploration of *purdah* as a nuanced practice within a framework of new patriarchal expectations resonates with historical and contemporary conversations, within various popular literary discourses, about women's access to public spaces.

Education and mobility in political life

Women also fashioned themselves outside patriarchal spaces through educational pursuits. Both novels show how obtaining an education, within institutions outside of the home, signified increased mobility. In the first part of *Sunlight*, Laila defends reading by stating that 'these books will be garlands of gold round my neck' (17). The symbolism of 'garlands of gold' taps into Indian fashions – jewellery was indicative of wealth and institutionalized within marriage. Here, Laila is also attempting to forge an alternative value system where knowledge is wealth.[17] In *Heart*, sisters Sughra and Zohra attend the Punjab college and Zohra is 'looking forward to becoming the first lady graduate in her family' (6). Both Laila and Zohra, in their respective narratives, pursue postgraduate education; Laila continues with 'uncle's indifferent consent and [her] aunt's passive disapproval' (225), and Zohra prepares for a master's degree (253). Nawaz and Hosain, amongst the first Muslim Indian women to graduate from university, exposit the education women receive through their protagonists. Zohra's higher education is shown to be an innovation, but the inequalities between the education Muslim men and women receive are highlighted; Zohra becomes 'prominent in the social life of her town' but is envious of her Hindu friend Rajinder, who has studied at Oxford (253). There was much debate, even within families, about the nature of women's education (Jackson, 'Gender and social class in India' 127). This debate is portrayed in both novels; in *Sunlight*, Zohra is taught enough to become an attractive marriageable prospect, and Zohra's cousins in *Heart* are educated within the home. *The Heart Divided*, however, goes further to debate the precise kind of education women should receive. Sughra debates with a *purdah* lady, who protests that girls are 'thoroughly spoilt in schools. They will never make good wives and mothers,' to which she replies, 'how wrong you are . . . educated women make better wives and mothers' (370). This conversation reflects the discourse on new patriarchy about the kind of education women should receive in order to fulfil their familial roles. Nawaz and Hosain engage in a realist social critique of women's education and mutable models of learning. Indeed, there was a whole host of reformist literature on education for Indian women; literature which would be familiar to the authors, their families, and within popular readership.[18]

Nawaz also directly borrows from the political achievements of her mother to illustrate how women could re-orient themselves to serve the nation. A 'well-beloved Jahan Ara,' a namesake for her mother, runs for member of the constitutional assembly in her novel (306). Nawaz utilizes facts from the immediate past to show female progression in political life; Habib states, 'times are changing. . . . Some Muslim ladies in other parts of India actually took part in the Civil Disobedience movement last year, and even from our own Province, a Muslim lady had gone to the Round Table Conference' (73). In *Sunlight*, Hosain also depicts the elections, political manoeuvring, and the precarious role of *talqudars* (landowners) in the government (225). However, in contrast to the sisters in *Heart*, Laila is more of a spectator in political conversations who occasionally critiques both Congress supporters and Muslim Leaguers. Hosain's observations, through a passive narrator, convey a historical account and exposit how women were still politically disadvantaged as colonial citizens. Alongside political involvement, both authors also show alternative paths to public activity: Sughra undertakes social work in middle-class homes during the Second World War (467), and Nadira, Laila's friend, becomes a social worker for refugees (304). Nawaz's own political activities included taking part in freedom marches and setting up a women's wing of the Muslim League in Delhi to encourage women's political mobilization and education. Her socialist involvement in welfare centres in Amritsar's factories also percolates into Zohra's involvement in factory strikes in *Heart* (Nawaz 1957 v).

Negotiations of the marriage framework

In deconstructing the transition between feudal norms and the codified behaviour of new patriarchy, Nawaz and Hosain explore marriage as an unequal social institution. Hosain succinctly portrays this in *Sunlight*: 'The cure for a good girl is to get her married quickly; the cure for a bad girl is to get her married quickly' (29). In *Heart*, Sughra has limited choices within her marital home, and her mother-in-law puts any unconventional behaviour down to 'these modern girls!' (118). However, both novels also indicate how the 1930s and 1940s were a 'period of transition' (332) for elite communities through their exploration of cross-generational changes in the selection of spouses. In the first part of *Sunlight*, Hosain presents the reader with an inter-generational debate about marriage. Aunt Abida insists that both nieces are present when discussing a marriage proposal for Zohra, much to the disapproval of an elder. She states, 'the girl cannot choose her husband,' but 'she can be present while we make the choice, hear our arguments, know our reasons, so that later on she will not doubt our capabilities' (21). Abida's bitter insistence that young girls should 'know our reasons' and 'hear our arguments' may reflect on her father's choices whose fastidious nature had left Abida unwed. The presence of Zohra is certainly portrayed as a departure from tradition. Yet, the notion of 'love' before marriage, especially if expressed by a young woman, was outrageous. Laila mentions love in defending a girl who had run away from home and describes how ' "love" was like a bomb thrown at' her aunt and her friends (134). Zohra's mother in *Heart* declares that 'girls of respectable families don't fall in love until after marriage' in response to Zohra's assertion, 'it's for me and the young man . . . to decide' and 'when I do marry, it shall be for love and I will choose my husband' (310–11). Her mother believes that the problems of making suitable matches have been 'created by this new education' (332). Laila and Zohra meet the disapproval of families in their choices of middle-class men. Zohra chooses Ahmad, whose father had been Jamaluddin's head clerk, propelling a debate on class and religion in which her siblings oppose their parents, insisting that such distinctions are rejected in Islam (490). The disapproval of Laila's choice mirrors Hosain's own choice; her mother vehemently disagreed with her choice to marry her cousin, Ali Bahadur Habibullah, in 1933 and this affected her dowry (Habibullah xii). All three cousins, Saleem, Kemal and Laila in *Sunlight* make their own choices and, Zohra and Habib of *Heart* make unconventional choices; Habib marries Najma, 'a divorcee' (418). Nawaz also disrupts the marriage framework by presenting paid work as a viable alternative for women. In the second part of the narrative, Zohra 'takes a salary' after her family 'give into her' (334–36) and then takes a job in Amritsar (409). Sughra defends Zohra's choice by claiming that 'lots of girls earn their living nowadays,' to which her mother responds, 'but Zohra does not need to' (410). Women working for money, as opposed to taking up voluntary work, was considered unrespectable for high caste and class women as it questioned the wealth and provision of their families. The narrative trajectory of Zohra's story closely mirrors that of Nawaz in her pursuit of higher education and financial independence. Nawaz also never married, and Zohra's consternations about marriage could indicate Nawaz's own anxieties about the institution.

Although written in English, *Sunlight* and *Heart* are indicative of a trend within Indian languages of exploring Partition through social critique. Mohammad Hasan argues that Urdu writers, from 1930s into the post-partition period, such as Qurratulain Hyder, Jilani Bano, and Iqbal Majeed, 'have all been haunted by this theme and have experienced the particular anguish of this trauma' (108). Social critique in Urdu, which attempts to understand and reconcile Partition and communalism, falls into what Hasan calls 'new forms of sensibility, which marks its identity and distinctiveness from contemporary literatures of other sister Indian languages' (111). In their critiques of expected conformity to new patriarchy, educational boundaries and the marriage framework, the work of Nawaz and Hosain can be situated alongside the realist fiction of Rashid Jahan and Ismat Chugtai, who scrutinized the multi-layered oppressions of cultural, religious, and patriarchal forces that women faced. Indeed, Hosain was heavily influenced by the *Anjuman Tarraqi Pasand Mussanafin-e-Hind* (Progressive Writers' Movement of India), who attempted to 'speak truth to power' in their focused socio–religious critique. This influence can be observed in her literary observations of class and gendered privilege within *Sunlight*, and more acutely in *Phoenix Fled*, a short story collection published in 1953.[19] Jackson has also argued that the writing of Muslim women in English, both colonial and contemporary, have not be considered in the same way as their non-Muslim counterparts like Nayantara Sahgal and Anita Desai because of the 'oppressed Muslim woman' narrative that endures when engaging with Muslim women's writings (Jackson, *Muslim Indian women writing* 157).

Essentially, by employing the social realist form, both authors take inspiration from their own lives and craft fictions that are autobiographically inspired realist fictions. Writing about their 'everyday,' this creative labour of women writers can illuminate historical narratives, not just about Partition but in the examination of Muslim women's lives as colonial and gendered subjects. Thus, this chapter argues for reading *Heart* and *Sunlight* as genre fiction; both novels are enjoyed within the corpus of historically immediate and realist narratives and a pre-partition gendered discourse. All three themes, new patriarchy and the negotiations of *purdah*, education and mobility, and the marriage framework, figure into notions of gendered citizenship, which look to self-fashioning quotidian practices and reconfiguring ways in which women would fit into nationalist conceptualizations of a state as equal citizens. As Niraja Jayal notes, 'a language of universal citizenship, and resentment at being treated as a "reservable" category . . . pervades the documents that emanated from women's organizations through the 1930s' (Jayal 190). As such, both Nawaz and Hosain contend with what Independence and a Pakistani nation would mean for women as gendered beings as well as Muslim persons.

Pakistan as an idea and Muslim experiences of partition

Attia Hosain has revealed how her editor Cecil Day Lewis cut lengthy sections on socio-political developments from her novel; she had countered 'that it is life,' to which Lewis replied, 'life is not art' (Hosain, *Distant Traveller* 6). In contrast, Nawaz's novel was published with relatively limited editing. Having an unedited version, written from 1943 and finished between 1947 to 1948, gives a unique insight into Nawaz's attitudes towards the Muslim League. There are long passages of dialogue between characters which map political debates, Hindu–Muslim tensions, and resistance against the British. Many conversations take the form of arguments or older family members informing young members about Indian history. A discussion about British rule and anti-colonial resistance in the Kaul household starts early on in the novel (18). Later, another occurs between Zohra and her father about the non-involvement of Muslims in civil disobedience activities after the rejection of Jinnah's Fourteen Points (41–46). Diviani Chaudhuri argues that historical discussions 'strains the form of the novel,' yet Tarun Saint maintains that the novel 'presents a lively and readable account of the way important debates in the sphere of high politics of the 1930s and 40s percolated into middle-class life at critical moments' (Chaudhuri 8; Saint 75). These speeches do disrupt the flow of the novel in places; however, they evince how elite Muslim families perceived unstable political developments. In the novel, Sughra has always been interested in Muslim history and starts leaning towards the Muslim League, resulting in disputes between Zohra and Sughra (341–344). Zohra finally decides to join the Muslim League wanting to 'work among Muslim women' (503). The parallels with Nawaz's own political trajectory are evident; she joined the Muslim League in 1942, and her mother depicts this as a great win for the cause (J. Nawaz 186). Alongside familial tensions, Nawaz also conveys assessments on the political climate; the Congress and the League are vying with 'one another in intolerance and prejudice' (436). Indeed, the novel was re-published in 1990 by a feminist publisher precisely because it could explain the recent history of Pakistan better than some contemporary textbooks (Chakravarti 124).

In *Sunlight*, Laila is an observer to socio-political changes rather than an active participant. Hosain depicts lively debates between her college friends, who all take *different* positions; Nita is active in anti-imperialist struggles (124), Nadira contends that 'Muslims had to defend their heritage,' (126) and Joan views herself as an Anglo-Indian but maintains that England is home (127). Hosain, through the perspective of Laila, depicts a subtler shift in political allegiances than Nawaz's direct confrontations; perhaps due to an editor's influence (one does wonder what a first draft looked like). Within *Ashiana*, familial tensions are ripe, no-one talked but 'everyone argued,' and 'a new type of person now frequented the house. Fanatic bearded men and young zealots' coming to speak to Saleem (230). Generational clashes routinely occur at the dinner table between old 'feudal attitude[s]' and separationist ideas (234). Similar to *Heart*, one can see political opinions forming through conversations: Congress has an 'anti-Muslim element' (Saleem), 'I always found it was possible for Hindus and Muslims to work together' (Uncle Hamid), and 'British rule is better than being ruled by Hindus' (Aunt Saira) (233–34).

Pakistan, a separate Muslim nation, is seen as imminent in Nawaz's novel: 'the great controversy began in India, the controversy that was to mould the destiny of the country' and 'the demand for Pakistan was voiced by a larger number of people' (435). Rituparna Roy argues that official histories of Pakistan subscribe to the narrative that the 'Pakistani nation was the inevitable crystallization of the desire of the Muslims of the Indian subcontinent to remain a distinctive community,', citing Aitzaz Ahsan's *The Indus Saga and the Making of Pakistan* (1996) as articulations of this theory (13–14). This two-nations theory is framed as 'inevitable' throughout the second part of *Heart*. Zohra muses that the name Pakistan 'was strange for her and did not arouse a deep tenderness like the word "India"' but finally comes to pursue an ideal of "peoples Pakistan' (496). A 'peoples' state suggests a kind of gendered citizenship within an egalitarian nation that encapsulates different identities and notions of belonging. David Willmer has examined how Pakistan is represented as a utopia within a narrative driven by a 'sense of telos'; one that views the attainment of Pakistan as a 'vehicle for resolving the contradictions of modernity' (416). Although *Heart* ends before Partition, we get a glimpse of these ideals as the novel ends with 'Towards Pakistan!', (506). Mohini's brother Vijay also foreshadows the violence of Partition (Zaman 85). There is no such musing on what a separate Muslim nation would mean in Hosain's articulation of Pakistan. Her allusions to it are understated, and Pakistan is not explicitly mentioned until Part Four of the novel. This part takes place in 1952 when Laila comes back to visit the neglected *Ashiana*. Hosain interweaves descriptions of the Second World War, Independence, and the ensuing migration of people and communal violence within a series of flashbacks. This part of the novel has been described as 'future-past' (Stewart in Burton, *Dwelling in the Archive* 129); as Laila moves through the house, she uses different rooms as intimate sites of change. She reflects on the changing skyline of 'hasty' urbanising Lucknow in the form of 'ugly buildings,' described as 'ill-digested modernity' (270). This 'future-past' tells the reader how Saleem left for Pakistan a few months after Partition and how Aunt Saira could not adjust to the loss of power and privilege: 'her eyes refused to see dust and decay' of her Lucknowi house and her pre-Partition world (275). This section is nostalgic, not for feudal society but for an unpartitioned, cosmopolitan India. The journey through *Ashiana* is simultaneously a tableau of intricate relationships and a memorialising metaphor of nation – a nation interminably altered by Partition but rooted in familial connections (Burton, *Dwelling in the Archive* 132; Jain, *Margins of Erasure* 181).[20]

Expressions of Pakistan as an idea within the authors' respective narratives hint at their own political feelings about Partition and Muslim-Hindu (dis)unity. Kashmir is ubiquitous in Nawaz's narrative, both the Kaul and Jamaluddin families travel to its hills for respite. During Partition riots, Nawaz worked to organize relief efforts for Kashmiri refugees (J. Nawaz 233). Her trip to New York in 1948, on which she met her untimely death, was scheduled so that she could be present for the Kashmir Question discussion at the UN Security Council Session (J. Nawaz 239). The primacy of Kashmir's loss pervades the text alongside other Islamicate locations, including Delhi and Agra. In *Sunlight*, Laila withdraws from society and buys a cottage for herself in the hills as 'a refuge from my loneliness' after the death of Ameer (316). Hosain herself decided to stay in England because, in her words, her mind 'could not accept the division of India,' and this choice allowed her to visit both India and Pakistan (Hosain, *Distant Traveller* 5). This contention of borders is depicted in the novel through a discussion about requiring visas to 'cross national frontiers' after brothers Kemal and Saleem make their respective decisions (287). Anuradha Needham notes that Laila neither 'derides nor diminishes those who make different choices because of their different beliefs and locations' (105). Indeed, Laila's visit to *Ashiana* in Part Four of *Sunlight* can be read as Hosain's own reconciliation with her decision to remain in England in defiance of the border-making of Partition. Hosain has confessed that 'subconsciously, to console myself for the maiming sense of loss of identity, I began to write' (Hosain, *Distant Traveller* 5). Her writing is a cathartic act of closure that mirrors Laila's visit to *Ashiana*; Hosain visits India through the act of writing to, and about, home. Her writing process reveals a similar trend amongst authors writing in Urdu, such as Saadat Hasan Manto. Kamran Ali locates Manto's writing within the 'contesting voices of uncertainty and confusion' in newly formed Pakistan (2). Essentially, Nawaz depicts a 'heart divided' whereas Hosain's world literally 'cracked apart' (277). These intimate articulations of identity and trauma by elite Muslim Indian women can certainly add to the voices of Partition in a similar way to Urvashi Batalia's *The Other Side of Silence* (2000) and other popular post-colonial fiction.

Conclusion

This chapter's interrogation of *Sunlight on a Broken Column* and *The Heart Divided* as autobiographically inspired realist fictions has shown how fictional writing can be used to supplement the archives on Partition and provide insights into processes of identity formation in South Asian history. Both narratives map how women contended with conflicting modernities. Readers can trace shifting notions of respectability and social mobility within the lives of women as new notions of citizenship, power, and belonging were being conceptualized within public and political discourse of the early to mid-20th century. On an individual level, their works reflect their lives as pioneers in education and their navigations of value systems, between being *sharif* and 'modern' and within Eastern and Western traditions. As popular genre fictions, the appeal of *Sunlight* and *Heart* lies in their relatable navigations of private and public spaces, both historically and contemporarily, especially for women. Therefore, the multi-layered designation of autobiographically inspired realist fiction, as a symbiotic category that includes rather than excludes texts, allows both novels to be situated within a wider conceptualization of popular genre fiction within South Asian literature. As Willmer notes, a text as rich in social and historical meaning as Nawaz's *The Heart Divided* is deserving of a plurality of readings (419). As a mainly unedited manuscript, it needs to be published and interrogated outside the subcontinent. Likewise, delving into a collection of new fiction, essays, and short stories by Attia Hosain titled *Distant Traveller* (2013), published by her children, would serve as a way of revisiting and re-assessing Hosain's literary oeuvre as a realist writer.[21] Indeed, a reading of Hosain's unfinished novel *No New Lands, No New Seas*, about lives of Indians in Britain, can help us think about displacement in *Sunlight on a Broken Column* and *Phoenix Fled* (Hosain, *Distant Traveller* 16–71). These inclusions enable South Asian Muslim women writers to occupy various spaces and embody mutable identities across the multiple temporalities of South Asian literature.

Notes

1 Harappa interview (1991). See bibliography.
2 Siobhan Lambert-Hurley, in a recent book titled *Elusive Lives: Gender, Autobiography, and the Self in Muslim South Asia* (2018), undertook the first in-depth survey of women's autobiographies of South Asian Muslim women in the subcontinent, but fictional writings and diaspora texts are beyond this scope the study.
3 Following on from analyses of life writing in Arnold and Blackburn's *Telling Lives in India: Biography, Autobiography, and Life History* (2004). See bibliography.
4 Antoinette Burton has also read Hosain's novel as autobiographical fiction. See Burton, Antoinette, "'An Assemblage/Before Me': Autobiography as Archive," *Journal of Women's History*, vol. 25, no. 2, 2013, pp. 185–88.
5 Judith Brown proposes that using life accounts as 'sources to probe the lives and concerns of individuals is a way of eavesdropping – listening to the intense debates that such people had within themselves and with each other over crucial issues' (Brown 589).
6 Hosain's parents, Nisar and Shahid Hosain Kidwai, were from feudal landholding families. Nawaz's parents, Mian and Jahanara Shah Nawaz, were politically active in Lahore.
7 There are a few comparisons including a doctoral thesis which compare domestic Islamicate interiors (Diviani) and an article examining Muslim feminist consciousness in fiction (S.). See bibliography.
8 Domestic fiction (Gopal), Partition (Mushiral Hussain in Burton, "Dwelling in the Archive"), and feudalism and colonialism (Kaul and Jain).
9 Nawaz tragically died at the age of 35 when her plane, bound for America, crashed over Ireland.
10 Nawaz had intended to write a sequel documenting 1942 to the Partition.
11 The *zenana* as an institution emerging from elite Mughal practices has been considered by Sarla Palkar (see Works cited).
12 Rochona Majumdar has examined this 'new conjugality' (Majumdar).
13 Cornelia Sorabji wrote about working with *purdahnashins* as a Lady Assistant to the Court of Wards.
14 Magazines include *The Indian Ladies Magazine* and *Roshni* journal.
15 Writer Rashid Jahan has recalled removing her *burqah* in spaces she would not be recognized (Jalil 26).
16 See *The Burkha* by Rokeya Sakhawat Hossain (2015).
17 The trope of jewellery is also critiqued as an extension of elite sensibilities in *Sunlight*: Nita, a Hindu friend of Laila, states, 'how typical of your class! You think a degree is a piece of jewellery, an additional adornment to be listed in your dowry' (125).
18 Prescriptive reform literature included Thanvi's *Bahishti Zewar* (1905). See bibliography.
19 The AIPW, which was later reorganised in Pakistan by Progressives (Ali 7).
20 *Ashiana* functions as a living, physical archive of Partition (Burton 135).
21 Hosain's daughter Shama Habibullah feels that 'Attia has come home' through the publication of *Distant Traveller* in India (Habibullah xxiv).

Work cited

Ahsan, Aitzaz. *The Indus Saga and the Making of Pakistan*. Oxford UP, 1996.
Ali, Kamran Asdar. "Progressives and 'Perverts': Partition Stories and Pakistan's Future." *Social Text*, vol. 29, no. 3, Sept. 2011, pp. 1–29.
All India Women's Conference. *Roshni: Journal of the All-India Women's Conference*. Central Office of All-India Women's Conference, 1940–1946.
Amin, Amina. "Tension Between Restriction and Freedom: The Purdah Motif in Attia Hosain's Sunlight on a Broken Column." *Margins of Erasure: Purdah in the Subcontinental Novel in English*, edited by Jasbir Jain and Amina Amin, Sterling Publishers, 1995, pp. 119–30.

Arnold, David, and Stuart Blackburn. *Telling Lives in India: Biography, Autobiography, and Life History*. Indiana UP, 2004.

Baldick, Chris. *Realism*. Oxford UP, 2008, www.oxfordreference.com/view/10.1093/acref/9780199208272.001.0001/acref-9780199208272-e-954. Accessed 25 July 2019.

Brown, Judith M. "'Life Histories' and the History of Modern South Asia." *The American Historical Review*, vol. 114, no. 3, 2009, pp. 587–95.

Burton, Antoinette M. "'An Assemblage/Before Me': Autobiography as Archive." *Journal of Women's History*, vol. 25, no. 2, June 2013, pp. 185–88.

———. *Dwelling in the Archive: Women Writing House, Home, and History in Late Colonial India*. Oxford UP, 2003.

Butalia, Urvashi. *The Other Side of Silence: Voices from the Partition*. Hurst and Co, 2000.

Chakravarti, Uma. "Betrayal, Anger, and Loss: Women Write the Partition in Pakistan." *Speaking of the Self: Gender, Performance, and Autobiography in South Asia*, edited by Anshu Malhotra and Siobhan Lambert-Hurley, Duke University Press, 2015.

Chatterjee, Partha. *The Nation and Its Fragments: Colonial and Postcolonial Histories*. Oxford UP, 1994.

Chattopadhyay, Bodhisattva, et al. "Introduction: Indian Genre Fiction – Languages, Literatures, Classifications." *Indian Genre Fiction: Pasts and Future Histories*, edited by Bodhisattva Chattopadhyay et al., Routledge India, 2018.

Chaudhuri, Diviani. *The House in South Asian Muslim Women's Early Anglophone Life- Writing and Novels*. Binghamton University-SUNY, 2016, https://orb.binghamton.edu/dissertation_and_theses/13/ Accessed 20 Aug. 2019.

Dey, Arunima. "The Domestic Sphere in Attia Hosain's Sunlight on a Broken Column (1961): The Home Mirrors the World." *The Grove- Working Papers on English Studies*, no. 23, Dec. 2016, revistaselectronicas.ujaen.es. DOI: 10.17561/grove.v23.a4.

Didur, Jill. *Unsettling Partition: Literature, Gender, Memory*. U of Toronto P, 2006.

Gopal, Priyamvada. *The Indian English Novel: Nation, History, and Narration*. Oxford UP, 2009.

Habibullah, Attia. "Seclusion of Women." *Our Cause: A Symposium by Indian Women*, edited by Şyama-Kumara Nehru, Kitabistan, 1937, pp. 205–211.

Hasan, Mohammad. "The Wounded Sensibility – Urdu Writing in the Post-Partition Era." *India International Centre Quarterly*, vol. 15, no. 1, 1988, pp. 107–11.

Hosain, Attia. *Distant Traveller: New & Selected Fiction*. Edited by Aamer Hussein and Shama Habibullah. Women Unlimited, 2013.

———. "Harappa Interview." 1991, http://old.harappa.com/attia/muslimleague.html. Accessed 18 July 2019.

———. *Phoenix Fled, and Other Stories*. Edited by Anita Desai. Virago, 1988.

———. *Sunlight on a Broken Column*. Virago, 1988.

Hossain, Rokeẏā. *Motichur: Sultana's Dream and Other Writings of Rokeya Sakhawat Hossain*, edited by Ratri Ray and Prantosh Bandyopadhyay. Oxford UP, 2015.

Jackson, Elizabeth. "Gender and Social Class in India: Muslim Perspectives in the Fiction of Attia Hosain and Shama Futehally." *The Journal of Commonwealth Literature*, vol. 53, no. 1, Mar. 2018, pp. 124–39.

———. *Muslim Indian Women Writing in English: Class Privilege, Gender Disadvantage, Minority Status*. Peter Lang, 2018.

Jain, Jasbir, and Amina Amin. *Margins of Erasure: Purdah in the Subcontinental Novel in English*. Sterling Publishers, 1995.

Jalil, Rakhshanda. *A Rebel and Her Cause: The Life and Work of Rashid Jahan*. Women Unlimited, 2014.

Jayal, Niraja Gopal. "A False Dichotomy? The Unresolved Tension between Universal and Differentiated Citizenship in India." *Oxford Development Studies*, vol. 39, no. 2, 2011, pp. 185–204.

Kabir, Ananya Jahanara. "Gender, Memory, Trauma: Women's Novels on the Partition of India." *Comparative Studies of South Asia, Africa and the Middle East*, vol. 25, no. 1, July 2005, pp. 177–90.

Kaul, R. K., and Jasbir Jain. *Attia Hosain: A Diptych Volume*. Rawat Publications, 2001.

Lambert-Hurley, Siobhan. *Elusive Lives: Gender, Autobiography, and the Self in Muslim South Asia*. Stanford UP, 2018.

———. "Life/History/Archive: Identifying Autobiographical Writing by Muslim Women in South Asia." *Journal of Women's History*, vol. 25, no. 2, June 2013, pp. 61–84.

Majumdar, Rochona. *Marriage and Modernity: Family Values in Colonial Bengal*. Duke UP, 2009.

Makinen, Merja. *Feminist Popular Fiction*. Palgrave Macmillan, 2001.

Malhotra, Anshu, and Siobhan Lambert-Hurley. *Speaking of the Self: Gender, Performance, and Autobiography in South Asia*. Duke UP, 2015.

Minault, Gail. *Secluded Scholars: Women's Education and Muslim Social Reform in Colonial India*. Oxford UP, 1999.

Nawaz, Jahan Ara Shah. *Father and Daughter: A Political Autobiography*. Nigarishat, 1971.

Nawaz, Mumtaz Shah. *The Heart Divided*. Mumtaz Publications, 1957.

———. *The Heart Divided*. 2nd ed. ASR Publications, 1990.

Needham, Anuradha Dingwaney. "Multiple Forms of (National) Belonging: Attia Hosain's Sunlight on a Broken Column." *MFS Modern Fiction Studies*, vol. 39, no. 1, 1993, pp. 93–111.

Palkar, Sarla. "Beyond Purdah: Sunlight on a Broken Column." *Margins of Erasure: Purdah in the Subcontinental Novel in English*, edited by Jasbir Jain and Amina Amin, Sterling Publishers, 1995, pp. 106–18.

Roy, Rituparna. *South Asian Partition Fiction in English: From Khushwant Singh to Amitav Ghosh*. Amsterdam UP, 2010.

S, Asha. "Muslim Feminist Consciousness in Indian English Fiction of the Nationalist Era." *The Criterion: An International Journal in English*, vol. 6, no. 4, 2015, pp. 1–10.

Saeed, Humaira. "Affecting Phantasm: The Genesis of Pakistan in The Heart Divided." *Journal of Postcolonial Writing*, vol. 50, no. 5, 2014, pp. 535–46.

Saint, Tarun K. *Witnessing Partition: Memory, History, Fiction*. Routledge, 2010.

Sathianathan, Kamala, editor. *The Indian Ladies Magazine*, 1901.

Sorabji, Cornelia. *Typescript of Report as Lady Assistant to the Court of Wards, Bengal. 1919–1920*. Indian Office Records, British Library, Mss Eur F165/133, 1920.

Thānvī, Ashraf 'Alī. *Bahishti Zewar or Heavenly Ornament*. Taj Company, 1983.

Walsh, Judith E. *Domesticity in Colonial India: What Women Learned When Men Gave Them Advice*. Oxford UP, 2004.

Willmer, David. "The Islamic State as Telos: Mumtaz Shah Nawaz's Narrative of Pakistan and Modernity." *The Indian Economic & Social History Review*, vol. 32, no. 4, Dec. 1995, pp. 413–27.

Zaman, Niaz. *A Divided Legacy: The Partition in Selected Novels of India, Pakistan, and Bangladesh*. Oxford UP, 1999.

SECTION III
Postcolonial genres

10

'OBEDIENT DAUGHTERS' AND THE DEPLOYMENT OF GRAPHIC STEREOTYPES

Christel R Devadawson

An exciting phase in the development of a genre occurs when it summons up its best-known critical commonplaces and positions them for scrutiny by the thoughtful reader. It is a strong temptation to discuss such images as tropes, along the lines of Visual Studies that conjure up the afrotope, a 'neologism referring to . . . recurrent visual forms that have emerged within and become central to the formation of African diasporic culture and identity' (Copeland and Thompson, n p). This chapter, however, does not wish to get ahead of its data-field by ascribing such a critical resonance to the images that it studies. It will retain the term 'graphic stereotypes' to place them within a context that is perhaps historic rather than poetical. Such a phase provides a valuable vantage point, not merely for an individual text but for the genre within which it domiciles itself. Author and reader alike can review received wisdom, scrub away the overlay of truism that might conceal important truths, and anticipate the possible evolution of the genre as fresh contexts reconfigure well-known themes. This chapter argues that Ayesha Tariq's 2015 graphic text *Sarah: The Suppressed Anger of the Pakistani Obedient Daughter* provides a pictorial documentation with precisely such a moment. The text casts troubling but important cross-lights on a range of concerns as it visualizes personal identity, familial relationship, and state-formation in contemporary Pakistan. This chapter focuses on conversations that develop around the genre, around the nation-state, and around the constituency – defined by age and gender – with which the text engages. It also tries to speculate on directions that these lines of inquiry might take in the future.

The title of Tariq's text ties together a set of operative phrases that outline the major critical issues with which it seeks to engage. To begin with, the single name 'Sarah' indicates possible continuities as well as discontinuities within the sub-genre of graphic memoir. It signals that this is going to be a narrative about a person other than the author, so that we cannot mindlessly blur distinctions between self-writing

DOI: 10.4324/9781003002062-14

and testimony. This nudge in turn leads the reader to think of the eponymous hero as a character within a precisely imagined context of her own, rather than as an alternative self for the author. The title goes on, however, to introduce two qualifying terms. The first is the subtitle, 'The suppressed anger of the Pakistani Obedient Daughter.' It signals a three-cornered affiliation: a state of mind, a nation-state, and a particular kinship-bond positioned within both these spaces. The second qualifier takes the form of the inscription that dedicates the text to 'all the Pakistani Obedient Daughters; you are not alone.' Clearly, the author intends to walk the line between the individual and the collective, between cultural formation and fictional space. Tariq's illustrations literalize metaphor to underscore this point. The cover page – which carries the title – literally corks the smothered rage of the group in a transparent jar. The name 'Sarah' arches itself above the jar, as though – through the act of representation – an individual might just escape imprisonment. In contrast, the dedication comes on a later page beneath a jar that is unsealed but quietly filled with ink. The squeeze of the bottleneck is no longer apparent. As the colloquial idiom of 'bottled-up rage' is visualized in this way, we realize that we are looking at a textbook solution to the standard problem before an illustrator, of how to endow an abstract concept with the visual reality of line and color, or how to ensure that 'a visual quality may be experienced as the equivalent of a moral value' (Gombrich 1963, 4). Gombrich is a valuable authority to employ here because he represents canonicity at its most intense, and makes it possible for the reader to gauge the nature and extent of the change involved in pictorial representation. The protagonist perhaps is now free, and the inscription holds out a reassurance of solidarity to her anxious sisterhood. The text spans this relationship between the individual and the collective. On her side, the reader needs to identify and understand the various stages of this journey if she is to make it alongside the eponymous protagonist.

Tariq's text takes its rise from the domain of graphic crossover. The author positions her protagonist carefully. On the one hand, she constructs Sarah as the type of the middle-class South Asian school leaver who – as she still lives at home – needs to conform to the wishes of her parents and lend a hand with household chores. As such, Sarah is a little like Betty in the Archie comics: friendly, hardworking, and dependent financially on her parents. Unlike her brother, Sarah cannot get the car keys any more than she can get permission to go out of an evening. The attractiveness of the colour-palette that Tariq uses, the veneer of teenage commentary, and the impulse to fictionalize through social comedy suggest that the text owes a good deal to the comic book format. On the other hand, however, Tariq is also careful to include more disturbing markers, such as the relationship between religion and state-formation, a patriarchy so encoded as to become almost acceptable, and the framework of middle-class capitalism. These serve as indices of social documentation and suggest the way in which Tariq positions her text on the cusp between the teenage comic book and cultural commentary. The hallmark of Tariq's text is thus an ability to demonstrate how micro-processes of political and personal conflict intersect and shape the lives of young adults. The protagonists set up – with the clarity of retrospect – visual and literary records of these patterns of convergence and divergence. Within this field, Alison Bechdel's 2006 *Fin Home: A Family Tragi-comic* is the closest predecessor of Tariq's text. Bechdel's text discusses the crises of personal identity built around professional and sexual choices within the larger context of familial pressures. The unforgiving accuracy of hindsight allows Bechdel's first-person narrator to ruminate on the way in which a father's manipulation of material surfaces and moral relationships can both entrap and liberate his daughter. 'In the circus, acrobatics where one person lies on the floor balancing another are called "Icarian games." In our particular re-enactment of the mythic relationship [between Daedalus and Icarus] it was not me but my father who was to plummet from the sky.' (Bechdel 4–5) Bechdel thinks through the way in which her slow and partial recognition of her father's paedophilia seems to move alongside her awareness of her sexual orientation. As she uses Joyce's *Ulysses* to work through the multiple ironies of filial relationship, Bechdel's narrator thinks about the deeply fraught relationship between parent and child. 'He did hurtle into the sea, of course. But in the tricky reverse narration that impels our entwined stories, he was there to catch me when I leapt' (Bechdel 231–32). The text plays out a personal narrative against the background of social and cultural movements, from the self-congratulation of the American Bicentennial to the claustrophobia of suburbia. Bechdel insists throughout that this is a piece of self-writing. The dedication to her mother and siblings sounds the autobiographical keynote, to which the text returns repeatedly, 'We did have a lot of fun, in spite of everything' (Bechdel vi). The author deliberately sets up her family as both the theatre and the cast of this unfolding tragicomedy of identity-revisionism.

In contrast, Malik Sajad's 2015 graphic memoir *Munnu: A Boy from Kashmir*, which is contemporaneous with Tariq's text, makes two choices – visual and literary – to complicate the relationship between personal and group identity; Sajad represents all his major characters – except Munnu's first love – not as human beings but as humanoids with the features of the *hangul*, the Kashmiri red deer. This is an author-illustrator's response to two related concerns. One is the erasure of humanity in Kashmir. The other has to do with the wilfully obtuse international anxiety about an endangered animal species in a conflict zone where human life has no value. Although Munnu's life story is substantially that of Sajad, the partial beast-fable blocks off casual one-to-one identification between author and character. Even when a critical issue – Sajad's use of his homely scrapbook to represent Kashmir – is under discussion, what we see is a *hangul* humanoid reaching for his work: 'Sajad avoided reading the news: it was daunting. Instead he relied on his personal scrapbook, in which he had collected pictures of the newsmakers in Kashmir' (Sajad 169). The collaborative hierarchies of visual politics – particularly the dramatization of international crisis within personal space – are thus a central theme particularly at the time of Tariq's text, and it is to this text that we now turn.

The most obvious point that strikes the reader is the way in which the visual grammar of representation keeps in step with the verbal grammar of narrative. The reader is unlikely to share the condescension implicit in the canonical acceptance of graphic narrative as valuable because of 'the linguistics of the visual image' (Gombrich 1960, 7) that it articulates. Gombrich indicates the extremely closed terms on which graphic narrative is traditionally accepted. Only then can we understand Tariq's divergence from canonicity. It is necessary to understand the dynamics of this relationship between the visual and the verbal. Sarah steps out to meet the reader by turning her back on a hinged mirror that simulates a book opened at the middle. Notice that Sarah's introduction of herself to the reader is gauche to the point of banality. 'Hi! I'm Sarah. I'm almost eighteen years old and I live in Pakistan. Living in Pakistan can be tough, especially if you're a girl. But even so, I have lots of dreams.' However, two points emerge almost at once. The first is that – by practically stepping out of the pages of a two-panel mirror – Sarah is living out the statement that her life is literally an open book. This is again an example of how Tariq literalizes metaphor not merely to evoke a smile but also to underscore the precarious nature of the existence of her protagonist. In everyday life, Sarah does not enjoy the luxury of theatrical hyperbole or dramatic gesture. What one sees is what one gets: a subsistence level of expression in speech, dress, and movement. At any rate, this is what it seems to be, until we realize that Tariq's use of the hinged mirror allows her to present three different images of the protagonist. These correspond to the conventional literary modes of character-analysis: how the individual sees herself, how others see her, and how the reader sees her in a way that she cannot see herself. Tariq's choice of the comic book mode of representation is exciting. It compels the reader to engage immediately with the core issue of seeking to know not just the characters but also the mirrors that both shape and distort their identity. To begin with, there is the full-face frontal representation of an unhappy Sarah. She confronts the reader, left arm resting aggressively on her waist, balanced neatly by a single conformist plait hanging down on the right. There is also the Sarah whose right profile – distinctly reticent – greets the reader. Finally, there is the rear-view depiction of a faceless Sarah with an evenly draped *dupatta* or neck-scarf, as though this ready-to-hand marker of tradition functions in the absence of any sign of individual personality. It is also noteworthy that Tariq eschews the traditional modes of decoration to take forward the 'visuality of the inauspicious' (Varughese xiii), which is the staple of much Indian graphic documentary. Instead, she reaches out for the comic-book style of clean line, bright colour, and angular perspective. This is a realistic illustrator's choice as it is in keeping with the ambition and rebellion of her urban young adult protagonist. It is also a pragmatic narrator's choice as it prioritizes velocity and clarity while relying on that quintessential comic-book quality of 'amplification through simplification' (McCloud 1994, 30). The principles of comic-book characterization – that signals through colour and movement – may emerge more clearly however in a relatively minor but complicated character like Sarah's father Abu who repays close attention.

Sarah's introduction of her father is both like and unlike her presentation of herself. The three-part sequence reappears, as the author positions her character successively through a full-length frontal representation, a depiction from the rear, and a left-facing profile. There is, however, no support from a mirror in the background this time, so that there is no illusion of depth. This is appropriate, as Sarah's presentation of her father is correspondingly abrupt. 'Abu. My dad is a retired army officer. He's very strict and dresses in the stiffest of *shalwar kameezes*. It's like every day is Eid with him' (Tariq n p). The staccato sentence-construction mimics a military tattoo or drumbeat. The olive-green *kameez* signals a continued affiliation to the army on the part of this retired officer, and recalls – again through its color – the national flag of Pakistan. This visualization helps us contextualize Sarah's story. It does not belong to newly independent Pakistan with its complete dependence on military might. During that early phase Jinnah believed that 'the army was what he needed most of all to clamp central authority over Pakistan's provinces' (Jalal 299). That time is past, as is another, more acerbic phase of which the epic catalogue of military heads of state appeared interminable. 'Number one, Ayub, number two, Yahya, number three, Zulu [Zia ul Haq], And now we are on number four. O Pakistan!' (Suleri 2002, 124). Tariq's text speaks to a nation in which military and religious pressures signal their presence without necessarily operating as official agencies of the government. The full significance of the comment 'It's like every day is Eid with him' (Tariq n p) will emerge later, but for now it is worth noting that possibly disturbing affiliations arrive in the company of each other.

A further dimension to the location of Sarah's story appears with the description of her home. Sarah explains that she lives on the highest floor of a mid-rise building that can function without an elevator. The apartment complex looks upmarket enough to belong to a Pakistan that is in the process of coming to terms with a certain phase of market-driven capitalism. Despite the fact that this is a society where consumerism is rampant, it does not make the lot of women particularly easy. As a canny analysis explains, consumerism does not necessarily mean a reduction in women's chores: 'Women work harder than men whether they are Eastern or Western, housewives or jobholders. A Pakistani woman spends sixty three hours a week on domestic work alone, while a Western housewife, despite her modern appliances works just six hours less' (Wolf 23). Moreover, in this phase of its socio-economic evolution, Pakistan typifies the crisis of urban planning that marks contemporary South Asia in which real estate development pushes nature and humanity alike to the fringes of survival. 'For technology, nature holds no secrets: this is an approach to the natural world in which all of the given forms, all natural boundaries, are erased and the very materiality of existence is construed as . . . a resource available for re-formation' (Dwivedi 52). The landscaping of the apartment block looks ludicrously like a glossy brochure from a land-development authority. Sarah indicates her practically inaccessible floor with curved arrows, so that the reader can share her experience. The rotors of a helicopter in the summer sky turn in giddy surveillance, sharing the perspective but not the grief of the author-illustrator. Below, a couple of trees try gallantly to compete with five mid-rise apartment blocks. A fountain leaps out of a roundabout, and multi-speed traffic spins chaotically around it. For good measure, this mapping of locality sprawls across a double-spread. Sarah's story belongs to a period when the constraints of economic liberalization make themselves apparent. Capital – that should liberate its consumers – drives them to extinction. 'An important point of the neo-liberal reforms is to extend the role of the market and reduce the role of the state in the economic affairs. It is based on the assumption that the market is always right' (Siddiqui 34).

As Sarah draws the ground plan of her own home, a more dismal picture emerges. A sympathetic reviewer first drew attention to the likeness between the ground plan and Askari Apartments 2 in Karachi, an old home of the author. The review quotes Tariq's remark that 'the illustrations involved a lot of photographic references and sketching' (Salahuddin, www.dawn.com/news/116796). Her family, like many others, is hostage to ungenerous home-buying policies and to its own bourgeois desire to maintain appearances. The floor plan tells its tale. 'Its really hot, really small and impractical' (Tariq n p). To create an illusion of space for different individuals in the family – with their various needs and aspirations – the architect maximizes shared fluid space and minimizes individual fixed space drastically. Effectively this means that common turf within a home overruns private turf, so that individuals have no privacy. They have to make common cause with the family at all times for 'the dining area and the lounge have no boundaries' (Tariq n p). In consequence, women – who have the least bargaining power – get the worst accommodation. As there is no proper provision for a store room the family converts its staff-quarters into storage space. This makes it impossible to hire staff, so Sarah and her Amu (mother) share the household chores. The kitchen – which is their space – is dark and imprisoning, the dungeon of the family-castle, to which it consigns its womenfolk. While Sarah's present room is large enough, her family consider relegating her to the storeroom so that her room can become a television-lobby. Unsurprisingly, her brother does far better: 'Of course he has the biggest room, the biggest hi-tech writing table and an exercise machine that he doesn't use. Of course he also has a queen-sized bed' (Tariq n p).

Where does the problem of sibling rivalry yield to the larger question of the gendered lines along which accommodation seems to operate? Austen's 1814 novel *Mansfield Park* is a pioneering response in women's fiction to the skewed expectations of gender and class that shape accommodation. Austen details the way in which the occupant and her work bestow or withhold a certain status on each room in a home. To illustrate this point, Austen recounts the fate of the school-room in which the governess once instructed the daughters of the house. The moment Maria (the eldest girl) turns 16 – and gives up her lessons – she calls it the East Room to extend her newly acquired dignity. When Fanny Price – the poor cousin of the family – gets the room, it bespeaks a minor rise in her status in the household. The room, however, continues to be unpopular, as Fanny never enjoys the privilege of a fire. Only when Fanny attracts a worthwhile marriage proposal does her uncle assign the East Room a load of coal, which again indicates an improvement in her status. Housing is thus a critical variable that is particularly vulnerable to distortion by class and gender. The best-known feminist trope in this connection is that mobilized by Virginia Woolf in her 1929 lectures on the relationship between accommodation and creativity. Woolf insists that – if a woman writer is to do justice to herself – she must have 'a room of her own and five hundred [pounds] a year' (Woolf). For a woman to compete successfully as an artist, economic independence alone is not enough. Space is essential. Woolf's contemporaries differed vigorously on this point with the most famous riposte coming from her best-known antagonist Arnold Bennet. He expostulated, 'I have myself written long and formidable novels in bedrooms whose doors certainly had no locks and in the full and dreadful knowledge that I had not five hundred a year of my own – nor fifty' (Majumdar 259). The larger point though has not been lost on subsequent writers. Personal space becomes one component in the ongoing struggle for freedom. Bechdel's response to this motif shows us the other face of the coin. Even while Bechdel and her family have enough space and creative solitude for each member to turn out something of value, their gothic mansion groans under the weight of unspoken secrets, placing a heavy burden on their imaginative talent. 'Our home was like an artist's colony. We ate together, but otherwise we were absorbed in our separate pursuits. And in the isolation, our creativity took on an aspect of compulsion' (Bechdel 134). Notice the very high price that Bechdel's narrator pays for freedom of the mind. On the one hand, a room without familial support is barely distinguishable from a prison cell. On the other, familial pressure may marginalize a young woman's quest for her own space within the house as a whole. Sarah's story is important because of the quality of the witness it bears to the power politics of domesticity, a core concern of women's writing. Family narrative connects to cultural history, so that 'artefacts (like house and home) are carriers of memory, and the narratives people tell about them are the stuff of history' (Burton 27). In this connection, a woman's configuration of domestic space and her account of personal space within it become critical modes of witness and self-reflexivity, which is why this segment of Sarah's narrative is important.

Sarah's story dramatizes the participative quotient of 'the stuff of history.' The sequence around Bakra Eid, or Eid al Adha, plots a fine argument that moves rapidly between personal identity-construction on the one hand and cultural formation on the other. The sequence carries a heavy emotional and cultural charge as it both analyses and internalizes the notion of sacrifice. Consequently, visual and narrative registers work in close coordination with each other. The author needs to keep the central character close to the reader – despite a surrounding ensemble-cast of family and neighbours – so that we never lose sight of Sarah's predicament. This is a common difficulty for the comic-book writer. '[Sometimes the protagonist] must appear in every panel, no matter what. The requirement never to lose sight of the protagonist creates real narrative challenges' (Gravett and Stanbury 49–50). At the same time, the larger issue of renunciation and self-surrender needs comprehensive representation on its own terms. Tariq handles this difficulty by showing us the way in which the realization of her predicament gradually dawns on Sarah and on the reader. We first meet two sacrificial lambs – decked for ritual slaughter – in conversation. One muses, 'I feel so objectified,' while the other responds, 'I feel like an ass' (Tariq n p). The reader – who has just met a set of despicable suitors for

Sarah's hand – automatically reads these asides as pointers toward Sarah's rejection of a marriage arranged by an unpleasant broker. Sarah herself – as she dices meat for a commemorative meal angrily – confesses that she finds the entire process revolting. A lecherous visitor exploits the event to grope Sarah, which makes her feel of a commodity than ever before. When she prays that Eid should end because of the countless chores she needs to complete, Sarah is close to casting herself as the scapegoat wearing the same colours of red and green as the sacrificial lamb. Unlike Ibrahim, there will be no scapegoat waiting to take her place. She is to be the ritual offering at the altar of the bourgeois expectations of her parents. Sarah's explosion 'I am done!' is the textbook embodiment of a distinguishing feature of graphic documentation: its 'transformative aesthetics' [or] the recovery of the everyday and its exposure to the light of day and its inclusion within the universe 'of scholarly discourse' (Saha and Sethi ix). Through Sarah's explosion, Tariq mobilizes anger as a possible vehicle of change in the hierarchies of power and relationship within the institution of the family. The remaining segment of the text tests the possibilities of change latent within the situation.

This concluding section begins – as have the preceding phases – with Sarah's bottled-up temper threatening to explode. Earlier segments have had lighter colours, such as yellow, orange and vermillion. As Sarah is now in a towering rage, the colour of the double-spread is a deep red. She storms out with furious thoughts running through her head. 'I'll give them a piece of my mind. They can't keep doing this to me' (Tariq n p). Just as Sarah gets ready to stride from left to right across the double-page, a curious turnaround takes place. A grey inset with a black full-length silhouette of Sarah's mother appears in the far right. The status of this figure is arguable. She might be a figment of Sarah's self-censoring imagination, in which case Sarah will be her own worst enemy because she prevents herself from thrashing this matter out with her parents. Alternatively, Ami (Sarah's mother) might guess that Sarah is about to complain, and so take the pre-emptive action that she does. This, however, seems unlikely, as she has not appeared either particularly sensitive or manipulative before. Nonetheless, we cannot rule out this possibility. We might not know whether Ami's conversation is the product of genuine maternal affection, or something of a pre-emptive strike, designed to evoke precisely the response of re-confirmed compliance that it does. Given the cramped domestic space of their apartment, and the fact that Sarah and she have worked alongside each other throughout, it is hard to believe that Ami does not know that Sarah is livid, or indeed, that Sarah intends to complain. At this strategic moment, for the first time Tariq gives us a character – literally – in shades of grey. When she stands in the passage, ahead of Sarah, Ami is a shadowy, ambivalent presence. She emerges in her true colours again only when she speaks to Abu, Sarah's father. This conversation makes Sarah check her step and stop to overhear. Once she does that, she pulls back from a position of revolt. Ami speaks appreciatively to Sarah's father of Sarah's efficiency. 'Wasn't Sarah amazing today? She handled the whole lunch! Didn't complain even once! She is the perfect daughter (Tariq n p). Her husband caps this by remarking that Sarah's future husband will be a lucky man.

This is the moment of dramatic reversal. Sarah cannot believe her ears. She persuades herself – against her better judgement – to value what she has overheard. 'They called me the perfect daughter! If I say anything now, they will be heartbroken!' (Tariq n p). As she returns to her daily round, Sarah seems to grow taller in stages, as she articulates one platitude after another. She begins by saying, 'They're not so bad,' and ends by assuring herself, 'They do care about me' (Tariq, np). As she makes this last remark, she is tall enough to cork up her rage, and place the jar on a row of shelves where it joins a host of others. Like the Alice of Lewis Carroll and John Tenniel, Tariq's Sarah pays the price for growing up to a point when she can reach the magic shelf and put back a bottle that she had once taken down. She has not reached the point at which she will uncork the bottle. She believes that it is simply not worth the thought and energy that she has invested in action. Sarah beats down her anger and persuades herself, as she has done in the past that her parents love her and do not exploit her desire for affection. The shelves stacked with jars from the past remind us of the repetitive and never-ending cycle of domestic abuse. Her woebegone face turns toward the reader for one last time and testifies to the price that she – and all Pakistani 'obedient daughters' – have to pay. No lamb taken to the slaughter could be more silent. The epithets scribbled across the jar speak, but the character has nothing more to say.

Two questions arise out of this conclusion to the narrative. The first concerns the genre as a whole, while the second concerns this particular text. A central characteristic of graphic documentation is the way in which it needs to negotiate a middle space between the difficulties of the collective to which it speaks and the achievements of the individual who chronicles her life as a kind of case study for the group. The text needs to work out an approach between the depression that is a consequence of perceived hardship, and the elation that arises from the narrator's ability to story her lives and connect to her readership. A successor to Tariq's text, the 2018 *Hey Kiddo* indicates both extremes in its subtitle: 'How I lost my mother, found my father, and dealt with family addiction.' *Hey Kiddo* is always conscious that it is a memoir with a duty before itself. It needs to show that the hero makes something of his life despite having an absentee father, a mother who battles substance abuse and promiscuity, and a grandmother who deals with alcoholism. The hero's quest is his creation of a graphic memoir in which he tries to make sense of a home that often seems on the brink of collapse. 'I often wondered who my father was and never quite knew where my mother was. But that entire time I had two incredible parents right there before me. . . . They just happened to be a generation removed' (*Hey Kiddo* 297). Krosoczka's text earns its triumphalism through its tale of a specific individual, his talent, and the agency of graphic memoir in his self-realization. The individual triumphs and reaches out to the tortured constituency of young adults from broken home, to assure them that his success can be theirs. In contrast, the principle of Tariq's text is that of the shared failure of a specific group – the 'obedient daughters' of the title – owing to the institutionalized callousness of family and nation alike. There can be no easy triumphalism here, as systemic failure skews the equation between the eponymous hero and the collective to which she belongs. Escapism is not an option, unlike Aaron Haroon Rashid's 2013 Pakistani animated television series, *Burka Avenger*. Here a committed teacher transforms into a superhero – complete with the mobility, strength, and costume of fantasy – to develop the theme of women's education. Even the more recent anti-hero of Shahan Zaidi's 2014 *Bloody Nasreen* requires the accoutrements of super heroism to deal with Karachi. Sarah soldiers on without the support of any face-saving fantasy to do the dishes, wring out the clothes, or pour out endless cups of tea. This adherence to realism leads us to understand the second question – the nature of Tariq's particular text – a little better. The core paradox of Tariq's text is that it needs to dramatize endemic failure if it is to succeed. It is thus an unsparingly realist subject.

This becomes clear if we compare Tariq's handling of the mother–daughter relationship to a similar motif in Reshu Singh's short graphic narrative of 2015, titled 'The Photo: My (Mother's) Marriage.' As a close analysis of Singh's text points out, there is a certain amount of emotional bonding between mother and daughter, even when they discuss the vexed subject of marriage. They have widely different views on the subject, but share a sofa, and occasionally shuffle costumes. In this way, 'the imagining of these women as each other' (Varughese 107) enables some slight sense of connectedness. Sarah, however, is clear that her mother is in denial on a range of issues – marriage, academics, social acceptance – that no conversation can take place.

Can an emotion like the 'suppressed anger' of Tariq's title help facilitate social change? It would seem to be all too subjective and fragile to accomplish anything of consequence. At the same time, however, two points emerge. The first has to do with the difficulty of sustaining emotion as an agent of social progress. As a 2016 graphic commentary on the aftermath of the 2002 Gujarat riots shows, anger does not last. Fear may drive it out, or apathy may help it fade away. When Pragya Tiwari and Pia Tiwari interview survivors who become first-time voters in 2014, they expect the survivors to show anger or at least demonstrate a political will to change. This does not happen. 'All three of them are polite and pragmatic to a fault. I find no sense of outrage or injustice over what happened to them in 2002, not even a hint of anger. It is as if they know they are second-class citizens and have adopted that reality' (Sen and Sabhaney 318). Tariq's text may appear to downplay emotion, but refuses to blink. To that extent, it insists that the reader take cognizance of emotion. This moves the focus of graphic documentation just a little away from social commentary as an end in itself to social commentary that rides on the heartbeat of an emotion. Tariq's text is able to enable this change.

An interesting representational choice that Tariq deploys is to have Sarah protest against parental restrictions that are traditional rather than specifically Islamic. Except for one remark by her father relating to prayer, and the extended Bakra Eid sequence, Sarah's complaints are specific to her position as a young adult growing up in Pakistan rather than to a young adult growing up under Islam. In doing so, Tariq addresses two important issues. The first is the care that she takes in placing her text specifically within contemporary Pakistan that chafes at excessive regulation rather than an older and more romanticized Pakistan, such as that which Sarah Suleri sometimes evokes. 'Leaving Pakistan was, of course, tantamount to giving up the company of women. . . . My reference is to a place where the concept of woman was not really part of an available vocabulary: we were too busy for that . . .' (Suleri 1). The second decision that Tariq takes is to sidestep the controversy around the use – or neglect – of the *hijab* or headscarf. This is a judicious choice because recent graphic and narrative accounts address this issue at length. The global *manga* comic-book explosion studies the issue of youthful consciousness and sartorial/religious representation. The idiom used for this purpose comes across as being 'child-like without de-aged characters' (Saha and Sethi 119). Sarah's story as an urban, middle-class teenager might not have added much of value to this debate, so Tariq does not need to handle the matter of religion and a dress code. Besides, Sarah's story addresses possibilities of escape – collective-solidarity, writing, and illustration – rather than certainties of imprisonment. This is again in keeping with the fact that its protagonist is a young adult, rather than an older, more disillusioned speaker, who might say of her life in Pakistan, 'I knew that I would never be able to leave. My life would turn out just like my mother's' (Javeri 152). Sarah, like Nigar Nazar's Gogi, tackles the world of the 'urban, emancipated Pakistani woman living in a male-dominated society' (Rehman 1). Tariq's achievement is that she trains her readers to look at Pakistan rather than at Islam as the primary factor in the fashioning of identity. This is a crucial change in the practice of reading Pakistan, and ultimately it is perhaps the most difficult stereotype that Tariq reconfigures.

Works cited

Bechdel, Alison. *Fin Home: A Family Tragicomic*. Mariner, 2007.

Burton, Antoinette. *Dwelling in the Archive: Women Writing House. Home, History in Late Colonial India*. Oxford UP, 2003.

Copeland, Huey, and Krista Thompson. "Afrotopes: A User's Guide." *Art Journal*, vol. 76, no. 3–4, Taylor and Francis (12 Feb.), 2018.

Dwivedi, Divya, and V. Sanil. *The Public Sphere from Outside the West*. Bloomsbury, 2015.

Gombrich, Ernst. *Art and Illusion*. Phaidon, 1960.

———. *Meditations on a Hobby Horse*. Phaidon, 1963.

Gravett, Paul, and Peter Stanbury. *Great British Comics*. Aurum, 2006.

Jalal, Ayesha. *The Sole Spokesman: Jinnah, the Muslim League and the Demand for Pakistan*. Cambridge UP, rpt 1994.

Javeri, Sabyn. *Hijabistan*. Harper Collins, 2019.

Krosoczka, Jarrett H. *Hey Kiddo!* Scholastix, 2018.

Majumdar, Robin and Allen McLaurin, *Virginia Woolf: The Critical Heritage*. Routledge, 1975.

McCloud, Scott. *Understanding Comics*. William Morrow, 1994.

Rehman, Sonya. "Pakistan's First Woman Cartoonist Shapes Young Minds, and Society." *Asia Society*, 7 Nov. 2014.

Saha, Ananya and Navneet Sethi. *Trajectories of Popular Expression: Forms, Histories, Contexts*. Aakar, 2018.

Sajad, Malik. *Munnu: A Boy from Kashmir.* Harper Collins, 2015.

Salahuddin, Zahra. "Are You An 'Obedient' Pakistani Daughter?" 9 Mar. 2015, www.dawn. com/news/116796. Accessed 8 Apr. 2019.

Sen, Orijit, and Vidyun Sabhaney. *First Hand: Graphic Non Fiction from India*, vol. 1. Yoda Press, 2016.

Siddiqui, Kalim. "Experiences of Capitalism in India and Pakistan." *Research in Applied Economics*, vol. 3, no. 1, 2001, pp. 1–49.

Suleri, Sara. *Boys Will Be Boys.* Penguin, 2003.

———. *Meatless Days.* Collins, 1989.

Tariq, Ayesha. *Sarah: The Suppressed Anger of the Pakistani Obedient Daughter.* Penguin Books India, 2015.

Varughese, E. Dawson. *Visuality and Identity in Post-Millennial Indian Graphic Narratives.* Palgrave Macmillan, 2018.

Wolf, Naomi. *The Beauty Myth.* Chatto & Windus, 1990.

Woolf, Virginia. "A Room of One's Own." https://archive.org. Accessed 8 Apr. 2019.

11

CONTEMPORARY POLITICS AND PREHISTORIC PAST THROUGH POPULAR GENRES

Maha Khan Phillips' novels

Mohammad Asim Siddiqui

There are some elements which are common to the works of all Pakistani writers writing in English. Arguably the most important thing to note about this writing is that most Pakistani writers have not skirted political questions, and as a result Pakistani fiction in English is intensely political in nature. Almost all the novels which have appeared in the last two decades show engagement with political issues facing the Muslim world, Pakistan in particular. *Granta* magazine's special issue devoted to new Pakistani writing (issue 112, 2010), even though it offered a lot of variety, was noted for its political content. 'More often than not, this writing,' as one reviewer wrote, 'is framed within the unforgiving narratives of political repression, internecine savagery, and terror that overwhelm this collection' (Akbar). This fixation on power politics can be seen in different genres of fiction. The novelists have usually tried to address issues of terrorism, media representation of reality, and the conflict in Pakistani society between the forces of conservatism and modernity.

One very important subgenre of Pakistani political writing centres on the effects of 9/11. Though 9/11 has influenced the entire world in one way or the other, with its impact on Muslim countries being especially very important, Pakistan's case is distinctive as not only was this country an ally of America in its war on terror but also a country where Osama bin Laden took refuge before he was killed. Some important Pakistani works addressing the impact of 9/11 include Mohsin Hamid's *The Reluctant Fundamentalist*, Kamila Shamsie's *Burnt Shadows*, Nadeem Aslam's *The Wasted Vigil*, and H. M. Naqvi's *Home Boy*, all four novels marked by the writers' use of irony directed at the new situation they find themselves in a changed world.

It is because of Pakistan's uneven relationship with the Western world that Pakistani writers display this ironic and ambivalent attitude towards the machinations of power by powerful groups. Talking about *The Reluctant Fundamentalist*, *Burnt Shadows*, and *The Wasted Vigil* and employing Judith Butler's idea of framing which 'calls certain fields of normativity into question,' Daniel O. Gorman posits 'that the

DOI: 10.4324/9781003002062-15

novels by Hamid, Aslam and Shamsie work to shift dominant framings of the war on terror in the opposite direction, and in doing so *challenge* such narrow 'modes of recognition' . . . They do this by attempting to enact-while simultaneously undercutting-an 'authentic' representation of Pakistan' (113). H. M. Naqvi's *Home Boy* perfects this genre by its ambivalence and deft use of irony directed at the dominant discourse on 9/11.

II

Maha Khan Phillips' two novels *Beautiful from this Angle* (2010) and *The Curse of Mohenjo Daro* (2016) focus on different subjects employing different genres. Whereas the first novel, set in Pakistan and written in a realistic mode, is basically concerned with the world of media, the second novel, flirting with realistic-fantastic-thriller modes, talks at length about issues of history and historiography. However, at the deeper level, both the novels address the question of power, exploring its functioning in both ancient and contemporary times. Both novels take up the role of media in the world and the class conflict in Pakistani society. They also show familiarity with the contemporary power situation in the world and the discourses that surround it. And most importantly, both novels demonstrate her concern to present serious political content in a popular genre. The title page of both books carries Kamila Shamsie's praise of them as unputdownable, a word usually used to describe popular forms of writings.

The political status of Maha Khan Phillips' *Beautiful from This Angle*, which reads like a popular thriller, is derived from its characters' consciousness about living in post-9/11 world. The novel talks at length about issues arising out of 9/11, particularly the conflict in Pakistani society between the forces of conservatism and modernity. The question of terrorism and the misrepresentation of issues in media, in Western media in particular, is also addressed by this novel. In an interview with Maheen Basheer, Maha Khan Phillips stated:

> I touch on the issues that keep making an appearance in the western media. I really just set out to write something funny that turned the idea of western perceptions of Pakistan and oppression and terrorism on its head. I wanted to write a satire and say, look, women are capable of exploiting other women too.

The political status of the novel is clear from its beginning. Early in the novel, there is a reference to terrorism and characters' consciousness about living in post-9/11 world. Monty Mohsin, a minor character in the novel, is producing a reality TV Show titled *Who Wants to Be a Terrorist?* which will feature many actors trying to become an actual terrorist. He knows that such shows are in demand in the post-9/11 world. In a world driven by market forces, Monty realizes the business potential of such ventures. He is not too bothered by the charge of opportunism because he knows that in the end the United States of America, the great imperial power that it is, will be able to milk all this money from the likes of him and his countrymen.

The impact of 9/11 can be felt in different ways in literary writings. After 9/11, the discourse on clash of civilization got some momentum in popular writings, if not in academic writings. The Orientalism of old returned in different ways to haunt people living in non-Western countries. This also resulted in the popularity of a certain genre of fiction which can be called 'oppressed woman's novel.' It tries to see the world in binary terms conceiving the East as backward and the West as the beacon of light. This kind of fiction revolves around the experiences, or ordeal, of a Muslim woman who is living in a Muslim land where women are a suppressed lot.[1] In some cases, the woman in question may be a Western Muslim woman forced by circumstances to live in a Muslim country. The entire Muslim land becomes a kind of prison for this miserable woman. This kind of fiction could interest readers because after 9/11 there was a sudden curiosity about Islam and Muslims. There is a clear relationship between this genre of fiction and the kind of reality show that Monty Mohsin is producing in *Beautiful from this Angle*.

Amynah Farooqi, a journalist by profession and the central character in the novel, also tries her hands at writing this oppressed woman's novel. Her attempt at this genre is more of a parody of this genre and displays her ironic consciousness about the figure of oppressed Muslim woman. In fact, the reference to this subgenre of fiction in *Beautiful from this Angle* offers a peep into Maha Khan Phillips' own interest in searching for a popular genre which will attract readers and which will also enable her to present her ironic view of power. Most journalists have the ambition of writing a novel, but Amynah, being the intelligent person that she is, knows the potential of her story. Though she is not as opportunistic as Mumtaz, she knows that her oppressed woman's novel will hold an appeal for the audience in the post-9/11 world.

Beautiful from this Angle can be understood only in the context of the media – created reality of the 21st century. Putting it differently, the novel is set in a post-truth world where the distinction between the authentic news and fake news has completely blurred.[2] The title of the novel offers an ironic commentary on the world of the media where everything is reduced to being a spectacle. The novel makes the point that the very things that we consider real are controlled by media barons and that we live in a world of mediated reality. Monty Mohsin's television programme *Who Wants to Be a Terrorist?* apparently shows the Waziristan region of Pakistan, but in reality it has been shot in a farmhouse owned by him. He has provided all possible props to convince his American bosses of the authenticity of his location. Not that the Americans themselves are too particular about honesty and transparency in the novel, as the episode involving the Fox News journalist, who comes to visit Mumtaz, suggests.

A much more prominent example of how camera can lie and media can invent a reality is provided by the documentary made by the three friends Mumtaz, Amynah, and Hina. Inspired by the success of *Who Wants to Be a Terrorist?* the three friends, led by Mumtaz, decide to make a documentary on 'honour killing' in

Pakistan. For this they need a face for their programme. This face is provided by Nelofar, the maid-cum-friend of Hina who narrates to her a painful, though half false, story of her captivity and exploitation. The West appears all too eager to pounce on such examples of the backwardness of women in Muslim societies. Interest in the practice of honour killing, a classic example of Oriental difference and its backwardness, can also make a very good copy. Such examples can justify the West's 'we care for democracy and justice' stance. This documentary becomes very successful because of the freak arrest of a terrorist from the land on which this documentary had been shot. The snobbery and dishonesty of Western media comes on the surface when Chip, the Fox News journalist, comes to interview Mumtaz and Amynah about their experience of having shot that documentary. Chip represents the aggressive and cocksure nature of American media and would not let Amynah present her version of Pakistani reality. Trying to control news in a very blatant manner, he uses props for his programme very arbitrarily without caring at all for truth.

Amynah is not too amused by Chip's manipulation of news. Chip would like his viewers to read that everything in the Muslim world is backward and that everybody is a potential terrorist. He speaks of terror inside Muslim homes. Amynah does not agree with his view of considering Karachi the most dangerous city in the world and the Muslim world as breeding potential terrorists. She is also very unhappy with Mumtaz's capitulation to forces represented by Chip and the Fox News. It may be recalled that Mumtaz lied before the camera to convince everyone that Nelofar is dead and that her husband is responsible for the murder of Nelofar. It is too much for Amynah to tolerate this kind of manipulation of news. Mumtaz also accepts the Western version of reality willingly as it suits her commercial interests and her ambition to become famous in her country. The break in their relationship is Amynah's way of telling that on the surface she may appear indolent but at the deeper level she is honest and truthful.

The Western perception of the Muslim world is also treated critically in the episode involving Mumtaz's father. A drug lord, he has all along been a kind of outcast in the respectable society of Karachi. His disappearances were seen with suspicion by everybody in Amynah's circle. Amynah is surprised to know that he is the nephew of a famous Afghan drug lord. However, America's war on terror benefits him in material terms, and from being a pariah he becomes useful for Americans. The opium trade went down drastically during the period of Taliban's rule in Afghanistan. American bosses find it useful to utilize this shady character for his contacts in Afghanistan for their shady activities.

III

Maha Khan Phillips continued her interest in exploring the machinations of power in her second novel *The Curse of Mohenjo Daro*. This novel also shows her success at finding an appropriate genre to contrast the functioning of power in both ancient and contemporary times. *The Curse of Mohenjo Daro* has been promoted as a thriller, if one believes the description of the book on its back page. Since the novel centres on Mohenjo Daro, it will be more accurate to consider it a combination of a thriller and a historical novel. After writing *Beautiful from This Angle*, Maha Khan Phillips said in many of her interviews that her next book would be a thriller. On other occasions she has talked about her fascination for the ancient site of Mohenjo Daro, which she first visited as a child and which ignited her mind and imagination. True to her intention, the novel is a thriller and right from its beginning to its end, it is enveloped in an air of mystery and suspense about how an explosion was caused in present day Mohenjo Daro, resulting in the disappearance or death of a team of archaeologists and their support staff. Following the conventions of a thriller, the novel progresses in time, backward and forward, to solve the mystery of the disappearance of this team of archaeologists, weaving into its narrative the events leading to the tragedy and tying all loose ends at the end.

Though all novels can be discussed in generic terms and there is little doubt about this novel's status as a thriller, good novels also re-work and flout the conventions they stem from. A good novel is also the result of a writer's staying within the conventions of a genre at the same time as putting his own unique signature on his work. There are definitely details and incidents in the novel, especially in its treatment of the present, which appear a formulaic emulation of a thriller. Thus, the entire sequence, where Nadia pursues Marianne Riviere and fools the receptionist to capture Riviere's bag containing the ancient tablet, appears formulaic.

The Curse of Mohenjo Daro, however, is saved from becoming a formulaic thriller by its imaginative use of history and archaeology and its attention to some contemporary concerns about the functioning of power and people's gullibility to fall prey to power's machinations. Ordinary people's willingness to just believe in anything, if presented well, is a motif that binds the past and the present. It has, in fact, become worse in the present, putting a question mark on the assumption of moral progress of mankind. The very choice of Mohenjo Daro as the subject of the novel contributes to building an atmosphere of mystery in the novel. The distance in time and the lack of agreement among scholars about the nature of language, religion, culture, and society of the Indus Valley Civilization is a position of advantage for a novelist to exercise her imagination. In her author's note, Phillips herself acknowledges how she has depended on some important studies on the Indus Valley civilization and how she has taken liberties with a number of 'facts' about Mohenjo Daro:

> I have taken some liberties with its history for the sake of plot. The city dates back to 2500 BC, not 3800 BC. However, recent efforts to date the site suggest it might be much older. These studies are not yet conclusive . . . What has been excavated thus far shows a society that does not seem to have had a military, and which was far more prosperous and equal than I have suggested.
>
> (Author's note 438)

Maha Khan Phillips attaches great importance to the pre-history of Mohenjo Daro.[3] The novel offers a number of interesting perspectives on the value and use of history through different characters. Layla feels some inexplicable pull of ruins. It was because of her fascination for the Indus Valley that she decided to become an archaeologist. 'She felt the ruins permeate themselves through her bones, become a part of her psyche. It was ridiculous. And yet, she couldn't help how she felt. Perhaps she had been here, in another life' (6–7). Marianne Riviere, formerly a banker but now the head of a dubious organization 'Indo Foundation,' which sponsors history projects, puts her viewpoint about history which, though in this particular instance, cannot be faulted: 'Our history often defines our future' (107–8). A different perspective is offered by Liam O' Rourke, a linguistic anthropologist who was part of the Mohenjo Daro project in the novel, when he cautions about the misuse of history. Commenting on historian Davenport's thesis about the possible presence of nuclear weapons and the rumour at one time about Hitler being interested in Mohenjo Daro's ancient technology, Liam puts his point very succinctly: 'I don't believe in ancient weapons. But I do believe in modern ones. And I believe that it is easy for those who covet power to try to claim the past' (201). Liam's succinct comment clearly explains how ultra-right ideologies of nationalism thrive on claiming and inventing the past.[4]

In a new country like Pakistan there remains an anxiety about its past. Which is the relevant history for its present needs and its future use? Is the history of ancient India before the coming of Muslims in the subcontinent important for Pakistan, which was created in 1947? History textbooks in Pakistan glorify the medieval period in history and view Pakistani identity in religious terms, pitting the Muslims against the Hindus, often replicating the British binary of Hindu and Muslim periods in Indian history. Because of this question of national identity viewed in its opposition to India, Pakistan has not been able to claim its ancient heritage. Haroon Khalid is of the view that the term 'Ancient Pakistan,' which includes the Indus Valley Civilization, the Mauryan Empire, and other ancient Indian empires, is the victim of this anxiety. The term ancient Pakistan is not used and has not gained any currency, because Pakistan is not comfortable with the Hindu past of the subcontinent. Making a case for a collective heritage of the subcontinent, Khalid believes that 'in this simplistic framework, contemporary India becomes the modern-day incarnation of the ancient civilization that is India' ('Ancient India'). Khalid also argues that Pakistan is more comfortable accepting its pre-Islamic history when it is separated from the Indian influence. Harappa and Mohenjo Daro become important in this discussion because they existed before the Vedic period and before the rise of Brahmanism. 'In this new order that emerged, the Indus Valley civilization acquired a unique significance, for this was not as "Hindu" as some of the other historical sites and buildings in the country' ('Indus Valley').

Some of these concerns and anxieties with regard to ancient history are taken up by Maha Khan Phillips in *The Curse of Mohenjo Daro*. There are two different kinds of strands in the presentation of this ancient history. The rational, scientific voices of Liam and Nadia rely on the available evidence, collected through diggings of the site. The other voice, that of the Hindu nationalists and Sohail, who spent some time with them in India, believed that 'India had once been a center for space, science, genetic technology and health innovation' (253). Taking a cue from the Hindu nationalists, Sohail's organization advocated the concept of genetic memory, of the evolution of human race even before the Ice Age, and of the power of mind and human will to increase their psychic powers.[5] Jahanara refers to the tales in *Ramayana* and *Mahabharata* and how they are appropriated by the Hindu nationalists for building their narrative:

> The story's recordings date back to the fourth and fifth century BC, but the tales are far, far older. They were passed down orally from generation to generation, long before they were put to paper. It's where the Hindu nationalists get their ideas from, though these stories are far older than even they imagine
> (259–60)

That these stories are older than the recorded history of Hinduism and that Mohenjo Daro does not present any evidence of any Hindu temple or that its link with latter day Hinduism is tenuous are facts in favour of a Pakistani historian eager to reclaim the collective heritage of the subcontinent for the modern state of Pakistan. In fact, the very act of setting this novel in Meluha may be considered an effort in the direction of claiming for Pakistan the collective heritage of India and Pakistan.

Liam's observation about the control of history reflects his anxiety about its misuse by dictators and demagogues in the present day world. Most authoritarian states try to control history, appropriating past icons, inventing a past and interpreting the past to suit their present concerns.

There are two simultaneous narratives, intertwined with each other and equally balanced in their presentation in *The Curse of Mohenjo Daro*. The various threads of the two narratives, of the ancient city of Meluha in the Indus Valley, and of the present day England, USA and Pakistan, come together in the end of the novel, much in the fashion of any thriller. The historical period is built round known details about Mohenjo Daro, like the Citadel, the mother goddess, the unicorn, and the headdress, discovered after extensive excavations. The author further builds the historical context by dwelling on the relationship of Meluha to other places like Chanu, Arrapha and Dilmun. Dilmun, as is now established, was located in Persian Gulf on a trade route between Mesopotamia and the Indus Valley and it had trade links with Mohenjo Daro. Arrapha was a place in ancient Iraq. Chanu better known as Chanhudaro, which refers to its post urban phase, was close to Mohenjo Daro. The author obviously takes liberties with the time period of these places and collapses their difference in time.

The representation of the Indus Valley in the novel is achieved in multiple ways: the description and details provided by the omniscient narrator through Jaya's perspective, the comments of various characters like Iaf, Rafa, Jay, and Liam, and most importantly through a supposedly authentic history textbook that Layla was reading and that Nadia 'reads' to the reader. Thus Jay informs Nadia about Indus script being one of the three oldest scripts in the world, about Indus Valley Civilization being older than Egypt and Mesopotamia and about there being not too many excavations, especially because of Pakistani government's denial of permission for excavations. Liam, a sceptic, comments on various theories about the decline and end of the Indus civilization, some of them are considered conspiracy theories by historians. He refers to Indus river changing course, people abandoning the place because of frequent floods, Aryan invasion, and even the atomic destruction theory advanced by historian David Davenport in his book *Atomic Destruction in 2000 BC*.[6] The use of Layla's textbook as a novelistic device 'reads' for the reader so many important details about the Indus Valley Civilization in one single paragraph:

> The people of Mohenjo-Daro were advanced for their time. They had a sophisticated social structure, a priest king or council which ran the city, numerous technological capabilities such as heated plumbing and metallurgy, a perfectly planned city on a grid, and some very interesting games for children, which was important because in most cultures, 'childhood' was not a concept which existed until the 1800s, according to the authors. But in reality, not much was known about the culture, for the Indus language was still undeciphered

(196)

History is as much about the past as about the present. This is also true about the genre of historical fiction as most novels about history and historical periods reveal a lot about their period of composition. In terms of ideas treated in the novel, both the historical period and the present touch upon the issues facing the present day world. Despite the writer's inclusion of the general facts of the Indus Valley Civilization, such as its symbols, its iconography, its deities, use of barter system, the novel, even when talking about the Ancients, stays close to modern consciousness. Thus, the narrator mentions the presence of crocodiles in the river and how once a little boy lost his arm and part of his shoulder after a crocodile attacked him. The modern consciousness is reflected in the narrator's amazement at the skill of Meluha's healers to save his life. The institutionalized corruption of society in Pakistan is present in Meluha too in equal measure. In order to be Clanned ordinary folks have to pay the Elders who have to pay the priests.

The neat division of society into the Clanned and the Unclanned groups and the Clanned's further categorization into clearly recognizable groups according to their roles and characteristics refers to the caste system in India and the tribal organization of society in Pakistan. However, the tension between various clans, the intense class struggle, and the feeling of unrest are all present day concerns in places like India, Pakistan and even Britain. The novelist brings in the contemporary problem of forced displacement of population in her references to the problems of migrants in the novel.[7] The relationship between the growth of urban culture, development and the movement of people from one place to another seen in the novel is also a major contemporary concern. Half of the Unclanned people in Meluha are immigrants and, as Rafa explains, 'they come here because the places they have left behind are worse' (315). The problems that these migrants have fled from are manifold. Their children are forcibly taken by the priests in Chanu and their women are openly sold in Northlands. Meluha offers them some hope, but even that hope, as Jaya knows, is illusory.

An important strand in the novel is the universal lust for power which results in the dominance of one individual or group over others and the destructive nature of power. This sinister hold of the power of a leader over his flock is treated through the representation of Giving of Light Foundation, founded and developed by Sohail, Nadia's father. Sohail wrote the manifesto of this foundation, a Bible of his movement, in his book titled *Awakening the Light*,[8] GoL, dismissed as a dangerous cult by Nadia, believes in using the collective knowledge of the world to fight disease, poverty and disasters. It believes that humans appeared on the planet much before what the evolutionary theory of Darwin would like everyone to believe. Interestingly, GoL in the novel is seen through the perspective of Nadia, who often dismisses her father and his ideas as 'insane, pompous, a diatribe against any kind of establishment,' but it is the character of Sohail and his cult that is a novelistic triumph in the novel. Much like Milton becoming a Satan's party through his powerful representation of Satan's character in *The Paradise Lost*, the telling resorted to by Nadia appears weak compared to the showing of the cult in the novel. At other times, the arguments of Nadia quoted against Sohail appear more convincing. Thus the following:

> Wasn't it strange, suggested Sohail, how the 1 per cent managed to keep the fortunes, while the poor never succeeded in rising up? Why did capitalism still exist even though it suppressed so many people? Why, every time there was a moment of peace, a new threat would be identified, a new paradigm of world politics would begin? Who was controlling the world
>
> (94)

The power that Sohail commands is also the power of a demagogue, which is a common phenomenon in contemporary times. The idea is that people can be duped easily; they can believe anything; they can follow a mesmerizing speaker uncritically. They lose their ability to distinguish between fact and fiction and true and fake news. This is a common enough phenomenon in many advanced democracies today. The author, fully conversant with this phenomenon because of her experience as a financial journalist, has also spoken about its danger in her interviews while talking about her novel.[9] Sohail's lust for power unites him with Iaf's lust for power in the past just as Nadia's affinity with Jaya pits her against Sohail. Both Iaf and Sohail are equally ruthless in their pursuit of power, not averse to getting their own followers killed. Both GoL and the clan of Iaf, which ironically is matrilineal, are autocratic, self-centred, and patriarchal in which women must be subordinated to men.

Another aspect which binds the two organizations in a sinister relationship is the control of finances. GoL controls enormous amount of funds; it can sponsor archaeological diggings; it has on its payrolls leaders, officers and professors. In the same way, the power of Iaf depends a great deal on his ability to control the finances. As Iaf tells Jaya, 'We are strong because we have power. And power comes from wealth, does it not' (155). Meluha receives tithes from important cities like Dilmun, Chanu, and Arrapha without doing enough for the inhabitants of these lands. Meluha is on the verge of a revolution only when the financial structures of the city collapse and people start starving.

The novel has a female protagonist in Nadia as well as a number of other female characters, which include Layla, Jahanara, Jaya, and Merrianne. However, as the issue of gender is seen in relation to the distribution of power in society between men and women, most of these female characters exercise power in their limited domain. In her portrayal of Jaya and her prehistoric times, the novel uses the present discourse on gender. The empowerment of women is very much the concern of the novelist but equally important is her understanding of patriarchal control that modern women face in traditional societies.

Muslim female characters in the novel are very different from the stock image of Muslim women in popular media. Both Layla and Nadia, though of Pakistani origin, are British citizens having received the best kind of education. They do not show any self-consciousness about drinking or having a relationship with men. However, there is a hint of Layla's discomfort with pork. Jay, Layla's friend who shares his flat with her, tells Nadia that Layla 'doesn't let me smoke in the flat. Or fry bacon, though she just about stomachs the smell of chicken in black bean sauce' (88). Nadia in particular refuses to be browbeaten by patriarchal control. In the representation of Muslim women, Maha Khan Phillips casts a sideways ironic glance at their representation in the Western media.

To conclude, it can be said that Maha Khan Phillips's two novels are deeply political as most Pakistani novels in English are. They join the debate about the representation of Pakistan in the Western media. They also show her understanding of history, historiography, contemporary politics, and the machinations of power in different times. Her intervention becomes successful because of her skill at handling the genres of thrillers and popular novel.

Notes

1 The most prominent example of this genre of writing is Jean Sasson's *The Princess Trilogy*. Sasson's very problematic representation of the Muslim world relies on all possible Orientalist tropes in a very simplistic manner.
2 The phenomenon of fake news and its use to capture and control power, facilitated by the new technology, rise of social media and availability of cheap smartphones, and easy access to internet connectivity, is undoubtedly the most common phenomenon in both authoritarian states and advanced democracies.
3 The cities of Harappa and Mohenjo Daro, though extensively researched by archeologists and historians, have not exercised the imagination of as many creative writers and film-makers from the subcontinent as one would expect, considering the significance of the

two cities in world's prehistory. A Google search for films set in ancient Egyptian period throws a list of hundreds of films, whereas a similar search for films set in Indus Valley meets with almost no results. In fact, Ashutosh Gowarkar's 2016 Hindi film *Mohenjo Daro* is the only worthwhile effort to put this ancient civilization on the celluloid. As for literary fiction, prolific Hindi writer Rangey Raghav wrote *Murdo Ka Tila*, while in Urdu Yakoob Yawar's *Dilmun* and Mustansar Hussain Tarar's *Bahao* have been set in the Indus Valley. Some other notable works set in Indus Valley civilization include *Winter on the Ghosts: A Novel of Mohenjo Daro* by Eleen Kernaghan, *Trade Winds of Meluha* by Vasant Dave, and Satyajit Ray's story *The Unicorn Expedition*.

4 The idea of a glorious, uncorrupted past has been used by right-wing parties in a number of countries which include India, Turkey, France, Britain, and others in recent decades.

5 In recent years a number of statements of many leaders in India have tried to link many modern inventions to ancient wisdom of India. Thus, speaking to a gathering of doctors at a Mumbai hospital in 2014, Prime Minister Narendra Modi referred to Karna's birth out of his mother's womb in Mahabharata and credited it to genetic science of the times and fixing of an elephant's head on Ganesha to plastic surgery. Other leaders have talked about the existence of internet in the days of Mahabharata, nuclear tests in the 2nd century BC, and Sita as a test tube baby.

6 All these theories about the end of Indus Valley Civilization are a matter of intense academic discussion. In her Author's Note, Maha Khan Phillips specially credits David Davenport's book *Atomic Destruction in 2000 BC*: ' . . . It was references to that book which first piqued my interest in setting a thriller in the Indus Valley' (439).

7 One of the greatest crises facing the 21st century is the issue of migrants, refugees, and internally displaced people in almost all parts of the world.

8 In her Author's Note, Maha Khan Phillips sheds light on the sources used for Sohail's beliefs: 'Many of Sohail's beliefs in this novel stem from the Forbidden Archaeology movement. The specific examples used by his cult to prove that human beings have lived on earth for billions of years came from the books and writings of Graham Hancock, David Hatcher, and Michael A. Cremo and Richard L. Thompson,' p. 439.

9 Thus, in an interview to Jaya Bhattacharji Rose, Maha Khan Phillips said: 'I've always been fascinated by cults. How do they work? Why on earth do people fall for charismatic leaders, giving up everything, even their lives in some cases? I suppose in my mind, there's a resonance with the political world now. People have started positioning themselves with these myopic identities and ideologies and aren't willing to broaden their thinking. Cults are very much about "Us and Them" and I feel the world is heading in that direction too. Look at all the fake news we have been seeing, and how quickly it's being disseminated as gospel through social media. Look at religious extremism. And, perhaps the best example – was there ever a cult leader as successful as Donald Trump? I don't know what's in the Kool-Aid he's been handing out, but he's tweeted his way to cult like devotion amongst his followers, in my opinion – providing them with an ideology that will not help them, and yet spinning the tale so well that they believe life will get better.' Bookwitty 7 March 2017. www.jayabhattacharjirose.com/pakistani-author-maha-khan-phillips-on-her-new-novel-the-curse-of-the-mohenjodaro/ Accessed 8 July 2019.

Works cited

Akbar, Arifa. "*Granta* 112: Pakistan, Edited by John Freeman." *Independent*, Friday 17 Sept. 2010, www.independent.co.uk/arts entertainment/books/reviews/granta-112-pakistan-edited-by-john-freeman-2081186.html. Accessed 8 July 2019.

Gorman, Daniel O. *Ambivalent, Fictions of the War on Terror: Difference and the Transnational 9/11 Novel*. Palgrave Macmillan, 2015.

Phillips, Maha Khan. *Beautiful from this Angle*. Penguin Books India, 2010.

———. "Interview to Maheen Bashir." *Newsline*, Feb. 2001, http://newslinemagazine. com/magazine/interview-maha-khan-phillips/ Accessed 8 July 2019.

———. "Author's Note." *The Curse of Mohenjo Daro*. Pan Macmillan, 2016, p. 438.

Khalid, Haroon. "If Pakistan Shuns the Term 'Ancient India', is it Entirely to Blame?" *Scroll. in,* 31 Aug. 2018, https://scroll.in/article/892597/if-pakistan-shuns-the-term-ancient-india-in-its-history-books-is-it-entirely-to-blame. Accessed 8 July 2019.

———. "In Pakistan, Appreciation of the Indus Valley Civilization." *Scroll.in*, 24 Aug. 2018, https://scroll.in/article/891655/in-pakistan-appreciation-of-indus-valley-civilisation-ties-in-with-attempts-to-erase-its-hindu-past. Accessed 8 July 2019.

12

OCCUPYING EDUCATIONAL AND INTELLECTUAL SPACE

Woman as radical flâneuse in Zahida Zaidi's campus novel *Inqilab ka Ek Din*

Aysha Munira Rasheed

Introduction

In *Oxford Triumphant* (1954), Norman Longmate comments on the production of campus fiction in and about the University of Oxford, 'Oxford has been fortunate in her novelists; they have rarely been brilliant but they have never been unkind' (Longmate 153) is interesting and may be accurate in its context. However, all the campuses may not be as fortunate as the Oxford in the matter of literary, especially, fictive representation. Looking at the production of campus fiction about the Aligarh Muslim University, it will be unfair not to notice conspicuous lacunae, which is sparingly filled by some sparks of brilliance by a handful of writers. Literary representations of campus life of the Aligarh Muslim University such as Ismat Chughtai's *Tedhi Lakeer* (first published in 1943), *Kaghazi Hai Pairahan* (first published in 1988), Mohammad Hasan's *Gham-e-Dil, Wahshat-e-Dil* (2003), Ali Sardar Jafri's *Lucknow ki Paanch Raatein* (2013), Punathil Kunjabdullah's *Aligarh Kathakal* (2012), and Asif Naqvi's *Ajeeb Din Thae* either devote just a few chapters to it, or can be categorized as memoir, biography instead of campus fiction. It is probably only two novels, both written by women writers from the campus, Zahida Zaidi's *Inqilab ka Ek Din* (1996) and Namita Singh's *Ladies Club* (2011), which belong to the genre of campus fiction, being academic in their thematic occupation with the Aligarh Muslim University as their setting. These novels, the former written in Urdu and the latter in Hindi, diarize and describe the hopes and aspirations of female characters, their assertion of independence and their claiming space in the campus which is caught between the forces of tradition and modernity. Zaidi's *Inqilab ka Ek Din* is focused on one female character who is allied with the progressives of the time, defies the social norms that restrict women's movement, claims her subjectivity and looks on and around with a gaze which is appreciative as well as critical.

DOI: 10.4324/9781003002062-16

Zahida Zaidi considered herself a poet and is known as a translator of continental drama and a critic rather than a fiction writer. Zaidi was a professor in the Department of English, Aligarh Muslim University, Aligarh, India and a member of the Progressive Writers' Association. She was also an active member of the Students' Federation and the Marxist Study Circle. *Inqilab ka Ek Din* (A Day of Revolution) was written during a time in which the mission and struggle for education of women had reached a point when an opportunity was open for women to assert themselves in various social spaces, namely educational, literary, intellectual, academic, and the ideological. It was a time when the role of women was still defined in traditional terms, and yet a space in the external world was gradually being claimed and created for expansion of what women could do; and the extension of women's domain of work from four walls of household and boarding houses to the sprawling space of university campus was being accepted. The perceptible transition from tradition to modernity offered women potential of educational and intellectual as well as ideological assertion. *Inqilab ka Ek Din* delineates characters of young women laying an unabashed and rightful claim to the intellectual space instead of the affective and emotional. In order to understand and put this transition into perspective, the chapter traces, in brief, the history of the movement for women's education, and the issue of *purdah* and women's independence, for one cannot be discussed without the other in the context of Muslim society. It looks into the expansion of women's physical mobility as a by-product of the movement and concludes that Zaidi's bike-riding independent female protagonists, despite being rare and avant-garde, is a possibility and a potential reality.

The female characters in *Inqilab ka Ek Din* are the fruits of the labour which the champions of women's education had invested into a mission of carving a modern society out of a traditional Muslim set-up. The young female character in the novel is in possession of a subjectivity which enables her to glance around at the space she occupies in order to know it, examine it, analyse and understand it, making her claim to a prominent niche legitimate. The novel also highlights the fact that the countercurrents to the progressive ideas embodied by the narrative voice in the novel are also available drawing attention to the fact that regressive interpretations of religion are atavistically present threatening women's freedom.

Women's education and the Aligarh movement

Sir Syed Ahmed Khan understood the state of women, their mental caliber in relational terms, in terms of their being unsuitable companions for men. To him women in their present condition were like beasts with whom men had to spend their lives without any joy. In an article '*Hindustan ki Aurton ki Halat*' (The Condition of Indian Women) in *Akhbar Scientific Society*, (*Aligarh Institute Gazette*), 14 April 1876, he begins with a statement, which sounds misogynistic, calling women 'weak in intellect.' However, he goes on to compare them with birds of flight who are caged since their young age (Panipati 188). It is an idea which surprisingly adumbrates Simon de Beauvoir's observation in *The Second Sex* (first published in

1949): "Instead of giving a 'substantive value' to 'to be,' which the current condition of a particular person or people in bad faith, 'to be' must be understood in the sense of the 'Hegelian dynamic' (Beauvoir 32). She further adds, 'women in general are today inferior to men; that is, their situation provides them with fewer possibilities: the question is whether this state of affairs must be perpetuated' (Beauvoir 32). The mention of the above two thinkers, seemingly in diametrical opposition to each other in probably every possible respect, may sound incongruent to many. Sir Syed Ahmad Khan was a visionary of his time, but is often perceived as falling deficient in thought and action in the matter of women's education. However, his statements vis à vis women's education put in the perspective of his time and seen in the context of the entire gamut of his statements, otherwise smacking of misogyny, may sound pardonable. Sir Syed touched upon the idea of creating space for women to grow as human beings and yet could not do much about it. Other people associated with Women's Education Section of Mohammedan Educational Conference took over from where he had left.

The reformist movement of Aligarh with its focus on women's education had started to pick up momentum since the end of the 19th century and became stronger in its demand for availability of formal education and institution with the advent of the 20th century. Ghulam Saqlain, Karamat Hussain, Mumtaz Ali, and Shaukat Ali were among the most active leaders for the cause. Sheikh Abdullah, who got married to Waheed Jahan, alias Ala Bi, a home-educated girl from a Delhi aristocratic family, became the secretary of Women's Education Section in 1902 and started to make efforts along with his wife to establish a madrasa or school for girls (Bano 608). Ismat Chughtai in her memoir, *Kaghazi Hai Pairahan* (The Papery Attire), mentions that as a student she often got the opportunity to talk to Ala Bi or Begum Waheed Jahan. Ala Bi shared with her that she always dreamt of establishing a girls' school and had opened an informal school at home for the children of servants and girls of her locality. When she married Shaikh Abdullah, she found a kindred spirit in him (Chughtai 158). The most important concern the founders of the girls' school at Aligarh initially faced was the issue of purdah. The primary concern people had vis a vis girls' education was the possibility of the norms of modesty and purdah being flouted. Hence purdah instead of being shown as a hurdle to education was put at the heart of the campaign for female education. It was claimed that the purdah the champions of female education believed in followed *Sharia* (Islamic code of conduct) more accurately, and girls within the four walls of a residential campus were safer from potential threat of mixing with the other gender in comparison to when they lived with their families.

Sir Syed Ahmed Khan's views on purdah sound intriguing. In his article 'Purdah,' he says that he considered purdah a fine practice among Muslims, but regards the discussion whether purdah was mandatory for women according to the Quran quite improper since discussions around Quranic edicts to be followed by men were not as much popular (Panipati 186–87). One of the greatest ironies still is that after the passage of more than a century, women are still perceived as repository of male honor, and the hypervisible identity markers graded in various degrees of piety are considered more important than other religious commands meant for men. *Inqilab ka Ek Din* touches upon the subject of purdah with irony and humour, but does not fail to make a clear statement about it.

Unveiling and *Inqilab ka Ek Din*

Chughtai started her writing career as a student in the Aligarh Muslim University at the time of colonial India, while Zaidi came of age around the middle of the century in the nascent nation of independent India. The dream behind the struggle of the Aligarh Movement for transition from tradition to modernity in Chughtai's *Kaghazi Hai Pairahan*, a text covering almost a life time with the description of the third decade of campus life in Aligarh, is witnessed in Zahida Zaidi's *Inqilab ka Ek Din* as an accomplished reality. It is not to say that the project of women's emancipation and the space for assertion of female subjectivity on the campus and various other academic and intellectual spaces are accomplished in absolute terms. The novel in fact focuses on the incomplete nature of emancipation post 1947. The narrative voice in *Inqilab ka Ek Din*, Sadqa, a 22-two-year-old master's degree student in the department of English, is instrumental in getting the screen between boys and girls removed. The novel also mentions that she achieves the same '*kar-nama*' (feat) when she is a student in the department of Education (Zaidi 37).

Inqilab ka Ek Din mentions that in case of the *purdah* there were movements going on for as well as against it. Among women, who were the stakeholders, contestatory attitudes and conflicting ideas and movements were to be found on the campus of the Aligarh Muslim University. The characters such as Shaheena and Shafeeqa Haee take upon them the onus of protection of girls from male gaze, make wearing light coat fashionable for girls of their clique, but ironically, as Sadqa claims, attract more male attention (Zaidi 36–38). Interestingly Shaheena justifies the use of coat as a sartorial choice for women students relating it with the tradition of the University of Oxford and Cambridge, where students then wore coats. She has a growing clique of followers among female students who try to convince Sadqa to follow the norm of wearing a coat they try to establish. For Sadqa Oxford and Cambridge traditions were to be followed when she would go there. As mentioned earlier, the movement for female education around the end of the 19th century and the beginning of the 20th century revolved around the concept of *purdah* which was based on the Islamic code of conduct. This narrative presents a big irony regarding the clash of ideas in the matter of female students' sartorial choice: it is that with the passage of time it is not only the tradition of purdah which is flouted, but also the very rationale of a version of *purdah*, the use of a light coat itself shifts from the *Sharia* to the Oxford as its inspirational source. Obliquely the young narrator informs the readers that her protection from male gaze is her self-confidence, out-spokenness, and independence; for Saheena and Shafeeqa Haee it is the visible coat. The narrator's emphasis throughout the novel is on her subjectivity and her ability to view, observe, examine, scrutinize, and comment on people she interacts with; her intellectual and academic space; and local, national and international politics.

The radical flâneuse

Sadqa, the young female narrator in *Inqilab ka Ek Din,* is limited neither to the four walls of her house nor to the boundary of the campus of the university in her intellectual as well as social space: she resists what she considers unnecessary vestiges of the past, participates in a communist party school meant for bourgeois girls aiming at taking them out of the bourgeois comfort zone, and pedals around peddling books of literature, Marxism and revolutionary ideas. Unlike Dorothy Wordsworth (Pascoe 165), she is a guilt-free ambler, one who is a viewer as well as viewed. As readers we see the narrator biking through the streets of the campus and outside it, its houses, faculties, departments, libraries, seminar halls, the market place of the Numaish ground (Exhibition ground), and the country side where she attends a party school like an intellectual flâneuse with a purpose. The narrator, one of the revolutionary girls riding bicycles depicted on posters (Zaidi 106), redefines or expands the role of a flâneur who serves as a 'modern archetype' (Lauster 140), a 'figure of the modern artist-poet,' and as 'an amateur detective and investigator of the city' (Shaya 47). Sadqa of course does not avert her gaze from her field of action to the display windows of the market place as Walter Benjamin alleges that flâneur does with 'the triumph of consumer capitalism' (Shaya 47). She consciously attempts to serve 'as a vehicle for the examination of the conditions of modernity – urban life, alienation, class tensions, and the like' (Stephan 2013). Of course, the narrator protagonist is herself a subject of her observation, while she examines the clash and conflict between tradition and modernity, and her social alienation especially from her peer group, and attains at least a theoretical understanding of class conflict through her participation in the communist party activities such as her three day long stay in a village to attend party school. Her detachment from the grass root condition is a result of her affiliation to the university space which, especially in case of a woman, means privilege and entitlement which is denied to women outside her space.

Inqilab ka Ek Din recounts the events of a single day in the life of the radical flâneuse, Sadqa. The novel is a slice of life describing a day in the life of the protagonist from the morning till the sunset. It describes an ordinary day in the life of the narrator which by no means is ordinary given the fact that, oscillating between tradition and modernity, she bikes to the university, lectures in the Marxist Study Circle, and peddles revolutionary books taking them from the book stall of the Communist Party (Zaidi 18). While the novel's commentary on the ideological conflicts between the right and the left on the campus evidenced through witty and humorous, and anecdotal observations is important, its elaborate discussion and narration of internal politics within the radical circle of communist party is as much worth appraisal. Sadqa is critical of the authoritarianism, which marks the party leadership. In a detailed account of her secret meeting with an underground party leader, Comrade Lal Salam, she asserts her right to stage an adaptation of Krishan Chand's *Anyadata* (*The Food-Giver*), for which she does not seek permission. The leader calls her vain and bourgeois, while she remains unrelenting in her aesthetic and ideological pursuit and is not willing to forsake an inch of her socio-cultural space (Zaidi 61–66).

In order to describe Sadqa's stepping out of her house to occupy space on the campus, Zaidi repeatedly uses the Urdu word '*muhim*,' which means campaign, mission, or battle (Zaidi 19, 23, 27, 83). Sadqa and her sisters' involvement and party activities land them in jail. The area of her scrutiny and examination reaches the inner circles of the communist party. As a young woman, with freedom, despite restrictions, to move in the intellectual, ideological, and physical spaces beyond the four walls of domesticity through radical activities to inside the prison walls, the radical flâneuse makes a long journey much beyond the traditionally defined role worth calling '*muhim*.'

While Sadqa and Saleha Alvi are able to create their niche in the academic and intellectual circles of the university, another sister Sadia who was married off at the age of 19 and has a child, feels deprived and unhappy. Sadqa categorizes her sister Sadia as a non-serious student in her college life, mixing with girls who were interested in fun, frivolous activities and parties (Zaidi 22–25). It is apparent that after marriage she comes to know the value of freedom, education, individual identity and respect. The 'four walls' of marital household makes her feel 'incarcerated' (Zaidi 22). Deprivation makes her realize the importance of education and motivates her to the extent that she is able to complete her graduation while she is expecting her first child (Zaidi 22).

Although the social space Sadqa and Saleha Alvi negotiate was gradually shunning the practice of gender segregation, continuities of the past in the mental landscape of the society could still be witnessed. Women, being bound by a stricter law of the threshold than men, keep their distance from men to be taken seriously and avoid marriage altogether if possible. Sadqa takes pride in her lack of interest in romance and emotional subjects. 'Staying away from emotions was a special quality of Sadqa's personality, and she had become an expert in boring her lovers' (Zaidi 29).

The narrator projects herself as distanced from the affective. She appreciates poetry of a particular university teacher, Baqar Ansari, for its brevity and intellectual content. Nevertheless, she mixes freely with men who were definitely in majority on the campus and connects with them at an intellectual level. Her own assessment is that despite her acceptable looks, she lacks the 'sex appeal' that attracts a man to a woman. In fact, the obvious is just hinted upon: it is her merit, independence, and her claim to intellectual space as a student which make her look intimidating to men. Of course the desired hierarchy of male-female relationship is still set at centuries old dominant-passive, intellectual-emotional, knowledgeable-innocent, superior–inferior, powerful–weak, and subject–object dynamic, around which gendered desires are constructed. The fact that Sadqa and Saleha Alvi claim intellectual space and shun the affective make them look radical in a society which considers domestic sphere as a natural domain for women.

The protagonist waits for an ideal partner who could affect her emotionally and intellectually. In fact, the way Sadqa scrutinizes young men on the campus, makes it clear that she is an observer and examiner of intellectual merit of the university dwellers, and uses a yardstick which declares that men need to work and grow mature. She is fascinated by some radical youth, such as Arif Majid and Salman Zuberi, but is not ready to sacrifice her freedom to get a man.

Claiming the intellectual space

All the discussions that Sadqa has with her sister Saleha Alvi, teachers, friends and colleagues revolve around literary criticism and political ideology. She is of the opinion that Wordsworth's *Lyrical Ballads* and Hali have ideas in common, which is a claim she makes in her essay she submits to Asrar sahab, a teacher in her department. In an article Sadqa submits to Professor Mahboob Ali, who is a patron for left workers in the university, she claims that Hamlet is a revolutionary and is on the lookout for justice and truth, and Hamlet's internal conflict is a universal conflict (Zaidi 32–33). As mentioned earlier, she is busy directing a dramatic version of Krishan Chand's story titled *Anyadata* (Food-giver) for the annual function of the Girls' College (Zaidi 33).

Sadqa's main concern and thematic engagement in most of the conversations she has with the academics including her sister Saleha is related to literature, culture and the local, national and international politics. With Saleha her talk is based on a request to discuss Dostoevsky's *Idiot*. Professor Mahboob would like to share with her a new book, *Underground Man*, on Dostoevsky (Zaidi 36). She tells him that she plans to work on *King Lear*. Her gift to her married sister Sadia is not any household item or some make up kit; it rather a collection of stories by Anton Chekov (Zaidi 23). Sadqa's interaction with the young women of her age is also primarily related with activities such as dramatic performances. She claims the limelight of prominence in socio-cultural spaces, she moves in, self-assertively and relentlessly.

Saleha Alvi, another important character who serves as an ideal for the main character, has completed her education America where she was offered a merit-based scholarship. She becomes senior lecturer in the department of History at a young age and is considered an academic par excellence. Her taste of music ranges from Mozart to Paul Robinson and other African-American artists. The novel gives a detailed account of an extension lecture on the topic 'American Democracy and Human Rights,' delivered by Saleha Alvi at the request of a respectable academic, Professor Abdul Majid, who respected only serious and brilliant academic. Saleha Alvi points out in her lecture that capitalism hinders proper functioning of democracy due to the fact that apart from voting rights common people do not get other benefits which democracy can ensure. As an example, she criticizes American democracy which despite its tall claims does not provide space for dissent, and McCarthyism is the political position America follows (Zaidi 52–53). She denounces the fact that African-Americans do not have the same rights, and the communists are targeted what has been called in Arthur Miller's *Crucible* as with-hunting. She pins hope on protest literature, revolutionary art, poetry and theatre, and black music (Zaidi 54). The third person narrator focuses on the impact Saleha

Alvi creates on the audience with her felicity of language and her ability to present a thorough analysis of human rights concerns, she thinks, American has. To broaden the space of influence for Saleha Alvi, she decides to suggest to Professor Mahboob Ali to invite her to lecture in the department of English, where Sadqa is a student. Sadqa is engaged in a constant struggle to expand the reach of ideas of dissent, protest, resistance and revolution in the academic circles on the campus. Interestingly, for her it is not the domestic which extends to the outer space; it is rather the academic and the literary which extends to the domestic. At home her mother writes and recites her self-composed religious poems at the dining table, which Sadqa decides to publish despite the risk of evoking the ire of the party leadership (Zaidi 57–78).

Zaidi's main character Sadqa has an aversion for women whose primary preoccupation in life is to be an object of male desire. Shaheena, her classmate in the final year of master's degree in English, is most popular and is the cynosure among male students. Her *purdah* is a light coat as mentioned earlier, and she observes head-covering and is a delicate feminine character. On the other hand, Sadqa is more popular among teachers since she is outspoken, confident and active, and is the topper of her class: she views more than she is viewed. Sadqa highlights Shaheena's feminine qualities: her coyness and her delicateness, through a tongue-in-check description of 'the beautiful Shafeeqa Haee' and a humorous anecdote related with her and her admirers. Shaheena is saved from the romantic overtures of an admirer by paternalistic protectionism of a teacher. Sadqa reminisces and narrates an anecdote about romantic overture made by a male student with a poetic bent of mind. As she highlights the comicality of unrequited love of a romantic young man and his poetic expression of romantic attraction as it unfolds in the traditional society of Aligarh, she provides information available only to insiders about how romantic emotions and interactions are expressed, repressed, postponed, and sometimes monitored and censured by parents and teachers even after gender segregation is done away with. An admirer of the girl referred to as beautiful scribbles a couplet of Ghalib: '*Nahin nigar ko ulfat, na ho, nigar to hai!/rawani-e-rawish-o-masti-e-ada kahiye*' (*Though love does not exist in the heart of the beloved, the beloved does/ Let's call it flow of stream and intoxicated coquetry*) and also the dedication 'for beautiful Shafeeqa' on the blackboard in the classroom. What transpires later is that Professor Abdul Majid and the object of desire, Shafeeqa, enter the classroom from different doors on the opposite sides, and the professor, after reading the romantic couplet, beats the boy with his attaché full of heavy books in front of the whole class (Zaidi 37–38).

In fact, Sadqa does not rule out the possibility of a romantic association with a person who is compatible with her, but her reality does not seem to provide her such an opportunity points out that the society has not grown up on par with women like Sadqa and hence it offers little opportunity for an equal partnership that young emancipated women can enjoy. Women glancing at their society with confidence, trying to examine, scrutinize and understand it, are women who are feared as well as desired. For such women, the atavistic tendency in the society evokes fear, while the futuristic leanings evoke desire. She claims the space from the campus to the exhibition ground, looks around, sometimes assesses male colleagues as possible partners. Instead of serving as Varda's 'cliché-woman' and 'feminine masquerade,' (3) examined by Janice Mouton in the essay titled 'From Feminine Masquerade to Flâneuse: Agnés Varda's Cleo in the City' in full feminine characteristics, Zaidi's Sadqa confidently claims subjectivity and flânerie in various kinds of social space around her.

Inqilab ka Ek Din as a campus bildungsroman traces the development of the main character as she graduates to a level of transcendence from the earthly and mundane life on the campus to philosophical questions about life and nature. By the end of the novel, the mood of the narrative voice turns more reflective and pensive. Her transcendence appears in form of her detachment from the vindictive, sexual politics which lurks around the corners of the departments and streets on the campus especially targeting women who are radical and intellectual flâneuse like her, or academics like Saleha Alvi, or students active in party schools and *mushaira* (poetic session) namely Salma and Khalda. The novel is autobiographical in essence, and could in all probability be describing a day in the life of the writer. However, I have not tried to find real life parallelism, and by exercising 'negative capability' with a disregard to hankering after factual or real life correspondences, and have read it as campus fiction representing the lifestyle of radical freewheeling women in a society undergoing revolutions in terms of transformation from tradition to modernity in the spheres of education, especially women's education, gender roles, and class struggles.

Despite being a prolific writer, translator, and critic, Zahida Zaidi had to face opposition from the upholders of traditional norms and values from her social/institutional circle or campus. She did not make herself popular in a predominantly traditional social milieu of Aligarh by being a radical in her thoughts and actions. Despite her having ardent admirers who look at her as a breath of fresh air in a society caught between forces of tradition and modernity. Mushirul Hasan, in his 2002 essay, 'Aligarh Muslim University: Recalling Radical Days,' reminisces:

> Amidst the cacophony of noises, it is quite remarkable that a number of women teachers and students occupied the cultural spaces. Though the butt of ridicule and criticism, the three Zaidi sisters, as they were known, actively organised mushairas and music concerts and staged plays. Unconventional in their demeanour and often provocative in their style, especially when one of them would light a cigarette in full public view, they were serious academics and at the same time, activists. Grand daughters of the leading poet and writer, Altaf Husain Hali, a contemporary of Syed Ahmad Khan, Sabira, Sajida and Zahida broke away from family traditions to bring much richness to Aligarh's intellectual and cultural ambience.

(54)

On the campus of the Aligarh Muslim University, Zahida Zaidi mentored artists as prominent as Naseeruddin Shah and was known as a feisty person who was determined, resolute, bold and courageous. Zaidi's Sadqa, is patterned on her young self, about whom she writes with pride, with no trace of fear and regret. Zaidi's bicycle riding flâneuse, Sadqa, is full of dreams about a future that may bring emancipation yet to be attained, working hard to usher in a dawn of revolution for the bound and unfree. After all, Sadqa believes in what Iqbal say: '*jis mein na ho inqilab maut hai wo zindagi*' (life bereft of revolutions/changes is akin to death) (124).

Work cited

Bano, Shadab. "Reform and Identity: Purdah in Muslim Women's Education in Aligarh in the Early Twentieth Century." *Proceedings of the Indian History Congress*, vol. 73, 2012, pp. 607–14.

Beauvoir, Simone de. *The Second Sex*. Translated by Constance Borde and Sheila Malovany-Chevallier. Vintage Books, 2010.

Chughtai, Ismat. *Kaghazi Hai Pairahan*. Publications Division. Wazarat-e-Ittelaat-o-Nashariyat. Hukoomat-e-Hind, 1994.

———. *Tedhi Lakeer*. Kitabkar, 1967.

Hasan, Mohammad. *Gham-e-Dil, Wahshat-e-Dil*. Takhleeqkar Publishers, 2003.

Hasan, Mushirul. "Aligarh Muslim University: Recalling Radical Days." *India International Centre Quarterly*, vol. 29, no. 3/4, India: A National Culture? (Winter 2002–Spring 2003), pp. 47–45.

Jafri, Ali Sardar. *Lucknow ki Paanch Raatein*. Kitabnuma, 2013.

Kunjabdulla, Punathil. *Aligarh Kathakal*. Matrubhumi, 2012.

Lauster, Martina. "Walter Benjamin's Myth of the Flâneur." *The Modern Language Review*, vol. 102, no. 1 (Jan.), 2007, pp. 139–56.

Longmate, Norman. *Oxford Triumphant*. Phoenix House Ltd, 1954.

Mouton, Janice. "From Feminine Masquerade to Flâneuse: Agnès Varda's Cléo in the City." *Cinema Journal*, vol. 40, no. 2 (Winter), 2001, pp. 3–16.

Naqvi, Syed Asif Akhtar. *Ajeeb din thae*. Zahida Publisher and Printer, 2010.

Panipati, Ismail. *Maqalat-e-Sir Syed*. 2nd ed. Majlis-e-Taraqqi Adab, 1990, vol. V.

Pascoe, Judith. "The Spectacular Flâneuse: Mary Robinson and the City of London." *The Wordsworth Circle*, vol. 23, no. 3 (Summer), 1992, pp. 165–71.

Shaya, Gregory. "The Flâneur, the Badaud, and the Making of a Mass Public in France, Circa 1860–1910." *The American Historical Review*, vol. 109, no. 1 (Feb.), 2004, pp. 41–77.

Singh, Namita. *Ladies Club*. Samayik Prakashan, 2011.

Stephan, Bijan. "In Praise of the Flâneur." *The Paris Review*, 2013, https://www.theparisreview.org/blog/2013/10/17/in-praise-of-the-flaneur/. Accessed 5 May 2020.

Zaidi, Zahida. *Inqilab ka Ek Din*. Educational Publishing House, 1996.

13

MAKING SENSE OF CONVERSION TO CHRISTIANITY IN 20TH-CENTURY PAKISTAN

Two women's co-authored autobiographies as crafted accounts

Madeline Clements

Introduction: writing religious conversion in post-colonial Pakistan

Co-authored, Anglophone autobiographical accounts of conversion from Islam to Christianity in Pakistan present readers interested in the perspectives they can offer of Christian lives in the post-colonial Islamic Republic with a number of interpretative problems. This is particularly the case when these narratives are published under neo-Orientalist covers by foreign presses years after the events they recall have supposedly taken place. Considering autobiographical accounts of conversion to Christianity in 19th-century India, Hephzibah Israel observes: 'one's life becomes . . . an object that acquires a life of its own, which can be probed and investigated for "religious truth," "genuineness," and "usefulness" both by oneself and others' (400). Yet such testimonies, she goes on to argue, 'cannot be treated as unmediated records of convert voices' because of their colonial provenance: they have been 'translated, edited, revised and extracted' by European missionaries who would deploy them to support their own evangelizing projects (400).

In a post-colonial Pakistani context, accounts of turning to Christianity, 'written' by Muslim women with the help of western co-authors or ghostwriters, similarly demonstrate a desire on their protagonists' part to make narrative sense of personal experiences of spiritual inspiration and affiliation, social exclusion, fellowship and homecoming. Like their colonial antecedents, these later-life writings have multiple uses: for the converts themselves, as they reflect on their experiences and bear witness; for publishers seeking to profit from the sale of their remarkable stories; for religious readers in search of guidance; and for academics seeking to understand the social and political implications of the public narration of religious translations. But such accounts must always be read with the kind of consciousness Israel encourages

DOI: 10.4324/9781003002062-17

of their mediation – in this case by near-invisible Anglo-American co-authors – into consumable, literary forms.

This chapter focuses on the narrative sense made of conversion to Christianity by two little-discussed autobiographical accounts elicited from Pakistani Muslim women of affluent family backgrounds, namely *I Dared to Call him Father*[1] by Bilquis Sheikh 'with Richard Schneider' (1978) and *The Torn Veil*[2] by Gulshan Esther 'as told to' Thelma Sangster, an author of inspirational non-fiction (1984, 2004). *Father* may have been based partly on the English-speaking Sheikh's diary accounts, referred to in her narrative as a way of safeguarding her story for posterity: 'I had no idea what might happen to me once word got out that I had become a Christian – at least I wanted this record of my experience to remain' (1978 edition, 59). However, it appears from the book's 'Foreword' that the version published by Chosen Books in 1978 may be based on no more than an oral 'outline . . . given to the world' by her American Christian friends, and that Schneider worked fairly independently on the manuscript (Marshall in Sheikh 1978, 9–10). Esther describes her own life history as 'my story,' but this claim is likewise complicated by the acknowledgement on *Veil's* front cover of the ghostwriter, Sangster, and references in the text to Esther's lack of an English education (2004 edition, 129–120, 149).[3] Hence, this chapter exercises caution when it comes to attributing authorship solely to Sheikh and Esther.

Both accounts begin with their reclusive protagonists' discovery and acceptance, through reading scripture, revelatory dreams and seeming healing, of the figure of Jesus and the Christian faith during the rule of Pakistan's modernizing dictator, Mohammad Ayub Khan (1958–1969). They conclude with Sheikh's and Esther's departure to join Christian communities in England and the United States at the time of the subsequent socialist rule of Zulfikar Ali Bhutto (1973–1977) and Islamic conservative regime of General Zia-ul-Haq (1978–1988). In terms of context, then, the period between these women's conversions and their experiences' recollection and re-composition in memoir form was one in which Pakistani national culture and politics were transformed, as Saadia Toor acknowledges, by a shift to the 'religious' right (157–158).[4] By the time of Sheikh's and Esther's accounts' publication in the late 1970s and early 1980s, Zia-ul-Haq's state-sponsored efforts to 'construct a new Islamic "national culture" free of obscenity, and of supposedly treacherous "Hindu" and " 'western" elements,' had resulted in an 'inject[ion] . . . of puritanism' into Pakistan's 'historically tolerant and open society' (151). Literature and the arts in Pakistan, which traditionally presented a challenge to the establishment, including its ideas about cultural and religious purity, were being subjected to acute moral scrutiny and strict political censorship, and efforts made to marginalize 'elitist' English as an official language and educational medium (Toor 151; Shamsie 163, 260). The composition of texts such as *Father* and *Veil* in English, and their detailing of acts of apostasy popularly construable as blasphemous, would have made their circulation in Pakistan at the time of their publication at the very least contentious.[5] Indeed, *Father* and *Veil* continue to present awkward reading in the present, when minority religious affiliations within the majority-Muslim (but not Islamic) state remain a pressing national issue, as President Imran Khan's 2019 Minorities Day speech against the enforced conversion of non-Muslims to Islam demonstrated (*Dawn*, no page). As it stands, *Father* and *Veil* are 'virtually unknown in Pakistan,' although more as a result of their Anglophone composition, foreign publication, and the fact that they cater to the tastes of largely English-speaking, Western, and Christian audiences, than of any direct, political censorship (Shamsie 573). Nevertheless, these Anglophone, diasporic texts by Pakistani women authors remain part of a wider body of literature in English, which reflects on the state of interfaith culture and freedom of expression in Pakistan in the later 20th century; as such, they offer more than the evangelical, Anglo-American agendas which may account for their provenance.[6]

The ensuing discussion of *Father* and *Veil*, and their implications for under-standing how, through such co-authored texts, the place of Christians in mid-to-late 20th-century Pakistan may be represented, is divided into three parts. Firstly, it considers how the narratives order their protagonists' personal experiences of religious transformation in post-colonial Pakistan so as to make personal sense of the women converts' altered lives. Secondly, it goes on to ask how Sheikh's and Esther's memoirs account for the meaning of their authors' spiritual trans-formations for the wider domestic, familial, and national communities in which they are invested. Lastly, it considers the problems of using these co-authored autobiographies, in which 'narrative design and historical truth' may 'come into conflict' (Wright 93), as 'evidence,' whether of the 'spiritual understanding' of women of 'eastern heritage' or of the extent of Pakistani Muslims' capacity to co-exist alongside Christians (Marshall in Sheikh 1978, 11). It argues instead for a reading of such life-writings as implicated in 'complex negotiations with com-peting cultural regimes': individual and collective, Western and subcontinental, 'Islamic' and evangelist (Israel and Zavos 363). It concludes that despite their limitations, they have the capacity to undermine wholly pessimistic assessments of the place and prospects of religious minorities in Pakistan in the late 20th century. At a time when the question of both Muslim and non-Muslim minorities' future in the region remains a matter of significant local and international concern, they warrant closer consideration.

1 Making sense of personal experiences of religious transformation

In his overview of Anglophone Pakistani life-writing, Tariq Rahman (874) briefly considers Sheikh's relatively unknown *Father* as an autobiographical work alongside *Confessions of a Native-Alien* by the more significant and secular poet and novelist Zulfikar Ghose (1965). Rahman deems Sheikh's prose comparatively 'undistin-guished' but considers both books interesting:

> Exceptions in the genre as practiced in Pakistan; others – mostly by generals, politicians and sports figures – are about the doings of the social persona of

the subject and offer no glimpse into either the personal and intellectual life
or the intimate recesses of the psyche of the writer

(874)[7]

Rahman's rare, academic mention therein positions Sheikh's account as providing a novel insight into the mindset of an educated, upper-class Pakistani woman
whose conversion is the result of 'psychological crisis' (874). As a historian of
Pakistani literature in English, he is preoccupied by her book's introspective divergence from the superficial autobiographies of Pakistani celebrities, rather than its
convergences with narratives of transformation produced to 'meet the religious
needs of those "looking for an order and a meaning in life"' (Wright 92). Rahman's position is interesting because of the alternative, private perspectives of Pakistani subjectivity it suggests such autobiographies are capable of revealing.[8] For the
purposes of this current section, however, it must also be acknowledged that, as
they try to trace meaningful patterns in personal experiences and weave them into
coherent wholes, Sheikh's and Esther's co-written autobiographies also echo and
speak to long-established and emerging traditions of writing religious transformation. These stretch from 4th-century Latin confessions to narratives of re-formed
selves created in colonial South Asia, and to inspirational life stories produced
by Anglo-American Christian publishers since the 1970s 'to help millions to live
Spirit-empowered lives' (Israel, Wright, Baker Publishing Group). The 'intimate'
accounts of spiritual discovery, fellowship, marginalization, and reconciliation in
post-colonial Pakistan which emerge should be read as shaped by this variety of
literary trends and antecedents.

Originally published six years apart by American and British Christian imprints,
Father (1978) and *Veil* (1984) bear many similarities, which reflect their generic
construction as conversion narratives. Both tell from a first-person perspective, and
through a series of chapters with signpost headings common to other evangelical titles, the story of an affluent, educated Pakistani woman removed from her
influential and religiously conservative Muslim family and experiencing existential
uncertainty: Sheikh following separation and divorce, Esther as a result of the failure
to find a cure for paralysis incurred in infanthood.[9] In each, the convert-protagonist
is led as a result of illness, death, and peculiar happenings to seek beyond the
Qur'an for a God to whom she feels she might speak as a friend and father. Each
woman experiences dreams and visions in which she encounters Jesus. Through
illicit procurement of copies of the Bible in Urdu and in English, both protagonists
engage in intense self-study and make contact with foreign missionaries and indigenous Christians. These acquaintances provide practical support, spiritual guidance, and fellowship. But they also urge caution on the basis of assumptions about
the prevalence of hostility towards apostasy (the rejection or abandonment of Islam,
the majority faith in the fledgling post-colonial nation) and Christianity (a religion
with historic colonial and low-caste associations). These concerns surface in particular when the newly converted Sheikh and Esther express their determination
to be baptized and bear witness to their religious transformations. Each woman

experiences a loss in status, periods of ostracism, and threats to her personal safety as a result of her change of faith, but is ultimately reconciled with members of their family, who are also miraculously converted.

The narratives end with Sheikh and Esther taking up invitations to share their stories with Christian communities in Britain and North America, and some last attempts to order and place a conclusive, retrospective gloss on the often confusing and contradictory events of their transformed lives. In her final chapter, Sheikh (with Schneider) accepts as God's plan her initially temporary departure from Pakistan in 1972, 'brought . . . out of my homeland, like Abram,' Genesis' archetypal man of faith (1978, 169). Nostalgia for all she appears to have lost is overwritten by 'such a feeling of *completion!*', strongly reinforced by animated typography. Yet a distinct hint of wistfulness lingers in the 'Epilogue,' which offers a further framing of events six years after she left:

> The knowledge that I would not see Pakistan again [on leaving for the US] was prophetic.
>
> I have not been back. My friends have warned that it is best for me. . . . I have been given similar messages from others in authority. . . . It's evident I would not be welcome back in Pakistan now.
>
> Most important, the Lord has made it clear that I remain here . . . I must encourage Americans to appreciate their freedom to worship Christ. And I must pray for my own country . . .
>
> [The ancestral estate of] Wah is now behind me. . . . For now my home is in the Lord.
>
> (171–73)

Ironically, the inclusion of these somewhat muted musings threatens to undermine the triumphal conclusions about leaving Pakistan for America which the foreign-published conversion narrative would encourage. At the end of *Veil*, Esther (with Sangster) proclaims with seemingly greater clarity and certainty:

> The great fear in my aunt's mind, when I first testified to my healing by Jesus, was that I should go to England. Well, here I am . . .
>
> I can see that the pilgrimage [to Mecca] that my father embarked on with me was the start of my soul's quest of knowing God . . .
>
> Today I am witness to the power of God to reach people who are behind the veil of Islam. That veil can be torn away, so that they can see Jesus, hear him and love.
>
> (Esther 2004, 147)

Unlike Sheikh, Esther makes no direct attempt in these summative passages to make sense of the highly contradictory (and controversial) part played by Pakistan in her life story. In *Veil* it appears as a brutal place where, as is shockingly and belatedly divulged, a Muslim neighbour can appropriate a Christian convert's property and shoot dead her adoptive daughter with seeming immunity.[10] Yet it also functions as a unifying location where Esther's Muslim brother, resurrected following an illness, can be reconciled to the idea of following Jesus, and so to his estranged sister. Nevertheless, in Esther's narrative, the focus remains on the significance of a loving Muslim daughter's conversion to Christianity and on her capacity to communicate to global listeners the universality of her life-lesson. For, according to Esther, if Jesus 'can penetrate the dark world of the Muslim faith that [she] was in, he can help you too' (152). Although her message, as this quotation suggests, is ultimately quite Islamophobic, the violence of the supposedly 'honorable' Pakistani men, the sudden volte-faces of the estranged family, and indeed the 'torn veil' metaphor which *Veil* features, appear ill-fitted to Esther's personal narrative, which, it may be argued, is at its core more a story of bildungsroman-like maturation and progression than one of rupture (150).

In both *Father* and *Veil*, Sheikh's and Esther's literacy – their ability to read on literal and metaphorical planes – is central to how their conversions take place, to the growth of their faith, and to their capacity to interpret and attribute symbolic significance to the experiences they recollect. In his consideration of how religious autobiographies 'construct . . . the self' in the European tradition, Wright asserts that they are 'at least in part the products of "intertextuality"' and that 'their authors can only "find" themselves and God in the literary forms which have been evolved for self-discovery and theological understanding' (93–95). He describes the Bible as one particular text that 'provid[es] models upon which . . . readers' might base their interpretations of religious experience (96). Wright also looks to the significance of Augustine's 'extremely intertextual' 4th-century conversion narrative, *Confessions*, in patterning out an emotional mode of responding to the Psalms and the Gospels, which brings the reader into a 'most intense awareness of himself and of God' (96–97). Sheikh's and Esther's accounts, produced at a time when the 'supremacy of scripture' was being ranked above all other priorities by 20th-century Western Evangelicals, are similarly punctuated by citations from scripture which elicit spirited responses and affirmative actions (Bebbington 19).[11] When the aggrieved Sheikh is troubled, for example, by hatred for her ex-husband (concerning which, she reports, a quotation from the Qur'anic 'Surah Al-Baqara' has provided no comfort), a citation surfaces from the Gospel of Matthew: 'My yoke is easy and my burden is light' (1978, 27, 68). This initiates a tearful confession and reconciliation with God. Sheikh describes her response to the Bible excerpt in the same metaphorical terms: 'Slowly, deliberately, I swung my terrible burden over. . . . I sensed a light rising within me . . . Once again I found myself living in His glory' (68). Here the scriptural 'literary form' and 'biblicism' so fundamental to Evangelical religious experience indeed appear to 'fashion [Sheikh's] religious experience, providing the structure' through which she comprehends her altered feelings and her place, as God's follower, in life (Wright 106; Bebbington 19). She describes herself as prepared to 'obey . . . Him explicitly, with the Bible' – presumably the Phillips modern English translation of the New Testament she was given by American missionaries – 'as [her] only check' (Sheikh 1978, 77).

Following this intertextual visitation, and again appearing instinctively to adhere to Evangelical priorities in keeping with those of her American publisher and co-writer, Sheikh proceeds to draw a henna cross on each hand as a reminder 'never . . . again . . . [to] step away from His company' (1978, 69).[12] The literal inscription of her conversion onto her body anticipates the highly symbolic, and narratively central, issue of her baptism. She understands the latter as 'the one unmistakable sign' to Muslims 'that a convert has renounced his Islamic faith to become a Christian' and hence as 'a difficult testing point' on her spiritual journey (71). Israel points to how, in Protestant narratives of high-caste conversions published in English in India during the early 20th century, 'events, including errors committed by others, are retrospectively assigned providential value,' ordered in such a way that 'the narrating I [can] "recognis[e]" itself as in a mirror, a fully formed individual chosen by divine grace" (411). These dynamics certainly appear to be at play here, in *Father*, and also in Esther's *Veil*, where she reflects on her childhood as 'Gulshan' (literally, "flower garden"), a Pakistani Muslim Sayed's beloved, devout, and 'cripple[d]' daughter (2004, 10–11). From the start, Esther's narrative appears to cast her as receptive to religious messages and in search of God's healing: 'looking back now, I can trace a purpose in those captive years, when my mind and spirit unfolded like rosebuds in our well-watered garden' (10–11). Reading religious transformation as preordained enables convert (and co-author) to finesse the narrative, smoothing the transition from Muslim to Christian so as to present it as possible to readers, even as its adversity is highlighted.

My focus here has been on European and Evangelical traditions of religious life-writing as shaping influences in Sheikh's and Esther's personal narratives. However, it is important also to emphasize that their accounts of conversion to Christianity may also be read in relation to traditions of (co-)writing religious conversion and women's autobiography in the context of colonial and early post-colonial South Asia, such as those discussed in the special section of the journal *South Asia* entitled *Narratives of Transformation: Religious Conversion and Indian Traditions of 'Life Writing,'* edited by Israel and Zavos (2018) and referred to throughout this chapter; in *Telling Lives in India: Biography, Autobiography, and Life History*, edited by David Arnold and Stuart Blackburn (2004); and in *Speaking of the Self: Gender, Performance and Autobiography in South Asia*, edited by Anshu Malhotra and Siobhan Lambert-Hurley (2015). The memoirs co-authored by Pakistani women converts and Western ghost writers which I consider partly replicate and occasionally re-write tropes identified in these critical volumes as female South Asian subjects attempt to make sense of their transformed lives. But Ether's and Sheikh's accounts also perhaps diverge in subtle ways from earlier models.

In the last of the three aforementioned publications, for example, Sylvia Vatuk (2015, 33–55) emphasizes the role of reading, in this case of Urdu novels, in the construction of a young Muslim girl's sense of self in pre-independence India. For Vatuk's Zakira Begum, 'the kinds of books [she] particularly enjoyed' and whose 'fictional worlds helped . . . other young girls of her time . . . to construct a sense' of self were 'not readily available in her religiously conservative home': although religious learning was highly valued and taught to children of both sexes, it was her mother's love of Urdu, taught to Begum after she had mastered Arabic, that instilled her life-long passion for Urdu literature (33, 37). In Sheikh's and Esther's accounts, the capacity of literate, upper-class Pakistani women to make sense of the experiences that lead to their conversions is similarly portrayed as substantially indebted to their Muslim Pakistani families' established traditions of religious education and approach to holy texts and, although their turn to reading the Bible is characterized as a rebellion, continuities are emphasized. Sheikh, the well-travelled ex-wife of Pakistan's former Minister for the Interior, has read the Qur'an in Arabic as a child and in Urdu as an adult; Esther, the daughter of a Shia Pir raised in purdah, has also read the Qur'an in its original language. Sheikh proceeds to study the Bible in Urdu and English, and Esther to obtain Urdu versions of the Qur'an and the Bible, although she claims that her father's anti-colonial 'prohibition' prevents her reading English (Esther 2004, 129–30).

What comes across in both *Father* and *Veil*, albeit in different measures, is an inherited reverence on the part of both women, their friends and family, for the divine texts of people, such as Christians, designated *Ahl al-Kitāb* ('people of the Book'). This renders them open to pursuing a search in and beyond the Qur'an for the 'prophet and healer, Jesus' and receptive to perceiving 'a prophecy' in chanced upon passages, whether of the Qur'an or of the Bible – although both of their accounts characterize the Bible as easier to interpret 'without guidance,' and as providing greater comfort (Esther 2004, 50, 79; Sheikh 1978, 26, 31–32, 27 cf. 67). Indeed, it might be argued that Sheikh's and Esther's facility with the Qur'an is portrayed in their post-colonial accounts as laying the foundation for their highly intertextual, emotional and intellectual conversions to the faith of a people deemed perhaps theologically 'wrong' but still 'sympathetic' by their Muslim Pakistani families because they possess and 'share the same book' (Esther 2004: 15). This is certainly one more positive interpretation of their trajectories towards which (largely western, Christian, and post-Vatican II) readers of their assisted, Anglophone autobiographies are encouraged.[13] However, Sheikh's and Esther's accounts also emphasize their religious translations' other more complex and more troubling meanings for the Pakistani communities within which their events are primarily situated.

2 Making sense of conversion's meaning for wider communities

When highlighting how *Father* differs significantly from other, mostly male, Pakistani celebrity autobiographies, Tariq Rahman implies that the value of this literary work lies in the deeper insight it offers into the 'psyche of the writer,' unspecified 'taboo areas,' and family affairs, rather than Pakistani 'history [and] general culture' (874). This idea is interesting, but needs to be approached with caution. As he privileges what the upper-class Sheikh's account can reveal of her interior intellectual, domestic world, Rahman perhaps both echoes and contradicts long-established, European, anthropological traditions of (mis)interpreting South Asian identities and life-writing as 'collective.' Arnold and Blackburn observe that in this area of scholarship (South Asian life-writing) 'a paradigm . . . has tended to prevail' in which 'identities founded on caste and religion dominated to such a degree that individual agency and selfhood were [assumed] marginal to South Asian thought and behavior' (2). According to this perspective, only 'a few privileged individuals might be [considered] sufficiently exceptional – or Westernized – [so as] to . . . be able to compose their own self-narratives' (2). As neither 'generals, politicians, [nor] sports figures' (Rahman 874), but, nevertheless, educated women from influential, landowning families, Sheikh and Esther may be understood as privileged enough to be able to testify to their self-led and idiosyncratic experiences of conversion and to participate in their transcription into English.[14] Yet their narratives provide more than the cloistered insight into a 'psychological crisis' leading to private conversion and transgression, which Rahman might set as Sheikh's literary and apolitical limit: they additionally reflect (on) the implications of their protagonists' personal transformations for a variety of communities in which their authors are situated (874). Israel and Zavos, in their discussion of Indian traditions of writing religious conversion, identify the genre as multifaceted, comprising 'personal narratives . . . that serve to construct collective narratives,' which in turn 'construct an account of . . . others, and point to what it meant for each community at specific historical points to be identified as devotees of a particular god' (365). How Sheikh's and Esther's narratives account for the meaning of their conversions for the wider familial and adoptive communities in which, in the late-1960s and 1970s, post-colonial Islamic Republic, they are situated, is the focus of this chapter's ensuing section.

As women raised in large, affluent, and powerful Muslim families, whose forbears had chaperoned 'heroes' of the British Empire and whose ancestry might be traced to the descendants of the prophet Mohammed, both Sheikh and Esther express in their narratives repeated concerns for how their conversions will be received by their immediate kin and wider Muslim society (Sheikh 1978, 39–40; Esther 2004, 7). By the late 1960s, when Sheikh's and Esther's conversions took place, the secularism of Pakistan's founder Muhammad Ali Jinnah – and, with it, the idea of the newfound Muslim nation as a place where people of different faiths and ethnicities might be considered equal citizens – had undoubtedly become devalued as a result of its association with Ayub Khan's unpopular military rule (Toor 95). Anti-Western and anti-imperialist sentiment had also deepened as a result of Pakistan's involvement in the Cold War as an ally of the US (97). Nevertheless, Pakistan as a nation remained considerably more open to an understanding of its culture and society as diverse and syncretic in the late 1960s than it was following the populist Bhutto's rejection of the Commonwealth, alignment with Saudi Arabia and designation of the Ahmediyya sect as non-Muslim in the mid-1970s (121–122, 124). The country also had yet to experience the Islamizing regime of General Zia-ul-Haq, when the uncompromising views of religious intellectuals such as Abul A'la Maududi regarding the Pakistani state's 'true' ideological Islamic basis, were 'mainstreamed' (108, 150). Hence perhaps Sheikh's, and to some extent Esther's, concerns appear in many ways more post-colonial and class-based than religious in nature.

For example, Sheikh and Esther worry about the effect on the family's prestige and prospects of their association with 'poor,' socially peripheral 'missionaries' and low-caste, indigenous Christian sanitation workers (Sheikh 1978, 40, 54; Esther 2004, 94, 144). Sheikh's account, with its perhaps pointedly affiliative title, makes clear that she understands her fate and that of her family as tragically tied: 'In the east, the family becomes *biraderi*, one community, with each member responsible to the other . . . they would have to live in the shadow of my decision if I chose to join the "sweepers"' (Sheikh 1978, 54). Both Sheikh's and Esther's narratives do also express concern for their personal safety and the future of their adoptive children, household (including servants) and property, particularly as a result of the anticipated aggression of aggrieved male relatives and of groups of young Muslim men, when their decision to convert is discovered. This said, the youthful, unmarried Esther is considerably more fearless and defiant than her counterpart, the wealthy divorcee and grandmother, Sheikh. Assumptions are made by both the protagonists of *Father* and of *Veil* about the dangers to be incurred by their conversion and baptism (glossed by Sheikh as meaning 'to the Muslim' renunciation of 'his [or her] Islamic faith') and apparent change in belonging (1978, 71). These are also reiterated by Muslim relatives, friends, servants, and foreign Christian mentors. Such interlocutors appear either to subscribe to the myth of a 'pure' Pakistan, solely populated by Muslims (Jesus' 'people,' in these Muslim characters' understanding, being located in western countries), or to accept it as a land where Christians can live only as 'secret believers,' nervous of accusations of apostasy and blasphemy (Esther 2004, 61, 66; Sheikh 1978, 139).

Yet the majority of the potential threats identified in *Father*, both from Sheikh's family and from her wider community in the village of Wah in northwestern Punjab, remain unrealized. Sheikh's account is punctuated by reprimands from loved ones, periods of ostracism, attempts to persuade her to revert to Islam, and expressions of grief at her perceived loss as a Christian convert, but no relative attempts to murder her on the grounds of offended 'honor,' contrary to her fears. Certainly, several of her timorous servants leave the household, and she receives threatening anonymous phone calls and 'vitriolic' hate mail ('true believers, the letter said, had to burn me out like gangrene') (97). One night, too, a pile of pine boughs left leaning against the side of her house is set ablaze in an apparent and disturbing attempt at arson (153). But these, although terrible, occur in the narrative as rare, exceptional incidents and, in general, Sheikh is seen to continue unmolested. Her utilization of her newfound faith to bring comfort to bereaved relatives, and her extension of her doors to 'maids, day laborers and school teachers and business people,' Christian and non-Christian, who might be interested in hearing her message, is received initially warily, but then warmly, suggesting a greater degree of tolerance and receptivity amongst the general populace than anticipated by Sheikh and her many acquaintances (97, 112–13, 133).

Sheikh is a privileged and propertied South Asian woman who continues passionately to view Pakistan as 'my land, my people' and yet considers her position jeopardized by the rise of Bhutto's Islamic socialist PPP and 1972 Land Reforms (146–47). One explanation for Sheikh's quite positive portrayal of her community's broad acceptance of her change in faith may be a desire to stake her claim to belonging in Muslim-majority Pakistan. Like her Hindu counterparts in pre-Independence India, Sheikh presents a story of 'reconciliation . . . post-conversion' which 'emphasis[es] connections' with, 'rather than interruptions' to, her Muslim past (Israel 416). However, Sheikh's depiction of her reception is also surely reflective of the political and religio-cultural status quo in Pakistan in the late 1960s and early 1970s. As is highlighted by Toor's discussion of efforts made by leftist intellectuals such as Faiz Ahmad Faiz towards the construction of a 'progressive Pakistani nationalism' under the government of Ayub in the late 1960s, ideas then in circulation proposed Pakistani culture as inclusive of:

> The 'religion of Islam which provides the ethical and ideological basis for the people's way of life', the 'indigenous cultures of various linguistic regions,' 'elements of Western culture absorbed since the days of British occupation' and 'distinct cultures of minority groups who form a part of the Pakistani nation.'
>
> (Faiz in Toor 110)

Converts to Christianity such as Sheikh, although conscious that a plural vision of post-colonial Pakistani culture like Faiz's would be 'anathema' to groups on the religious right, such as Maududi's *Jama'at-e-Islami*, might find in such public attempts to displace 'religio-centric' definitions reassurance of the legitimacy of their pursuit both of a marginal, non-Muslim faith and of the notion of being Pakistani (Toor 111, 114).[15] Nevertheless, the last perspective her narrative offers of Christian belonging in Pakistan ultimately remains ambiguous: when she takes her leave at the autobiography's close, en route to the US in 1972, Sheikh describes her 'heart' as 'caught' by the sight of her 'country's flag,' with its 'star and crescent' of light and progress, 'on its green' Islamic 'background' (167). As she asserts: 'I would always respect that flag, my people, and their Muslim faith,' although the white band signifying Pakistan's religious minorities appears, like Sheikh herself and Mahmud, her grandson, to have been evacuated from the scene (167). The lingering implication of her narrative is that to be identified a devotee of a Christian god in Pakistan by the late 1960s and early 1970s, in which Sheikh's narrative concludes, is to be confined to a parallel, peripheral life on the margins of the society one would serve: to feel, but no longer to be seen as, Pakistani.

Veil concludes a decade later than *Father*, in early 1981, two to three years into General Zia-ul-Haq's now notorious rule. This is widely acknowledged to have been a particularly perilous period for women and for non-Muslims 'whose presence within the body politic had always been a source of cognitive dissonance' since Pakistan's inception (Toor 137). As Toor (among others) argues, Zia's regime, with its introduction of punitive and discriminatory laws, such as the Hudood Ordinances on adultery and sexual offences such as rape (1979), and stricter prohibitions on blasphemy (1980–1986), 'effectively cast' such marginal groups legally and morally 'outside of the state' (137). Because Esther's account spans a longer period than Sheikh's and the events re-collected in it are largely undated, it is difficult to draw precise connections between her portrayals and the historical context in which they should be understood to have taken place. However, the post-conversion episodes must predominantly have occurred in the 1970s when, prior to the advent of 'Islamisation,' Bhutto's 'Islamic socialist' government, with its populist slogan of 'Islam is our faith, democracy is our polity, socialism is our economy' began to 'set in motion . . . forces which reversed many of the democratic gains of the late 1960s, setting the stage for [Zia's] radically new . . . regime' (Toor 118).[16] The genteel Sheikh's focus is predominantly on the effect of her conversion on her herself, her family, her household, and to some extent the Christians she befriends and cultivates within the village community over which she presides, largely in Ayub's era. However, the young, unmarried Esther's account encompasses, additionally, the more cautious and censorious responses of wider groups she encounters in the decade after Sheikh left Pakistan. These include indigenous, church-going, city-dwelling Christians; well-to-do Muslim family 'friends'; Muslim children and teachers at a school for the blind at which she helps; and colleagues at the magazine where Esther temporarily works. The tense encounters Esther recalls having had with her Muslim compatriots, like the dramatic familial exchanges she also describes in *Veil* (unlike Sheikh, she is threatened at gunpoint by brothers she loved and respected), appear to provide a means by which she can rehearse what it means for her, and for the Pakistani Christian communities to which she affiliates, to be identified as Christian by their Muslim peers and hence – for the majority as characterized in her narrative – as apostatical betrayers of caste, religion and nation (Esther 2004, 120).

The period of her employment as an interviewer of affluent ladies at a magazine in Lahore's Old Anarkali district, for example, offers for Esther a useful means of presenting a window on the contradictory and at times hypocritical responses she encounters as a Christian in mainstream Pakistani Muslim society in the 1970s. At first, Esther is told by her employer that her newfound faith 'doesn't matter so much' in the journalistic profession, given her education, and she relishes the liberty she has in Pakistan's changing society to be a woman asking women questions for a national publication with the potential to impress and inspire female readers (2004, 128–129). Yet soon the magazine's editor refuses to publish Esther's articles under her Christian name; she is 'teased' for her 'polytheistic' faith in 'three gods,' and pressured to revert to Islam if she is to keep her job (131–33). Although Esther's employer is not unkind – he offers to help her if she is 'destitute' – he can only conceive of her faith as an insurmountable stumbling block: for him, and for many of his Muslim peers, so long as she persists in staying a Christian, 'this problem of religion will remain,' and with it her exile from mainstream society (134). It is surely not insignificant that it is at the end of this difficult chapter of her life that Esther identifies her 'own particular Promised Land' as lying in wait for her (134). She does not directly explain what she means by this, but within a few swift pages she has 'ended up in England and Canada, preaching to groups of Asian and English people' and 'looking back over all the way that [her] heavenly Father has led' her (147). Hence, we must presume Esther's 'Promised Land' to be comprised of these western localities (147). Her aunt's reported conviction that Christians can only live in Christian countries thus becomes a self-fulfilling prophecy. *Veil* does undoubtedly touch on episodes of sympathy and acceptance extended particularly by female relatives who find 'solace' in Esther's Biblical message (115). Yet ultimately, like *Father*, it strongly suggests that Christian subjects who demur – whether actively or by virtue of following a minority religion – from the 'terms of [a] normative Pakistani Muslim identity regulated by a society constructed around exclusive models of [Muslim] piety,' will automatically be relegated to a realm of foreign un-belonging, regardless of their geographic location (Cilano 104; Ashraf, 'Honour,' 56).[17]

3 Problems of evidence: playing into and complicating cultural discourses

In *Telling Lives in India* Arnold and Blackburn observe that 'one reason for the broad appeal of life histories, to the scholar as to the wider public, is . . . that they straddle the elusive divide between personal narrative and objective truth' (4). Personal accounts, 'far from being [read as] mere fabrications, are seen to be imbued with', and valued for, a potent sense of 'veracity,' informed as they are by lived experiences (4). Arnold and Blackburn go on to identify 'a further reason for attributing an underlying veracity to life histories' as being, somewhat counter-intuitively, 'that, even when written, they seem to speak directly to us, without the distorting mediation of an author, without editing or censorship' (4). The implication – that something of the subject's 'voice' can somehow transcend various forms of control and communicate directly with the reader – is of course contentious, as Arnold and Blackburn are aware. This is particularly the case when it comes to reading South Asian women's narratives. For, as Vatuk (2004, 147) observes, drawing on the work of the Gayatri Spivak, they may be composed 'in a language that is by definition not [their] own,' use 'forms of discourse [which] originate in male modes of thought and expression,' and be 'constrained' in terms of content 'by cultural prescriptions.' In the case of Sheikh's and Esther's accounts, the mode of expression used, a charismatic American English, as practiced by their professional co-authors, appears additionally remote from the South Asian, Muslim, and primarily Urdu-speaking women, whose elicited confessions they purport to unfold.

As I have signalled, co-written autobiographies such as Sheikh's and Esther's, although apparently reporting actual occurrences, must be understood not as providing straightforward 'evidence' of certain spiritual and persecutory experiences. Rather, we should read them with caution, 'wary of the partisan telling and selective recollection of events' (Arnold and Blackburn, 4). In other words, we must be prepared to acknowledge them as accounts carefully crafted with the aid of Western ghostwriters to convey a particular perspective to global audiences of South Asian Muslim women's experiences of conversion to Christianity, and to interpret for that audience the meaning of such a transformation for Pakistani society. This said, although the individual narratives considered in this chapter partly bolster stereotypical western perspectives of Muslims and Islam, they also point to alternative subject positions which complicate the Evangelical, Islamophobic and exoticist discourses in which such accounts may be implicated. In this way, Sheikh's and Esther's life-writings encourage, perhaps unintentionally, subtler readings of their Muslim-turned-Christian protagonists' personal, familial, and social lives than might be anticipated, given their provenance and production. It is to a summation of these complexities — of these co-constructed narratives' simultaneous confirmation and complication of stereotypes as they attempt to account for experiences of Christian conversion — that I now turn in this final section.

Father and *Veil* undoubtedly invite predominantly western, Christian readers to discover within them self-affirming stories of spiritually inclined 'daughter[s] of the East' leaving a supposedly strict Islamic culture and finding liberty and solace in the Biblical God, and are structured so as to sustain such readings.[18] The strapline, for example, on Sheikh's (1978) front cover reads, 'An incredible journey of discovery begins when a high-born Muslim woman opens the Bible,' while Esther's asserts, 'Christ's power breaks through to a Muslim girl,' reflecting a prejudicial perspective that sees Islam as belated and Christianity as the desirable, enlightened spiritual destination (1984). The sense of a bildungsroman-like 'progression' from Islam, through adversity, and into God's truth introduced here is further reinforced (as earlier noted) by the sequencing of life events into chapters with titles such as 'To Mecca,' 'The Strange Book,' 'The Baptism of Fire and Water,' 'The Witness' and 'Flight,' which would prescribe and constrain their stories' meaning (Sheikh 1978, 'Contents'; Esther and Sangster 1984, 'Contents'). Gerard Genette has suggested that liminal, paratextual zones, such as these chapter headings, located between the interior of the 'text' and 'the world's discourse about it,' are always 'at the service of a . . . more pertinent reading of [the text] (more pertinent, of course, in the eyes of the author and his allies)' (2). Although the confessional narratives provided in *Father* and *Veil* circulate under the auspices of Bilquis Sheikh's and Gulshan Esther's 'authentic' and 'eastern' authorial names, considerable responsibility for their construction and promotion as inspirational insights into trials and triumphs of turning Christian in a hostile, Muslim country surely lies with their Anglophone co-authors and publishers. The hand of the co-author is also present, as I have pointed out in the above readings, not only at a paratextual level but also in the body of the text. It is visible, for example, in the colorful 'explaining' of Pakistani Muslim religious and cultural traditions and practices (in 'Ramzan . . . Muslims fast from sunrise to sunset until . . . we load ourselves with delicacies'); the posing of dramatic rhetorical questions which counterpose Islamic and Christian priorities ('Would I yield to the fear of being treated as an outcast . . . or would I obey Jesus?'); and in the portentous metaphors of enlightenment so seemingly central to the narratives' overall message (of Islam as the 'veil that can be torn away') (Sheikh 1978, 58, 71; Esther 2004, 147).

Nevertheless, this chapter has proceeded on the basis that 'the dialogic quality of such [mediated] narratives needs to be recognized, not the erasure of the mediator, or a search for a (false) authenticity of a text' (Malhotra and Lambert-Hurley 18), and that 'however biased and incomplete these personal reflections may be . . . [such] life histories [can] open up an experience of the self-in-society unrecorded elsewhere' (Arnold and Blackburn 23).[19] Conscious of the problems of reading Sheikh's and Esther's selective, melodramatic, co-authored Anglophone accounts as indicative of 'true' experiences of interfaith revelation, contestation, and conflict in post-colonial Pakistan, this chapter seeks an acknowledgement of these women's orchestrated life-writings as both implicated in 'complex negotiations with competing cultural regimes' and capable of undermining binary oppositions which pit Christian against Muslim, West against East, and individual against collective (Israel and Zavos 357, 363). One final, concluding example may best illustrate this: the unorthodox occasion of Sheikh's baptism, which occurs in *Father's* climactic chapter, dramatically entitled 'The Baptism of Fire and Water.' This recounts at pace how Sheikh decided to perform her own baptism ceremony herself following a visitation while praying from Jesus in which he informs her that it is 'time . . . to be baptised in water' (1978, 71). Again here, the fears Sheikh expresses about the potential persecutory reaction from her family and community – 'of being treated as an outcast, or worse, as a traitor' – significantly stoked by the American missionary friends who advise and support her, and compounded by the warnings of avuncular Muslim relatives, play into prejudicial assumptions about Muslims' incapacity to entertain Christian difference which haunt both *Father* and *Veil* (Sheikh 1978, 71–72). Yet when patronizing foreign Christian associates and regional church bureaucracy conspire to thwart her desire for immediate baptism, the terms of the frank, confessional account also permit the divulgence of the single-minded Pakistani 'noblewoman['s]' dissenting behavior (dust jacket). As Sheikh (with Schneider) 'explains':

> What I proceeded to do may have some theological problems. But I wasn't thinking in theological terms. . . . I wanted more than anything else to stay in the Lord's Presence. . . . I walked into the bathroom and stepped into the deep tub. As I sat down, water rose almost to my shoulder. I placed my hand on my head and said loudly: 'Bilquis, I baptise you.'
>
> (76–77)

This ad hoc, idiosyncratic act negates both the concerns of (mostly male) foreign missionaries and the censure of Pakistani relatives, domesticating and – one might argue – 'decolonizing'[20] post-colonial religious practice for a short, intense moment.[21] Then the more celebratory and multicultural evangelical narrative trajectory continues, however, with Sheikh's official baptism by a Pakistani Padri at an Abbotabad mission, attended by an apparently unprecedented ecumenical mix of Pakistani Christians and North American expatriates from Baptist, Presbyterian, and Anglican denominations huddled together like first-century Christians 'in the catacombs under Rome' (78).

Israel and Zavos have pointed out that in academic and non-academic accounts of religious conversion in colonial South Asia 'the work of evangelical Christian missionaries is frequently projected as a paradigm of cultural domination' (353). As the scenes described above indicate, here, in the post-colonially composed *Father*, this no longer quite appears to be the case. Instead, the book recalls and reflects a time when overseas missionary organizations working in the new, independent nation of Pakistan had begun publicly to acknowledge that their role was 'not . . . to be "The Answer" . . . [nor] to put the church to rights or to convert,' but rather to seek 'to function as a member of [Christ's] Body' in nurturing 'a self-supporting, self-governing, self-propagating indigenous church' (Anderson and Hover 38, 5). Yet the relationship of the Christian converts in *Veil* and *Father*, and of Christians more broadly in post-colonial Pakistan, to the 'universal' (west-led) church is – like their relationship to their Islamic origins – more contradictory and complex than this quotation from a 20th-century missionary publication would suggest. This complexity may be revealed through what we could term Sheikh's 'displacing' and perhaps indigenizing, baptismal 'gesture,' and through other incidents, such as those discussed earlier, ambiguously reflected in Sheikh's and Esther's texts, which fail fully to fit either the celebratory or the persecutory narratives which would contain them (Spivak 63).

To try to make personal and collective 'sense' of a turn to Christianity, of being and becoming Christian, in mid-to-late 20th-century Pakistan, is to navigate between multiple potential interpretations and perspectives. Despite *Veil's* and *Father's* in many ways reductive framings and construction, the perspectives on religious translation they present function partly to undermine purely pessimistic assessments, both Western and Eastern, of the place and prospects of religious minorities in the Islamic Republic of Pakistan in the later 20th century. Rather, they point to possibilities of co-existence and co-habitation which have passed largely unremarked upon, unreported, and unimagined. Hence, it is my argument that such narratives continue to warrant closer consideration, particularly in a present-day period of intense concern, both internally and internationally, for the future well being of such people.

Notes

1 Hereafter referred to as '*Father.*'
2 Hereafter referred to as '*Veil.*'
3 The British Library catalogue entry for the 1984 Marshalls edition of *The Torn Veil* (1984) provides the alternative subtitle of 'the story of Sister Gulshan Esther / as told to Thelma Sangster; with Noble Din, interpreter' for this first edition of the autobiography, suggesting a further (and male) involvement in shaping her story.
4 Sheikh converted in 1966 and Esther in 1969.

5 Attitudes towards apostasy, or the renunciation or abandonment of Islam in Pakistan, are by no means homogenous. As was noted in a recent report by *The Law Library of Congress* (11–12), 'there is no specific statutory law that criminalizes apostasy [i.e. the renunciation or abandonment of Islam] in Pakistan.' As early as the (arguably secular) 1954 Munir Report into agitation against the Ahmadiyya Muslim minority in Punjab, which led to the imposition in Lahore of martial law, the incipient Pakistani State – via Chief Justice Muhammad Munir – was at pains to distance itself from calls for the greater policing and punishment of apostasy and defend freedom of thought and belief. Munir's report (quoted in Ahmed, 435–36) emphasized that 'The Qur'an again and again lays emphasis on reason and thought, advises toleration and preaches against compulsion in religious matters; but the doctrine of *irtidad* [apostasy] as enunciated [by members of the *ulema* or Islamic clerics in favour of Pakistan's recalibration as an Islamic State] . . . strikes at the very root of independent thinking when it propounds the view that anyone who, being born a Muslim or having embraced Islam, attempts to think on the subject of religion with a view, if he comes to that conclusion, to choose for himself any religion he likes, has the capital penalty in store for him.' Nevertheless, as Sana Ashraf notes (in accordance with the above-mentioned report by *The Law Library of Congress*), today in practice, '[e]ven though there is no punishment for apostasy in the Penal Code of Pakistan, the offence of apostasy . . . is understood as blasphemous, and more particularly as an insult to the Prophet' (*Moral Anxiety*, 97–98).

6 I use 'evangelical' here in the broad, adjectival sense, that is: 'of or denoting a tradition within Protestant Christianity emphasizing the authority of the Bible, personal conversion, and the doctrine of salvation by faith in the Atonement' (*English Oxford Living Dictionaries*). When referring to individuals as 'Evangelical,' I do so with a consciousness of the particular emphases of the Christian church's evangelical tradition in the late 1970s on Christians as ' "Bible people" . . . [who] possessed a gospel to proclaim' (Bebbington 18–19).

7 Vatuk's 2004 essay on an Indian Muslim woman's life-writing corroborates this perspective on the limited range of lives showcased by the genre

> 'South Asian women's autobiographies . . . provide a window into the lives of only a select sample of the region's female population: mainly, women of the upper socio-economic strata who enjoy some public prominence (in politics, the professions, social reform . . .) or are closely related to notable men in the same fields of endeavour. They have been used by historians mainly as primary documents for answering questions about such matters as the development of women's education or their political participation'
>
> (148)

8 Although, it is worth noting, the perspectives in which Rahman is interested do not appear to encompass minority religious ones. As in his *A History of Pakistani Literature in English*, Rahman's primary interest is in cultivating appreciation of this writing as a 'literary' (cultural and aesthetic) as opposed to 'non-literary' ('Islamic, nationalistic, traditionalist' and political) phenomenon (11, 15).

9 'Signpost' chapter headings include 'To Mecca,' 'The Book,' and 'The Crossroads' (Sheikh 1978; Esther 1984: contents pages), which closely resemble those in other inspirational accounts of conversion from Islam to Christianity by Muslim Pakistanis, such as Christopher Alam's *Through the Blood and the Fire* (1994).

10 These details are awkwardly appended in the elliptical afterword to the book's 2004 edition (149–52).

11 The priorities or 'defining attributes of the Evangelical religion' since the early 18th century, as identified by Bebbington, are 'conversionism, activism, biblicism and crucicentrism' (Bebbington 19).

12 Bebbington points to 'crucicentrism,' the emphasising of the significance of Christ's death on the cross and its role in bringing salvation, as a key Evangelical principle (36–41).

13 The Second Vatican Council's (or Vatican II's) *Nostra Aetate* ('Declaration on the Relation of the Church with Non-Christian Religions') was proclaimed in 1965, intended to 'promote respect for other religions and declare that they reflected "a ray of that Truth which enlightens all men"' (Fuchs 451). Specifically, with regard to postcolonial Christian-Muslim relations, it declared that:

> Since in the course of centuries not a few quarrels and hostilities have arisen between Christians and Moslems, this sacred synod urges all to forget the past and to work sincerely for mutual understanding and to preserve as well as to promote together for the benefit of all mankind social justice and moral welfare, as well as peace and freedom.
> (Declaration, section 3)

This proclamation has commonly been considered as a 'watershed' moment in interfaith relations, responsible for 'transform[ing] the Church's attitude towards believers from other religions' and 'continu[ing] to inspire and to guide Catholics [and other Christians] in forging relationships of mutual respect and collaboration' (The Australian Catholic Bishops Conference, 2).

14 I am, of course, aware of the problems posed by such a claim in relation to South Asian women's narratives, regarding which, as Vatuk notes, 'the question of whether and how the real "voice" . . . can be heard (and, if heard, deciphered) [remains] an issue of lively discussion,' particularly when 'the form of [women's] discourse originates in [western and male] modes of thought and expression, its content constrained by cultural prescriptions' (2004, 147). The problems of interpreting Sheikh's and Esther's co-authored, Anglophone accounts as unmediated expressions of Pakistani, Muslim female subjectivity, towards which I have alluded throughout this chapter, are touched on again in its final section.

15 *The Objectives Resolution,* adopted in 1949 by Pakistan's Constituent Assembly, declared that 'Muslims shall be enabled to order their lives in the individual and collective spheres in accord with the teachings and the requirements of Islam as set out in the Holy Quran and the Sunna,' but also that 'adequate provision shall be made for the minorities to profess and practice their religions and develop their cultures' (Article 2 (A)). The effect, according to Ispahani, was 'to define the state in Islamic terms, opening the door for . . . interpretation[s] of Islam,' such as the narrow, theocratic ones supported by Maududi and his followers, which would further erode minorities' rights and status as equal citizens (loc. 569). However, as Toor emphasises in her discussion of Faiz's engagement in debates with the religious right in the late-1960s, 'while the relationship between Islam and Pakistan was actively under contention, and had been so since the very beginning, the idea that "Islam" (however understood) was a major constituent of Pakistani nationalism was not' (115). In other words, although 'difficult and complex,' it was still possible at this moment to conceive of a national culture – and hence a nation – built on, and inclusive of, diverse (including pre- and non-Islamic) cultures and histories (110, 114–115).

16 For example, in 1973, Bhutto oversaw changes to Pakistan's constitution, as a result of which 'All existing laws shall be brought in conformity with the Injunctions of Islam as laid down in the Holy Quran and Sunnah . . . and no law shall be enacted which is repugnant to such Injunctions' (*The Constitution of the Islamic Republic of Pakistan*, part IX, article 227).

17 Missing from partial accounts such as Esther's is a contextualization of such piety. As Ashraf endeavours to highlight through her study of expressions of Muslim religious offence in the Punjab, past and present, 'models of [Muslim] piety' performed within Pakistani society must be understood as complex, based, for example 'on a conjunction of cultural and religious values' such as 'honour, shame, heroism and a public display of faith/loyalty' that 'have been produced within [a particular colonial and post-colonial] historical and political context' ('Honour' 56). To attempt to convey

Esther's and Sheikh's more reductive perspectives in this chapter is to seek to understand them, not to endorse them.

18 The inspirational writer Catherine Marshall's 'Foreword' to *I Dared to Call Him Father* promotes a perspective of Sheikh that conforms to another, Orientalist, stereotype of Eastern spirituality. She states: 'I have marveled that a new Christian could have such depth of perception into the world of the spirit. Also, how odd that God would reach down for a Muslim woman in Pakistan to bring her to minister in the United States! Could it be that the eastern heritage and psyche is generally more fertile soil for spiritual understanding than that of Western man?' (Marshall in Sheikh 1978, 11).

19 Third-person accounts exist in English in the form of contemporary missionary-produced pamphlets such as *If Any Thirst: The Christian Caravan Hospital Comes to Pakistan* (Anderson and Hover 1963), and retrospective missionary memoirs (such as Pauline A Brown's (2006) *Jars of Clay: Ordinary Christians on an Extraordinary Mission in Southern Pakistan*). However, Sheikh's and Esther's accounts are rare first-person (although co-authored) examples from the period. Other accounts of conversion to Christianity in mid-to-late 20th-century Pakistan may exist in Urdu, and I hope to undertake collaborative research with the aim of identifying and drawing them to the attention of wider audiences.

20 By 'decolonizing' I mean to point to an attempt to 'claim and acknowledge the colonizing legacy of Christianity' (Duggan xiv).

21 It is also, however, construable as the stubborn and eccentric action of an enigmatic 'eastern' woman, see from a stereotypical western perspective. Marshall's framing 'Foreword' to *Father,* in which Sheikh is described and prized as a passionate, exotic advocate for Christ, who 'fits no established pattern,' certainly invites this reading (in Sheikh 1978, 11).

Works cited

Ahmed, Asad. "Advocating a Secular Pakistan: The Munir Report of 1954." *Islam in South Asia in Practice*, edited by Barbara Metcalf, Princeton UP, 2009, pp. 424–37.

Alam, Christopher. *Through the Blood and the Fire: A Muslim Fanatic Becomes a Fiery Evangelist for Jesus Christ*. New Wine, 1994.

Anderson, John Douglas Chalmers, and Peter Stephen Hover. *If Any Thirst: The Christian Caravan Hospital Comes to Pakistan*. Bible and Medical Missionary Fellowship, 1963.

Arnold, David, and Stuart Blackburn. "Introduction: Life Histories in India." *Telling Lives in India: Biography, Autobiography, and Life History*, edited by David Arnold and Stuart Blackburn, Indiana UP, 2004, pp. 1–25.

Ashraf, Sana. "Honour, Purity and Transgression: Understanding Blasphemy Accusations and Consequent Violent Action in Punjab, Pakistan." *Contemporary South Asia*, vol. 26, no. 1, 2018, pp. 51–68.

———. *Moral Anxiety in the 'Land of the Pure': Popular Justice and Anti-Blasphemy Violence in Pakistan, 2019*. The Australian National University. Unpublished PhD thesis, https://core.ac.uk/download/pdf/222805766.pdf. Accessed 23 Sept. 2020.

The Australian Catholic Bishops Conference. *Nostra Aetate: Declaration on the Relation of the Church to Non-Christian Religions*. Australian Catholic Bishops Conference, 2015, www.catholic.org.au/about/bishops/statements/1726-nostra-aetate-declaration-on-the-relation-of-the-church-to-non-christian-religions-50th-anniversary/file. Accessed 23 Sept. 2020.

Baker Publishing Group. "About Chosen." http://bakerpublishinggroup.com/chosen/about-chosen. Accessed 23 Sept. 2020.

Bebbington, David W. *Evangelicalism in Modern Britain: A History from the 1730s to the 1980s*. Taylor and Francis Group, 1989. ProQuest Ebook Central, https://ebookcentral.proquest.com/lib/tees/detail.action?docID=179445. Accessed 23 Sept. 2020.

Brown, Pauline A. *Jars of Clay: Ordinary Christians on an Extraordinary Mission in Southern Pakistan*. Doorlight Publications, 2006.

Cilano, Cara. *Contemporary Pakistani Fiction in English: Idea, Nation, State*. Routledge, 2013.

The Constitution of the Islamic Republic of Pakistan, no date, www.pakistani.org/pakistan/constitution/. Accessed 22 Oct. 2018.

Dawn. 'Minority Day: Those Who Convert Others by Force Do Not Understand Islamic History, PM Says.' 29 July 2019, www.dawn.com/news/1496888. Accessed 19 Sept. 2019.

Declaration on the Relation of the Church to Non-Christian Religions, Nostra Aetate, Proclaimed by his Holiness Pope Paul VI on October 28, 1965, 1965, www.vatican.va/archive/hist_councils/ii_vatican_council/documents/vat-ii_decl_19651028_nostra-aetate_en.html. Accessed 29 Sept. 2020.

Duggan, Joseph F. "Introduction to Postcolonialism and Religion Series: The Death and Rebirth of a Discipline: Taking Subalterns Seriously." *Decolonizing the Body of Christ: Theology and Theory After Empire?* Edited by David Joy and Joseph F. Duggan, Palgrave Macmillan, 2012, pp. xiii–xx.

Esther, Gulshan. *The Torn Veil: The Best-Selling Story of Gulshan Esther as told to Thelma Sangster*. Zondervan, 2004.

Esther, Gulshan, and Thelma Sangster. *The Torn Veil: The Story of Sister Gulshan Esther as told to Thelma Sangster*. Marshalls, 1984.

"Evangelical." *English Oxford Living Dictionary*, no date, https://en.oxforddictionaries.com/definition/evangelical. Accessed 4 Sept. 2018.

Fuchs, Maria-Magdalena. "Walking a Tightrope: The Jesuit Robert Bütler and Muslim – Christian Dialogue in Pakistan." *Islam and Christian – Muslim Relations*, vol. 27, no. 4, 2016, pp. 439–54.

Genette, Gerard. *Paratexts: Thresholds of Interpretation*. Translated by Jane E. Lewin. Cambridge UP, 1997.

Ghose, Zulfikar. *Confessions of a Native-Alien*. Routledge & Kegan Paul, 1965.

Ispahani, Farahnaz. *Purifying the Land of the Pure: Pakistan's Religious Minorities*. Kindle ed. HarperCollins India, 2015.

Israel, Hephzibah. "Conversion, Memory and Writing: Remembering and Reforming the Self." *South Asia: Journal of South Asian Studies*, vol. 41, no. 2, 2018, pp. 400–17.

Israel, Hephzibah, and John Zavos. "Narratives of Transformation: Religious Conversion and Indian Traditions of 'Life Writing'." *South Asia: Journal of South Asian Studies*, vol. 41, no. 2, 2018, pp. 352–65.

Jinnah, Muhammad Ali. "Muhammad Ali Jinnah's first Presidential Address to the Constituent Assembly of Pakistan." 1947, www.columbia.edu/itc/mealac/pritchett/00islamlinks/txt_jinnah_assembly_1947.html. Accessed 20 Sept. 2019.

The Law Library of Congress. *Laws Criminalizing Apostasy in Selected Jurisdictions*. Law Library of Congress, 2014, www.loc.gov/law/help/apostasy/apostasy.pdf. Accessed 28 Aug. 2018.

Malhotra, Anshu, and Siobhan Lambert-Hurley. *Speaking of the Self: Gender, Performance and Autobiography in South Asia*. Duke UP, 2015.

The Objectives Resolution, no date, http://www.pakistani.org/pakistan/constitution/annex.html. Accessed 13 July 2021.

Rahman, Tariq. *A History of Pakistani Literature in English 1947–1988. 1990*. Oxford UP, 2015.

———. "Pakistan: Life-Writing." *Encyclopedia of Post-Colonial Literatures in English*, edited by Eugene Benson and L W Connolly, 2nd ed., Routledge, 2004, pp. 874–75.

Shamsie, Muneeza. *Hybrid Tapestries: The Development of Pakistani Literature in English.* Oxford UP, 2017.

Sheikh, Bilquis, and Richard Schneider. *I Dared to Call Him Father: An Incredible Journey of Discovery Begins When a High-Born Muslim Woman Opens the Bible.* Chosen Books, 1978.

———. *I Dared to Call Him Father: An Incredible Journey of Discovery Begins When a High-Born Muslim Woman Opens the Bible, 1978.* Kingsway, 1979.

Spivak, Gayatri. "Can the Subaltern Speak?" *Can the Subaltern Speak? Reflections on the History of an Idea*, edited by Rosalind Morris, Columbia UP, 2010.

Toor, Saadia. *The State of Islam: Culture and Cold War Politics in Pakistan.* Pluto Press, 2011.

Vatuk, Sylvia. "Hamara Daur-i Hayat: An Indian Muslim Woman Writes Her Life." *Telling Lives in India: Biography, Autobiography, and Life History*, edited by David Arnold and Stuart Blackburn, Indiana UP, 2004, pp. 144–74.

———. "A Passion for Reading: The Role of Early Twentieth-Century Urdu Novels in the Construction of an Individual Female Identity in 1930s Hyderabad." *Speaking of the Self: Gender, Performance and Autobiography in South Asia*, edited by Anshu Malhotra and Siobhan Lambert-Hurley, Duke UP, 2015, pp. 33–55.

Wright, T. R. "Religious Autobiography: Writing God and the Self." *Theology and Literature*, Blackwell, 1988, pp. 92–110.

14

FEMINIST FUTURES AND THE SPECULATIVE FICTIONS

Umme Al-wazedi

A lion is stronger than a man, but it does not enable him to dominate the human race. You have neglected the duty you owe to yourselves and you have lost your natural rights by shutting your eyes to your own interests.

Rokeya Sakhawat Hossain, '*Sultana's Dream*'

[Sci-fi is] a wonderful way to think about possibilities. It's a wonderful way to explore exotic politics.

Octavia Butler, *Black Sci-Fi*

If any female feels she needs anything beyond herself to legitimate and validate her existence, she is already giving away her power to be self-defining, her agency.

bell hooks, *Feminism is for Everybody: Passionate Politics*

. . . a woman might travel into fantasy, in order to locate herself in reality.

Jennifer Wagner-Lawlor, *Postmodern Utopias and Feminist Fictions*

Introduction: speculative fiction and the use of Utopia and Dystopia

Science fiction utopias and dystopias have long been considered products of the Western world, yet it is only since the 1960s as Ralph Pordzik asserts, women writers have become more and more visible in the West: Margaret Atwood, Octavia Butler, Angela Carter, Ursula K. Le Guin, Sally Miller Gearhart, Charlotte Perkins Gilman, Joanna Russ, and Jeanette Winterson are but a handful of women science fiction writers who found critical and commercial success. The Western canon cannot claim exclusive rights to the genre, however, nor is speculative fiction exactly new to the Global South. Uppinder Mehan, while talking about

DOI: 10.4324/9781003002062-18

post-colonial science fiction, writes, 'These other fictions unsettle the accepted epistemological and ontological issues regarding the West's others. And doing so while at the same time making a genre of their own.' In 1905, Rokeya Sakhawat Hossain wrote '*Sultana's Dream*', a utopian novel in which women create scientific inventions to preserve the environment and end wars. Hossain's women characters who live in Ladyland resist age-old social norms and break the chains of the purdah (in its particular meaning of being secluded and kept from accessing education) that has them shackled, demonstrating that the possibilities are endless for any woman who realizes her own self-worth and questions the scientific reasoning behind a woman's biological construct. While addressing Rokeya Sakhawat Hossain's use of the utopian form, Suchitra Mathur, in her article 'Caught between the Goddess and the Cyborg: Third-World Women and the Politics of Science in Three Works of Indian Science Fiction,' states:

> "Sultana's Dream" thus envisions an end to the opposition between science and the feminine through feminizing of science. This is accomplished not merely through making the available body of scientific knowledge accessible to women, but also through a fundamental revisioning of its methodology and purpose. . . . In "Sultana's Dream," however, "the technological innovations are designed to work in collaboration with the nature instead of competing with it."
>
> (123)

Andaleeb Wajid and Bina Shah are taking Hossain's work further by challenging different aspects of the traditional idea of what a fantasy fiction from the Global South would look like. They are indeed Sultana's sisters who continue Hossain's dream that there will not only be education for women in general but there will be an education that 'enabled women to excel in science' (Jahan 5).

While talking about the Western science fiction, Pordzik, in his book *The Quest for Postcolonial Utopia: A Comparative Introduction to the Utopian Novel in the New English Literatures* (2001), establishes a timeline for contemporary women writing Science Fiction in the West and argues that women writers have been availing the utopian genre for a long time 'in order to envisage suitable alternatives to male-dominated social structures' (89). Jennifer Wagner-Lawlor, on the other hand, argues that 'contemporary speculative fictions have proven themselves powerful formal tools for revis(ion)ing the shape of history and revaluing the role of imagination' (2). In addition, Hope Jennings argues, 'For many contemporary women writers, the use of utopian and/or dystopian elements has become a preferred mode of interrogating current systems of oppression and violence while offering visions of resistance and possible (future) alternatives' (132).

Anna Gilarek contends that feminist science fiction is a form of speculative genre which addresses crucial issues in our present society that are important to feminists. She argues, feminist science fiction 'exposes the unfairness of patriarchal society and the mechanisms of its perpetuation, as well as the discrimination and marginalization of women' (34). In her May 2019 *New Yorker* article, 'Science Fiction doesn't have to be Dystopian,' Joyce Carol Oates deftly proves that there is an expansive range of topics available to science fiction writers, citing '[c]ontemporary issues relating to bioethics, virtual reality, free will and determinism, time travel, and the uses of robotic forms of AI' in Ted Chiang's collection of short stories. So, there are a range of subjects that a science fiction writer can focus on and decide how they want the genre to appear to their readers. Claire P. Curtis argues, 'The fiction of science fiction is primarily a fiction concerning how we get from one point to another. The description of place, the prescription for how to live, is the contextually rich thought experiment that we need in order to think about where and who we want to be' (161). In addition, Raffaella Baccolini defines dystopias as texts that 'maintain a utopian core at their center, a locus of hope that contributes to the deconstructing tradition and reconstructing alternatives' (13). Dystopian fictions are powerful because 'the construct of dystopia is needed to draw attention to the fragility and newness of women's voices, to keep us from taking our freedom to speak for granted, to urge the need for continuing the fight, and to highlight the courage and beauty of those who break silences' (Jones 11).

In other words, smashing the patriarchy isn't the only – or even the most important – reason women choose to write in the speculative fiction genre. With that in mind, this chapter explores the definition and application of speculative fiction through the works of two authors, both Muslim women. This chapter will consider three novels in total: the first and last novels in Wajid's coming-of-age *Tamanna* trilogy, *No Time for Goodbyes* (2014) and *Time Will Tell* (2014) and Bina Shah's dystopic *Before She Sleeps* (2018). Wajid's work is a coming-of-age novel while Shah portrays a dystopic world. In this chapter, I argue that both writers are trying to invent an alternative future. Wajid and Shah are using the form of speculative fiction, to use the words of Wagner-Lawlor, to prompt 'resistance to traditionally regulated spaces that define the particularities of their cultures' (156). Wajid uses time travel to tell the romantic story of her heroine and by doing so she is answering to Mehan's concern that 'Indian science fiction . . . wrestle[s] with the need for technological development' (64). She is writing in a genre that has long been thought of as a Western genre. On the other hand, Shah questions enclosed systems which restrains human freedom, particularly the freedom of women. The existence of the women in her novel almost denies them their lives. Yet, these women fight their way to their freedom. Both Wajid and Shah see the two cities – Bangalore of the past and Panah as refuge for their heroines. In addition, what I take from Wagner-Lawlor's comment is that South Asian women writers instead of adhering to the rules of writing simply a love story are challenging the idea that they are *only able to* write a story about love. They destabilize this narrative and thus create a new type of fiction that offers visions of resistance to oppression and suggests alternative futures. These alternative futures are imaginary and question issues of injustice, yet they are 'not only politically viable but also politically necessary' (Wagner-Lawlor 2).

Andaleeb Wajid and the idea of time travel

Andaleeb Wajid's *No Time for Goodbyes* (2014), the first novel of the trilogy, tells the story of Tamanna, a college student, who is accidentally transported to the past – to the Bangalore of 1982 – where she meets her mother, her aunts, and grandmother all over again. The reason for Tamanna's time travel can be explained through Curtis' argument. While visiting the Bangalore of the past, Tamanna describes a place and also narrates how people lived in the 1980s, which guides her to think about 'where and who we want to be' (Curtis 161). Tamanna learns from Manoj that his grandfather, Mr. Prakash, was trying to go to the future through a Polaroid camera; he was trying to 'time travel through photos' (72). But he is unsuccessful and, instead, he ends up bringing Tamanna to the past. In answer to Tamanna's question as to how she can get back to her future life, Manoj's grandfather says, 'I have to find the trigger' (71). Although the exact process of how Tamanna ends up in the past is not known in this book, the readers realize that there is a purpose for Tamanna to be here.

So, what happens when Tamanna comes to the past? – she records the day-to-day life of the people in her life, compares her life of the future to the past, and explores her love affair with Manoj. She has to pretend to be the pen-pal of Manoj, a young man who lives nearby her grandmother's house as she can't just explain that she is from the future. Tamanna sees a lot of difference in fashion and not so much of how life is lead differently. Her grandmother is as she was in her life in the future, 'she's always maintained a stoic smile and always indulged us whenever we visited her' (62). As she shares the space with her two aunts Reena and Vidya, and her mother Suma, she thinks about sharing living spaces with siblings. Again, she compares her life there to that of the future. She wakes up at her Ajji's house and looks outside the window:

> There's a tree outside the window and I can spot a couple of squirrels running up and down the while, a bird coos gently from somewhere above the dense branches. I don't remember the last time I saw or heard these simple things with such clarity. It could also be that the moment my eyes are open, my hands stray towards my phone where I quickly check Facebook for updates.
> (27)

Definitely, Wajid's intention is to show that even though we have progressed in the present world, we have moved away from enjoying the simplest things in our lives which reminds us of Curtis' argument about why anyone would want to write a time travel novel. So, while doing an interview when asked why she writes fantasy fiction, Wajid answers so that 'her character could actually feel nostalgia, be a part of the past' (Narkhede).

Yet, far beyond this nostalgia is Wajid's message about what is at stake when a city modernizes itself. While out and about, Tamanna notices the Bangalore of the past was much greener than the present Bangalore, 'I look out the window and breathe in the unpolluted air of the city, filling my lungs with it entirely. It feels so good to be outside the house! . . . On the other side of the road, there's a lovely cover of trees all along it. It looks so pretty that I'm a bit speechless. How could they have cut it all off for the Metro?' (45). This change in the cityscape is one thing that makes Tamanna answer Manoj's question about what the future looks like. Tamanna always replies in her head that the future isn't that great, ''Yes, lot of bad things happen but I have hope,' I tell him, thinking of the global warming and the terrorist attacks. I don't want to ruin his vision of the future' (39). While the Bangalore of the 1980s provides a calm refuge for Tamanna, once in 2020, she notices technological advancement but not that the people are happy. She finds a woman in a bubble: 'I peer closely as she walks right past me and I can see her lips moving soundlessly. She is talking to someone obviously, but I don't see any phone or earpiece anywhere. Then I realise that she's talking to someone whom she can probably see *in* the bubble' (Wajid, *Time* 102). This scene counters Mehan's comment about how South Asian writers may face challenges to creating technological inventions in their fiction. On the other hand, Dr. Arvind, the Psychiatric doctor, who travels with them, immediately thinks that they should observe all medical inventions and take it back to 2013. However, he also learns that his hospital was shut down five years ago and wants to go back to 2018 so that he can save his hospital. Although Tamanna finds Manoj in this advanced world, the future doesn't look good to Tamanna as she observes the faces of the people around her: 'The faces of most people are blank, tired and withdrawn. There is a general air of discontentment, like this is not what they'd bargain for' (Wajid, *Time* 129). One argument for the discontentment could be that it is a dystopic Bangalore. Although we only get to see the spectacular Bangalore of the future, Wajid doesn't portray the lives of lower-class people. Perhaps in her future world there is no class division. Yet, definitely Bangalore becomes a trope for the bulging urban civilization of the future. The woman in a bubble scene is so eerie that it almost seems that we are in the future; this might as well be a response to Covid-19. In addition, Dr. Arvind's interest in making a profit only alludes to the capitalist nature that one sees in many pharmaceutical companies.

Wajid is successful in locating the source of female empowerment firmly within the scenario described earlier. By the end of the first novel, we find Tamanna calm and giving herself up to the power of time travel. In addition, Wajid addresses another common fantastical motif, 'a quest for unity in a world whose wholeness has been lost to view' (Harter 28). The wholeness in Tamanna's world can only be achieved through her nostalgia of Bangalore of the past without its techno-modernity and her love for Manoj. Tamanna's love affair with Manoj is complicated, yet they fall for each other. Tamanna realizes that in 2012 Manoj will be 46 years old. Even though they don't know how their relationship will work out, they become close to each other. Tamanna and Manoj do end up in the future together through the grandfather's photography yet Manoj vanishes from the scene as soon as Tamanna's parents show up in their future life. Tamanna time travels back to the future but the scene is in the hospital. Once Tamanna wakes up, she is told that she has been in a comma. While she can't make sense of the reality of her experience, she asks her mother about Manoj and comes to know that Manoj has moved to Australia because he fell in love with a girl whose name was also Tamanna. Tamanna desperately tries to see if she has a picture of Manoj in her phone but with no luck. She travels again to the past after six months when Manoj takes a photo of Suma's graduation. Yet it is a short stay this time. And then, next time she meets Manoj at a beach. So, it seems that when Manoj takes a photo and Tamanna finds it in the future, it acts as the trigger and she travels to the past. However, by the end of the first book, Manoj loses his bag with the camera in it. We are left with the message that Tamanna may not be able to get back to the future.

What does Wajid achieve by writing a time travel trilogy? She is 'working to outline the foundations for productive, non-coercive, human communities' (Curtis 161). Yet these communities are messy and difficult, particularly when it comes to defining relationships. By the time we reach the third book of the trilogy *Time Will Tell*, we find that Manoj has travelled to 2020 instead of 2013. This time Rajat, the young man whom Tamanna meets in her college, and his father Dr. Arvind, the Psychiatric doctor who wants to benefit from finding information from the future, travels with her. Tamanna takes Rajat to her grandmother's house, where Manoj left the camera. They find out that they can only take three photos – one to go to 2020, one to come back, and one for emergency. The third book ends with many unknowns with a positive turn in the relationship between Tamanna and Manoj.

Bina Shah, destructive forces, and effort for alternative futures

Bina Shah's novel *Before She Sleeps* is much more sinister in its message than Wajid's adolescent escapade and love affair of Tamanna through time travel, yet love is not missing in this novel either. Moreover, environmental disaster and its effects are portrayed with intention and not just a casualty of progress like in Wajid's novel. Lastly, where Wajid gives prominence to nostalgia in her novel's space while indicating that advancement of technology may not make people happy, Shah is trying to delineate a world which has been altered or destroyed by the acts of male species and women are the ones who must think about alternatives to survive; women must intervene the situation and invent an alternative future.

In Shah's novel, we move into an imaginary beautiful green city somewhere in South West Asia. However, there is gender disparity in this world. The authoritarian government in Green City handles this 'gender emergency' by mandating every woman to have multiple husbands to ensure repopulation. A small number of women who are against this policy live underground in Panah, a semi-city which means 'sanctuary' in Persian. They provide night-time emotional companionship for powerful party leaders but not sexual partners. Ilona Serfati, one of the women leaders of the Panah, tells us that a nuclear war has destroyed the world and countries turned black in the satellite maps, carbons were released in the air that killed millions and 'The Green City was built on top of what was destroyed' (33).

Bunkers were built underneath the earth to safeguard people and then ultimately new treaties were formed, and new boundaries were made and 'Survivors aligned themselves not in federations, but in abbreviated trading corridors and economic zones' (34). Then came the gender emergency as women were engendered species and the leaders established the Agency and then the Perpetuation Bureau. The Perpetuation Bureau made a new law that to preserve humankind, women must marry once, twice, and thrice (35). The women of the Green City didn't protest and if they did then they were quickly brought to trials and consequently eliminated.

The Green City like Bangalore in Wajid's trilogy is also a trope for a bulging urban civilization, but unlike Bangalore, The Green City devours everything that doesn't abide by the rules. This city was once known as Mazun which meant 'clouds laden with rains' (Shah 13). Yet, it was a desert city. The leaders ordered the planting of thousands of trees and millions and gallons of cultivated water to create the Green City. It is the city of the future as Sabine recalls, 'On a busy day, with its myriad radio frequencies and optic lines, the buzzing of the high-efficiency cars cutting smoothly across fiberglass roads and planes and vibrating through the sky, Green city is a chorus of sound and site' (12). Yet, the city is so restrictive that it becomes a prison and the power of the city, to quote Elsa Bouet, is 'reproduced in the biological body' (51). Bouet argues, 'These authoritarian urban systems impose control, repression and confinement, detrimental to individual freedom and the welfare of the community' (Bouet 51).

By the time we are introduced to the heroine Sabine in the novel, we already know that the Bureau's rule has devasted the lives of many women. We come to know of a woman committing suicide. When this news is being reported, the woman isn't given a name but is called a Wife just like the handmaids in Margaret Atwood's *The Handmaid's Tale*. These wives are reduced to 'pure bodies or 'vessels' and thus denied any kind of personal identity'(Cataldo 161). The fact that she had committed suicide was a more criminal act then her having five husbands – this was the message that the Bureau wanted to announce. We soon know the reason for her suicide – she was soon to be married to her 6th husband. The Bureau sent out a note, 'Her children, five girls, and two boys, . . . will be taken to a care facility, informed of their mother's death, and treated for trauma before being returned to the house where the Wife lived with her husband. This particular family will be reassigned a Wife by the end of the month, along with compensation for the tragedy endured by them, by order of the Perpetuation Bureau' (11).

Yet, Sabine recalls that the Wives were treated extremely well. They were given nice dresses and were pampered yet 'they were bowed down, shrunken, and meek' and were always accompanied by two or three of their husbands (23) as they were kept under constant surveillance. They were given high doses of fertility drugs and as a result they gave birth to triplets and quadruplets. Though 'childbearing has assumed a sort of sacred value' in Green City (Cataldo 160), Sabine realized that motherhood was an oppressive aspect of a patriarchal institution. It was declared in the city that no contraceptive can be used, and no abortions were allowed. When Sabine would make eye contact with them in the city, she saw them giving her fixed and 'steely looks of recognition, as if they were saying to me, I was young and carefree like you. Treasure these days girl, they don't last' (24). Sabine's mother committed suicide as well when she learned that she will be getting her second husband. When Sabine grew up, her father decided to fast track her to the Bureau in the hope of either monetary reward or a wife. At that moment she decided to run away to Panah; she was 17.

Panah, a sanctuary, was created by Ilona Sarfati where she sheltered runaway women. This is where I see the invention happening through Sarfati – she created Panah for survival. Sarfati's design was, to use Baccolini's words, to 'maintain a utopian core at their center, a locus of hope that contributes to the deconstructing tradition and reconstructing alternatives' (13). Sarfati didn't want women to have multiple husbands and thought that being companions would be the alternative. The purpose of Panah was to provide service to men who wanted companions – not as sexual companions but as empathetic companions. These men are older high officials and who are not eligible to have wives. Most men were happy with the companions, yet Joseph, the man to whom Sabine gave company to wanted to be more than a companion. Joseph wished for more than what he could have. Moreover, there was jealousy and rivalry in Panah. Sabine was betrayed by a girl named Ruma. Sabine was drugged and sexually assaulted by Joseph and left outside. She didn't reach Panah but was rescued by Reuben, another man who received services from the Panah. After gaining consciousness, Sabine was told that she was pregnant, of which she had no knowledge. However, later on she realized that she was raped by Joseph. She couldn't understand how that happened because her friend and guardian Lin didn't tell her that she was mixing drugs in her tea to help her sleep. This drug if mixed with alcohol can create loss of memory. So, she was unconscious when Joseph raped her. After being in the hospital she got to know her doctor, Julian, and together they escaped from the Green City. As Libby Falk Jones argues, Sabine's revival to life represents 'the fragility and newness of women's voices, to keep us from taking our freedom to speak for granted, to urge the need for continuing the fight, and to highlight the courage and beauty of those who break silences' (11).

Shah focuses not only on the tragedy of human lives but also on the environment. As a dystopic novel, it provides a cautionary tale on what the Earth can become in the future. The reference to a nuclear war points to both India and Pakistan who have been in the mode of war since 1947. The reference to Sabine's rape only points to what a future without women will do to the community. In addition, sex selection in India and in many parts of the world can have havoc in the future. We already see this in the news in the form of 'Bride Trafficking' or 'Bride Kidnapping.' Because villages in many countries lack unmarried women, many women are being abducted and married to multiple men. Maggie Shen, in her novel *An Excess of Men/ A Novel*, writes about the same issue as Shah does. Manish Jha's 2003 film *Matrubhoomi: A Nation without Women* is a worrying reminder of the systemic infanticide in India. Through interrogating the fictional narrative that Shah presents, we can observe a range of perspectives on perplexing and crucial philosophical and political issues, one being: will we ever get to a time when we will have a nation without women?

Conclusion

Both Wajid and Shah through their fictional works are speculating and visualizing other possible worlds. These novels focus on the nature of responsibility and educate us both as individuals and as part of a larger corporate world and thus teach us about what Margaret Atwood claims, 'the full range of our human response to the world – that is what it means to be human, on earth' (qtd. in Wagner-Lawlor 4). They present imaginary futures that question political moves made by the state. To go back to Mehan's comment about what post-colonial science fiction entails, we see that these writers are reframing the concept of the fantasy fiction and are approaching the center from the periphery. Wajid and Shah reflect the four authors' view (quoted as epigraphs in this chapter) about women writing science fiction. They confirm Wagner-Lawlor's argument that women's fantasy fiction doesn't remain just as an imaginative art or creation, rather the writers take information from the real world through 'rational inquiry as well as imaginative inquiry' and 'propose risk' and 'anchor hope' (3). Their visions are not politically useless. Thus, Wajid and Shah have been successful in portraying political possibilities for women to show their agency in a futuristic future. These sisters of Rokeya want to motivate not only women, but men and the whole community 'toward self-realization and to persuade their society to not to obstruct their way to self-realization' (Jahan 3).

Works cited

Baccolini, Rafaella. "Gender and Genre in the Feminist Critical Dystopias of Katherine Burdekin, Margaret Atwood, and Octavia Butler." *Future Females: The Next Generation: New Voices and Velocities in Feminist Science Fiction Criticism*, edited by Marleen S. Barr, Rowman & Utdefield, 2000, pp. 13–34.

bell, hooks. *Feminism is for Everybody: Passionate Politics*. South End Press, 2000.

Butler, Octavia. "Black Sci-fi-Section 1." *YouTube*, uploaded by Doctor Zerkalo's Monitor Zone, 31 July 2013, https://www.youtube.com/watch?v=_lAXJQlmFUU.

Bouet, Elsa. "Architecture of Punishment: Dystopian Cities Making the Body." *Cityscapes of the Future: Urban Spaces in Science Fiction*, edited by Yael Maurer and Meyrav Koren-Kuik, Brill Rodopi, 2018, pp. 49–65.

Cataldo, Adelina. "Breaking the Circle of Dystopia: Atwood's *The Handmaid's Tale*." *Women's Utopian and Dystopian Fiction*, edited by Sharon R. Wilson, Cambridge Scholars Publishing, 2013, pp. 156–73.

Curtis, Claire P. "Rehabilitating Utopia: Feminist Science Fiction and Finding the Ideal." *Contemporary Justice Review*, vol. 8, no. 2, 2005, pp. 147–62.

Gilarek, Anna. "The Temporal Displacement of Utopia and Dystopia in Feminist Speculative Fiction." *Explorations: A Journal of Language and Literature*, vol. 3, 2015, pp. 34–46.

Harter, Deborah. *Bodies in Pieces: Fantastic Narrative and the Poetics of the Fragment*. Stanford UP, 1996.

Hossain, Rokeya Sakhawat. "Sultana's Dream." *Sultana's Dream: A Feminist Utopia and Selections from The Secluded Ones*, edited by Roushan Jahan, The Feminist Press, 1988, pp. 7–18.

Jahan, Roushan. *Sultana's Dream: A Feminist Utopia and Selections from The Secluded Ones*. The Feminist Press, 1988.

Jennings, Hope. "'A Repeating World': Redeeming the Past and Future in the Utopian Dystopia of Jeanette Winterson's *The Stone Gods*." *Interdisciplinary Humanities*, vol. 27, no. 2, 2010, pp. 132–46.

Jones, Libby Falk. "Breaking Silences in Feminist Dystopias." *Utopian Studies*, vol. 2, no. 3, 1991, pp. 7–11.

Mathur, Suchitra Mathur. "Caught between the Goddess and the Cyborg: Third-World Women and the Politics of Science in Three Works of Indian Science Fiction." *The Journal of Commonwealth Literature*, vol. 39, no. 3, 2004, pp. 119–38.

Mehan, Uppinder. "The Domestication of Technology in Indian Science Fiction Short Stories." *Foundation*, vol. 74, 1998, pp. 54–66.

———. "Introduction to 'the Other Sci-Fi.'" http://uppindermehan.blogspot.com/2011. Accessed 2 Apr. 2019.

Narkhede, Nikhil. "Andaleeb Wajid Trilogy – Time Will Tell Book of the Tamanna Trilogy." *WriterStory*, www.writerstory.com/andaleeb-wajid-interview-time-will-tell-book-of-the-tamanna-trilogy/. Accessed 5 Feb. 2019.

Oates, Joyce Carol. "Science Fiction Doesn't Have to Be Dystopian." *The New Yorker*, www.newyorker.com/magazine/2019/05/13/science-fiction-doesnt-have-to-be-dystopian?fbclid=IwAR1Kgh6lXLtkfHCufILkgMrTlOshU6Sw20hBnxN97KI423Vs-84K6Uk26Vfg. Accessed 9 May 2019.

Pordzik, Ralph. *The Quest for Postcolonial Utopia: A Comparative Introduction to the Utopian Novel in the New English Literatures*. Peter Lang, 2001.

Shah, Bina. *Before She Sleeps: A Novel*. Delphinium Books, 2018.

Wagner-Lawlor, Jennifer. *Postmodern Utopias and Feminist Fictions*. Cambridge UP, 2013.

Wajid, Andaleeb. *No Time for Goodbyes*. Bloomsbury, 2014.

———. *Time will Tell*. Bloomsbury, 2014.

INDEX